WITI
FROM TH
MID-CONTI
D1249622

BEYOND

THE BROKEN SKY CHRONICLES

BEYOND

BOOK 3

JASON CHABOT

TURNER

Turner Publishing Company
Nashville, Tennessee
New York, New York

www.turnerpublishing.com

Beyond: The Broken Sky Chronicles, Book 3

Cover design: Maddie Cothren
Book design: Glen Edelstein

Library of Congress Cataloging-in-Publication Data TK

Names: Chabot, Jason, author.
Title: Beyond / Jason Chabot.
Description: Nashville, Tennessee : Turner Publishing Company, [2017] | Series: The broken sky chronicles ; book 3 | Summary: While Elia continues striving to topple the oppressive monarchy, she is finally reunited with Hokk but their reunion is tainted by the fact that they belong to different realms.
Identifiers: LCCN 2017009008 | ISBN 9781681626079 (pbk. : alk. paper)
Subjects: | CYAC: Science fiction. | Survival--Fiction. | Love--Fiction.
Classification: LCC PZ7.1.C468 Bg 2017 | DDC [Fic]--dc23
LC record available at https://lccn.loc.gov/2017009008

9781681626086

Printed in the United States of America
15 14 13 12 11 10 9 8 7 6 5 4 3 2 1

Dedicated with love to Shawn,
for the light you shine.

Chapter 1

HOKK TANGLED HIS FINGERS in the horse's mane and squeezed his thighs to press himself back into the saddle. The stallion had tucked its wings, ready for a nosedive. Together, they plunged straight down. Dense mist swirled wildly around them. As they sliced through the underbelly of the cloud cover and emerged into the open, a frigid wind slammed against their bodies, howling like an invisible beast fighting to defend the boundary between Above and Below.

Pummeled by horizontal rain, Hokk was immediately soaked. His tinted glasses were useless in such a raging storm. He had needed them to protect his eyes against the blinding sun traveling across Elia's sky, but down here, the dark lenses filtered out the feeble daylight and had become so splattered with water, they now impaired his vision. Daring to free one hand, he yanked the glasses off and stuffed them into a pocket, then squinted at the land racing up, hoping he could spot Elia falling through the air ahead of him.

You're too late! She has already hit the ground!

Hokk's mind was still grappling with the disturbing scene he had witnessed just moments earlier—Elia, her clothes smeared with blood, struggling in the clutches of an Imperial

Guard before somehow breaking free and dashing up to the top of the Grand Bridge, where she'd hastily climbed its low wall. She had glanced back at Hokk, ever so briefly, with a look of utter hopelessness that made his heart seize. Yet she turned away, and as Hokk screamed for her to stop, she leapt off the ledge. The next instant, Hokk had vaulted onto the back of the closest horse to fly down after her.

But why had she committed such a desperate act? What could have gone so horribly wrong for her to choose almost certain death over being captured by Imperial Guards?

As Hokk had been anticipating, his stallion's rapid descent now stalled as the animal became caught in a layer of the atmosphere where gravity played by a different set of rules. Here, the wind was a mere caress. Even the raindrops seemed to hover around them.

Hokk knew this band of near-weightlessness would've momentarily slowed Elia down too. However, would it have been enough for her to survive a second fall to Below?

Dropping his gaze, Hokk could only make out solid terrain far beneath him. He wished instead that he could see the ocean, which might offer a softer landing. No matter the outcome, though, he had to find Elia—to retrieve her dead, broken body, if that's all he would discover.

Glancing overhead at the oppressive sky, Hokk saw churning clouds every shade of threatening gray, hanging heavy with the burden of the storm's deluge still waiting to be released. The bottoms of the two floating islands pierced this thick blanket of mist, their rocky undersides poking through like inverted mountain peaks. The larger one was Kamanman, which Elia called home; the other, following close beside it, was the Isle of the Noble Sanctuary, where she had previously been a laundry girl, working many floors beneath the Mirrored Palace.

Hokk finally registered the tug of gravity once more, so he urged his steed with a sharp kick in the ribs. The horse began flapping its wings and soon escaped the opposing force that had been holding them suspended. Descending swiftly again through the battling wind and rain, they sped toward the ground.

Yet the closer they got, the more baffled Hokk became. What lay below looked like nothing he had ever observed. The landscape was far different from the grasslands where Hokk had lived in exile for so many years. In all directions, the entire area was covered by what appeared to be garbage, with no traces of rock or plant life. And most surprising of all, this large mass rose and fell as if a perpetual earthquake were rolling across its surface.

Then Hokk realized what he was looking at. This wasn't some vast, treeless plain spoiled by litter and debris. It really was the ocean! An ocean filled with undulating garbage!

Less than a hundred feet above the water, Hokk pulled the horse's mane, wrenching its neck to make it stop flying. The animal back-pedaled the air with its wings while Hokk leaned over in his saddle to study what he saw. As he had suspected, the majority of the tangled rubbish was plastic—plastic of all types and sizes—bobbing up and down. In some places, the trash had become piled in heaps like small mountains pushed up by the wave action; in other spots, there were gaps where he could see through to the deep, clear water.

Hokk raised his eyes to the horizon, trying to comprehend the magnitude of this colossal island of snarled garbage, which had likely formed over countless decades.

He fretfully wiped the wetness streaking down his face. Elia could have landed anywhere. And if he couldn't find her on the surface, then that meant only one thing—she had slipped through a hole in the buoyant layer of trash and was now trapped beneath it. Drowning.

Chapter 2

RAYHAN WAS NUMB. GRIPPING his helmet tightly in one hand, he struggled to process the commotion around him. Everything seemed to be happening at half speed.

Only a few minutes ago, he'd watched his sister, Elia, with blood on her sleeves, jump from the edge of the Grand Bridge. He had almost grabbed her in time. He could have saved her!

The other Imperial Guards, most of them trainees like himself, were equally stunned, each staring over the side of the wall in disbelief at the spot where Elia had plunged into the white clouds. But then that pale young man with dark glasses—the one who had earlier shouted "Don't do it!" to Elia—proceeded to steal a stallion so he could fly after her. For every witness who saw these two courtiers sacrificing their lives to face death at the hands of Scavengers . . . it was unfathomable!

Not that Elia was really a courtier. Rayhan had no idea how she, a servant in the laundry room, could have shown up again being chased out of the palace by guards. She was dressed in a billowy, white silk dress, and except for her short-cropped hair, she looked like a noblewoman. However, such a rise in status was unheard of. Certainly out of the question for anyone from a family as poor as theirs. So what could possibly have led up to that astonishing moment when Rayhan realized he had caught his sister in his arms?

It had been many weeks since he'd last seen her. Elia had inexplicably vanished around the same time his mother had gone missing too. Regrettably, Rayhan hadn't been immediately aware that anything had happened since he no longer lived in the family's humble shack on a small island floating at the end of a suspension bridge. As far as he knew, Sulum and Elia were working as usual in the lower levels of the palace while he carried on harvesting waterballs in the dewfields, just as his father used to do. But then Greyit, a trusted family friend, had tracked him down on the plantation and shared the troubling news: both his mother and sister had disappeared.

Subsequent events had unfolded in a blur. Before Rayhan could make contact with his grandfather, who was now left on his own, Greyit insisted that Rayhan's formal training as an Imperial Guard start the very next morning, even though, up until that point, Rayhan had been just a volunteer Shifter. The old man explained that becoming a guard was the only way to ensure Rayhan's protection, though he would not elaborate further. Greyit had always had a surprising level of influence, but even still, Rayhan had wondered if his promotion could really be arranged in such short order. So he was very much surprised the following day when he reported to the palace and discovered that his arrival was expected. His newly issued uniform complemented the boots he had already received a few months earlier as a Shifter—footwear that painfully pinched his toes—but he was especially pleased to be given his helmet. With its stern, sculpted faceplate of polished metal, it not only identified him as an Imperial Guard, but also allowed him to go into hiding just as Greyit had intended. Behind the helmet, Rayhan became perfectly indistinguishable from the many other men who wore one.

Ever since, he had been enjoying his daily training schedule. A high-ranking guard, a man named Blaitz, had just been assigned as the new commander of the Royal Regiment, following the untimely and mysterious death of Commander Wrasse. Rayhan had never met Wrasse, but he knew enough about the man's tyrannical reputation to appreciate his own good fortune in not having to serve under him.

Now, glancing back toward the palace, Rayhan noticed Commander Blaitz arriving on the scene. He was easily recognizable by the distinct metal spike protruding from the forehead of his polished helmet. As other guards crowded around, probably explaining to Blaitz what he had just missed, Rayhan hurried down the bridge to speak with him.

"I have to follow after her!" Rayhan exclaimed as he pushed through the crowd. The numbness in his mind was gone. He knew exactly what he had to do.

"Who? Where?" Blaitz asked as he too removed his helmet.

"I'm taking a horse down into the clouds to start looking."

"Don't be ridiculous," the commander replied coolly.

"That was my sister! I have to at least try!"

The commander's eyes flashed. "The girl who jumped . . . was your sister?"

"Yes. So I request permission to—"

"No! I cannot let you leave," Blaitz said. "There is absolutely no need for it."

Surprised, Rayhan dared to challenge him. "But there could still be time. Maybe a Scavenger hasn't stolen her yet."

"I forbid it!" the commander shot back. "I can't lose men to foolish pursuits. Whatever is within these clouds is off limits to everyone. None of our citizens should ever go below the islands. That includes Imperial Guards!"

Something about his manner made it seem as though he was lying. Had his harsh expression cracked ever so slightly?

Were his lips tense? Had his eyes flitted away for a fraction of a second?

As if guessing Rayhan doubted him, the commander began stabbing a finger just inches away from his face. "I mean it!" Blaitz roared. "You'll be arrested if you disobey me! I'm giving you a direct order. Do you understand?"

Rayhan scowled.

The commander grabbed him by the collar and twisted. "*Do . . . you . . . understand?*" he said with a snarl.

Rayhan jerked backward, away from the man's reach. "I do."

Blaitz nodded.

Just then, Emperor Tael himself emerged from the palace, catching everyone's attention. The blind man's steps were halting, as if his legs struggled to support him. He swung his white cane from side to side to clear his path, but his free hand—in fact, the entire lower arm of his shirt—was covered in blood. Much more blood than Rayhan had seen on Elia.

But whose blood was it? The emperor's or his sister's?

As guards, including Blaitz, hurried to Tael's side, Rayhan didn't move. His thoughts remained on Elia. What had she done? What kind of mess had she become mixed up in? All he could guess was that someone had tried to assassinate Tael. Yet surely Elia couldn't be guilty of such a crime.

His eyes focused on the clouds that drifted beneath the bridge and pressed up against the banks of the two islands connected by this crossing.

She's still in those clouds! The Scavengers might not have found her yet!

The thought of such fearsome creatures sent a shiver ricocheting between his shoulder blades. Scavengers were monsters with curved spines, lips pulled tight over toothless gums, and bulging foreheads, but no eyes. They came up through the limitless, misty depths of Below to cling to the sides of islands, waiting to snatch people over as new specimens for their collections. Whenever citizens of the Lunera System died—like Rayhan's grandmother not so long ago—their bodies were carefully wrapped and released over the edges of the islands to appease the creatures' desires so they'd be less likely to steal anyone living.

If there was still a chance, Rayhan couldn't imagine not trying to save Elia from these monsters. That other young man, whoever he was, hadn't thought twice before diving into the clouds to pursue her.

Rayhan put on his helmet and returned to the flying stallion that had been assigned to him for his training. The animal, with jet-black feathers, was still waiting at the base of the bridge where he had left it when Elia first appeared. He quickly led the horse up to the crest of the arched crossing and down the other side to where the gate opened to the City of Na-Lavent. Normally patrolled by guards, the gate was unmanned. All the activity was on the other end of the bridge, which was exactly what he'd been hoping for.

He mounted his stallion and kicked his ill-fitting boots into the stirrups. He shoved his hips forward to signal the horse to prepare for flight. It opened its wings and began to flap, rising above the cobblestones and then moving out over the mist.

Without looking to see if he had been noticed, Rayhan pitched his body forward and dug his heels into the horse's sides.

The animal dove, gliding down at a steep angle, its wings tightly tucked.

Swirling clouds enveloped Rayhan in an instant. His view dissolved into gray nothingness.

Chapter 3

THE GUARD GRIPPED TASHEIRA'S arm more tightly than he had to as he whisked her inside through the back of the Mirrored Palace, guiding her away from the turmoil around the Grand Bridge where she had just witnessed madness.

"Should you really be touching me?" she scolded, yanking herself free.

He didn't try to reach for her again. "I'm simply ensuring your safety."

It seemed, rather, that she was being taken to meet someone. But who?

Tasheira glanced over her shoulder and saw, a few steps back, her cousin being escorted by his own guard. Fimal, who, until today, she had thought was dead, had arrived at the palace earlier in the morning, exhausted after traveling non-stop to get here. He had shared an almost unbelievable story about flying down to Below, then explained the shocking truth he had discovered about both Elia and her friend Hokk, who were apparently not who they said they were.

Their guards now led them toward the front reception hall that connected the emperors' two towers, only to discover a melee of alarmed courtiers. *They must have heard about the attack on Tael*, thought Tasheira. To avoid the crowd, the guards ushered her and Fimal into a wing of the palace opposite the banquet hall, where just a few flustered servants darted about.

The corridor branched off into another hallway, this one empty, and Tasheira's guard opened the first door they came to. She halted, but did not go into the room. She had a sinking feeling as she watched the second guard pass by with Fimal and open a door for him much farther down the same passage.

Tash spun on the man beside her. "Why can't we wait together?" she asked, wishing she could see his expression instead of her own features glaring back, reflected on the front of his highly polished helmet.

The guard said nothing, but simply gestured for her to enter.

"Do you know who I am?" she asked loudly enough for the other guard and Fimal to hear too. "I'm Baron Shoad's daughter, Lady Tasheira!" She nodded in Fimal's direction. "And that's his nephew."

"Just ensuring your safety," the guard repeated in his deadpan voice. "We've been ordered to keep watch over you, given the circumstances."

Tash put her hands on her hips. "I want to see my father. *Now*!"

"He has been sent for."

"Then I'll wait with my cousin until he arrives!" said Tash as she tried to continue along the corridor.

The guard blocked her.

"Move out of the way!" she yelled.

"It's all right, Tash," Fimal said, just as he was about to step into his own room.

Why was he being so cooperative?

"I don't like what's going on!" she shouted back.

"They're doing this for security purposes, not to harass us," he replied, sounding much more calm and composed than she felt. "If an assassination attempt really was made this morning, then caution is paramount. We could be the next targets if we're not careful."

Tasheira bit her lower lip. He was absolutely right. They could both be in danger too. But wasn't that all the more reason to stay together?

"Besides, we're only a few rooms apart," Fimal added. "I won't be going anywhere."

Tash sighed. "Fine," she said. She turned to her guard. "Then I want you staked outside my door at all times."

The guard nodded.

Tasheira dramatically whirled around to make the hem of her dress flare up and strode into the richly decorated room as the door closed behind her. She flung herself into an ornately carved chair with a thickly padded seat and kicked her feet up onto a low glass tabletop, catching the lip of a nearby serving dish with the heel of her shoe. The bowl, filled with waterballs, bounced and dropped with a loud crash, and one of the jiggly, transparent globes rolled out. Tash leaned forward and caught it before it fell onto the floor.

She pursed her lips on the waterball's surface and sucked a mouthful of the gelatinous, thirst-quenching fluid. She then squeezed the thing in her hand as she became increasingly consumed with anxious thoughts.

Did anyone else know that Elia and Hokk were imposters? Surely no one would actually blame her for bringing them to the palace, would they? Yes, she was the one who had found them on the Isle of Drifting Dunes; yes, she'd convinced her father they should be saved. But how was she to know they had both invented stories to fool people? If anything, she was just another victim of their trickery.

Tash was actually embarrassed now to think how easily she had been deceived by a lowly servant girl. Pretending to have lost her memory, Elia had claimed to have no recollection of how she'd ended up stranded in the sand dunes, her winged horse dead, her clothing torn, and her head injured. Tash should have been more suspicious, but at the time, she was preoccupied, wondering if Elia belonged to an influential family who could help boost Tasheira's status within the Royal Court. And the whole situation surrounding Hokk, the young man from the moon—Tash still didn't know what to make of all that. Was he somehow connected to Elia and her sinister plans to infiltrate the palace? It seemed unlikely. Since he was so unusual looking, with his pale, extremely sensitive skin and his single eyelids, it was perfectly plausible to assume he might be from some far-off world. That's why Tash had been so certain he belonged to the wreckage she'd found in a crater deep within the desert, especially after watching pieces of that burning vessel fall from the same sky where the shattered moon hung suspended. Then there was that strange padded suit, plus Hokk's special message that he was so keen to deliver to the Twin Emperors—a cryptic message of unity.

Yet, according to Fimal, Hokk was from Below. *Actually from Below*! And Fimal knew because *he had been there himself*! Though Tash had no reason not to trust her cousin, it seemed impossible that Fimal could have gone to Below and lived to tell the tale. What about the Scavengers? How could such monsters not exist when Tash had been warned about them all her life?

No doubt, Elia was the real monster. She had attempted to murder Marest, Tasheira's personal attendant, so clearly the girl was capable of trying to kill the Twin Emperors, Tael and Tohryn. And regrettably, just by her association with Elia, Tash feared her own reputation was now in jeopardy.

The door to Tasheira's room suddenly opened and a guard came inside. Was it the same man who was supposed to be stationed out in the hallway, or a different one? Tash hated how, with their expressionless faceplates, they all looked the same.

"What?" she asked harshly.

The guard closed the door and slid a deadbolt across to lock them in.

"Why did you do that?" Tash asked uneasily, tossing aside the waterball in her hand. She stood up and moved closer to confront him. "What do you want?"

He remained silent and stationary.

Tash's eyes narrowed with suspicion, and her heartbeat quickened.

Then she heard footsteps in the corridor. She cocked her head to listen. Someone spoke, and she immediately recognized her father's voice, right outside.

"So my daughter saw it all happen?"

"That seems to be the case," replied some other man with him.

"And is Tasheira in one of these rooms?" asked the Baron, his words and his footsteps fading as he moved farther down the hallway.

"No. She's elsewhere, but safe. As a lady-in-waiting, she's in lockdown with Empress Faytelle while we sort matters out."

Stunned by the lie, Tash lunged for the door. But the guard was faster, grabbing her around the waist. He held Tasheira in an inescapable embrace and clamped a gloved hand over her mouth.

"Just so long as my daughter is not in danger," Tasheira heard her father say while she kicked and squirmed, fighting in vain against her captor.

Chapter 4

ELIA RUBBED HER SCRAPED elbow and favored her twisted ankle as she hobbled along the stone platform joining Kamanman with the Isle of the Noble Sanctuary. This ledge of rock, submerged under the cloud cover, was at least twice as wide as the Grand Bridge that arched directly overhead in the sunshine. Down here, however, Elia could distinguish nothing more than the bridge's silhouette through the sparkling mist.

Just moments earlier, in a state of desperation, Elia had thrown herself off the edge of the man-made crossing, fully expecting to fall all the way to Below. Landing on this moss-stippled formation was simply a stroke of pure luck. She had always been told the two islands were separate masses that would have drifted apart if not for the Grand Bridge that connected them. It had never occurred to her to consider other possibilities.

So did anybody else know about this span of rock? Were any of the Imperial Guards aware of its existence? Should she be prepared for men swarming down the slopes at either end because they knew where to find her?

The thought of being captured prompted Elia to quicken her pace. She had already seen the shadow of a winged horse and its rider slip by, flying straight down, as if sent to Below to look for her. She feared her window for making a getaway might be rapidly shrinking.

She continued to limp toward the opposite slope, where she was planning to climb up and escape into the City of Na-Lavent. She stepped over large cracks in the rock, as well as loose cobblestones that had fallen from the bridge deck above, all the result of damage from a recent earthquake that had forced the evacuation of the Mirrored Palace's lower levels when Elia still worked there.

Arriving at the steep incline, she started to ascend, but her injury slowed her progress. Because her sore ankle couldn't bear much weight, Elia had to use her one free hand to pull herself higher. The fingers of her other hand clutched her precious telescope.

The coveted instrument, which reputedly had the power to reveal secrets capable of toppling the monarchy, had been smuggled out of the palace over a month earlier by a young lady-in-waiting, who had given it to Elia while she worked among the clotheslines. This unfortunate woman had ultimately paid with her life for trying to ensure the telescope's safety. Elia had been spared a similar fate, despite coming dangerously close to her own death on several occasions.

Though Elia had looked through the telescope often, expecting each time to see something either scandalous or profound, the device had always failed to deliver on its promise. Her most recent and unsuccessful attempt had been first thing that very morning when she snuck into the private quarters of the blind emperor, Tael, who was supposed to be at breakfast. Hokk had helped her gain access to the lavish rooms, but was called away before he could make sure she safely emerged. Unfortunately, the emperor returned to his suite much sooner than expected and caught Elia in the middle of her fruitless search. Fearing that Tael would call out to his guards for backup, Elia had thrown a bottle of red ink at him to buy herself a few extra seconds to run away. Yet her feet were temporarily rooted to the floor in shock after watching the emperor quickly catch the bottle in mid-air before it could hit his head. That one action alone immediately made the situation much more dangerous for Elia—what she had witnessed dispelled years of lies surrounding the emperor's claim to blindness, so there was no telling what the man would do to prevent the secret from getting out.

With the ink dripping down his arm, Tael had lunged for Elia, smearing the sleeve of her dress with the crimson red liquid as if it were blood spilt during a violent struggle. Yet she was able to break free of his grasp unharmed, and she quickly fled to the back of the palace, hoping to cross over into the city and disappear.

But then she'd been forced to jump and had miraculously ended up here, below the bridge. As for the telescope, however, her hard landing cracked the glass at its widest end. After everything she'd been through to protect it, she'd felt like such a failure. Looking through the broken eyepiece, Elia had realized right away that its capacity to magnify was ruined.

Discouraged, she had almost given up, ready to abandon the thing, when a remarkable—downright inspired—thought came to her. All this time, she had assumed it was necessary to look *through* the telescope. But that was a huge mistake. Instead, she needed to look *inside* it.

So with no hesitation, she had proceeded to smash both ends of the instrument until she could peer into the collapsible cylinder. And then her eyes caught sight of something curled up within! She crammed two fingers as deep as they'd go, just enough for the tips to touch the hidden documents. She pulled them out and hurried to unroll the pages, yet just as quickly realized her inability to decipher what was written on them; she had never been taught how to read. Elia did recognize, however, the emblem of the royal seal stamped on each sheet. The symbol matched the purple tattoo on her own forehead, which was still obscured by the crusty scab she had given herself after trying to gouge out the despised marking, all in an attempt to hide her true identity as a palace servant.

Besides the insignias, however, it was the last page Elia unrolled that she had found especially intriguing. Pressed onto the paper in black ink were the handprints and foot-prints of an infant. But what made them so significant? For that matter, why were any of these documents important enough to warrant hiding them in the telescope so they could be smuggled out of the palace?

She needed to find someone trustworthy to interpret their meaning. But who? Any number of people, for all sorts of reasons, might be after these very pages, willing to stop at nothing to possess them.

As Elia now climbed higher toward the city, another dark shadow—a second winged horse with its rider—swept down from overhead, plummeting to Below. She had assumed the first was an Imperial Guard. Could this be Hokk? She'd seen him at the base of the bridge as she looked back at the palace one last time. He had shouted for her not to jump. Maybe he had decided to follow the guard down, hoping to find her himself.

The fog around Elia gradually began to brighten, then dissipated altogether as she reached the top of the slope. She could imagine the strange sight she'd be if somebody on the mainland was watching as her head, then the rest of her body, slowly rose out of the white, murky soup of clouds pressed up against the island's sides. And with the large smear of red ink on the white sleeve of her dress, like splattered blood, anyone would naturally assume she was the victim of a Scavenger attack, struggling to pull herself free of the monster's claws.

Before she rose too high, Elia scanned the vicinity to confirm no one was around. She didn't want to raise any alarm that might draw attention her way. She had emerged a safe distance from the bridge and its patrolled gates that restricted access to the Noble Sanctuary, and it was now late enough in the morning for the day laborers to have reported for work. Regardless, Elia kept careful watch as she heaved herself out of the clouds and swung her legs up.

After another quick glance to make sure she hadn't been spotted, Elia ducked low and hurried into the nearest alleyway as fast as her swollen ankle would allow. Dilapidated buildings lined the filthy lane, making it dark and narrow, but Elia felt relieved to be in its protective gloom. Ahead, she could see a few homeless people sleeping in the passage or picking through garbage. In some ways, it almost felt as if Elia belonged here too. A spot where people could blissfully be forgotten and hide. A refuge for society's castoffs. A place where no one would think to come looking for a lowly servant girl tasked with an important mission.

No! I do not belong here! Elia scolded herself. She began shuffling down the alley as if to challenge anyone who might confront her.

I am not like my father and never will be.

Chapter 5

SEARCHING ON HORSEBACK FROM such a height over the humongous island of debris, flying back and forth over the same large area, Hokk worried he had somehow missed seeing Elia. But where else could she have fallen? With the wind, torrential rain, and surging waves, the situation was beginning to feel hopeless. And to make matters worse, the islands of Kamanman and the Noble Sanctuary were currently being carried away by the storm's upper airstreams, so he was starting to lose his bearings.

Hokk remembered Elia had been wearing white, therefore he tried focusing on anything that could possibly be the fabric of her dress. But white was by far the dominant color in the jumbled trash swirling directly below him. It was maddening. Something white would catch his eye, and he'd fly his horse lower for a better view, only to discover more flimsy plastic bags snagged in the current.

Then he noticed something a short distance away that he was absolutely sure had to be her. Wasn't that Elia's sleeve sticking up as if she were trapped under the water?

"Elia!" he screamed.

Hokk dragged his hand over the stubble on his scalp. Maybe it was already too late.

Or maybe not.

Get down there and save her!

Hokk knew he wouldn't be able to carry out a rescue unless he set his horse down on the surface. But what surface? Any firm or compact site could unexpectedly drift apart and expose deep, open water.

Surveying the turbulent scene, Hokk spied a more densely packed mountain of garbage that wasn't too far away. Though the huge mound bobbed with each passing ocean swell, it was holding together and looked like a safe enough place to touch down. He flew closer and tried to make the horse land, but it resisted. Hovering above as the spot rose and fell beneath them, the animal reared and kicked in protest.

"Do it, you stupid thing!" Hokk shouted, jabbing his heels repeatedly into the beast's rib cage until the animal finally surrendered and perched itself precariously on top of the heap.

Hokk launched himself from the saddle. He half ran, half stumbled down the side of the rubbish pile. Arriving at water level, he struggled to keep his balance as he gazed out, hoping to pinpoint where he had seen Elia's sleeve. But the rolling peaks and valleys of the ocean were more extreme than they had seemed from the air. One moment, the crest of a massive wave would raise the surrounding garbage, Hokk included, to a point higher than where he had abandoned the horse. The next minute, he would dip down into a trough until he entirely lost sight of the restless horizon.

He began to second-guess his decision to land. He had sacrificed both his ability to move quickly and his aerial vantage point.

Damn it, you're down here now! he thought angrily. *Find her!*

Drenched by the rain's stinging assault, Hokk tried to maintain his footing as he jumped from one snarled mass of plastic debris to the next, leaping over patches of dark, frothy water, yelling Elia's name, all the while hoping he was going the right way. He rode up on another crest. He anxiously scanned the area and—

There! There she is!

"Elia!" he shouted again.

Hokk fixed his eyes on the spot, hoping not to lose sight as the wave dropped. He rushed forward before the sea could climb once more to block his view, but he only made it a few steps. His foot slipped through a gap in the layer of garbage, plunging his leg into water up to the knee. The heaving surge knocked him onto his backside. He felt an instant panic, as if something below the surf had caught hold of his ankle and was attempting to pull him under. He fought frantically until he could pull his leg free and scramble to his feet. *Don't be such a fool!* he scolded himself. *There's nothing down there that can get you!*

Still shaken by the burst of adrenaline, he staggered on, his wobbly legs making it doubly difficult to keep steady.

Yet as he drew near, Hokk was filled with dread. Given the pull of the undertow, Elia appeared to be more deeply submerged than he had initially believed. He could still see only her sleeve. There was no way she was getting air.

Taking a running start before he could think twice, Hokk plunged headfirst into the frigid ocean. Shocked by the cold, he swam nonetheless through the trash toward Elia as opposing currents threatened to carry him away. He battled against them with powerful strokes and tried to keep his eyes open, despite the stinging salt water. Closer, he dove under, reached out, and grabbed Elia's sleeve. Unfortunately, he hadn't actually caught hold of her arm, so a handful of material would have to do. The most important thing was to hurry and get her back up to the surface.

Hokk felt resistance, but he continued to pull. He held his breath to the verge of rupturing his lungs, until Elia's body was finally released from whatever held it. Demanding one last surge of strength from frozen, exhausted muscles, Hokk vigorously kicked his feet and erupted above the water.

He choked and sputtered, but quickly focused on getting Elia's head high enough so she was exposed to the air. Yet as he yanked her up, he grabbed only more handfuls of fabric. He paused, almost allowing himself to sink, as he became sickened with the realization that he did not have fabric in his hands. This was not Elia's dress. It was only more plastic! A thick bolt of the stuff!

"No!" Hokk slammed his fists into the water, creating a large spray. "Elia, where are you?" he bellowed.

The immense piece of plastic he had dislodged kept floating up from the deep and started to envelop him. Hokk panicked a second time. It was wrapping around him, like a clinging shroud. He could barely move! So with the momentum of another upswell, Hokk hurled himself toward the closest clump of garbage, paddling hard to reach it. He grabbed hold, hoping the mass would not break apart as he pulled himself up. Panting, he stared at the plastic sheet growing ever larger as it spread out.

"Where *are* you, Elia?" he whispered miserably.

Then he reminded himself about the pledge he'd made while flying to Below. He was here to find Elia, even if all he could do was retrieve her body. He had to see her for himself—it was the only way he'd be able to accept her fate. And the sooner he could get airborne and carry on, the better.

He quickly stood just as another wave carried him higher. At its peak, Hokk looked through the rain for his horse.

Wait! Who is that?

Hokk stretched as high as he could on his tiptoes without slipping off. Unfortunately, with the ever-undulating ocean, he descended too quickly to confirm the sighting.

But he was certain he had just seen another person on this floating island of trash!

Unless he was hallucinating. He'd been plagued by

corrupt visions in the past. If they had been somehow triggered again, it was a very disheartening prospect. Why would they be coming back today?

Hokk steadied his emotions and waited for the next big wave to boost him skyward. This time he was ready.

Yes! No doubt about it! He could now see *two* people! Though strangely, they appeared to have plastic wrapped around their arms and legs. It was as if they were camouflaging themselves to blend in with their surroundings.

Hokk lost sight as he again sank into a basin formed by walls of water.

Had they seen him as well? He didn't think so. They hadn't been looking his way. But they were definitely interested in his horse . . . as if they were hunting it!

The next moment, Hokk looked up to see his horse rising into the air. It was flapping its wings wildly as if startled.

This couldn't be happening! Without a horse, he would lose his only means of finding Elia and returning her to her home.

But he felt sure now that Elia couldn't possibly be alive. Not anymore. So without her, what reason did Hokk have to return to Above?

Nym, he thought. Nym was his reason. Hokk had left the little fox in his room at the palace, tucked safely in the nest he had made in the bottom drawer of a cabinet. He had lost so much in his life, and now to think of living without Nym's company . . . well, that was unbearable. He had to find a way to get back up there.

His gaze followed the horse as it grew smaller, abandoning this stormy hell to ascend to its home on the other side of the clouds.

Yet it wasn't alone. Hokk was stunned to see a second horse in the sky, as black as night! This one, however, was *descending* to Below, with a rider on its back.

Hokk wasn't going to be stranded down here after all!

As Hokk's fleeing horse passed by, the other stallion

seemed to hesitate briefly, as if its passenger were debating whether or not to continue down or to follow after it up into the clouds.

The rider, whoever he was, decided to fly lower.

As man and beast got closer, Hokk stiffened. Despite the wretched weather and the remaining distance between them, there was no mistaking the mirrored helmet of the Imperial Guard sitting in the saddle.

Yes, of course a guard would be sent down once again to cross the forbidden border of mist dividing Above from Below! Nothing in the past had stopped them searching for Elia, all the way to the City of Ago, so why would they give up now?

But if the guard was so clearly obvious to Hokk, then probably Hokk could be just as easily spotted from the air. That was the last thing he wanted. He had learned, through hard experience, to be extremely cautious in the presence of these fierce, masked men.

Hokk immediately crouched and scanned the surface. He saw a space between the drifting debris that was just wide enough, so he quickly slipped into the water and clung to pieces of tangled plastic to stay afloat, rising and falling in the current with the rest of the trash.

He kept his eyes trained on the approaching guard. The man's stallion was not far overhead when he redirected his steed to a different area. The guard leaned over in his saddle, looking down as if he too had seen the other people out here.

Perfect! A distraction! Hopefully the guard would forget all about him, as well as Elia.

But then Hokk saw a most unexpected sight—a net hurtling high into the air, tossed up from the ocean. It spread out, spinning in a circle, until the weights around its perimeter pulled the thing down, catching one of the horse's beating wings. With its rhythm interrupted, the animal pitched to the side.

Hokk rode a wave higher, giving him a better view. He could see the same two people camouflaged with plastic. One of them was twirling another net in his hands.

Above, the black stallion flailed with its free wing. The guard fought to stay on.

Below, the hunter released the second net, and like a twirling, sticky web, it completely ensnared the horse and rider.

As the wave sank lower, Hokk watched the stallion drop out of the air, catching a glimpse just in time to see the animal and its passenger hit the surface of the water.

Chapter 6

TASHEIRA SAT FACING THE locked door, frustrated and angry, unable to either move or speak. She was gagged, and her ankles had been tied to the legs of a chair, her wrists to the armrests. An Imperial Guard stood opposite, watching in silence.

Well, at least she had put up a good fight—she could be proud of herself for that. In fact, Tash had fought so hard against the guard's restraints that the commotion had alerted another guard outside, who'd needed to come in and help. Now, however, she had given up struggling altogether. It was better to save her energy for when it might make a difference.

But what or who was the man waiting for? Why was she being kept here?

Father will be furious when he hears how they've been treating me!

Then suddenly, a banging at the door made Tash jump in her seat. She hoped it was the Baron. But as the guard unlocked the door and swung it open, her eyes widened to see their visitor.

The blind Emperor Tael.

He was alone, holding the white cane he always used to clear a path in front of him. The guard moved out of his way, and the emperor seemed to flinch, ever so slightly, as he stepped into the room. Just for an instant, Tasheira could have sworn he looked directly into her eyes. Yet it could only be an illusion. The emperor couldn't actually see her sitting there—he was merely staring right through her.

To leave no doubt, though, Tash moaned so he'd know she was in the room.

Typically an upbeat, jovial man, Tael now scowled. "Who's in here?"

"A suspect we've detained for questioning," replied the guard.

"Who is it?"

"The daughter of Baron Shoad."

"Well, allow her to speak!" the emperor demanded.

"Yes, of course."

As Tael found a chair for himself, feeling carefully with his hands for the back of it, the guard approached Tasheira and lowered her gag.

"I'm outraged!" Tash immediately roared, undaunted by the inappropriateness of such an outburst in the presence of an emperor. "Where's my father? I demand to see him. I was promised protection, and then I get treated like a common criminal! No, worse—like an animal!"

Emperor Tael gripped the arms of his chair until his knuckles turned white. "All in good time, my dear," he said in a frigid tone. "If you cooperate, then everything should be fine. But there are other important matters to deal with first. If I understand correctly, you know the young lady who broke into my private suite this morning. Is that correct?"

Tasheira hesitated before answering as she glanced at the splatter of red on the man's sleeve. If it was blood, it had to be Elia's. Tasheira could see no wound on his arm, or any tear in the fabric of his shirt.

"Was she a companion of yours or wasn't she?" Tael asked with greater severity.

"Calling her my companion makes it sound as though we were friends," Tasheira replied with more control. "And that could not be further from the truth. She acted alone. I knew nothing of her plans."

"You're getting ahead of me," the emperor replied, raising his hand to stop her. "To start with, what is her name?"

"Elia. Her name is Elia. Or at least that's what she told me," said Tasheira, softening her tone even more. She would have to approach this interrogation wisely if she hoped to get through it unscathed. To come across as believable, as someone whom Tael could trust, she would have to sound sincere. Fortunately, she was good at faking it.

"I'm so sorry, Your Excellency," Tash continued. "I wish none of this had happened. I'm upset because I'm just so worried about your well-being. Has the girl done something to harm you? The right arm of your shirt is all bloody."

Emperor Tael touched his sleeve and appeared to be surprised, as if feeling the wetness for the first time. He sniffed his fingertips and then nodded. "This is only ink," he explained. Tash decided he must be relying on his obviously keen sense of smell, which would compensate for the loss of his vision. "I'm assuming it must be *red* ink if you've mistaken it for blood."

"Thank goodness. That's a huge relief," she said with a sigh. "I feared the worst. I only found out this morning what this Elia girl is truly capable of. My cousin arrived from my father's estate with crucial information about how dangerous she might be."

The emperor leaned forward, his interest piqued. The aim of his gaze missed its mark, however, directed just over her shoulder. "Tell me everything you know about her."

"She tried to murder my dear, faithful attendant, who happened to discover the truth about her. Elia isn't from a noble family. That's what she wanted everyone to believe, but she's really just a lowly palace servant—"

"Wait. From this palace?"

"Yes. But somehow Elia ended up on the Isle of Drifting Dunes, claiming that she had lost her memory and had to be reunited with her family, whoever they might be. Thinking about it now, she must have stolen a horse from your stables to make her getaway. Perhaps she stole other things as well, though I only ever saw a telescope in her possession."

As she said this, the emperor all of a sudden became very tense. Then his head spun around, trying to judge where the guard might be. "Leave us," he ordered sternly. "I want to be alone with her."

The guard hesitated, then moved to the door and opened it. Yet he didn't leave. He closed the door as if he had stepped outside, but he remained in the room, standing perfectly still.

Tasheira couldn't believe such shocking disregard for a direct order. She was about to call the man out on his deceit, but somehow Tael was already aware.

"I know you're still here," he growled viciously. "You must be incredibly foolish to defy me."

Even though the guard's face was hidden behind his mask, Tasheira could tell he was shocked. With no choice but to obey, he made a quick exit.

"He's gone," said Tash.

"I know," replied the emperor, straightening his back to sit taller. "Now, what were you starting to tell me? Something about a telescope?"

"I'm not sure what I can really say about it. Elia never really showed it to me, or let me use it, though I have to admit, I didn't ask if I could. I wonder if a telescope like that can hold any value."

"More than you can imagine, I'm afraid. But it won't be long before I have the thing safely in my custody."

"Is that really possible? I doubt you can retrieve it," said Tash. She could see from the emperor's expression that she had offended him. "Please, forgive me," she quickly added.

"I only assumed it would be a problem to find the telescope since Elia was holding on to it when she jumped from the Grand Bridge. What she was thinking I'll never know. And then to see Hokk fly after her—"

"What do you know about this Hokk fellow?"

"Not too much."

"Weren't you the one who found him? You convinced your father to bring him to the palace, along with the girl, didn't you?"

Tash swallowed a lump in her throat. Why had she been so determined to make sure everyone at the Royal Court knew she was the one who had discovered Hokk after he crash-landed in the desert?

"I did," she reluctantly admitted. "But I'm sure if anyone else had witnessed the fiery debris falling from the moon, then found the wreckage and Hokk barely surviving, with such awful burns to his body, they too would have believed his story without doubting it. Only now am I questioning Hokk's motives. I don't know for certain whether he had any real connection with Elia. To be honest, I don't even think he's from the moon because—" Tash cut herself off. Her face contorted with a grimace of regret. Fortunately, she thought, the emperor wouldn't see her frustration. She wished she had shut up sooner. She'd been on the brink of telling Tael everything Fimal had shared with her—how Hokk was really from Below, and how Fimal had been beneath the clouds to confirm such a place existed. She realized, almost too late, that keeping this information confidential could ultimately prove to be a benefit to her.

Unfortunately, though, Emperor Tael was now too interested to let the topic drop. "You suspect he's not from the moon because . . ." he prompted.

Tash rolled her eyes and frowned as she tried to think of an answer, again thankful Tael could not see her struggling. "Well . . . I guess because he's so pale. He doesn't look like anybody else. So how, then, can he share a common ancestry with us?"

Tael nodded thoughtfully. "Hmm. That's a very interesting question. One that I hadn't considered, though I did have my suspicions about the young man from the start. I even had him followed in case—"

The door abruptly flew open and banged against the wall behind it. Tael's identical twin brother, Emperor Tohryn, stormed in with an Imperial Guard at his heels. Tasheira could not tell if it was the same guard as before, but how else would Tohryn have known they were here?

"Brother, I'm glad I have found you," he said. "I've heard what has happened. The entire palace is in turmoil. Is this the perpetrator?"

"I am *not* the one to blame!" Tash declared vehemently. "There's been a misunderstanding. I want to see my father."

Tohryn gave her a contemptuous look before turning his attention to his blind brother, who remained seated and composed, with just the hint of a smile on his face.

"Everyone is horrified to think you've been the victim of an assassination attempt. There are rumors you've been killed."

"Yet as you can see, I'm perfectly fine," said Tael, dramatically raising both arms but continuing to gaze blankly ahead.

"It's best you present yourself to the court, as soon as you feel capable, to put an end to this speculation before it gets out of hand."

"No, it's best we find the girl who was in my suite," countered Tael. "That is of far greater importance."

"I've been informed that the girl in question jumped from the Grand Bridge. She's dead. She is no longer a threat."

"I want the city searched for her," said Tael.

"What?" exclaimed Tohryn.

"I said, my dear brother, that I want the city searched. That's where she'll be found."

Tohryn glanced at Tasheira, as if she might understand

this reasoning. But she was just as baffled. To look for Elia within the City of Na-Lavent—it made no sense at all!

"So what do you propose?" Tohryn asked with a large sigh. "What will the order be?"

"All available reinforcements will be dispatched to search every street and alleyway. We need posters up with her image for people who might have seen her, a town crier to publicly announce what's going on for those who can't read, and a reward for information."

"We'll need a good description to reproduce her likeness."

"Lady Tasheira, here, will help us with that, I'm sure. She knew this Elia girl more personally than any of us. And when Lady Tasheira is done, I want her untied from this chair and released," Tael added firmly as he stood and stretched his arm out with his cane. "For goodness' sake, we're not barbarians!"

Chapter 7

THE DEEPER ELIA MOVED toward the heart of the city, the more anxious she felt. She ducked from one alley into another, always hugging the walls, limping along within the shadows. Every time she came across someone, she would hurry past, afraid she'd be recognized and stopped. Her steadfast resolve was quickly slipping away. Her hands trembled. The pace of her heartbeat had doubled. With each minute, her condition deteriorated more, and she knew exactly the reason why.

She craved incense.

And she hated herself for needing it!

Elia could not deny how dependent she'd become. Inhaling the fragrant smoke had seemed completely harmless at first—even Tasheira had indulged, despite relentlessly harassing her mother for the woman's addiction. Yet Elia had lit a stick of incense only a couple of hours ago, and now here she was, already struggling to cope. Its calming effect had worn off much too soon.

And that was supposed to have been her last stick of incense *forever*! She had promised Hokk.

You don't need incense! You're being too weak. Just carry on like you used to!

Perhaps she'd be better able to manage the nagging desire if she could find something to eat. She was already heading toward the market.

But Elia stopped mid-stride. Was that really a place she wanted to be? With all the people who might see her? With the possibility of running into her father along the way?

She reconsidered and changed direction. It would be a different situation if she had a few coins—she could discretely enter the market, buy food, and then disappear again. Yet Elia had no money, and nothing to trade. All she had was the telescope in her hand and the clothes she was wearing.

So what should she do instead?

Leave the city. Return to what she used to call home. Maybe life for the rest of her family hadn't fallen apart as badly as Elia was assuming. Perhaps she'd find her mother, or even her brother, waiting in the shack on its island that floated at the end of a suspension bridge. Think of the joyous reunion!

But what if no one was there? What if they were truly missing or imprisoned? Or dead? Could Elia handle being on her own in the empty home, filled with so many memories, worrying about what had actually happened to her family?

One night. She could deal with one night. It would give her a chance to rest and figure out her next move. Then, if neither Sulum nor Rayhan showed up by morning, Elia would leave and never look back.

Unfortunately, the trip to get there would be long and arduous because of her sore ankle. She'd have to get to the outskirts of the city, travel past miles of farmland, then cut through the forest along the path that led to her home. It was a journey Elia and Sulum had always done on their bicycles, riding both ways, to and from work. And a bike was precisely what she needed to pull this off.

Steal one!

But where could she find a bicycle without getting caught?

Despite its risks, she knew the market was her best bet.

Elia changed course yet again. This could work. The marketplace would be busy, but with lots of distractions. And it didn't mean she would have to run into her father.

After several more blocks, Elia came upon the public square, which was full of midday shoppers, farmers pushing carts through the throng, stray dogs chasing each other, and vendors calling out their wares or cooking over fires. She found the tantalizing smells an unbearable torment. *You've been much hungrier than this, she reminded herself.*

Elia continued on, keeping to the outskirts, until she spied a cluster of vulnerable bikes behind a stall where several family members—the ones too old or young to work in the fields—were selling melons of all shapes and colors. Their harvest had drawn a sizable crowd of prospective buyers, and the family was busy exchanging produce for money. She waited for the right moment.

A quarrel started when a purchaser dropped a melon, splat, on the ground, and then refused to pay for the damaged fruit. Before the fuss could die down, Elia grabbed the handlebars of the nearest bicycle, kicked one leg over, and planted her feet on the pedals. Her balance was shaky as she began pedaling hard.

"My bike! Thief! She's stealing it!"

Elia didn't stop or turn to look—she just kept going. She maneuvered as best she could through the curious crowds. No one tried to interfere. Ignoring the pain in her ankle, Elia soon found herself racing down an alley, speeding away from the market as fast as her legs would take her.

She rode for at least an hour until she arrived, exhausted, at the edge of the forest. And then her heart seized with nostalgia, knowing what she would find at the end of the trail. The weeks that had passed since she had last been here felt like the memories of some other lifetime.

As she cycled down the path, the front wheel of her rickety

bike wobbled precariously as if it might fall off entirely, and the tree roots made the whole contraption rattle in protest. But it all held together.

Elia arrived at the turn where she and her mother had discovered Opi blocking their way that one evening when the poor old man was panicked because Omi had gone missing. Later that same night, Elia had found her grandmother dead.

Trying not to think about it, Elia kept pedaling.

She came to the spot where she used to climb trees with her father at the end of a long workday, before his troubled mind distorted the man she had loved and admired.

Elia suppressed this memory too and continued on.

Then she rounded the last bend, where she'd finally see their family home up ahead.

Elia screeched the bike to a halt. Her heart drummed against her chest.

Launching herself from the seat, she pitched her bike to the ground and hobbled the rest of the way on foot.

She couldn't believe her eyes.

The path ended where there should have been a suspension bridge!

Just a few frayed fibers from where the rope had been cut now dangled over the edge of rock, hanging down into the mist.

No house. No small floating islet. Only clouds and nothing more, stretching out to the endless horizon.

Chapter 8

IF ONLY THIS WERE a nightmare—then he could wake up from it. But Rayhan had witnessed smells, sights, and sounds beyond what his mind would be capable of conceiving in a dream. So it had to be real! All of it!

Rayhan guessed well over an hour had passed since he had disobeyed Blaitz and descended with his horse through the visually impenetrable clouds. Disoriented by the gray void ahead of him, he had stayed on high alert for Scavengers, who could attack from any direction. His heightened anxiety only grew worse, though, when he saw no sign of either his sister or the young man with the dark glasses. Something horrible must have happened to them. He feared the same fate for himself. But then, at last, he had emerged through the mist, completely unscathed, and the immensity of the new world that spread below him was both thrilling and terrifying.

Yet how could any of this be possible? Dark clouds were suspended overhead instead of level with the ground, and drops of falling water, like tiny waterballs, were blasted sideways by a raging wind to soak his uniform. Incredible! The land itself seemed as vast as the sky, although at first,

Rayhan couldn't figure out its true nature since it gave the bizarre impression of being both solid and liquid.

Then, in that one heart-stopping moment, he had seen them—the Scavengers!

They looked, however, nothing like the descriptions he had heard since childhood. Perhaps they were minions of the more ferocious creatures he feared. They had a recognizable human form and appeared to be foragers who combed through the staggering quantities of . . . what was it? Garbage? He saw it everywhere. They were even dressed in the stuff!

And now, he was their prisoner.

They had taken his helmet and forced him into something resembling a cage, but not one with bars of metal or wood. Instead, a crude dome of interlaced netting, like the material that had snared him, held him captive. The lightweight walls were constructed from countless rings made out of a semi-translucent substance—a very unusual material Rayhan had never encountered before, like strong, flexible rope, but without any discernible fibers. Each loop was almost big enough to stick a hand through, if his wrists hadn't already been tied behind his back. Six rings at a time were joined seamlessly, two by three, into a rectangular shape, with hundreds of these same rectangles lashed together to create the web of his inescapable enclosure.

The bottom of this flexible cage was a tangled mess of more floating garbage. It held together well enough for him to stand and not slip through, but his boots were thoroughly soaked. Actually, everything he was wearing was wet, and Rayhan shivered from the extreme cold.

But at least the water's surface had calmed down, no longer moving up and down in violent, nauseating waves. And the droplets falling out of the sky had stopped too; only a few occasionally dripped onto his head from the top of his cell. Tasting somewhat like waterballs, they were refreshing when he licked them from his lips, though not enough to satisfy his growing thirst.

Rayhan lowered himself onto his knees and balanced carefully as he dipped his face into a chilly puddle. He sucked a big mouthful and swallowed, and then immediately retched from the water's extreme saltiness. His stomach convulsed to rid his gut of its vile contents. Groaning, he collapsed onto his side, soaking himself even more. Since his hands were bound, he couldn't wipe away the awful stomach acid and salty mucus that lingered on his tongue and dribbled over his chin.

What had he just tried to drink? This wasn't water! It was something else!

He became overwhelmed with despair. How was he ever going to escape from here? Feeling doomed, he thought about the riderless horse he had seen flying back to Above, just before he was taken prisoner. His instinct had been to take it as a sign that he should return home. To avoid Below at all costs! But then he had thought of his sister.

Maybe Elia was also being held as a prisoner somewhere nearby.

He struggled to his feet, then peered through one of the walls. He could see mounds of trash, bobbing gently, but none that looked like a similar enclosure where Elia could be kept. In the distance, almost as far as the horizon, he noticed several plumes of smoke rising into the sky, as if small fires had been started—the only clue that other people existed out here.

Rayhan heard a startled neigh behind him, which made him jump. He splashed across to the other side of his cage and pressed his face against the mesh. He could see his black stallion tethered not too far away, its wings wrapped with nets. The animal pulled against a rope tied around its neck, and stamped one hoof. Something was making it anxious.

Then Rayhan noticed two additional legs—the legs of a person standing behind the stallion. It could only be one of the bandits who'd attacked him.

"Hey!" Rayhan yelled. "Get away from that animal!"

Caught by surprise, the culprit crouched to the ground as if attempting to hide. But Rayhan could easily see him beneath the horse's belly, and he couldn't believe his eyes. It was the young man from the palace who had earlier been wearing dark glasses!

"Come and help me!" Rayhan shouted.

The young man looked left and right, as if unsure from which direction the voice was coming.

"Over here!"

The other fellow didn't move.

"I can see you!" Rayhan called out again.

Their eyes finally locked.

"Break me out of this thing!" he demanded.

Cautiously, the young man stood and came around the stallion. Then he sprinted toward Rayhan, leaping over gaps in the garbage where the water was exposed. As soon as he reached him, the youth's hands shot through the webbing, stretching two of the rings, and he grabbed Rayhan around the throat, yanking him up against the wall.

"Shut up!" the young man hissed, frantically glancing around. "Are you a complete idiot?"

"Let . . . go . . . of me!" Rayhan gasped. The rings of the enclosure were cutting into his face.

"Do you want them coming back?" he asked, tightening his hold as if to stop Rayhan's breath.

Rayhan shook his head. With his wrists tied, he could do nothing to pry away his attacker's hands. And now so close to each other—face to face with only the netting between them—Rayhan was suddenly aware just how much this pale young man resembled the creatures who had captured him.

When his adversary's grip loosened just enough, Rayhan pulled free. He choked, but could not rub his sore neck. He wished he could launch himself at his opponent to strike back.

Just convince him to get me out of here, Rayhan thought to himself. *I can retaliate later.*

"Why have you followed me down to Below?" the young man whispered angrily.

"Because I'm looking for the same thing as you," Rayhan croaked. "We're on the same mission."

"And what's that?"

"I'm trying to find Elia."

The young man's rage flared, and he lunged at the wall again, sticking both arms through, but this time he couldn't reach Rayhan. "Leave her alone! What could you possibly want with her?"

"She's my sister, damn it!"

The face in front of him flashed with surprise. "I don't believe you," he murmured, letting his arms drop.

"It's true. Elia is my sister," Rayhan repeated firmly. "And together we can save her."

Chapter 9

HOKK CLENCHED HIS JAW as he scrutinized the young man in the plastic enclosure. He was missing his helmet but was otherwise dressed in the uniform of an Imperial Guard. "How can I know for sure you're telling me the truth about your relationship with Elia?" he finally demanded.

"You can't," the guard replied.

"Exactly!" said Hokk, making up his mind at that very moment to be done with all this. "That's the problem here." He turned and started heading back to the horse he had come to steal. It was his only means of getting away from this dreadful place.

"No, wait! Stop!" the guard shouted. "I swear, I'm not lying!"

Immediately spinning around, Hokk charged toward him again, each footstep splashing up a spray of water. "Shut your bloody mouth!" he fumed. "You're too loud! You're going to alert the savages! Then what? They'll definitely be back to see what's going on."

"Exactly!" said the guard shrewdly, mimicking Hokk's earlier response. "I'd say that's the *real* problem right now for *you*!"

Hokk threw his hands in the air, frustrated to be caught in this predicament. In order to escape on the stallion, he'd first have to untangle the netting around the animal's wings, but he'd never accomplish anything with this bastard raising such a commotion. It would ruin everything. And the guard knew it too.

"You're going to make this as difficult as you can, aren't you?" said Hokk.

"Guaranteed."

Hokk sighed. Always vigilant, he scanned the surrounding area.

"What's your name?" the guard asked.

"Hokk," he replied grudgingly.

"I'm Rayhan."

The name sounded familiar.

"Do you think you can get me out of here?" Rayhan asked.

"It's just plastic," Hokk said with a snide chuckle. "You don't realize just how easy it can be."

"Show me. My hands are tied."

"No! First, a few questions."

"Like what?"

Hokk frowned as he tried to remember things Elia had told him about her family. "How long have you been an Imperial Guard?"

"Several weeks now. More than a month, I'd say."

"See, right there, that's not what I understood from Elia," Hokk said to challenge him. "She never mentioned you were actually a guard. That's a really significant detail for her to leave out if it were true."

"My training started right after she disappeared. Before that, I was a volunteer Shifter."

The term meant nothing to Hokk. "Were you part of the search party that came to Below to look for her that first time?"

"The *first* time?" Rayhan repeated with surprise. "I don't know what you are talking about. You mean she's been down here before?"

"Yes. She fell from the edge of her island. The ground shook so badly, it crumbled beneath her feet when she was hanging laundry . . . or something like that."

Rayhan's eyes widened as if Hokk's description had sparked a sudden realization. "Of course! I remember that day. And I remember hearing about the damage to the grounds of the Noble Sanctuary. I just never made the connection that it could be the reason why Elia went missing."

"Fortunately, she landed in the ocean and was washed up onto a beach. That's where I found her shortly after."

Rayhan's brow wrinkled. "What's the ocean?"

"You're standing on it now!"

Puzzled, Rayhan looked down at his feet.

"No, I don't mean this garbage floating on the surface. I'm talking about this entire body of water," Hokk clarified, sweeping his arms in a wide circle to encompass the horizon.

"This can't be water! It's far too salty. And there's so much of it."

"Trust me, that's exactly what it is."

Rayhan seemed to be struggling to comprehend this. But he also had other questions on his mind. "So, have you been with Elia from the start?"

"Yes, I rescued her and kept her safe." Hokk felt his chest tighten to think of their first few days together on the prairies when he had treated Elia so poorly. If only he could have a chance to do it all again differently. "We flew back to Above roughly a week ago. We had access to a horse that had been abandoned by a regiment of Imperial Guards. They were down here tracking Elia so they could capture both her and that thing she was protecting."

Rayhan gave him a side glance. "What thing?"

"I'm not saying. That's a test for you."

"I have no idea."

"Then perhaps you can tell me more about the old man

whose dead body Elia and I found after it was bundled up and thrown to Below."

Rayhan appeared genuinely confused.

"Elia referred to him as Opi."

Rayhan's expression sagged with grief. He stepped closer to the wall. "That was my grandfather," he murmured sadly. "But he can't . . . is he really dead?"

"You should at least know that."

"Unfortunately, I know very little. It's been incredibly frustrating. Elia disappeared around the same time as my mother, but I only found out about it several days after it happened. I haven't been able to learn anything more. I've been in hiding ever since."

"Hiding?" That didn't make any sense to Hokk. "So, what is it? You've escaped from where you were being concealed?"

"No, I mean I've been hiding behind my uniform. My mask. You never know who's really on the other side of a mirrored helmet."

Hokk peered into the cage of plastic webbing. "Where is your helmet, anyway?"

Looking around, Rayhan shrugged. "They took it."

Then a thought came to Hokk—a question that would decide things once and for all. "Your grandfather had a small pouch around his neck. Can you identify what its contents were?"

Rayhan considered it for a moment. "Let's see . . . there was probably a coin or two, a set of false teeth made out of wood . . . some other odds and ends. Oh, and he also had an orange jewel. No, wait," he added. "He might have given that away."

"He could afford an orange jewel?" Hokk asked curiously. "I was told your family has always been poor."

"We were. We are. Extremely poor. It wasn't an actual jewel, just a piece of polished glass my grandfather once found in a sand dune."

That was the answer Hokk had been waiting for. Inspecting Elia's brother more closely, Hokk could perhaps even see a hint of a family resemblance—or was it just the dark skin and blond hair that made him and everyone else from Above look so similar?

"I believe you're the person who you say you are," Hokk admitted.

"Good. Because there's no other reason to risk coming to Below except to save my sister. Have you seen any sign of her? Is she with you now?"

Hokk's face clouded over and he glanced toward the distant skyline. He took a moment before being able to respond. "I'm afraid there's no hope for her. Too much time has passed."

"That can't be!"

"Then where is she?" Hokk asked gravely. "Where could she possibly be in this vast wasteland? If the fall didn't kill her, she most likely slipped through into the water and has drowned. I'm trying to prepare myself for the reality that all we can do now is locate and retrieve her body."

Rayhan shuddered, but then he looked up at Hokk with determined eyes. "Let's find her . . . together." He stepped closer. "Will you tell me now how I can get out of here?"

Hokk nodded. "As I said, this cage is made of nothing more than plastic. It stretches. You can tear right through the stuff."

To demonstrate, he crouched near the bottom, grabbed the flexible wall and started pulling the rings apart. They didn't tear as he described, but they did slowly stretch to create one larger hole. When the space was big enough, Rayhan awkwardly slithered out with his hands still lashed behind his back.

"Here, let me help," Hokk offered.

Rayhan turned and Hokk removed the plastic straps around his wrists by stretching them until they were loose enough to slip off.

Rayhan faced Hokk again. "Thank you. If I'd known it was that easy, I could have done that from the . . ."

His voice trailed off. He was staring over Hokk's shoulder, his face igniting with alarm.

Even as Hokk turned, he knew exactly what to expect. Still, every one of his muscles went rigid at the sight.

A small group of men and women, numbering half a dozen, had snuck up behind them. Looking like a gang of ragtag bandits, their limbs and torsos were wrapped in garbage, and they had pieces of trash tied around their heads. It was as if their entire wardrobe was made of plastic bags knotted together.

In silent unison, they raised the weapons in their hands, and then they charged forward, war cries wailing from their throats.

Chapter 10

TASHEIRA WAS PANTING AND sweating by the time she'd climbed the stairs to the top floor of Tohryn's tower. But what a relief to finally be back in her shabby little room. She slammed the door, making a loud point of cutting herself off from the guard who had followed her up, then she collapsed onto her bed. The plain mattress, boasting one measly thin sheet, sat directly on the floor, surrounded by a large number of boxes containing Tasheira's clothes and belongings shipped from her old bedroom at the Baron's estate.

She stuffed the bed's only pillow under her head and began massaging her sore wrists where the rope marks were still obvious. Thankfully, as the blind Emperor Tael had promised, she had been released from her restraints after assisting the artist who was summoned to their meeting room. The man had earned a reputation for painting portraits of nobility and seemed completely unfazed to work with someone tied to a chair as he swiftly sketched a reasonable likeness of Elia from Tasheira's descriptions. Elia's short hair, the scab in the middle of her forehead, and the metal piercing in her eyebrow were all important elements that helped pull together the final picture—an image destined to be copied and posted throughout the city.

Tasheira had been asked, not ordered, to return to her room for her own protection. She didn't argue. She knew she had no choice. The blind emperor had explicitly said that he wanted her kept out of sight until both he and his twin brother had a chance to address the Royal Court about the morning's events. Tasheira could tolerate this isolation for the time being, but only because she had also been promised that her father and her cousin would be sent up to see her as soon as they were located. Tasheira couldn't understand what was taking so long—the Baron had walked right outside the room where she'd been detained, and supposedly Fimal was still just a few doors down the same corridor. Whatever the case, she would just have to be patient and take advantage of this chance to catch up on some rest.

Tasheira drifted in and out of sleep, but eventually she was roused by bright sunshine bathing her mattress, reflected from the mirrored surface of the second soaring tower a short distance outside her window. Overheated and groggy, she forced herself to sit up and clear her head. Though she couldn't tell exactly how much time had passed, she was surprised that neither her father nor Fimal had shown up yet. Was Fimal in the middle of his own interrogation? The Baron too?

Above all, Tasheira was most keen to see her father. Everything that had happened over the past few days had made up her mind for good—life at the palace was not for her. She would return to the family's estate when the Baron was ready to depart. In fact, the sooner they could go, the better. She didn't want to face Empress Faytelle, the wife of Emperor Tohryn, or her own half-cousin, Lady Jeska, and have to explain anything. She couldn't risk being pressured to change her mind or, even worse, being forbidden to leave. Tash just wanted to make her escape and put as much distance between herself and this place as quickly as possible, with the least amount of fanfare.

But of course, leaving didn't mean that she had failed. Being a lady-in-waiting simply did not suit her temperament. At the moment, she no longer cared about rising in the ranks of the nobility, or finding a suitable husband with an enviable status. She just wanted her old life back. Her mother had always despised the gossip and politics of the Royal Court, and surprisingly, Tash now felt sympathetic toward the Baroness in a way she would have never believed possible. To realize how much they were alike was both enlightening and depressing.

Tasheira got to her feet, stretched, and approached the window. Staring straight ahead at the opposite tower, she marveled at just how far her room was above the ground. Could anyone be over there on the top floor of Tael's tower, looking back at her? She doubted it. Surely no one else was assigned to live at such a ridiculous altitude.

Her gaze drifted down the tower's glass panels until she could see the courtyard where she had arrived several nights earlier. The area outside the main reception hall was filled with horses and floating stone platforms, like the ones that had been used to bring her things here. Brimming with sudden excitement, Tasheira knew exactly what she was seeing. The Baron was preparing to leave!

Praise the sun!

Although Tash couldn't recognize any faces from such a height, she was absolutely certain both the Baron and Fimal were down there, making arrangements for their journey—it explained why they hadn't come up to see her yet. And she was pleased that almost all of her personal items were still in crates, because there'd be no time wasted organizing things. Maybe they could be airborne, heading back toward her father's estate, within the hour!

A knock at the door made Tash spin around. "Come in," she said cheerfully.

When it opened, she saw two guards standing in the corridor.

"It's time to leave, isn't it?" Tash asked with a wide grin.

"That's correct," said one of the men, sounding almost surprised.

"And I'm assuming all this will be brought down for me?" she asked, waving her arms around her. "No need for me to do anything with it?"

"Uh, yes . . . it will all be taken care of," the same guard replied, as if not quite sure. "Just come as you are."

Tash took a final look around her wretched room, thrilled to know she'd never see it again, and then stepped out into the hallway to join them. "Good. Let's go."

This is also the last time I'll have to take these miserable stairs, Tash thought to herself as the three of them began to descend, one guard leading, the other following behind. Flight after flight, they continued down but encountered no ladies or noblemen along the way. Tash suspected everyone in the Royal Court was assembled for the special audience the emperors wanted to hold. It was ideal! The fewer people who would see her leaving, the better.

By the time they reached the ground floor, Tash realized she had seen very few servants. She would have expected a large group of them to be heading up to her floor to start bringing down the boxes. Yet perhaps, since it was such a sudden departure, it would take some time to assemble enough staff to handle the volume of work.

Crossing through the main reception hall—a massive atrium of glass that connected the emperors' two towers—Tasheira started heading toward the revolving doors that opened into the courtyard and the gardens beyond. One of the guards, however, gently touched her elbow to redirect her. "The Baron asked to meet you at the stables. For security reasons, we'll take you through the back way."

"Fine," said Tasheira.

They passed through the same corridors that Tash and Fimal had taken earlier when they followed Elia out to the

Grand Bridge, moments before the girl jumped, presumably to her death. Now, however, the guard walking ahead of her stopped at the top of some stairs. The steps, which appeared to be carved out of solid rock, led underground.

"Down the stairs!" he ordered, his voice suddenly threatening.

In the split second it took for Tasheira to realize her situation, it was already too late. The guard behind her grabbed hold of her shoulders.

"No!" Tash yelled in terror, trying to break free. "Let go of me!"

The guard pushed her forward and Tash stumbled down the first few steps before recovering her balance. But the man was right there again, shoving her hard.

"Help me!" she shouted as she was half dragged, half carried to the next level beneath the main floor of the palace. Hauled past the kitchens, Tash noticed cooks and serving staff. "Please, somebody help me!" she screamed.

Startled faces turned in her direction, but no one dared to move. Instead, they frowned and quickly cast their eyes down, continuing to work as if they had seen nothing.

Desperate, Tash started to kick, scratch, and flail her limbs. The pair of guards picked her up, one squeezing her arms to her body and one holding her ankles tight, as they continued down to greater depths of gloom. They arrived at another floor of kitchens, and then below that, at what appeared to be the palace laundry. Here, there were no traces of natural light, only the feeble glow of torches on the walls. It was as though she was being delivered to her death.

And then they arrived at the very bottom of the stairs, in front of a massive wooden door. With his gloved hand curled into a fist, one of the guards knocked—*boom, boom*—and a small slat slid across to allow a pair of eyes to peer out. The slat closed and the door opened with a chilling creak. The dungeon keeper—not an Imperial Guard with a polished metal helmet, but rather a colossal brute with a leather hood over his head—stepped aside to let them enter.

"Got another one for you," said a guard as they dropped Tash on the damp stone floor.

"Same orders?" the warden asked.

"That's right. The very same."

Tasheira leapt to her feet and attempted to bolt. The beast of a man easily caught her. Tash screamed, trying to fight him off, but her efforts were no match for his strength. Once the guards had left, he held her with one hand and used his other to close the dungeon's main door with a thunderous crash. Then he flung her over his shoulder, grabbed a torch, and carried her down several more staircases and winding corridors. Though hanging inverted with blood rushing to her head, she could distinguish cell doors along the passages, some with inmates clinging to the bars, staring out silently at the commotion, mere phantoms of the people they used to be.

Tash pounded on the man's back with her fists. It made no difference.

He seemed to bring her as deep as they could possibly go. When they reached her cell, he tossed her to the floor without a word, then quickly slammed the door before she had a chance to get to her feet.

Tash threw herself onto the metal bars, her arms reaching out, trying to stop him. "You can't do this to me!" she roared.

But the dungeon keeper disappeared around a corner, his torchlight growing ever fainter as the darkness closed in, like a demonic shadow, to envelop her in this tomb beneath the palace.

Chapter 11

ELIA SAT SLUMPED ON the ground with the telescope in her lap and her legs hanging over the side of the island. Not that long ago, before she knew better, she never would have dared to approach anywhere near such a dangerous edge like this, let alone risk dangling her feet into the clouds where Scavengers could grab hold and pull her over. Certainly, if anybody from Above came across her now, they'd think she had lost her mind, or given up on life entirely.

And she did feel like giving up. She was overwhelmed with grief and worn down by setbacks. How could she carry on? Why should she even bother trying?

With hands trembling from the effects of incense withdrawal, she absent-mindedly picked the frayed ends of rope still tied to the spikes wedged into the ground beside her. Though she stared straight ahead, her unblinking eyes had stopped registering the view. Instead, her focus had turned inward as she imagined every possible scenario of what could have happened here. But her mind always came back to an especially troubling theory—Imperial Guards must have visited in the middle of the night and slashed the bridge's ropes while Elia's mother was asleep. Bathed in the glow of the shattered moon, the small islet upon which the home sat would have floated away into the clouds, but this time with no rescue team to tow it back.

And it might not be just Sulum out there, either. Maybe Elia's brother was with her too. While it had been a few years since Rayhan had left home to live closer to his work in the dewfields, it was very possible he had started spending the nights again with their mother. Perhaps Sulum needed his company, plus the added security, if she was struggling to live alone after Elia's disappearance and Opi's unexplained death.

So, have my worst fears actually been realized?

Elia thought she had prepared herself for losing her family, but now to really comprehend the magnitude of what that would mean in her life . . . her mind refused to accept it. *I can't be the only one left! Have I really lost everybody I care about?*

No . . . not everyone. There was Hokk. Just the thought of him stirred something within Elia, like a bud of tenderness that went beyond sympathy, gratitude, or the ease of familiarity. If only he could be with her now. Somehow it seemed so wrong to be separated once again on what had started out as a journey together—a journey she'd believed they were destined to complete side by side. Elia took comfort in knowing Hokk was alive, but where had he ended up? Above? Below? Would they ever find each other again?

And there's still my father.

Elia dug her fingernails into her palms. She might be alone, but she saw no reason to go looking for her father. Not today, or tomorrow. Hopefully, not ever.

Yet Elia knew of another man—a father figure himself—who might very well give her the assistance she needed. She should try to find Greyit. It was a much better plan than simply sitting here, doing nothing. In addition to being reliable, he might understand how to decipher the documents hidden inside her telescope. And maybe she'd also be able to convince him to share whatever secrets about her family he kept locked away in his mind. Surely he knew something. Elia had never forgotten that curious look Greyit and her mother had given each other when they were reunited on the mainland after Elia's home accidentally broke away during the night and drifted off the first time. Their silent exchange, spoken only with their eyes, had betrayed painful memories, as if a hefty price was once paid for something in their past. Sulum had then made a comment that immediately stood out as odd and intriguing: *We are indebted to you once again.* Again? What could her mother possibly have been referring to?

Elia made up her mind. Grabbing the telescope, she got to her feet and backtracked along the forest path. She retrieved the stolen bicycle and turned off the trail to cut across the spongy, moss-covered ground. As she walked, her sore ankle slowed her down, and she had to lift her bicycle over fallen trees blocking the way. All the while, she tried not to think about the last time she had been out here: that day she searched for her lost grandmother, only to find Omi dead.

Greyit lived deep within the forest, though Elia had little more than a general idea of the direction. She'd discovered his place by accident many years ago, before her mandatory work in the palace laundry had started at the tender age of five. In those earlier days of freedom, she regularly roamed these woodlands, but always by herself because the rest of her family worked from early morning until dusk. On rare occasions, Elia's father would arrive home ahead of the others and he'd playfully chase her up into a tree, then sit with her on one of the branches to share stories of the islands in the Lunera System he had visited as a young man. She used to love being with her father back then, just the two of them. But after everything that had happened, including his assault, arrest, and eventual abandonment of his family, the memories were bittersweet.

Shadows began to stretch as the afternoon ripened. A warm breeze picked up and carried with it a scent of green foliage and soil.

Coming across a narrow yet well-worn path, Elia decided it looked promising. She got back on her bicycle and followed the trail for what seemed like several more miles. Around each bend, she expected to see Greyit's home, but it was only when she was about to lose hope altogether that the trail curved and she finally spotted a building farther ahead, nestled among the trees. *Praise the sun!* She had found it! The rough-hewn walls framed a weathered door painted with large blue-and-white checkers, just as she remembered.

No doubt, as soon as Greyit heard about the lost islet and the possibility that Elia's mother and brother were missing, he'd spring into action. She was sure he would arrange a search party. Initially, Elia had assumed the ropes had been sliced several days ago, but it could have happened just last night. There might still be time!

Elia's eagerness waned, however, as she got closer to the modest building. The door and the home's one window were closed tight. If Greyit were actually home, he would have left them open to let through the cooling breeze. Elia wondered how long she should wait for his return—unless he already knew the suspension bridge had been cut, and he was launching a rescue attempt this very moment! Yes, of course, that's what he was probably doing! Greyit visited her family regularly, and after Opi died, he would have probably started dropping by more frequently to check on Sulum. Elia must have just missed him. He could very well be at the edge of the island right now, where she had been sitting earlier, waiting with a bunch of Shifters for another team of flying horses to tow her home back to where it belonged.

Having come all this way, however, Elia wanted to double-check that he really wasn't around. She leaned her bike against the wall and cupped her hands to peer through the window. She was surprised and disappointed to see Greyit napping in a chair.

Though tempted to rap her knuckles on the glass to wake him, Elia decided against startling the old man. She went to the door instead and knocked lightly, simultaneously turning the knob and slowly opening the door.

"Greyit?" Elia asked softly. "Are you awake?"

She remembered he was a sound sleeper.

Elia crept forward. A plate of half-eaten food sat on a small table next to his chair. She crouched beside him and gently shook his shoulder. "Greyit, it's Elia," she said, realizing she'd look very different to him from the last time he had seen her. "I've returned. I need your help."

She shook a little harder and Greyit's head rolled toward her on a limp neck.

One look at his face was all she needed.

Elia shoved herself away from the chair and the dead man sitting in it.

Chapter 12

RAYHAN BRACED HIMSELF, READY to launch a barrage of fists against this howling pack of attackers. Escape was impossible. Even if he tried fighting off half of them, while Hokk confronted the others, they were still outnumbered three to one.

He took a defensive step backward, but found no solid footing. One leg plunged into the frigid water, and his boot became trapped in the garbage. He lost his balance and toppled over. Panicking as he struggled to pull himself free, Rayhan looked up just in time to see Hokk take a running leap, then dive headfirst through an open space in the drifting debris before disappearing with a splash beneath the surface. Quick thinking on Hokk's part; Rayhan wished he had done the same.

The next moment, he was swarmed by the feral gang of men and women who tugged him free of his boot and lifted him into the air. His limbs were pulled in different directions by many hands, as if to tear him apart. He screamed and kicked someone in the head with the heel of his remaining boot, before it was snatched off. His wrists and ankles were tied together with plastic straps that dug painfully into his flesh.

Longer pieces were then hastily wrapped around his body to keep his legs together and his arms cinched to his side.

Once securely bound, he was dropped onto the wet, ever-shifting surface, and the human scavengers abandoned him to circle the spot where Hokk had escaped. Seeing nothing, they scattered to explore other open holes in the vicinity, peering into the deep, dark ocean for any sign of him.

"He's got to come up for air!" one of them shouted.

From where he was lying, Rayhan craned his neck and scanned the area intently. He too saw nothing—no head poking above the water, no eye-catching ripple or displaced piece of trash moving ever so slightly.

The others were clearly growing frustrated with their search. Some held clubs, but those holding spears began stabbing their pointy shafts through the layers of garbage.

"I see him!" a young woman finally yelled. She drove her spear down with all her weight as her five companions gathered beside her and started clearing away the rubbish to retrieve Hokk's skewered corpse from beneath the water.

But Rayhan could only worry about himself. He desperately looked to the left and right for options. His tethered horse, with its wings still caught in a net, stood not too far away.

The next instant, Rayhan was rolling as fast as he could. A blur of gray sky and then garbage, gray sky and then garbage spun past his eyes. Thankfully, the others were too preoccupied with pulling their catch from the ocean and shouting encouragement to each other to hear the splash of the puddles he tumbled through or the crunch of debris beneath him. But would he make it?

Suddenly, a shadow darkened his vision. As he had hoped, it was the belly of his stallion overhead. One more full roll and he was on the other side of the animal, the horse now separating him from his enemies.

Glancing back, he neither saw nor heard any commotion to suggest his departure had been noticed. Rayhan looked down at himself and was surprised to discover that his rolling had caused the strips of plastic lashed earlier around his body to loosen and unravel. He wiggled out of what remained, and then, with his bound hands, stretched the plastic around his ankles until he could finally kick his legs free. He carefully stood, using the horse to steady himself as the surface of the ocean bobbed beneath his bare feet. He peered over the animal's back. He could see six bandits, but none were looking his way. Instead, they had pulled something out of the water, though it was too difficult to tell whether or not it was Hokk's body.

Hurry! I'll be next!

He only had to free his hands. Bending over, Rayhan inserted one foot as a wedge between his wrists, then pulled his arms up hard to force the ties to stretch. For greater leverage, he leaned backward as he focused all his strength—and that's when his attention was suddenly diverted skyward, causing his pulse to run wild.

Flying stallions! Just below the boiling clouds. A small formation of them was gliding down toward the ocean from two colossal floating rocks—clearly, the pointed undersides of Kamanman and the Noble Sanctuary. And though the animals were still quite a distance away, Rayhan had no doubt the riders on their backs were Imperial Guards. They had descended to rescue him! These were the reinforcements he needed! Now he just had to survive long enough for the team to reach him.

Worried the bandits might have noticed the stallions too, Rayhan looked again over the horse's back. Wait—there now appeared to be only five people present. Or was he mistaken?

Stripping the loosened ties from his wrists, Rayhan spun around, but there was nobody sneaking up to surprise him. He turned again and quickly counted heads, straining to confirm whether a bandit was missing or if one person was just hidden behind the others.

And then he felt a hand grab him. Like a claw reaching out of the ocean, it dug into the tendons around his ankle, ready to pull him under.

Chapter 13

ELIA SAW NOTHING TO suggest that Greyit's death was suspicious. But given the circumstances, she had a terrible feeling that things were not right. Somebody could have so easily made it look as though the man had passed away of natural causes. Was the food on the plate beside him poisoned? Was his neck broken? Had he been suffocated, then arranged on the chair as if nothing sinister had happened?

It seemed everyone connected to her was doomed to meet an unfortunate end. And how much time did she have before those dangers caught up to her? Could she stay a step ahead long enough to get her questions addressed? Or had the last chance for answers perished with Greyit?

The old man must have died recently, otherwise a more horrendous smell would have fouled the air, much stronger than the stale scent of his unfinished meal. But it wouldn't be long before the situation with his corpse became exceedingly unpleasant.

Elia wanted to get away as soon as possible. Being alone with a dead body didn't bother her, but she certainly did not want to risk an encounter with whoever might bear the blame for this suspected act of violence against Greyit—somebody who was just as likely to be on the hunt for her.

Deciding to simply abandon the corpse, Elia quickly stepped out through the door, but then paused to reconsider. Why leave before searching the place for some useful supplies? Maybe she could even uncover information about the puzzling questions that she still faced.

Not surprisingly, Greyit had very few possessions. He had been a bachelor, living in the same kind of poverty as most other rural citizens of Kamanman. Elia found more food on the verge of spoiling, as well as a dusty waterball with a few mouthfuls still left in it, but her suspicion about poison made it easy to ignore the urge to eat or drink. It wasn't worth the risk.

Finding a wooden chest beneath a blanket, she opened the lid and discovered a leather saddlebag sitting on top, which was just the right size to hold her telescope. When she opened one of the bag's side pockets, she was excited to see a few coins hidden inside. Perfect! They'd be enough to buy some fresh food to last for at least a couple of days.

She rummaged deeper in the chest and found a few pairs of old pants, wrinkled shirts, a hat, another blanket, a pair of boots, and—

Elia gasped. She couldn't believe it!

A mirrored helmet, wrapped in a threadbare towel! The kind of helmet worn only by Imperial Guards!

Elia promptly dropped the lid as if to prevent the contents from escaping. She glanced at the body in the chair, then back at the chest, as her mind raced.

Had she ever before heard the slightest indication that Greyit had once been a guard? She didn't think so. She thought he had always been a farmer—that's how he knew her father and Opi so well. But as a young man, perhaps he really had been a member of the Royal Regiment. That might explain the important connections he seemed to have. Given his age, however, Greyit would have been an Imperial Guard during the reign of the Empress Mother, not her sons, the Twin Emperors.

Now feeling an even greater separation from the answers she wanted, Elia raised the lid of the storage chest again and carefully rebundled the helmet with the old towel. Except for the saddlebag and the money, which she would keep, she repacked everything as she had found it. To leave his belongings looking undisturbed felt like a measure of respect for Greyit—albeit a very small gesture. But she could not afford wasting any more time.

She touched Greyit's shoulder before she headed to the door where, for the briefest moment, she allowed herself to look back one last time at him sitting in his chair.

And then she was gone.

Chapter 14

HOKK REACHED UP TO grab a handful of plastic to pull himself out of the water. But to feel human flesh in the grip of his ice-cold fingers was an absolute shock. He immediately let go and dropped his arm back into the ocean.

He opened his eyes again underwater and could tell through gaps in the rubbish that he was almost right below where the horse was standing, just as he had intended. But had his efforts been in vain? Had he foolishly grabbed the leg of one of those strange, vicious garbage collectors?

Hokk was running out of oxygen—he could not swim to a different hole. Another moment or two, and he'd be forced to surface right there for his next breath, regardless of who was waiting for him on top.

Still, he held out a little longer, delaying the inevitable in case a different plan came to mind. He glanced around. His eyes stung from the salt water, but he strained to keep them open. It was a whole different world beneath the surface, a nightmarish dreamscape of inverted mountains of garbage that descended to ever-greater depths, disappearing into the bluey-blackness. Maneuvering through this jumbled maze had not only been extremely difficult, but also terrifying. He could so easily have become entangled in the floating debris. If Elia had fallen into a similarly snarled, sunken wasteland, she might have been hopelessly trapped, likely unable to break through the trash for a breath.

Hokk had already come up once for a quick gulp of air, after dodging the spears that had suddenly started piercing the garbage. When he had poked his face out for that brief instant, he'd been able to gauge in which direction to swim to reach the horse. Flying away on the animal was his only chance to escape with his life. He would leave Rayhan behind if necessary.

Now his lungs felt seriously close to giving out. His ears were plugged. All sound was muffled except for his racing pulse, which thumped against his eardrums. Then it occurred to him that the onslaught of spears behind him had stopped. Except for plastic bobbing in the current, everything was still.

They're just waiting for me to emerge.

Unable to delay any longer, Hokk extended his arms straight above his shoulders and kicked with a last spurt of energy despite his muscles screaming from the cold. He aimed for an opening that was just wide enough to burst through. Erupting above the water, he gasped for air and clawed at the surrounding plastic. He felt the viselike grip of a hand clamp around his wrist to drag him out of the ocean.

"He's by that large bird we captured earlier!" someone shouted.

"They're both there!" yelled another.

Sprawled beside the ink-black horse, Hokk sputtered to catch his breath. He could hear the splash of footsteps running closer. Wiping his eyes, he looked up at the person standing next to him, anticipating either a blow from a club or a spear impaling his rib cage. But thank goodness! It was only Rayhan!

Rayhan quickly hauled Hokk to his feet. "Your timing couldn't be better," he said grimly as he peered over the stallion's back. "Or worse."

The garbage collectors were charging toward them, brandishing their weapons as before.

Then Rayhan did a most unexpected thing. He stepped out from behind the tethered horse and held one hand up to them, palm forward, fingers splayed, as if the gesture could stop their advance. Keeping his arm raised, he pointed up to the clouds with his other hand and screamed, "Not another step! There are plenty more like me on their way here!"

The six attackers halted abruptly, their expressions twisted with confusion. Still keeping their weapons at the ready, they turned in unison to gaze where Rayhan was pointing.

Hokk stared as well, and his mouth fell open. The view of the sky was reminiscent of what he had once observed with Elia on the prairies, only now, he was witnessing it with her brother. Far above, a group of Imperial Guards were flying on horseback, gliding down to Below, no doubt to search the ocean just as Hokk had been doing. While he didn't know whether he should feel relief or dread, the inhabitants of this gigantic floating heap of garbage were clearly disturbed by the sight.

"It's more of those enormous birds," screeched one of the women as she spun on Rayhan, wielding her spear again.

"Who are they?" demanded another man with a scruffy beard. "And who are you?"

"I'm from Above," Rayhan yelled fiercely, now pointing up to the floating islands in the distance. "I am a soldier, and those are members of my regiment. They are descending in order to find me. They'll be here soon, and they're very dangerous. If you don't back down, you'll lose your lives!"

The same man, whom Hokk judged to be the oldest person in the group, combed his fingers through his long whiskers as he reassessed the situation. "Why have you come?" he asked. He lowered his club, which made him seem less threatening—less like a savage. "We want nothing to do with you."

"So why have you captured me and held me prisoner?" Rayhan retorted.

The woman who had spoken earlier waved her spear. "We are trying to decide what to make of you two brutes," she said distrustfully. "You have trespassed on our territory. You are unexpected and unwelcome."

The bearded man held up a calming hand in front of the woman before he took a cautious step forward. "We were hunting for food when my wife first spotted your huge bird," he started to explain. "A bird like that could feed us for many weeks."

"It's a horse," Rayhan said curtly.

The word apparently meant nothing—all six faces were blank.

"And nobody eats a horse," he added with disgust. "It's cruel and uncivilized to even suggest it."

Hokk noticed the bearded man clench his fists as if insulted by Rayhan's comment and tone. He must be the father, thought Hokk, and the rest of them were his family. Whatever their connection, Hokk now felt compelled to intervene before Rayhan escalated an already difficult situation into something much more dangerous. He would have to play these people carefully to his advantage.

Hokk circled around the stallion to present himself. "My name is Hokk," he offered, deepening and softening his voice to sound more conciliatory. "And this is Rayhan. We ask that you stand down, at least long enough for us to fully explain our circumstances."

The father hesitated as he considered the request. He glanced at his wife, who nodded; then he did the same. "We'll listen."

"As you can see from my skin color, I look very different compared to my companion, Rayhan. That's because I'm not from Above." He was trying his hardest to sound sincere. "I'm actually from Below, just like you and your family."

"You sure don't look like one of us," growled a younger man whose eyes had narrowed.

"It's the truth. The only difference is that I come from a location very far from this area. Which makes me all the more curious to know—what is this place?" he asked, swinging his arms around for a broad sweep of their surroundings.

"Our home," the father replied simply.

"I mean, what's the name of it?" Hokk clarified.

"We call it the Plastlantic Mass."

"It's incredible," offered Hokk as a compliment. "Really! I can't believe how much area it covers. How far does it go?"

"It's huge. It stretches much farther than the horizon in every direction," said the man proudly, relaxing his shoulders slightly—a gesture that suggested to Hokk he was not as combative as his first introduction implied. "Most inhabitants have never journeyed far enough to reach its edges, but I am one of the few who has. I hope someday my two daughters and my two sons will have the same opportunity."

"Yes, I can imagine it must be quite an experience to see solid land for the first time," said Hokk.

"Solid land?" the man repeated, as though Hokk was speaking nonsense. "The only solid land I know of are the rock islands that drift by in the sky," he said with a snort, pointing to Kamanman and the Noble Sanctuary, which would soon disappear over the horizon.

"Actually," Hokk replied, "solid land does exist down here on Below. It's where I come from—vast, flat grasslands."

"That has to be a lie!" the man barked. "Where the Plastlantic Mass ends, there is only open ocean beyond. I have seen it! Nothing but water!"

"What kind of tricky business are you trying to pull here?" his wife demanded. "You can't fool my husband. He knows exactly what's out there!"

Hokk bowed his head in a deferential manner. He knew

he'd have no success arguing, so he changed his line of questioning. "Why do you not live closer to the edges?"

"The hunting is much better around here," the father brusquely replied. "Besides, the Mass is very unstable at the edges, and we can't build settlements there when the terrain is always breaking apart and drifting back together. The Mass is also constantly growing. As more plastic floats by, new pieces merge, so as time passes, our dwellings end up being farther and farther away from open water." The man cast a fretful gaze skyward and then frowned deeply as he scowled at the two of them and lifted his club to rest on his shoulder. "But like I said earlier, we want nothing to do with either of you, or those who are coming to retrieve you."

Hokk looked up to the clouds as well. The Imperial Guards were circling, but still at a height and distance that would prevent them from noticing this assembled group. Moreover, Hokk felt a few drops of rain, and after a lifetime gauging the weather, he could tell the storm clouds were on the brink of a deluge. The guards, unaccustomed to rain, would probably not remain here for long. To lose the threat of their presence in the sky could jeopardize Hokk and Rayhan's safety.

"We mean you no harm and we will leave as soon as possible. But first, we must ask you one thing of great importance," said Hokk. "We're trying to find a body that has dropped from one of the islands of Above. Have you seen anything?"

The husband and wife both appeared to be debating whether or not to disclose what they knew. After a moment, the woman spoke. "Are you asking about a body that has only just recently fallen?"

"Yes!" said Hokk. "That's right."

"A female? In white?"

"That's her!" Rayhan exclaimed. Then his body stiffened and his voice became strained. "She's . . . she's my sister," he mumbled.

Hokk also felt the weight of grief suddenly overwhelm him now that Elia's death had been confirmed. "If you've already found her," he said gravely, "we only want to collect her remains. Then we'll be gone."

The pair appeared very reluctant to cooperate. Again they glanced up at the flying guards.

The earlier smattering of rain was beginning to intensify. Already, the guards were converging as if preparing to leave.

Hokk could not let this opportunity slip past. "We'll give you this horse—or this bird, as you call it—in exchange for the body," he blurted out. He heard Rayhan beside him inhale sharply, but before Elia's brother could stop him, Hokk quickly continued. "Do we have a deal? The girl's body for this animal? You'll be free to do whatever you want with the beast, and we'll leave you when the troops from Above arrive to collect us."

The man studied his wife and children. He then turned back and nodded. "Agreed!" he said decisively. "Come with us."

With his club in one hand, the man swung a bundle of supplies onto his shoulders. His wife untied the horse and began leading it away. The rest of the family followed, but only after each person was loaded up with provisions. Most of the stuff appeared to be various plastic objects—they seemed to be carrying an entire dismantled camp on their backs.

Together, Rayhan and Hokk fell into step behind the group. One of the sons held back and joined the end of the procession, probably to keep a close eye on them. Hokk didn't care. Though he was unable to guess how far they'd have to travel, the only thing that mattered now was the certainty that Elia's dead body awaited them at their destination.

Chapter 15

TASHEIRA HAD BEEN SITTING alone in the pitch-black for what seemed like hours. At first, clinging to the metal bars of her cell, she had sobbed until her body was completely drained. Then, after salvaging some emotional control, she'd crawled around her enclosure, feeling for where the wall met the stone floor. In the farthest corner, she found a board covering what turned out to be a small hole. Based on the smell emanating from it, Tasheira realized this would have to be her toilet. She resisted as long as possible before using it, and shed tears again when she did.

Besides the darkness, there was dead silence, too. Tash had noticed other prisoners in the cells on higher floors when she'd first arrived, but from what she could tell, she was the only person on this lowest level of the dungeon. She hated being so isolated. Would that man with the hood forget about her down here? Would anyone bring her food and water, or would they simply let her wither and decay?

It was staggering to imagine the suffering that prisoners—some of them surely just as innocent as she was—must have endured over the years in these cold, lonely, terrifying jail cells. This underground dungeon had probably always existed, but Tasheira hadn't given the place the briefest consideration, let alone spared any thought for the caged humans within it. She had lived in a privileged world high above, taking her blessings for granted and never guessing that the luxuries she had become accustomed to could be taken away so quickly and unexpectedly. Well, when she got out—when someone realized the horrendous mistake that had been made and finally came to rescue her—she would see to it that no innocent person ever had to go through what she had already suffered.

I'm the daughter of the Baron, for goodness' sake! I'm the last person who deserves to be imprisoned!

Planning her crusade for justice on behalf of unfairly accused victims of the state, as well as imagining the lavish apology that would soon be coming her way, were enough to keep Tasheira's hopes up for the time being. So long as she never saw her father or Fimal locked away—that would be more than she could bear.

Tash banished the troubling possibility from her mind. At this very moment, the Baron and Fimal were probably demanding that the palace be torn apart until she was found.

She decided to nap. Sleep would kill the hours she might still have to wait until her release.

Tash dozed restlessly, however, constantly shifting to find a more comfortable position on the hard floor. Whenever she did drift off, she dreamed about her sumptuous bed back home.

She had no idea how much time had passed when she was roused by the sound of rattling keys.

Her wait was over!

Tash stood and crept closer to the sturdy door of her cell. The corridor slowly brightened with sputtering candlelight, but her excitement plummeted when she recognized the voice of the dungeon master.

"There's just the one down this passage," he growled.

Who was he talking to?

A door slammed, but the light from the hallway steadily grew brighter.

Tasheira's eyes widened in anticipation of the person who might come around the corner.

But it was only a servant girl, wearing an eye patch. A few years younger than Tash, she carried a bowl in one hand and a thick candle in the other. As she came closer and could see Tash in better light, the girl looked disappointed. "Oh, you're not who I was hoping you'd be," she mumbled.

"You have to get me out of here!" Tash softly pleaded.

The girl frowned and looked back along the way she had come. "There's nothing I can do. I just deliver the food," she replied as she lowered the bowl and slid it through a small gap under the bars. The dish was filled with watery brown broth and what looked like half a potato with a sliver of onion.

"I need you to deliver a message to my father," whispered Tash. She was certain he hadn't already left. He would've tried to say goodbye first, no matter what the circumstances.

"Who's your father?" the servant asked as she adjusted the patch over one eye and studied Tash with the other.

"Baron Shoad."

The girl shrugged. "The name isn't familiar."

"It doesn't matter. Just find the Baron and tell him that his daughter, Lady Tasheira—that's me—has been mistakenly arrested and hauled away to the dungeon. And you must hurry! I promise, you'll be compensated beyond what you can imagine."

Chapter **16**

GRAY CLOUDS TUMBLED OVER themselves in the upper atmosphere and wept an inconsolable torrent of water. The ocean had begun rolling again, but without the huge waves Rayhan had observed earlier in the day. Still, it was difficult to find stable places to plant their feet. He and Hokk slogged through the wetness, often leaping from one slippery pile of garbage to the next, trying to keep up with the others who had developed a natural rhythm for balancing on this moving mass.

At least he was rid of his boots. After so many months squeezing his feet into such painfully tight footwear, it was a relief not to wear them. Rayhan didn't care that the boots, as well as his polished helmet, were now in the possession of the wandering bandits. Of much greater concern to him was the horse. Hokk had acted like a madman when he'd promised it to those savages. Could they even be trusted to uphold their end of the bargain? His gut instinct told him this was not going to end well.

Upon first starting out on this trek, Rayhan and Hokk had followed the group toward the distant columns of dark smoke that Rayhan had noticed earlier, carried by the wind at an angle over the ocean. He guessed the family was heading toward an encampment, and that they would eventually find Elia's body along the way. But because of the water falling relentlessly from the sky—Hokk called it *rain*—any last vestiges of the thick plumes of smoke soon disappeared. Nevertheless, these nomads somehow knew which way to go without any landmarks to guide them. They marched on, undeterred by the miserable conditions.

Unfortunately, the weather had chased off the troop of Imperial Guards, who had returned to Above shortly after the rain began. Rayhan had been scanning the sky ever since, hoping to see them flying back beneath the clouds; however, that likely wasn't going to happen today. It was already starting to get darker with the onset of dusk, although to Rayhan's eye, Below seemed to wallow in a perpetual state of gloomy twilight. Of course, Hokk would be used to enduring this cold, wet, soul-sapping dreariness. He was probably perfectly content to stay in this godforsaken place—why else would he have so willingly offered up the flying stallion, Rayhan's only means of returning home?

Rayhan knew that Hokk, like these garbage people, could not be trusted. While the two of them were unavoidable companions for the time being as they traced Elia's fate to her tragic end, nothing about Hokk gave Rayhan any confidence. And it wasn't just because the pale young man was from Below. Rayhan couldn't pinpoint exactly why, but Hokk had a manner about him that suggested he was a schemer—that a hard life had taught him to survive no matter what the cost, without regard for anybody else. Rayhan, on the other hand, had certainly grown up in poverty, but he had still been able to develop a solid sense of compassion, decency, and good judgement—traits that Hokk seemed to be lacking. Hokk had already proven that he was unpredictable, and Rayhan would bet anything that he could be cruel, manipulating, secretive, disloyal . . . and dangerous.

All the right qualities to make him the ultimate Imperial Guard.

Rayhan was appalled that he could conceive such an offensive thought. Was that how he really felt about Imperial Guards? And what did it say about Rayhan, himself, having just started his training to become one? Was the pursuit dishonorable? *Absolutely not!* Did he think Hokk was better than him? *Never!*

"Surely these waterballs will eventually stop falling!" Rayhan complained loudly, hoping to quell the doubts that had suddenly rooted in his brain.

Hokk looked skyward and wiped his face. "Sometimes it can truly feel endless," he replied with a half-hearted chuckle. "But I've seen worse."

If Rayhan hadn't already experienced it before when the rain was blowing sideways, he would never have believed it could possibly get any nastier. Whereas the band of trash collectors ahead of them wore garments made of plastic that seemed to protect them well from the wetness, Rayhan's uniform and Hokk's clothing were completely soaked. Water ran through their eyebrows and into their eyes, down their cheeks, and into their mouths. Rayhan hoped wherever they were headed, they would soon find some shelter.

But when they reached that point, he'd have to deal with his sister's death.

Am I ready for that?

How could he ever really be prepared to see Elia's corpse?

Rayhan's footsteps slowed as images flooded his mind, beginning with his earliest memory of his younger sister—Elia no more than a baby and Rayhan just a toddler, playfully sticking his slobbery finger into her ear so that she would reward him with a laugh or cooing gurgle.

As the older brother, he had always been very protective of Elia. That's why, for all these years, he'd hated to think of her laboring so hard, so deep underground in the palace laundry. Those first few weeks after she'd started had been heartbreaking. No five-year-old should ever have been forced to work bent over a washtub, scrubbing out stains, or expected to deal with red, painful blisters like the ones that had broken out on Elia's sensitive skin from the harsh soaps and hot water. Those women and young girls working in the laundry were not much better off than the prisoners trapped one floor lower in the dungeon.

Rayhan had visited the laundry room just once, the morning their father had been beaten and arrested by Imperial Guards in the dewfields. While Greyit had left to try to find out where he'd been taken, Rayhan tracked down Sulum to tell her the news. Together, they had collected Elia and hurried home, spending the next few days in hiding and in constant fear, until Rayhan's father miraculously turned up again. That whole incident marked the starting point of their struggling family's downfall.

"Are you coming?" Hokk suddenly barked above the sound of the rain.

Rayhan looked up with a start. Without realizing, he had fallen behind the rest of the pack. He quickened his pace. When he reached Hokk, Rayhan noticed that farther ahead, everyone else had stopped to form a circle around something at their feet. A few of them were looking back at him expectantly as the stallion shook its head against the tight grip on its reins.

"Is that . . . ?" Rayhan began to ask.

Hokk nodded gravely. "I think it must be."

Rayhan took a deep breath, then clenched his jaw as he reluctantly trudged forward. Beside him, Hokk's footsteps matched his own. As he got closer, the others parted to make space for them.

He looked down and cringed. It was definitely a body, in the same white fabric Elia had been wearing when she'd come charging out of the palace. The wet material covered her head, obscuring her face, and in some areas, it had become twisted around her body.

Rayhan stood frozen, water dripping off his nose. He was reminded of the last time he had stared at a family member's bound corpse, moments before Omi was released from the Slope of Mourning. Had Omi's body also ended up somewhere in this ocean? To be discovered by these strange people who dressed themselves with garbage?

Hokk glanced at him, almost apologetically. "I'd better double-check to make sure."

Rayhan pressed his lips together and nodded.

Hokk crouched beside the body and slowly pulled back the soaked fabric to reveal the face of—

It's not her! This isn't Elia!

The startling discovery nearly made Rayhan's legs buckle, but he quickly recovered. "Is this supposed to be a joke?" he asked in a rage, squeezing his hands into fists. He had known all along these savages couldn't be trusted!

"Is this not who you were expecting?" asked the father, scratching the long whiskers on his chin.

"This is not my sister!" Rayhan bellowed. "I've never seen this person before in my life!"

Whoever she was, the middle-aged woman at their feet had been traditionally bundled for release from the Slope of Mourning, or someplace similar—except most of her wrapping had unraveled during the fall or after landing in the ocean, which created the illusion of a dress floating around her.

"This body is the only thing we've seen fall out of the sky over the past few days," said the father.

"Really? You saw nothing this morning?" Hokk asked. He moved to stand between Rayhan and the others, no doubt sensing—correctly, in fact—that Rayhan wanted to lash out. "Weren't there any signs of a girl falling from the clouds ahead of us just moments before we descended?"

The mother shook her head. "We saw nothing."

"You're lying," Rayhan fumed through gritted teeth. "There must have been something!"

The mother glared at him, her hands on her hips. “We—saw—nothing!” she growled.

Rayhan pushed Hokk aside and lunged at the woman. She stumbled backward. “Deal’s off!” he declared, grabbing the reins of his horse and trying to wrench them free of her grasp. But the woman held strong.

“Wait!” Hokk shouted, stepping in quickly to break up the tug-of-war before the husband got to them first.

“Wait for what?” Rayhan shot back at Hokk. “Where is my sister? What have they done with her? If I don’t get my sister, they don’t get the horse!”

“We’ve seen no one else out here!” the man fiercely exclaimed.

“Everybody cool down!” Hokk warned. He frowned thoughtfully. “Rayhan, I believe what they are saying. So there’s got to be another explanation.”

“Which is what?”

“I just . . . at the moment, I can’t think what it might be.”

“Elia couldn’t have simply disappeared in mid-air.”

“No, she couldn’t,” said Hokk. Then he tilted his head as if a new idea had struck him. He seemed hesitant, however, to say anything.

“What are you thinking?” Rayhan asked, both curious and skeptical.

“Well, I can’t say for sure how,” Hokk answered slowly, apparently still mulling over the notion. “But maybe we’ve gotten it all wrong. Maybe Elia never actually *fell* to Below after all.”

Chapter 17

ELIA SAW THE POSTER of herself shortly after arriving within the outskirts of the city. The illustrated face had to be hers—the pierced eyebrow made it undeniable—yet the image portrayed her as more mature than she imagined herself to be. Sketched on paper, she also came across as slightly dangerous. Even a bit demented. The fact that she had singed off her hair during her first visit to Below, to prove her worthiness to a band of Torkin marauders, probably added to the effect.

It was also strange to stare at herself. Without exception, in the past, she had always tried to avoid her reflection, relying instead on memories that had probably become distorted over time. It used to be easy when she worked at the palace laundry, but in the company of Tasheira or Empress Faytelle, Elia had encountered mirrors everywhere she went, forcing her to avert her eyes.

Elia's habit of avoidance hadn't developed because of any concern over seeing a plain or ugly likeness of herself. Rather, she'd always felt uncomfortable gazing into her own reflected eyes. She didn't like the scrutiny of her image staring back; it was an intimidating feeling, as though she were observing the very core of her being. From a young age, she feared the potential of what percolated deep beneath the surface, because sometimes her true nature—one of unrestrained anger, detachment, and calculating ruthlessness—would flare up from an unexpected and frightening place.

As for this poster nailed to the wall of a building, it had to come down. Cautiously glancing around to make sure she was alone, Elia tore the notice from its peg, then crumpled the paper and tossed it among the rest of the garbage littering the curb. She knew this had to be merely one bulletin out of many more posted throughout the city. Somebody at the palace must have realized, just as she'd initially feared, that she hadn't actually fallen to Below. Obviously, the authorities had wasted no time in sending out the alert. While it had only been this morning that she'd broken into Emperor Tael's suite, Elia hated to think how many people had already seen her image on identical notices.

Returning to Na-Lavent was a mistake. She realized that now. It had also been a huge mistake to steal the bicycle from the market in the first place. After creating such a ruckus, the shoppers and vendors who witnessed the robbery would have no problem identifying her as the wanted criminal. Public announcements had likely been made throughout the afternoon to alert the illiterate masses; she was certain too that money was promised to anyone who could turn her in. Similar broadcasts in the past always whipped up a frenzied response from citizens, everyone intent on claiming the cash reward as they searched the city for the guilty, or not-so-guilty, individual.

Elia's father had been a victim of that very scenario—the target of a city-wide manhunt. In the end, it had ultimately destroyed the person Elia used to admire and adore.

But he still turned his back on our family. A family who loved him and tried to help him heal. Never forget that!

With Greyit's saddlebag slung over her shoulder, and the money and telescope safely stashed inside, Elia abandoned the bicycle and quickly hobbled into an alleyway. The passage was extremely narrow, as if the occupants of each building could reach out of their dirty windows and almost touch their neighbors' hands across the way. The majority of these structures were several stories tall, yet so dilapidated that they teetered on the verge of toppling into the lane. It was amazing most of them hadn't already collapsed after the recent earthquakes that had violently rumbled across the islands. In a few areas, Elia did see piles of rubble. The families from these ruined dwellings were probably homeless now, struggling for survival in the streets.

As the strip of sky overhead darkened with the setting sun, Elia continued to creep farther into the city, pulling down posters whenever she came upon them. Though admittedly she was taking a huge risk to be here again, she couldn't lose faith in the plan that had formed in her mind after she'd left Greyit's. She had come back to reconnect with the last person who could possibly help. The only individual from her past with, perhaps, a shred of knowledge about what was really going on.

Cook.

Almost every working day Elia had ever spent in the laundry, she'd despised having to deal with that cranky woman. Cook managed her workers like a dictator, constantly forcing everyone to maintain a grueling pace to make sure the linens and clothing of the Royal Court were thoroughly washed, rinsed, and ironed, yet without allowing a drop of water, a soap pellet, or even a spare minute to be wasted. Stirring her cauldrons over the fires to melt each day's delivery of waterballs, Cook had always been miserable. She never greeted anybody, never addressed them by their names, never cared about health issues or family problems that could legitimately excuse a worker's absence. Young girls starting out were always terrified of her, and Cook seemed to thrive on their fear. People who dared to oppose her would suffer her wrath. Yes, the woman was an unquestionable tyrant.

But during the last few days she had spent with her, Elia had been startled to learn that Cook actually knew her name and was then further astounded when the woman reassigned her to the much easier task of hanging laundry out on the clotheslines along with Naadie.

Elia's apparently lucky break was marred by the threat of danger, though. Before she had been reassigned to hanging laundry, a bone tied with a blue ribbon had mysteriously shown up in her washtub. Soon afterward, a co-worker, Mrs. Suds, had been arrested. Somehow, Cook must have known something about the significance of these events. She had even selflessly risked her own life trying to prevent Mrs. Suds from being hauled away to the dungeon by Imperial Guards. From then on, Cook had paid careful attention to Elia and Naadie's activities, always questioning them about what they had encountered with the donkey procession on their treks into the hills to hang the wash. In fact, Cook had been so worried something sinister would happen to them that Elia could only imagine the crisis it must have created when Elia disappeared and never returned to work. Did Cook know she had fallen over the edge of the island? Was she aware that a lady-in-waiting had smuggled a precious item out of the palace, or that Commander Wrasse had hunted Elia to get his hands on it?

She'll be amazed to see I've returned.

Which was why Elia was heading toward the Grand Bridge. From a safe spot, she planned to watch all the palace staff arriving for work. Cook would be among them, and Elia would try to intercept the woman before she crossed over to the Noble Sanctuary. There'd be no chance for lengthy explanations, but perhaps they could quickly make plans to meet later. And depending on how things went, she might even show Cook the telescope and the documents inside—it would just depend how much Elia felt she could trust her former boss.

Between now and then, however, Elia would have to find some sort of disguise that would allow her to blend in with the other workers. She didn't want to catch the attention of the Imperial Guards, or anybody else keen on collecting a bounty for her arrest.

Continuing now along the back alleys, Elia remained alert, firmly gripping the saddlebag's strap. The streets were quiet. And thank goodness for the fading twilight—it would give Elia the cover she needed to steal some clothing from any vagrants she passed in the street. Yet she found it a challenging task and was only able to swipe a hat from a drunk man sprawled in the middle of the lane, as well as a scarf from a blind woman, which Elia could use to cover her face.

She arrived at the city limits. Straight ahead of her, she could see clouds level with the ground, glowing orange from the reflected sunset, the mist filling in the expanse between the Noble Sanctuary and Kamanman. Elia was separated from the edge of the island by a road that circled the perimeter of the city, so she scurried along it and ducked into the next alley, which was much closer to the bridge. She recognized the lane as the same one she had used this morning to escape after climbing out of the cloud cover.

Elia scanned the length of the passage and noticed she wasn't alone. Another homeless person was nearby, tucked up against a wall and covered with a blanket. She needed that blanket. It would get her through the cool night, and she could use it to conceal herself more fully in the morning.

Elia approached in silence. The person was breathing heavily as if sleeping. She crouched beside the body, but couldn't tell if it was a man or a woman since one bent arm shielded his or her face. Elia could smell urine and alcohol. She tasted the stench in her mouth.

She snagged a corner of the cover and slowly began to pull it off. The body remained still, except for the rise and fall of the chest. Inch by inch, the blanket slipped away.

Then, suddenly, a hand darted out to snatch it back. A second hand grabbed Elia by the wrist.

"Let go!" she snarled as she broke free.

"Thief!" the vagrant shouted, scrambling to stand upright. "Thief!"

She was caught by the shoulders and spun around.

Elia's eyes blazed wide with shock.

Both stood frozen, staring at each other as if viewing their mirror image. Then the man reached forward and pulled Elia into a tight embrace.

But Elia bristled. She could not allow herself to hug her father back.

Chapter 18

THE MORE HOKK PUZZLED over her disappearance, the more conceivable it became that Elia had never fallen to Below—that she had quite possibly devised a backup plan right from the start in case she needed to escape.

"How could she not have fallen?" Rayhan wondered incredulously, flicking raindrops off his chin. "It's impossible! We both saw her jump!"

"Yes, but perhaps that's what she wanted everyone to believe," said Hokk.

"So where is she?"

"I don't have any idea. All I know is that a few seconds after she stepped off the bridge, I mounted my horse and flew down to save her," Hokk replied. "And yet I saw no sign of your sister anywhere when I broke through the clouds."

As he thought about it now, the zone of weak gravity that existed midway between Above and Below should have slowed Elia down long enough for him to catch up—or at least for him to have had a better view of her dropping toward the ocean once the invisible layer had released her.

"If anything, Elia's white dress flapping in the wind should have caught my eye, but there was nothing. That says to me she couldn't have fallen as we originally assumed," Hokk explained. "It also explains why our escorts here didn't witness anything either."

The family members stood silently in the downpour, listening with interest.

Rayhan considered Hokk's suggestion. "If your theory's true, I can't imagine how she pulled it off," he finally said. "In fact, the whole situation has been difficult to piece together, right from the very moment I saw Elia running out of the palace, dressed like some upper-class lady, except with very little hair. I wonder what kind of trouble she got herself into. There was so much blood."

Hokk cringed to remember it. Even if she had somehow avoided falling to Below, it was very troublesome to think of the injuries Elia had obviously sustained. He hoped the incense he'd caught her inhaling first thing that morning hadn't caused poor judgement, ultimately ruining what she had set out to accomplish. Whatever happened, Hokk felt certain he bore some of the blame. He should have insisted Elia postpone entering the emperor's suite until tomorrow.

"Do you know why the guards chased her onto the bridge?" asked Rayhan.

Hokk shrugged. Though Rayhan was Elia's brother, he was also an Imperial Guard, so Hokk couldn't risk being too generous with his information. "I really don't know why she was forced to flee, or why she *chose* to jump. Maybe someone with a winged stallion was waiting just below the surface of the clouds to take her away. Or maybe something was rigged beneath the bridge to catch her.

Rayhan stared at the sky. "So then in all likelihood, my sister's still up there."

"Yes, probably."

Lowering his head, Rayhan scowled. His gaze shifted to the horse, whose reins were still in the wife's possession.

Hokk could guess what he was thinking: If Elia never left Above, then why were they down here?

The woman must have figured out what was going through their heads too. From the corner of his eye, Hokk noticed her twist the reins around her hands several more times, as if she'd never let go of her four-legged hostage.

Hokk needed to do some quick thinking. He turned to the family. "Listen, there's obviously no reason why my friend and I should be stuck here any longer when—"

"We brought you to the body. We delivered as promised," the mother of the family declared, stabbing her finger toward the bound corpse at their feet. "It's not our fault if this wasn't the person you were looking for."

Rayhan snorted with frustration, but Hokk held up his hands in a placating way. "No, I don't dispute that. We had a deal. All I'm asking now is whether we are close to some shelter. Perhaps we can bed down for the night and try to dry off a little bit. Then, in the morning, once our comrades return to pick us up, we'll leave."

"They're never going to—" Rayhan started to say.

Hokk cut him off. "They're never going to attempt it in this weather, yes, you're absolutely right," he said quickly, flashing his eyes at Rayhan as a warning. It was best to allow this family to think more guards could be coming. This threat gave Rayhan and Hokk an advantage, but clearly they both knew their chances of rescue were now almost zero. How would they ever be found, this little cluster of humans who were mere specks of white on this vast white terrain? Besides, the floating rock tips of Kamanman and the Noble Sanctuary had long since drifted off over the edge of the horizon. No, Hokk and Rayhan's only hope now was to steal the stallion for themselves before it was eaten.

"What are your names again?" Hokk asked, as if he had already been told.

The man hesitated for a second. "I'm Ahmet," he answered cautiously, then pointed to the rest of his family. "And this is my wife, Guri, and our four children."

"Thank you very much for so generously providing refuge for us," Hokk said, pretending the offer had already been extended. "It's greatly appreciated."

Ahmet and Guri shot uncertain glances at each other.

Hokk continued before they could decline. "Earlier we seemed to be heading in the direction of a settlement. I saw smoke drifting up into the air. Are we far away, or do you just set up camp wherever you find yourselves?"

"That's often the case if we're out wandering," Ahmet replied. "But not today. We still have to trek a few more hours to where we can join the others," he added, jerking his thumb over his shoulder.

Hokk could not see anything in that direction. "How many people live together?"

"Enough," was the cryptic response. "Sometimes we're all together, sometimes not, depending on migration patterns and our seasonal hunt."

"Is everyone gathering together now?"

Ahmet just shrugged.

"And when does your hunt start?" Hokk asked.

"Any day now," Ahmet said. "The main season comes around much later each year, and the wait we've had to endure over the past few months has been too long. We're suffering," he added with a labored sigh, as if the topic weighed heavily on him.

Guri nodded toward the horse. "Which is why we need this bird. We need to feed ourselves to get us through these lean times," she explained, shooting a stern look directly at Hokk.

"Then we'll have to have a feast," said Hokk, throwing a smile right back at her. "As you can see, there's a lot of meat on a bird like this."

Catching Rayhan's horrified expression, Hokk winked at him reassuringly. Though Rayhan seemed to notice, he didn't appear pleased with Hokk's approach.

"Once the rain stops, can we get a decent fire going to cook the beast?" Hokk asked. The chance to enjoy roaring flames, with their heat, light, and the crackle-pop of escaping gases was like a rousing elixir.

"We'll build a big fire and a spit large enough to roast the whole thing," said Guri with the hint of a smile.

Good. His scheme to win them over seemed to be working. And he knew now that hunger was their greatest weakness. If he wanted to deflect their suspicions and prevent the family from turning on them again, he'd only have to appeal to their stomachs.

The couple's children must have already been anticipating the feast because right away, they started off again on their trek.

Ahmet and Rayhan watched as Hokk reached over and took hold of the reins. He held his hand near Guri's for a second and then, with the slightest tug, he claimed the reins for himself. Guri shot him a quick look of defiance, but gave in. Both she and Ahmet turned and followed the lead of their children.

Hokk jerked his head at Rayhan to indicate that he too should fall into line.

The look Rayhan gave Hokk was murderous.

Rayhan leaned close. "I don't like what's happening here," he whispered with such animosity that the words sprayed from his mouth. "This isn't going to end well. I can sense it in my very core."

Wiping away the spit, Hokk didn't let Rayhan's concerns bother him—he knew if his plan was going to work, he had to be in control of the situation.

"You can trust me," Hokk reassured him in a patronizing manner. "I know what it's like to be these people. I've been isolated and hungry too. It's only desperation that makes them act out in a threatening way. It's not their true nature. I can get them to help us."

"I have no faith you'll be proven right," Rayhan replied coldly. "Mark my words, we're being led into some sort of trap."

With that, Rayhan stepped over the discarded corpse, which was simply going to be abandoned out here.

Hokk looked at the lifeless face of the dead woman at his feet, her wrapped body nestled in the trash. He then gazed skyward against the falling rain but still saw no floating islands.

As he stood staring back in the direction from which they had just come, planning what his next move should be, his eyes suddenly caught the briefest flicker of movement. Then it was gone. He waited, watching for it. Whatever it was materialized again for a few seconds, hanging low in the misty air just above the ocean, before it vanished once more. Hokk felt a knot of apprehension twisting in his stomach.

Am I hallucinating?

Yet the vision had seemed so real. He was positive he'd just observed a large pair of gray wings, their outline barely distinguishable as they flapped against the gray backdrop of the darkening sky and ocean. Maybe even the glint of a polished helmet through the downpour.

Don't forget how many times you've been fooled before.

Hokk spun around to see if perhaps Rayhan had noticed the flying stallion as well, yet Elia's brother was already quite far ahead, looking forward, not back.

Rayhan wouldn't have seen the horse because it doesn't exist! It's only your brain playing tricks on you!

Still, Hokk looked carefully again, hoping to see something to validate the sighting.

No, there was nothing. Only the rolling ocean, the garbage, and the clouds dropping their deluge.

The horse beside him pulled on its bridle. Hokk finally turned and hurried to catch up to the procession ahead of them. His internal voice, however, struggled to keep reminding him: *We are not being followed. Your mind is just damaged. We are not being followed!*

Chapter 19

WHEN ELIA'S FATHER RELEASED her, he had tears in his eyes. He quickly shrank back against the wall, his frail body seemingly incapable of standing up to her critical gaze.

A part of Elia's mind was shouting for her to bolt, but shock and overriding curiosity kept her feet glued to the ground.

It had been many years since they'd last talked to each other, and he was a fraction of the man he used to be, not only in size and physical strength, but in his overall manner as well. He was much more timid and beaten down than she remembered.

All the nagging questions that had always plagued her began flipping through her mind. Why had the palace issued the decree for his arrest when he was nothing more than an inconsequential dew farmer? Where had her father disappeared to before he was eventually found again, abandoned in the outskirts of the city? What could've possibly been done to the poor man to make him crumble?

He doesn't have to be this way, Elia reminded herself. He *chose* this life—or rather, this shadow of a life. He could have tried to get better after that awful episode when the Imperial Guards made an example out of him, but he had done nothing. And making no effort was completely unforgivable.

Nevertheless, Elia found it sadly fascinating to see him now in front of her. His clothes were stained and torn. His arms were badly bruised, and he had crusty scabs on his face and knuckles. The smell of alcohol wafting from him betrayed that he'd been drinking, and his emaciated frame was evidence that he had not filled his stomach with anything nourishing for many weeks.

I used to not care whether he'd starve in these filthy streets.

I still don't.

For years, whenever Elia's mother had enough money to purchase some extra food at the market, she would routinely set aside a portion for her husband, then pedal through the surrounding alleyways, trying to find him. Elia would trail behind on her own bicycle, always keeping back a safe distance, trying to avoid her father altogether.

Even now, Elia found standing near him like this very uncomfortable. Not wanting to feel obliged to speak to him, she swung Greyit's saddlebag over her shoulder, then pivoted on one heel to leave. He probably wasn't keen to deal with her either, so if she just left, she'd be making it easier for both of them.

She began walking away.

"I thought . . . I thought you were dead," her father nervously called after her.

Elia paused, keeping her back to him.

"Then I saw you climb out of the clouds this morning," he murmured. "Right up over the island's edge. I couldn't believe what I was seeing."

Elia slowly turned around. She took a few tentative steps toward him, yet remained silent, sucking on her lower lip.

Her father cast his gaze to the ground until he found the courage to look up again. He offered a weak grin, but it quickly vanished.

"You saw me?" Elia finally asked.

He struggled to maintain eye contact. "Yes. Then you raced right past where I was sitting, but . . . I was too startled to say anything." He sniffed and wiped his runny nose with the back of his hand.

"I didn't notice you," Elia replied, forcing indifference.

"How could you have known?" He barely uttered the words. Then he inhaled deeply to fill his lungs as if hoping that might muster his determination. "But it's different for me. I've always been on the lookout for you."

Elia flinched. "What do you mean?"

"I've done it for years now, watching morning and night for you and your mother to cross the bridge. It always made me feel good to see you both together, arriving for work or leaving the palace."

Elia crossed her arms over her chest and squeezed. "That can't be true," she said defensively, feeling increasingly flushed. "Mom and I always found you much closer to the market, more often than not passed out in a dark alley. Never on the edge of the city limits like this."

"That's only because each day after you crossed the bridge to head home, I'd move several streets closer to the market so your mother wouldn't have to backtrack as far to find me. Any other time of the day, however, I could be found waiting at the end of this lane so I wouldn't miss the two of you crossing over."

Elia's mind struggled to accept what he was saying. "Why did you never tell us this?"

"Your mother knew."

Numbness swept through Elia's body. Her breath, even her heartbeat, seemed to stop. Why hadn't her mother ever said anything?

"Besides, I realized you wanted nothing to do with me," her father added matter-of-factly. "Just like your brother. Obviously, I'm too much of an embarrassment for my children."

Elia's eyes brimmed with tears, and she tried to blink them away. Ashamed and unable to look at her father, she stared down the empty alley toward the center of the city.

"But that's okay, El," he added. "I understand. I accept

it. Most of the time, I don't want anything to do with myself either. I loathe myself."

Elia felt his gentle touch on her arm. Surprisingly, for all his anxiety and awkwardness, he didn't remove his hand as she swiveled her head to face him.

"I just can't believe . . . I mean . . ." Elia started to say, choking up. "I never would have guessed you've been here all this time, watching us come and go."

"I needed that connection, even if it was from a distance," her father replied. His eyes flitted about, never able to linger on her for more than a second or two. "Seeing you and your mother—confirming every day that you were still safe—was what kept me fighting to stay alive."

"Fighting to stay alive?" Elia blasted as she abruptly pulled away from him. "What a ridiculous thing to say! You've done nothing to help yourself all these years!"

Her father cowered and wiped his nose again.

"Why didn't you simply return to the family?" she challenged, her voice growing tremulous as raw emotions erupted. "Don't forget, *you're* the one who rejected *us*, not the other way around. We would have been there for you. To help you through whatever broke your spirit."

Her words seemed to break him now like falling bricks.

"I'm sorry," he whispered, wringing his hands as he looked at the ground.

"Why can't you just explain what happened to you?"

He shook his head but kept it lowered. "I can't."

"Why not?" Elia sobbed. "This whole affair has ruined our family, and you've only made it worse. You've made it unbearable!"

Anguish twisted his expression.

"So why don't you bloody well deal with it?" Elia spat defiantly, almost relishing this opportunity to be mean.

Her father was silent.

"Well?" she demanded.

"Even if I could let myself go there, to relive it all again . . ." But his voice trailed off. As if his legs could no longer support him, he slid down the wall until he was sitting on the ground, hugging his knees to his body.

Elia groaned and flung her hands up into the air. Nothing she could say was going to change anything. He was hopeless. She should just let him flounder in his own misery.

Yet, all the same, Elia couldn't deny her feelings of guilt. Here was a display of that malicious, terrifying side of herself, rearing up from the depths of her consciousness, taking control. This wasn't who she wanted to be. She could be better than this—couldn't she?

With a loud sigh, Elia sat down beside her father. She said nothing. She leaned back against the wall and stared straight ahead, clutching the saddlebag in her lap. The alleyway was swiftly growing darker. Before long, they would be able to see each other only by the glow of the shattered moon strewn across the night sky. Maybe her father would be better able to cope if she were little more than a voice coming from the shadows, instead of an angry face confronting him.

Many long minutes passed as Elia tried to think of what she could say to him. Was there anything that could encourage him to open up? Would memories of happier times help, or just make things worse? Or would they simply sit here all night as if the other didn't exist?

From an open window overhead, Elia heard a baby start to cry. From another building, the clatter of plates and utensils as food was served. Elsewhere, someone whistled. A dog barked. A door slammed. Distant laughter.

The ordinary, comforting sounds of families and neighbors. Sounds that made it glaringly obvious to Elia how much had been lacking in her own life for far too long.

She thought back to the last time she'd sat up in a tree with her father. She was just a little girl. Happy. Blissfully unaware of the poverty in which they lived. Not yet crushed by relentless days of back-breaking work. How unfortunate she couldn't go back to the days when she and her father always had so much to say to each other, when her imagination would flourish listening to his fascinating tales about visiting the islands of the Lunera System as a younger man.

"I've been to the Isle of Drifting Dunes," Elia blurted out. From the corner of her eye, she noticed her father turn with surprise. *Good.* It was a promising start. "The sand dunes were exactly as you used to describe," she continued. "Huge, and always shifting with the wind."

"And the heat?" her father asked, perking up beside her.

"Almost unbearable. I didn't think I'd survive."

"But truly a beautiful, unique landscape."

"Yes, it was."

Her father paused. "So . . . how did you get there?"

She had no intention of telling him everything too soon, if at all. "I flew over with a friend. He had always wanted to visit the spot too."

"Oh. But then how—?"

"His family has their own flying stallion, and he invited me to join him. There was really nothing more than that," she said firmly.

"So that makes three generations of our family who have traveled to the island," her father said with a weak chuckle. "Any luck finding a jewel?"

"No. Nothing like what Opi found."

"Did I ever tell you my father discovered that polished piece of orange glass in a mound of sand shortly before I was born?"

"I know. I used to love that thing." Elia wished she still had the keepsake. She had given it to Hokk at the Baron's estate, pretending it belonged to him, all part of a backup plan to explain why she had snuck into his room when he was still healing from his sunburns.

Another moment of silence descended. This time, her

father was the one to break it. "How are my parents?" he asked with a sense of remorse.

Elia grimaced. This was more information she was reluctant to divulge. "Omi and Opi are fine, all things considered. Of course, Omi's memory is not the best."

"And Sulum? I haven't seen her cross the bridge for weeks now."

Elia felt incredible sadness to hear this about her missing mother, but she didn't want to let on to her father how bad things had become. "Are you sure it's been that long?" she replied, trying to think quickly. "Mom did skip a fair bit of work recently because she was ill, so she's had to work longer hours to make up for it now that she's better. Lately, she doesn't arrive or leave the palace with everyone else, like you'd expect."

"Yes, that explains it, I guess. What about your brother? Has he become an Imperial Guard yet?"

"No. As far as I know, his training hasn't begun. I assume he's still working in the dewfields."

Her father nodded. Then his head turned and, even in the dim light, she knew he was studying her.

Elia didn't wait for his question. "As for me, I got reassigned. I'm working in the higher levels of the palace as a maid. That's why I'm wearing different clothing."

"Your hair's so short."

"It is," she replied simply, opting not to explain further. Hopefully, he wouldn't ask about her piercing.

"But you still look the same as I remember. Your eyes, your nose—really, your whole profile leaves no doubt about it. You're definitely my daughter." He sounded proud.

Elia scowled. Why did he have to say that? She hated it. She didn't want to be reminded how much she resembled her father since it always sparked fears that she could turn out like him in other aspects too—another reason to avoid her reflection.

Farther down the alley, the shadows of two homeless

people suddenly appeared, supporting each other as they staggered along, cursing and bickering. They were both intoxicated. One of them must have dropped his bottle on the street because Elia heard shattering glass. The noise made her cringe.

"Don't worry, just a bunch of harmless drunks," observed her father.

Harmless seemed far from an accurate description. The other man had started berating his companion for wasting alcohol, and Elia found the cruelness behind his slurred words very unsettling.

"I don't feel safe," she said.

"I know those two. It's always the same. But maybe you should start heading back home. Your mother might get worried."

"She's not expecting me," Elia replied. "And it's already too late. I'll have to spend the night in the city."

"You won't be comfortable here."

"But can I at least stay with you until morning? I'm afraid because . . . I just don't want anyone finding me during the night," said Elia, thinking about the bulletins posted around the city with her face on them. "I can't explain more. Can you help me?"

Her father hesitated. "Yes. I'll make sure that no one bothers us. Nothing will happen to you."

"I appreciate it," said Elia.

You owe me that much, she wanted to add.

Chapter 20

WITH THE DAYLIGHT FADING and the rain starting to ease, Rayhan trailed the family of six, trudging miserably through the puddles collecting on top of the garbage. At the very least, he wanted to stay well ahead of Hokk, who, for some reason, was now the one lagging behind, leading the stallion whose wings were still hindered by the plastic netting. But then Rayhan heard splashing footsteps of both man and beast catching up to him, and he frowned.

They sloshed alongside each other in silence, though from the corner of his eye, Rayhan noticed Hokk repeatedly craning his neck over his shoulder. What could he be looking at?

"I know it's getting dark, but have you noticed anything strange behind us?" Hokk finally asked, checking once more.

"What are you talking about?" Rayhan fired back, not bothering to turn.

"I think we're being followed."

Rayhan felt a rush of panic. Could it be the corpse-collecting monsters he had been fearing from the start? He whipped around and shielded his wet brow with one hand to survey the landscape. He saw no sign, however, of Scavengers closing in on them. "You must be seeing things," he said bitterly, swinging forward again.

Hokk flinched as if the comment was hurtful.

Rayhan knew he was just putting on an act. *It's all part of his deceitful ways. But what is he really scheming?*

"I thought . . . I thought maybe it was an Imperial Guard tracking us," Hokk explained as if he had read Rayhan's mind. "It sure looked like a pair of wings."

"That's ridiculous," Rayhan replied scornfully. *How gullible does he think I am?*

They walked at the same pace for a minute or two more until Hokk abruptly pulled ahead. "I think I'll catch up to Ahmet and Guri. I'm curious what more they might be willing to tell me," he said before breaking into a run and taking the horse with him.

Rayhan chased after them, not wanting to miss a thing.

Practically clipping Hokk's heels the rest of the way, Rayhan listened carefully to their conversation, knowing full well that Hokk was manipulating the husband and wife for information to drive his own agenda. What that agenda could be, Rayhan wasn't sure.

Still, it proved interesting to find out more about the family and how they lived. The settlement where they were headed now was one of several across the Plastlantic Mass. Despite the great distances separating them, the inhabitants were all considered part of the same tribe—a people who called themselves Merreens. They were nomads for many months at a stretch, scratching out an existence on the Mass. They banded together for their annual hunts, though the success of their expeditions had been declining steadily over the past decade.

According to Ahmet, the hunt involved spearing or netting something that he described as *fish*, though Rayhan could not comprehend what kind of animal he was talking about. Apparently, they lived *under* the water, yet for some reason could not survive above it. At certain times of the year, these so-called fish converged in great numbers, but they were otherwise very difficult to come by and usually only found tangled in the floating debris.

The animals were a topic that Ahmet clearly enjoyed discussing. "And if the legends are true, centuries ago, fish used to grow as long as your entire arm! Can you believe it?" he said enthusiastically. "As long as your arm!"

Hokk nodded earnestly, his expression seeming to beg for more details.

Ahmet obliged. "Now we're lucky to find anything half that size."

"And in much smaller quantities too," offered his wife. "We all worry what will happen when there's nothing left."

"*If* that day actually comes," said her husband.

"Oh, it will, I'm afraid," Guri replied. "Probably much faster than we would ever guess." As if to change the subject, she then pointed ahead of them. "Look. You can see it—we've almost reached the settlement."

Rayhan's eyes strained. By now, the rain had mercifully stopped, and as they rode the next wave up on a gentle crest, he managed to distinguish about ten formations in the distance that appeared to be just more large heaps of garbage, but arranged in an orderly fashion.

He saw some movement in the deepening twilight. And though the figures were still small from this outlying vantage point, they looked like animated pieces of trash with the debris they were wearing.

"How many families did you say live together?" Rayhan wondered, having not said anything until now since Hokk had been asking all the questions.

"Each of our longhouses can hold about eight to ten families," Guri confirmed.

"I'm surprised the number's so high," said Hokk.

Rayhan was thinking the same thing, trying to determine how many adversaries they might have to face.

A thin trail of white smoke began to rise out of one of the shelters. A few minutes later, the white suddenly changed to a thick black plume that billowed skyward, similar to what Rayhan had seen from his woven-plastic prison many hours ago, before the rain had started.

What could they possibly be burning to create such a dense column of smoke?

By the time they reached the settlement, two more of the dwellings had similar fires burning from within. But Rayhan was now more interested in the few Merreens standing outside, all watching their arrival with great curiosity. None of them were able to pull their gaze from the flying stallion being led by Hokk. Rayhan could see behind their eyes a smoldering hunger.

"Guri! Ahmet!" shouted one of the Merreens, running over to them. The man was festooned with elaborate drapings of plastic bags and other colorful pieces of garbage.

"Brother!" the couple replied cheerfully.

Rayhan wondered if they were indeed related, or if this was simply a customary greeting.

"What kind of incredible beast have you caught?" the man asked, clearly astonished.

"The biggest bird to ever take flight," Guri chuckled. "Although it will be even more impressive to see the thing turning on a spit."

"It's an omen," the man said decisively. "The best sign we could have hoped to receive for a successful hunt to come."

"When did you get here?" asked Ahmet.

"Yesterday," said the man, with a grin.

"We should plan on having a feast as soon as all the other families have arrived," Ahmet decided.

Praise the sun! It didn't sound as though the horse was in any immediate danger of being cooked and eaten.

"Is there enough room left in your longhouse for us to join you?" Guri asked the man. "Or should we just be neighbors?"

"Yes, there's still plenty of space. We can all stay together and . . ." The man stopped, staring at Hokk and Rayhan suspiciously.

Ahmet clapped his hand on the man's back and laughed. "I'll explain once we get inside."

Ahmet showed Hokk where to tie the horse, and Rayhan watched as his black stallion was secured to the side of the lodge. Then, all three followed the rest of the family as they entered the longhouse.

The walls of the lodge were constructed with dense, interlaced debris. Surprisingly, the floor itself was almost completely dry, so tightly woven that little water could seep through, even though the entire area moved with a subtle rippling motion from the currents beneath.

What was it like in here when the waves were raging?

The only light in the space came from a fire burning in the center. The fire sat on a battered sheet of metal, which, upon closer inspection, was floating on open water where a large hole to contain it had been cut out of the surrounding plastic.

Guri, Ahmet, and their four children were welcomed by others who stepped forward from the shadows, or who came in from outside. Rayhan held back, still dripping wet, and watched the smoke drift up to the ceiling, where it exited through a hole in the top. He then saw Hokk approach the flames as if to warm himself and dry off. He decided to do the same.

Holding his hands up to the heat, Rayhan glanced at Hokk beside him, sensing that same intensity that Rayhan had just witnessed in the eyes of the Merreens as they watched the stallion being led into their settlement. Hokk, however, appeared almost to be hypnotized.

"I didn't realize I was so cold," Rayhan said, testing him.

Hokk didn't respond—not even a nod or a blink to acknowledge his comment. Glassy-eyed, with an unsettling, frozen smile on his face, Hokk simply stared at the fire.

Behind them, Rayhan overheard Ahmet explaining how the family had encountered Hokk and Rayhan on the Mass, "as if they fell right out of the sky like a blessed gift."

Once again, the subject of solid land came up, and Ahmet shouted to Hokk to come over and tell his story about the grasslands, where he supposedly came from. The request seemed to break Hokk's trance. He turned around and joined the discussion. This time, rather than arguing that the existence of such a place was impossible, the Merreens were fascinated to hear his descriptions. Then Hokk described Above, and they were equally mesmerized, especially to learn that Rayhan's home was on the other side of the clouds.

As the conversation started to wane, one of the Merreens decided they had waited long enough. "Let's start eating!" the person called out.

Rayhan stiffened, once again fearing the slaughter of his stallion.

"Is there any food, though?" wondered Guri.

"Don't worry, woman!" Ahmet shouted jovially. "We'll eat whatever scraps we can find. Tomorrow, we feast! Tonight, we drink!"

The others hooted and cheered at the suggestion, obviously in the mood to celebrate their change in fortunes.

Every assembled family pledged to contribute a few fish, and the women scurried off to scrounge up whatever they could find in their meager stores. Soon they were back, and Rayhan moved closer to see what they had brought.

"Those are fish?" he asked in shock.

"Of course," Ahmet replied with a good-natured chuckle. "What were you expecting? Something with four legs?"

Rayhan shook his head in amazement. He certainly hadn't anticipated an animal with no limbs whatsoever! This creature was nothing but a head attached to a tail. How could it move? And what part of the thing could really be eaten?

The fish had silver skin, mushy eyes, and a gaping, expressionless mouth. It was about as long as the distance from Rayhan's wrist to his elbow.

"Try touching one," somebody said with amusement.

Rayhan reached out to stroke the specimen that Guri was holding. The cold skin felt surprisingly rough, almost prickly, yet when he tried to pick it up, the carcass slipped out of his hands as if squirming to be free. Rayhan leapt back with a start, and many of the Merreens laughed. He couldn't resist laughing too.

"We need a bigger fire than this! Let's throw another chunk of tire on and get these things cooked!" a woman encouraged as she skewered the fish on a metal rod.

"Leave that to me," said Ahmet as he took a small axe from his family's bundled supplies, then began hacking away at one of several large, black, circular objects sitting beside the metal fire pit.

Rayhan had seen tires in the past—the thin, half-deflated, practically treadless things on the bicycles that his sister and mother used to ride. Could these be similar, only much bigger versions? If so, what kind of contraption needed wheels so large and cumbersome?

Chopping off a sizable piece, Ahmet threw it on the flames, where the tire began to burn, immediately producing the same choking thick smoke that Rayhan had seen earlier. The impaled fish were then held over the fire, disappearing into the rising plume. After several minutes, they were pulled out and, with their skin now black and crispy, the fish were declared cooked.

By this point, dozens of Merreens had congregated in the lodge. People crowded around for their share as hunks of fish were cut and dropped into their open palms. Both Hokk and Rayhan were offered generous portions, and Rayhan had to pass the piece back and forth from one hand to the other, waiting for it to cool. Before taking his first bite, he sniffed the steaming, flaky flesh, charred on one side, and the strange smell made his nose wrinkle. Too hungry to let that stop him, he wasn't surprised when the taste matched the aroma—he couldn't quite describe the flavor beyond something oily, salty, and burnt. He almost choked on a few small bones, but he swallowed every bite.

Once all the food was eaten, and fingers licked clean, several of the men left and returned carrying bottles filled with liquid of various shades of green. Seaweed wine, they called it, and apparently, everyone had brewed their own concoction. The bottles began their journey around the lodge, passed from hand to hand, as men, women, and children gulped down mouthfuls. As each new fermented batch arrived in Hokk's possession, he took a swig too, probably wanting to stay on friendly terms with the Merreens. Rayhan, however, felt no such obligation, and he simply kept the bottles moving without indulging himself.

The mood in the longhouse quickly became boisterous, and listening to the raucous chatter, Rayhan only now began to appreciate something that he hadn't realized earlier—the Merreens seemed genuinely content. Surprising, really, for such an impoverished people. Perhaps it was because they knew no other life.

Many times in the past, Rayhan had envied the advantages enjoyed by the privileged classes of Above, and when compared to the situation of his own destitute family, the disparity was tremendous. But wasn't the simple existence of the Merreens much more appealing, living in ignorance of the miserable inequities that Rayhan knew first-hand?

Yes, he was sure of it.

But could he ever give up his old life to join these people? To live out the rest of his days here?

All he was certain of was that he had to get away from this place as soon as possible. And that he still couldn't let his guard down and fully trust these Merreens.

As more and more of the bottles were emptied, revelers with full bladders began going outside for relief. At one point, the urge must have hit Hokk too. Rayhan watched as he put his hand on his neighbor's head to stand up and balance himself before staggering toward the door of the lodge. Not wanting to let Hokk out of his sight for even one minute, Rayhan quickly followed. Ahmet, upon tipping back the bottle he was drinking from, noticed them leave, and Rayhan overheard him telling one of his sons to follow.

As they relieved themselves out in the near darkness, Rayhan noted the horse was still safe and tied to the side of the longhouse. Good. That was exactly what he wanted to see.

The fresh air seemed to have a sobering effect on Hokk, but heading back toward the lodge, his steps were still wobbly. He rested a heavy hand on Rayhan's shoulder for support. Clearly in a cheery mood, though, he leaned close to Rayhan so no others could hear him. "As you can see, my plan is working just as I intended."

"Is it?" Rayhan grumbled.

"Our horse is still here," he slurred. "They haven't eaten the thing, and we'll be long gone before they can make an attempt. Unless, of course, you want to stay," he added half-jokingly.

Rayhan groaned. "Not a chance."

Chapter 21

SINCE NIGHTFALL, ELIA HAD been tucked up against the side of the wall, using her saddlebag as a pillow. With her father dozing nearby, she had drifted in and out of sleep for several hours, yet was disturbed whenever she heard an unfamiliar sound in the alleyway or coming from the surrounding buildings.

But now, after finally entering a deep sleep, she was suddenly wrenched awake by somebody seizing her ankles.

She instinctively kicked her feet to break free and tried to sit up. Whoever was holding her legs yanked hard; her head snapped back and cracked on the cobblestones.

Where was the saddlebag to cushion the impact?

Her eyes shot open, but her pupils struggled to adjust to the light of several flaming torches held just above her face. A pair of hands grabbed her head and held it steady.

"Yeah, it's her!" exclaimed a gruff voice.

"Help me!" Elia screamed as she writhed about.

Where was her father?

She kept yelling and fighting until several people pinned her arms and legs to the ground. Then, as the torchlight was pulled back, what Elia saw filled her with nauseating dread.

Flames reflected off the many mirrored helmets that had encircled her, each identical face sculpted out of cold, lifeless metal.

She had been found.

With her soiled white dress bunched up to her thighs, Elia was flipped onto her stomach. Rope was lashed around her wrists and shackles clamped to her legs.

"Dad! Help!" she groaned, drooling as her cheek was pressed painfully into the gravel on the ground.

"Where's the cart?" asked a man standing above her.

"A few blocks over," someone else responded. "It's been summoned."

"Dad!" Elia screamed frantically, struggling to raise her head. She could not let them take her. "Help me!"

No response. He must have been captured too and already taken away while she was sleeping.

Or worse, maybe he had fled the scene, leaving her helpless to defend herself.

Elia heard the clatter of hooves and the grind of rolling wheels. The sounds grew louder, then stopped next to her. She was dragged by the chain of the shackles, which aggravated the pain of her sore ankle and scraped her cheek on the uneven stones. A man grunted as he lifted her, then flung her onto a flat cart with no sides. A donkey was harnessed at the front, its wings strapped down.

Elia clenched her jaw as a chain was secured around her waist to a metal ring screwed into the cart's wooden floor.

"Cover her head," ordered one of the guards.

As a man came forward with a burlap sack, she glanced past him for one last look down the alley—and there was her father! Cowering against the wall, in full view, he was standing within the ring of light cast by the torches. The guards paid no attention to him whatsoever. He was watching the commotion with a frown on his face but made no move to intervene.

Then Elia saw what he held in his arms—the saddlebag containing her telescope, the documents, and the little bit of money she'd taken from Greyit's home.

As the burlap sack was about to be pulled over her head, she saw an Imperial Guard approach her father. "I guess this is meant for you," the guard said, tossing a small drawstring bag in her father's direction. One arm shot out quickly to catch it. Elia heard the clink of loose coins inside—the bounty for her capture.

The bastard!

Chapter 22

STRETCHED OUT ON THE floor in the dark, resting her head on her bent arm, Tasheira heard the rattle of keys again, then the crash of a door swinging open. Curious, she crawled closer to her own cell door as the corridor gradually brightened and footsteps approached.

Was the girl with the eye patch bringing another meal? Probably not. Tasheira's stomach was aching like she had never experienced, yet she guessed it was still the middle of the night—of course, stuck down here, it was impossible to know for sure the exact time of day.

An Imperial Guard, carrying a torch, appeared around the corner. Behind him walked a prisoner, followed by another guard, with the hooded warden bringing up the rear.

Judging by the clothes, the convict was a female, but Tash could not see a face since the person's head was completely covered by a gunny sack. Whoever she might be, she wore a filthy white dress and hobbled along, accompanied by the sound of dragging chains.

The procession passed by, and the dungeon master unlocked a cell a bit farther down on the opposite side of the corridor. One of the guards turned the captive around to face the open entryway, and then, without removing the gunny sack over her head, roughly pushed the prisoner forward. Unable to maneuver easily with her feet chained, the woman stumbled and fell deep within the cell. Tash lost sight of her, but heard a thunk and a groan when her body hit the ground.

The hinges squealed as the metal door was quickly slammed shut and locked. Without an exchange of words, the guards and the warden departed. The heavy door at the end of the corridor then closed with a boom, and the sound echoed through the cavernous space, which was now, once again, as black as the dead of night.

Tasheira held her breath, listening for any noise coming from the new prisoner. At first she heard nothing, but as she strained to hear, pressing her head against the narrowly spaced bars of her door, she made out the faint sound of weeping.

Always inquisitive and never shy, Tash called out, "Hello? Can you hear me? Who are you?"

Nothing.

"Why have you been arrested?"

Silence.

"Are you as innocent as I am?"

Still no response.

Tasheira decided the prisoner was probably in the same situation as her. The inmate's arrival only strengthened the picture that was becoming increasingly clear in Tasheira's mind about the true nature of the Imperial Guards, as well as the Twin Emperors who directed their activities. Tash was sure this other woman was also a victim of a corrupt, perverted system, with no reasonable grounds whatsoever to warrant her confinement.

And Tasheira wondered again just how many of the other people trapped down here in these hellish, underground vaults were casualties of that same corruption.

Yes, her mind was made up. As soon as she regained her freedom, she vowed to expose anyone guilty of abusing their power. The justice served against them would be swift, systematic, and severe.

Chapter 23

RAYHAN FEIGNED SLEEP UNTIL the last Merreen had staggered off to a vacant spot on the floor and fallen into a deep, drunken slumber.

Hokk lay passed out beside Rayhan, his mouth wide open, snoring loudly. Rayhan knew he would not be waking up for many hours.

He waited patiently until little remained of the noxious fire in the center of the longhouse except for a few glowing embers.

Then he slowly rose to his feet.

As silently yet as quickly as possible, Rayhan tiptoed toward the lodge's entrance, trying with great care not to lose his balance as he stepped over people sprawled on the gently rippling floor. A few of the Merreens stirred, but nothing more.

Rayhan hurried outside and found it brighter than he would have expected—night was relinquishing its embrace with the approaching dawn. All of a sudden, though, he froze. He could hear the undeniable sound of a whinny and a neigh from his horse. The next instant, he saw wings extend into the air above the top of the lodge. No longer tangled, they stretched and flapped a few times as if the animal was preparing to take flight.

Damn it, someone's trying to steal my horse!

He dashed to the other side of the longhouse, ready for a fight. Yet coming around the corner, Rayhan halted in a puddle.

He couldn't believe what he was seeing—not just one stallion, but two! He had been in such a hurry, he had failed to realize that the outstretched wings had *gray* feathers. A second horse was standing beside his own black steed, whose wings were still caught in the plastic webbing first used to snare it.

And just as he had predicted, a person was with them, half hidden between the two animals as he tried to free Rayhan's horse.

"Who are you?" Rayhan challenged with a low growl, hoping no one within the surrounding lodges would hear him.

The person turned around, and Rayhan took a startled step backward.

An Imperial Guard!

But on second glance, he realized this was no average Imperial Guard. The man's helmet had a very distinctive spike poking straight out from the forehead of the polished metal faceplate.

Chapter 24

TASHEIRA SAT WITH HER shoulder pressed up against the bars of her jail cell, waiting with fretful impatience for light to appear again in the passage. She was starving and cold, and also exhausted, but couldn't sleep despite the absolute silence. The brief murmur of weeping from the other prisoner had stopped long ago, and Tasheira's ears had picked up nothing since, not even a sigh or the faint rustle of the woman shifting.

After an endlessly long stretch, Tash finally heard familiar sounds at the entrance of the cellblock: keys opening the lock, a crash of the door hitting the wall, the corridor brightening, footsteps on the stone floor. Tash watched with anticipation, but it was only the girl with the eye patch who appeared around the corner. Again, she held a bowl in one hand and a large burning candle in the other.

"Have you seen my father?" Tash asked anxiously, wrapping her fingers around the metal bars and stiffly rising up on her knees. "Have you been able to tell him where I am?"

"No, I haven't," the girl said flatly. "Though I've tried to spread the word to anyone who might know who he is."

Tash knew she was lying. The girl owed her nothing, and there were probably many prisoners in the dungeon who constantly professed their innocence—this servant must have gotten very accustomed to routinely shrugging off their attempts to negotiate their freedom.

The girl bent over to place the dish on the floor. With a scraping sound, she slid it under the bars. Tash quickly snatched the bowl and raised it to her lips. The lukewarm broth contained a few black beans and a quarter of a boiled egg with the yolk missing, but at least it was something to fill her stomach.

The servant girl watched her slurping the diluted soup. "I'll just wait until you're done so I can take the bowl back with me," she explained when Tash glanced up at her. "It'll save me another trip."

Tash wiped her mouth with her sleeve. "Aren't you returning with more food?"

"Prisoners only get a single serving at a time," she replied as she adjusted her eye patch.

"No, I mean there's someone else down here," said Tasheira, pointing in the direction of the other prisoner's cell.

"There is?" asked the girl, perking up with great interest.

"Yes. She was delivered late last night," said Tash. "At least I think it was during the night. What time is it now? Is it morning yet?"

But the servant girl ignored her. She hurried the few steps down the corridor to stand in front of the new inmate's door. She peered into the cell. As though unable to see properly, she stuck her whole arm through the bars while still holding the candle. Without saying a word, she yanked her arm out and spun around, a look of concern on her face.

"What's wrong?" Tash asked.

The girl scurried by, neglecting to collect Tasheira's now-empty bowl.

"Is she dead?" Tash called out after her, but received no response.

Chapter 25

"HURRY! COME QUICKLY!"

The shouting pulled Hokk from his sleep. He sat bolt upright, but immediately regretted it. His head was pounding and his mouth tasted vile.

Other Merreens around him were slow to react and Hokk heard much moaning.

"Everyone, wake up!" the same person demanded, raising his alarm from the entrance of the lodge.

Hokk turned his throbbing head ever so slightly to glance over at Rayhan—but Rayhan was not where he should have been, stretched out on the floor. He was nowhere to be seen.

He's gone. He's left me here!

The commotion began to increase as people were roused and got to their feet. Hokk could also hear a similar din outside, coming through the plastic walls. Obviously, the horse's disappearance was provoking outrage across the entire settlement.

While the welcome Hokk had received from the Merreens the previous evening had been far friendlier than he would have ever expected, he wondered how quickly they'd turn on him today now that their good omen had been stolen by Rayhan. In spite of the disappointment of their recent hunting expeditions, Hokk would undoubtedly bear the full blame for their misfortunes this year. So, what price would they make him pay?

"What's happening?" Guri asked the man standing in the entrance as she clawed unkempt hair away from her face and tried to focus her bleary eyes.

"It's starting!" the man yelled, unable to hold himself back any longer as he raced out.

For Hokk, this didn't answer anything, although many of the Merreens seemed to understand and became more animated.

"What's going on?" asked Hokk as he grabbed Ahmet's arm.

Ahmet looked rough, but whatever was happening seemed to excite him nonetheless. "The hunt!" he exclaimed. "I guess it's starting early!"

The man collected his wife and children as they and many others hurried outside.

Hokk groaned, his whole body aching and his mind struggling to piece everything together.

Nobody had yet mentioned anything about the fact that Rayhan was missing. Did they not realize he had escaped with the horse? Or did Hokk have it all wrong? Was it possible that Rayhan was still here, sober, already awake and waiting for him?

Yes, that had to be it.

And with everyone distracted, Hokk and Rayhan could now make their getaway!

Hokk staggered into the fresh morning air, free of the pollution that still hung inside the lodge from last night's fire. His head began to quickly clear as he surveyed the scene. The Mass rippled on top of timid waves while people raced about, organizing themselves as they grabbed spears and plastic nets.

And then Hokk's heart sank like a heavy stone into the well of his gut.

The black stallion was truly gone. Though no one else seemed to have noticed, a beast that size could not easily be missed. That meant Rayhan was gone too. Elia's brother had actually abandoned him here.

That bloody bastard!

Furious, Hokk kicked the side of the lodge, embedding his foot in the garbage before he yanked it free.

How could Rayhan do this to him? Were they not bound to look out for each other by their mutual connection to Elia?

But Hokk knew he was to blame. How could he have drunk so much last night? He should have exercised better judgement, kept himself under stricter control.

I make one bad decision after another.

"I said, aren't you coming?" Ahmet called to him impatiently.

Hokk glanced over, pressing his hands against his temples to stop the spinning. "Where are we going?"

"You must be blind!" said Ahmet as he pointed up into the sky.

Hokk did a double take. And if not for everyone else's reaction, he would have assumed he was suffering from another wretched hallucination.

Chapter 26

TASHEIRA SUSPECTED IT WAS well over an hour since she had been plunged once more into darkness. If there really was a dead body across the way, shouldn't someone have shown up long before now to remove it? Or would they just leave the corpse there to decompose?

She shuddered to think how horrible it would've been if she had discovered bones or other remains while blindly exploring her own cell. Surely her heart would have stopped on the spot. Even at this moment, she found it very unsettling to know death might be so close, as if, like a black cloud, it could drift through the bars of the neighboring cell to envelop her.

Which was why Tash felt immense relief when she finally heard a faint cough. The next instant, she worried whether she had just imagined it, so she listened for the sound again. Less than a minute later—

Cough.

Thank goodness! That had definitely been real. The woman was still alive, so Tash could stop worrying.

Yet it also raised more questions. Why was that girl with the eye patch so alarmed when she first looked into the cell?

And if the prisoner wasn't dead, why hadn't she returned with another bowl of broth? Had the kitchens run out of food for the dungeon, or did the servant girl simply forget? Or worse . . . was the convict going to be starved?

Maybe I should call out to see if she's all right over there.

But Tasheira stopped herself. How did she really think she could ease the poor woman's suffering across the distance that separated them? Besides, the prisoner could be a true criminal, in which case, Tash would want absolutely nothing to do with her.

A thunderous boom reverberating down the corridor suddenly pulled Tasheira from her thoughts. The next moment, she saw a different dungeon master march into view. He was shorter and fatter than the first man, but his face was hidden behind a similar leather hood, with holes cut out for his eyes, nostrils, and mouth, making him look frightfully inhuman in the torchlight.

Tasheira stiffened as he halted beside her cell. Her fears subsided, however, when he reached forward with a key.

She was being released! Finally, this horrendous mix-up had been sorted out. Soon she would be with her father.

As the door swung open, Tash tried to leave, but the warden stopped her. "Not a word to anyone," he warned fiercely. "Otherwise you will be brought straight back to your cell."

"I promise," Tash murmured with a solemn nod, though inside, she was laughing at his threat. He must be kidding. To be treated like this and not say anything? They had imprisoned the wrong person if that was the response they were hoping for! She could not be intimidated. Her outrage and vengeance would see no bounds!

Pushing past the man, Tasheira strode down the corridor as he followed. At the end, they turned the corner, exited through the solid wood door, and began climbing the winding stairs. When they reached the upper level of the dungeon, they backtracked along passages lined with more prison cells, and at first, Tash didn't notice anything unusual about them. When she did realize, however, her steps halted.

All the doors were open. Each cell was empty.

Puzzled, Tash glanced back at the warden.

"Keep moving," he ordered.

Maybe the entire prison had been emptied in an effort to locate her. It seemed the only logical explanation.

Still, Tash had an uneasy feeling. Her pace quickened. The sooner she could get out of here, the better.

Not far ahead, the passage ended at the main dungeon door, where a second hooded warden was standing, blocking the way. He pointed to a narrow side corridor that Tash hadn't noticed when she was first brought down yesterday. "Join the rest of them and get undressed."

"Undressed?" Tash exclaimed. "Am I not being allowed to finally leave?"

"Nice try," the man facing her snorted with contempt.

"What's really going on around here?" she demanded.

"Wash day," replied the other warden from behind. He pushed her shoulder to start her moving again.

Tasheira spun on him and tried to yank the hood off his face. She wanted to know what these men looked like when it came time for them to be punished.

But she was too slow. The man ducked out of the way as he caught her wrist and twisted it. "You're a very foolish girl," he growled, before shoving her with such force that Tash toppled backward and landed hard on the floor. Then he stepped over her, grabbed one of her arms, and began dragging Tasheira down the side corridor.

"Let go! Don't touch me!" Tash shouted. "You're all going to pay dearly for this!"

Yet her protests and flailing limbs made no difference as she was hauled about a hundred feet farther into a large chamber.

What she saw—after scrambling to her feet and looking around—was something she could never have anticipated. So many prisoners in one place, silent and expectant.

And all of them naked.

Filled with a surge of trepidation, Tash instinctively crossed her arms over her chest. What sort of nightmare had she entered?

Several hooded guards stood around the room's periphery, keeping watch over the group.

"Dirty clothes get tossed in there," said the fat man beside her, pointing to a line of tattered woven baskets along the wall, already overflowing with discarded garments. "A clean outfit will be delivered later to your cell."

"You can't expect—" Tash started to protest.

"You have no choice," the guard snarled. "The emperors demand cleanliness down here at all times. No foul odors that might offend them."

Tasheira had failed to pick up on it earlier, but it was true—except for her toilet, she had noticed no offensive smells since arriving. But still, to undress in front of everybody like this? How could she possibly do it?

"I demand some privacy, at the very least," Tash declared. "I'm a lady of the court. I'll simply wait until everyone else is finished, then wash up quickly on my own."

"Undress right now, *My Lady*," the man mocked. He raised his hand high over his head. "Or get a beating like you've never known."

Tasheira's insolence evaporated. She slowly undid one button of her dress, then another, directing her scowl toward any of the other prisoners who might dare to look over at her.

By any measure, they were a pathetic mob, dehumanized by their incarceration and shamed by their nudity. Some had physical ailments; others appeared to be suffering from mental conditions. The majority were men, of all ages and shapes, yet a few females waited among them too.

An old woman with white, scraggly hair, standing nearby on badly swollen legs, stepped closer. She glanced meekly at the prison guard for permission, and when he nodded, she turned to Tasheira. "Let me help you," she offered quietly.

"Thank you," Tash barely whispered.

The sympathetic woman must have read on Tash's face that she was near her breaking point. "It will be all right. You'll get used to it. In a few weeks—"

"Not a word!" the fat guard growled, raising his hand again as a warning.

The woman cringed, but remained silent as she helped unbutton Tasheira's dress along the back. Once it was loosened, Tash stepped out of the garment and tossed it onto the top of one of the heaping baskets. She turned but did not join the others. Though she wanted to cover herself with her arms, she resisted, as an act of defiance. Fear and embarrassment were what the hooded warden wanted.

Tash surveyed the assembled crowd as she stood tall, ready to challenge anyone who might try glancing at her naked body. But then she made eye contact with someone against the farthest wall who was staring unabashedly. Tasheira's fierce glare immediately withered. All hope drained away, as if she were deflating to nothing more than an empty sack of skin on the floor.

No, it can't be!

Though his features were swollen and bruised, there was no denying that face.

Fimal was now a prisoner too.

Chapter 27

"WE DON'T HAVE THE numbers we need!" shouted Ahmet, pumping his arms as he ran. "This wasn't supposed to happen for another few days!"

Guri sprinted beside him. "Maybe families trekking in other areas will see what's going on and can join us in time!"

Hokk tried to run just as hard to keep up. Queasy, panting, and ignoring the burning sensation in his leg muscles, he split his attention between what he saw in the air and the careful placement of his feet.

They had left the longhouses much farther back as they raced across the bobbing terrain of the Plastlantic Mass. Where they found themselves now, the garbage was less dense and entangled. In many spots, sizable gaps in the plastic had formed, which exposed open water, like large ponds with debris ringing their perimeter. Maintaining a straight path became impossible, so several times they were forced to circle around the edges to make any progress.

"This is the largest flock we've ever witnessed!" said Guri. "I'm sure we're going to have the best year yet!"

Hokk looked up once again at the swirling cloud of white and black, made up of hundreds and hundreds of birds, plummeting straight down toward the ocean before disappearing beneath the surface.

When the Merreens stopped at the edge of the largest hole of water they had yet come across, the cacophony of the squawking seabirds was nearly deafening. Those circling overhead dive-bombed again and again and again, like a volley of arrows at lightning speed, each bird tightly tucking its wings back to slipstream through the air. The water roiled with every splash of their entry. Returning to the surface with fish wiggling in their long beaks, the birds would paddle around as they stretched their necks skyward to swallow their meals whole. Then they were flapping their wings to get airborne before circling, screeching, and diving once more.

Meanwhile, many of the Merreens had fanned out in a ring around the open water, shouting orders and encouragement at their companions. Those with spears thrust them into the deep and pulled out fish. Others threw nets into the water to catch the squirming prey, or into the air to trap birds.

At first, all Hokk could do was rotate on the spot, taking in the entire scene with a smile and racing pulse. Then someone handed him a spear, and he crept to the edge, where he could see countless flashes of silver beneath the blue water. The fish moved fast and spearing them was tricky, but the game was exhilarating all the same, and when he impaled his first catch, he yanked the fish off, raised his spear into the air, and let out a loud whoop.

He noticed several of the younger Merreens hurrying about with baskets of woven plastic to collect the fish that had been caught, so Hokk added his own.

On his next attempt, he leaned out farther, bracing himself, ready to launch his weapon again when the moment was perfect.

Being overzealous, however, and still woozy from his night of drinking, he stretched too far and lost his balance. He tumbled into the ocean. The frigid temperature snatched his breath, yet it was the view underwater that was truly breathtaking. He watched huge clusters of fish moving in unison, spheres of fluid motion, each mass like one integral being. Then the spheres would split apart into innumerable flickers of silver, dispersing in an instant to avoid capture by the birds slicing through from above with enough momentum to carry them into the depths while trails of tiny bubbles rose to the top.

If not for the need to refill his lungs, Hokk would have stayed submerged much longer to watch this enthralling life-and-death dance between birds and fish, but he suddenly sensed a shadow moving deep beneath him. So startled, he sucked salty water into his mouth and started choking.

At the same moment, though, a hand reached down from above the water, grabbed him under the armpit, and hauled him out to safety.

Chapter 28

WITH HER WRISTS TIED together, Elia had been unable to remove the burlap sack from around her head. But she didn't care. Hours had passed, and while the tears she'd wasted over her father's betrayal had long since dried, Elia felt too discouraged and hopeless to do anything.

She knew without a doubt that she was imprisoned many levels below the palace, below the laundry room where she used to work. From the moment her head was covered, Elia had focused on clues that revealed where she was being taken: the grating sound of wheels bumping over cobblestones as they left the alley; the sense of elevation as they crossed the Grand Bridge; the feeling of cold, damp steps beneath her bare feet as she was escorted in shackles down many flights of stairs; the pounding of fists; heavy doors opening and slamming shut; the crackle and heat of torches; more stairs; stumbling forward; landing on the hard floor; metal hinges squealing as she was locked in.

Though crying had made her feel foolish and weak, it had been impossible not to surrender to her emotions. Her father turning her in for money was a despicable act, but she was just as upset that he had stolen the saddlebag with the telescope and its documents inside. He'd never comprehend their true value—measured not by what they could be sold or traded for, but by the many lives ruined to protect them. Such an awful waste.

Yet equally horrendous was ending up in the dungeon, a place where she had always feared to one day find herself.

I'm going to die in here. They set Tasheira free, but they'll never do the same for me.

Much earlier, there had been no mistaking Tasheira's strong, demanding voice as she talked to a servant girl who had come to deliver food. After Tash mentioned that a new prisoner had arrived during the night, the servant must have been curious because footsteps approached and stopped right outside Elia's cell. The glow of candlelight filtered through the fibers of the gunny sack. Whoever was standing didn't stay long, as the light soon disappeared. Then Tash called out, "What's wrong? Is she dead?" followed by the fading patter of footsteps, and silence. The stillness, broken only a few times by Elia's coughing, lasted quite a while, until she finally heard a guard opening Tasheira's cell door and taking her away after warning her not to talk to anyone. So it seemed that Tasheira had indeed been released.

But why was the girl imprisoned in the first place? If the Baron's daughter had been caught up in the Imperial Guards' web, then many others could also be in jail—Hokk, her mother, Rayhan. It was a frightening thought.

Now so consumed with worry—and trembling from the lingering effects of incense withdrawal—Elia was startled by the light of a candle shining through the burlap for a second time.

"Come closer so I can remove that bag," someone whispered gently. The voice belonged to a young female. It almost sounded familiar.

Elia struggled to sit up. Trying to control her shivering, she slowly dragged herself toward the metal bars and stopped when she felt hands touching her head. The hands dropped to the drawstring under her neck, quickly unlaced the ties, and pulled the sack off.

"Praise the sun, it is you!"

Elia blinked several times before she registered the eye patch on the face in front of her. "Naadie!" she croaked, stunned to see her former co-worker. "Am I dreaming?"

"I could ask the same thing," said Naadie. "Are you all right?"

"I guess. Definitely better now to see you."

"Good. I'm so relieved. We thought we'd never find you."

"We?" Elia repeated, her eyebrows knitted. "Who's *we*?"

"A bunch of us have been looking for you for many weeks," Naadie replied. "We had given up hope you were still alive until those posters appeared yesterday throughout the city. Then our efforts grew tenfold to find you before anyone else. Obviously, we failed."

"You're here now, though."

"Yes, by a turn of good fortune." Naadie reached through the bars. "Lift your arms so I can untie your wrists."

Elia obeyed, and Naadie began picking at the knots in the rope.

"Aren't you working in the laundry room anymore?" Elia asked. "How did you make the switch?"

"Cook was able to get me reassigned from the clotheslines as soon as you disappeared, just in case this is where you ended up. I'm so thankful she was right."

The loosened rope dropped away and Elia rubbed her sore wrists. "Have you seen my mother or brother down here? Were they imprisoned too?"

Naadie paused, biting her thumbnail as she looked back along the corridor. "Uh, no . . . not that I saw."

Why had she hesitated? Was she trying to avoid sharing the truth?

Before Elia could ask, Naadie turned back with mounting concern. "Listen, I'm worried we might not have much time. I have to leave before everyone returns from the showers. Thankfully, you were excluded from joining them, but whether it was because of direct orders, or because nobody seems to know you're down here, I'm not sure."

"Showers? What are you talking about?"

Naadie rushed on as though she had not heard the question. "You're in great danger. The same for me. So you'll have to listen carefully and follow my instructions exactly if we're going to break you out of here."

"I can escape?" Elia asked, resurrecting a spark of hope.

"You can."

Naadie reached up and removed two pins holding back her hair. She stuck both of them into the lock of Elia's cell door, and began fiddling with the mechanism. "Damn thing!" she grumbled after the first few attempts.

"Will it work?" Elia asked.

"Cook taught me how to do it a number of weeks ago. I've been practicing so I'd be prepared if this day ever came." Her tongue stuck out from the corner of her mouth as she concentrated for several more minutes, until finally—*click*—and the lock disengaged.

"What now?" asked Elia, leaning on the door to open it.

Naadie pushed it shut again. "No, you'll have to leave the door closed for the time being. We can't let anybody suspect that it's unlocked."

"So how do we escape? How do we make sure we aren't caught?"

"Unfortunately, we won't be able to do it together. You'll have to manage on your own, but I'll meet up with you on the other side once you're out. Are you willing to risk it?"

Elia nodded. "Of course. Should I make my getaway as soon as you leave?"

"My goodness, no! You'll have to wait until much later in the day when the timing is better. Near the end of the afternoon when my shift is over."

Elia looked past Naadie into the corridor, then around her enclosure, which was lit only by candlelight. "How will I be able to tell what time it is? There aren't any windows. For all I know, it could be the middle of the afternoon right now."

"I realize it's too dark in here, but we can get around that." From behind her ear, Naadie produced a yellow dandelion and handed the flower to Elia. "After I'm gone, keep pinching the bottom of the stem and wait for it to wilt. I picked a second one for myself. When the flower bends over far enough that you feel the petals touching your hand, you'll know the right amount of time has elapsed for you to slip away. Does that make sense?"

"Got it."

"Good. This way, we can meet up at approximately the same time. One of us may have to wait a short while at the other end."

"But when I leave, how do I get all the way through the dungeon without anyone seeing me? Surely I can't avoid the watchmen. They'll get replaced at the end of their shifts."

"Yes, someone is always on duty and guards are everywhere. But you will not be going out the same way you came in."

"I won't?" Elia asked with surprise.

"No, there's another option." Naadie pointed down the corridor, but in the opposite direction from where guards and prisoners entered. "Go to the very end of this passage. Remember, it will be too dark to see, so move slowly to avoid colliding with anything. When you can't go farther, you'll feel an old wooden door in front of you. If you were to see it in regular light, it would look so ancient you'd guess it could never open."

"Is it locked?"

"Definitely. But that won't be a problem." Naadie reached up and flipped her eye patch over onto her forehead, exposing an empty eye socket. A key was nestled in the cavity. "I couldn't risk the guards finding this if I was searched, which they sometimes do," she explained, noticing Elia's amazement. She pulled the key out and passed it through the bars. "Keep this very safe."

Elia studied the key. The thing was so small. "So this is all I need?"

"It is, but you won't be using it like you'd think. On the far right-hand side of the door, you'll feel a massive handle, as well as three heavy padlocks—one at the top, the bottom, and in the middle. But these are not real locks. They are just decoys to disguise the door's three hinges, and to distract anyone hoping to pick them—though, in truth, a person could spend a lifetime trying without success. The actual lock you want is on the left-hand side. It's nothing more than a small hole hidden in a burl."

"What's a burl?"

"A knot in the wood. You'd assume it's just a crack that's developed with age. It's really difficult to pinpoint, even when you have enough light."

"Can you show me now while we have your candle?"

Naadie frowned as she pulled the patch back into position. "It's too risky. I'd be afraid of getting caught. You'll have to figure it out on your own. Just feel carefully with your fingers. When you find the correct spot, however, the key will slip right in and turn with ease."

"So what will I discover on the other side? Stairs going up?"

"Just continue as far as you can go and stop when you get outside. Wait for me there. And remember—lock the door behind you!"

Chapter 29

TASHEIRA WANTED DESPERATELY TO approach Fimal, yet he cautioned her with a side glance at the guards that had circled the room. She held back, hoping for a better opportunity.

But what were they all waiting for anyway? It was absurd, really—men and women standing around with no clothes on, shivering in the gloom, while a few sputtering torches along the walls repelled the shadows. If this was a chance for everyone to bathe, what was the delay? Would they get soap? Would they be able to rinse themselves? Surely water was too precious to waste on prisoners.

"Is anything going to happen?" Tash whispered to the woman who had earlier helped unbutton the back of her dress.

"It should start any minute now," she replied, peering toward the ceiling.

A moment later, Tash heard gurgling sounds and she looked up too.

Then, from what she guessed to be a spout embedded in the rock overhead, a thin trickle of water fell into the chamber. The volume increased. Several people jostled to position themselves beneath the shower, raising their hands to catch the stream and rubbing their faces with the wetness as it splashed down on them.

A few more hidden ceiling spouts began to release water as well, yet the flow from each was sporadic. The streams would surge, then dwindle to only a few dribbles, followed by another gush shortly afterward, like a passing wave, all while the prisoners below scurried about as they tried to wash themselves.

With everyone distracted, Tasheira took the chance to inch closer to Fimal, ever watchful to avoid raising the suspicions of the men guarding the space. At one point, however, she was forced to stop when a startling rush of tepid water doused her head. As she was pushed aside by others who wanted to take advantage of the flow, Tash wiped the fragrant water from her face. Only when she felt grit on her skin and tasted soap on her tongue did she finally realize the water's source. This first level of the dungeon was the very next floor below the palace laundry, where workers were probably emptying their washtubs into the drains. The effluent was then running down pipes to fall on the expectant prisoners.

A raucous cry suddenly erupted at the chamber's only exit. Three men were attempting to storm out, but hooded guards fought them off, relentless in their retaliation and relishing the opportunity for abuse. The failed fugitives could do little to defend themselves, and soon they were battered and bleeding. Tash felt sickened to witness such brutality.

Keep people fearful and weak from hunger, thought Tasheira. That's how to eliminate any threat of a full-blown uprising.

But at least the commotion allowed Tasheira to take the final few steps toward her cousin.

There was no way of ignoring each other's nakedness.

"You're not supposed to be here!" she hissed. "This is terrible! I was counting on you to rescue me!"

"I was hoping you hadn't been imprisoned either," Fimal murmured unhappily.

Their eyes darted about, watching for anyone who might catch them talking.

"You look like you've been roughed up pretty bad," Tash whispered, judging that it was safe to speak so long as it looked as though they were busy washing.

"Would you expect them to be gentle?" he asked just as quietly. "I fought back, of course."

"When were you hauled off?"

"As soon as we parted ways."

Tasheira's eyes widened with surprise. "You mean you were never a few doors down the hall from where they first held me for questioning?"

"I was in that other room for only a minute. I guess they wanted to make it look as though that's where I was being kept."

A stream of water fell on them. The soap made Tasheira's eyes sting, and she rubbed them as she asked, "So you didn't see my father?"

"Unfortunately not."

"And you were never interrogated?"

"No. Who interrogated you?" Fimal asked, slicking the water out of his hair.

Tasheira frowned, but continued rubbing down her body. "The Twin Emperors. At first it was just Tael on his own, then both of them at the same time. They grilled me to learn everything I knew about Elia and what she was scheming to do. I cooperated with them the best I could and fully expected to be released after we were done. And I was let go, briefly, until guards arrived not long after to arrest me."

The flow of water started to dwindle from all the ceiling spouts. Soon, only a few drops were dripping throughout the chamber.

"Listen, we probably don't have much time," said Tash. "I'm sure my father has already left the Sanctuary, without a clue about what's happened to us. I saw his team of horses being assembled for the flight home."

"But the Baron was our only chance for freedom."

"Exactly."

"And nobody else knows where we are."

Tasheira nodded gravely. "So it's up to us alone to discover some way of getting out of here."

Chapter 30

GURI WAS THE ONE who had pulled Hokk to safety at the water's edge.

"Are you all right?" she asked. She held a spear with three wriggling fish impaled along its length. She had likely run them through with a single carefully timed jab.

Hokk spat the taste of salt from his mouth. "Yes . . . yes, I'm fine," he replied, half laughing, half choking. "Somehow, though, I always seem to end up under the water!"

"I thought maybe you were trying to escape again," Guri teased with a sly grin and one suspiciously arched eyebrow.

"Not with all this going on!" he replied enthusiastically as he bent down to retrieve his spear. "It's too incredible!"

Birds continued to plummet headlong into the ocean at breakneck speeds, splash after splash, no more than a blur of white and black swallowed up by a spray of water.

"You're right. It's like nothing we've ever seen!" Guri agreed. "Just more proof that you bring us good fortune. We can never let you go!"

Hokk had no clue why the Merreens credited him for this bounty of fish, but he wasn't going to argue. He would take any break that came his way. If they thought he was their lucky charm, they might treat him as an equal member of the tribe, regardless of how much he contributed to today's haul—and so far, for every dozen fish caught by a Merreen, Hokk might have caught one. He really needed to improve his aim.

More importantly, if Hokk was going to be stuck with these people—which seemed likely to be his fate now that Rayhan had taken the horse and abandoned him—then his survival depended on them sharing their food. That, plus making sure he didn't choke to death on the awful fumes of their fires. Perhaps he could convince the Merreens to find an alternative fuel to replace the tires they fed into the flames. Anything to avoid the billowing, acrid black smoke that had burned his throat last night and caused his head to throb, long before their bottles of seaweed wine were passed around.

And I'm swearing off the wine for good!

Then, very unexpectedly, Hokk sensed a shift in the atmosphere around him, and he hesitated, his spear poised directly over his head. It took only a split second for him to realize what was different—in an instant, all the birds had gone quiet. There was an eerie, unsettling calm. The Merreens seemed to feel it too.

The next moment, however, the silence was shattered by loud and riotous screeching as the birds paddling on top of the open water suddenly took to the air to join the others circling above. It seemed as if none of them dared to dive into the ocean.

But it wasn't the chaotic maneuvers of the birds riding the air currents that now captured Hokk's focus. His eyes widened, and he felt a combination of relief and apprehension to see two stallions flying toward him, soaring just above the water.

Somebody else spotted them too. "Look! Over there!" the person yelled as he pointed, triggering every other Merreen to abruptly turn.

Without question, an Imperial Guard was riding one of the horses. His mirrored helmet easily gave him away. But in the other saddle . . . was that . . . could it possibly be Rayhan?

"Stop them!" someone screamed. "They're after our catch!"

As the guard and Rayhan flew past, several of the Merreens started throwing their spears, yet each shaft fell short of its target. Cries of outrage rang out, but before any further shots could be made, the wet, unstable surface of the Plastlantic Mass suddenly rose beneath everyone's feet, as if a rogue wave were trying to boost them closer to the intruders.

Quickly spinning, but also struggling not to fall over, Hokk watched a bizarre and frightening scene unfold as if in slow motion.

The ocean under them bulged upward. Growing in size, it burst like a massive bubble, releasing a monstrous shadow trapped within.

Yet the shadow had substance. Black. Shimmering. Alive. Full of tremendous strength.

So impossibly huge!

The creature rose high up into the air, its open mouth stretched wide, its throat so distended it looked as if it could swallow several stallions at once.

"Whale!" a Merreen screamed.

With an immense swoosh of water and pieces of plastic raining down, the beast twisted in mid-air, then landed on its side. The colossal wave knocked people off their feet. Baskets of fish toppled over.

"Everyone retreat!"

The ocean was churning. No sooner had the first whale disappeared into the depths than a second one surfaced, rising clear out of the water as well. Its enormous tail crashed down against the Mass with a thunderous smack that sent more debris flying.

"Hokk! Jump on!"

Almost unable to pull his attention away, Hokk realized the command had come not from Guri or Ahmet, or another Merreen, but from right overhead.

"Come on, Hokk! Hurry!"

Though the voice was Rayhan's, it was the Imperial Guard who was hovering only a foot above the surge. The guard extended a hand to pull Hokk up.

Hokk hesitated. He glanced at Rayhan as if for confirmation.

Rayhan nodded.

Hokk felt the Plastlantic Mass heave violently again, about to rupture with another breaching whale.

"Grab hold!" the guard ordered.

Instinct told Hokk to turn and run. He had no idea who to trust. He wasn't used to having others save him. All he could think to do was put as much distance as possible between him, the horses, and the colossal beasts that were plowing out of the ocean to devour great quantities of fish.

However, a tidal wave carrying garbage overtook him as a third whale plunged below the water with a roaring splash. Hokk fell to his knees.

Scrambling to his feet, intent on following the Merreens who had scattered, he sensed beating wings directly above his head. The horse's legs were kicking right beside him, its hooves nearly touching the rippling surface.

A hand quickly grabbed Hokk by the collar. As the horse flew higher, Hokk was pulled up into the air with it, his breath almost completely cut off by the material twisted around his neck. He flailed his limbs and glanced down to see the Plastlantic Mass dropping away below him. As they climbed to greater heights, approaching the clouds, Hokk reached up to grip the guard's wrist, now afraid the man might change his mind and let go.

"Stop fighting!" the guard growled.

Rayhan's stallion flew alongside. "We're here to rescue you!" he yelled.

"I—can't—breathe!" Hokk gasped, clawing with his other hand to loosen the fabric cutting into his windpipe. "I—can't . . ."

With an extra burst of strength, the guard was able to lift Hokk a few inches, enough so that Hokk could grab onto the end of the saddle with his free hand.

"Now use your other hand to grab the saddle horn and pull yourself up!" the man ordered.

Hokk was reluctant to let go of the guard's wrist, but had no other choice. His hand shot forward and locked on the saddle horn.

Now to get a leg over the horse!

It took several tries, but finally, Hokk managed to get his heel firmly dug into the animal's rump, and he used this leverage to hoist himself into place behind the guard.

Hokk glared at Rayhan, who had watched all this, and shouted, "Where are you taking me?"

"Back to Above," Rayhan answered.

"Who asked you to?"

"I figured it was the right thing to do."

Hokk scowled. "I thought you were going to abandon me down there for good."

"I was," Rayhan replied fiercely. "Then I reconsidered. Just don't make me regret my decision."

Chapter 31

ELIA THOUGHT IT WOULD never happen. She squeezed the bottom of the dandelion stem as if to strangle the life out of it. Of all the weeds growing at the back of the palace, Naadie must have picked the most robust flower of the bunch. It was never going to wilt. This waiting in the dark would go on forever.

But then, finally, when she had almost given up hope, the delicate petals touched her hand.

Elia tossed the flower over her shoulder and grabbed Naadie's key, which she had been sitting on. She pushed against the door of her cell, half expecting it had somehow relocked itself. Thankfully, it swung open, though with an ear-piercing shriek from its hinges.

"What's going on?" demanded Tasheira, her voice drifting down the passage. "Who's there?"

Elia paused, debating whether to answer. She decided against it.

Earlier, Elia was so certain Tasheira had been set free that she was surprised to hear the girl being brought back to her cell. It had happened several hours ago, not long after Naadie's departure. But why had she returned? What could Tash have done between her cell and the dungeon's main entrance to make the guards reconsider letting her go? It must have been her strong will and sharp tongue working against her. But what kind of trouble had Tasheira become involved with to get herself arrested in the first place?

Sticking the key into her mouth for safekeeping, Elia slipped through the narrow gap in her cell's doorway and stepped into the pitch-black corridor, closing the door behind her. Unfortunately, her legs were still shackled and the sound of the chains betrayed her.

Tasheira called out again. "I can hear you!"

Elia cringed, biting down on the key, but didn't stop moving.

Tash must have guessed the direction she was going by the clatter of metal on stone. "Come back. Are you escaping? If you found a way, then please, you have to help—"

Elia tuned her out, focusing instead on her steps as she blindly reached forward into the darkness—one hand directly in front and the other high enough above her shoulders to make sure she didn't hit her head. As she hobbled along, she felt disoriented, as if she were in a limitless abyss, made all the more confusing by the echo of Tasheira's demanding voice.

How much farther? She should have found out from Naadie the length of this passage. She should've also asked the girl to pick the locks on her noisy shackles so she could be rid of the burden.

Then Elia's fingertips grazed a rough, splintered wood surface. She flattened her palms and carefully slid her hands across to determine that this was indeed a door. On the right, she confirmed the three padlocks, just as Naadie had described. They felt so real. So heavy and imposing. Making the locks fake—and therefore tamperproof—was the perfect way to confound any would-be escapers. Now, Elia just had to find the right hole to get herself beyond this barrier.

Yet such an old door had many cracks and pits in the wood, and without any light, it seemed impossible that she could find the secret spot.

Elia took the key out of her mouth and stuck it into whatever crevices she touched. Each time, she was unable to make it turn. One spot proved to be especially tight, and as Elia tried yanking the key out, she fumbled it between her sweaty fingers. It fell, and she heard it bounce several times with a metallic clatter.

She dropped to her knees and hastily began feeling around. As Tasheira continued to shout at her, Elia's frantic fingers accidentally brushed the key and sent it skittering across the stone floor.

"Come free me!" Tash ordered.

"Shut up!" Elia screamed as her frustration erupted as anger. She immediately regretted the outburst, however, and hoped Tasheira would not recognize her voice.

But had she lost the key completely? Had she ruined her one chance to escape?

Elia tried to calm her mind, glad that at least Tasheira was now quiet so she could think more clearly.

It must have bounced into a neighboring cell.

Elia crawled over to the nearest enclosure. She reached through the metal rails.

Please let it be within my reach!

Patting the floor, she had to move a few bars farther along before she finally, thankfully, felt something flat.

Praise the sun! She had found it.

Elia carefully picked the key up, gripping it tightly as she pulled her hand out of the cell. She then immediately stuck the key into her mouth again as she hurried back to the locked door.

Now focus! Let's make this happen!

Still, no matter how much she tried, Elia had no luck. Would she ever get this damn thing open?

Then a remarkable thought occurred to her. Elia had assumed the keyhole would be at a normal mid-level height. However, if this door was rigged to trick people, the actual spot she needed could be in a knot located *anywhere* on the left. Maybe Naadie had never actually used the door, or seen it for herself, to know exactly where it might be. Yes, that had to be the answer!

Elia stretched up and began feeling around much higher than she had before. When her fingers felt a raised knot, with a crack in the middle, close to the top of the door near the frame, her anticipation soared.

Could this be it?

She was about to remove the key from her mouth when Tasheira's distant voice made her freeze.

"Hurry. Someone's coming."

Elia looked over her shoulder. She saw only blackness, but she too could hear the very faint jingle of keys as someone was preparing to open the door at the opposite end of the corridor. Fearing she'd soon see light illuminating the passage, she stood on her tiptoes and, with a trembling hand, slipped the key into the crack. She almost couldn't believe it when the key turned. With a little extra pressure, she heard a subtle *click* and felt the door silently swing away from her as if weightless.

Too scared to look back, Elia pushed through, stepping from one black space into another. She slipped the key into a pocket and closed the door behind her.

Now what?

To help get her bearings, Elia spread her arms wide and determined that she was in a narrow passage. But where would it take her? She had no choice, however, except to trust Naadie. And even though her shackles impeded her stride, she ran. She ran for blessed freedom, as fast as she possibly could, despite not being able to see anything ahead of her. It felt as though she had never escaped the tunnels below the City of Ago.

I'm supposed to meet Naadie . . . outside.

Yet how could that be? It didn't make sense. If anything, the ground now beneath her feet was slanted downward, whereas Elia would have expected to find a secret set of stairs leading up, or at least feel herself climbing an incline to the surface.

But soon, in front of her, Elia detected the faintest orange glow. If her eyes hadn't been so used to the complete darkness, she might not have distinguished it at first. A source of light was definitely just a short distance ahead, growing brighter with each step.

It was the mouth of the tunnel! That was her way out!

Recklessly, she charged forward, and in the next instant, she was skidding to a halt at the very edge of rock. Another step farther would have sent her toppling over.

She was teetering at the precipice of a cliff, with a wall of mist in front of her, glowing yellow from shafts of piercing sunlight.

Chapter 32

AS SOON AS THE FLYING stallions tore through the uppermost layer of clouds, their three passengers began to roast in the blazing sun. Hearing a groan from Hokk, Rayhan glanced over. The pale young man had covered his eyes and was trying in vain to shield himself behind Commander Blaitz.

"Do you still have your dark glasses?" Rayhan called out.

"I lost them somewhere," Hokk replied, the suffering evident in his voice.

"Then maybe it's best we fly below the clouds again."

Blaitz's metal helmet bobbed in agreement. "We should. The horses will be able to last much longer if we can avoid the midday heat."

Descending quickly at a steep pitch, they soon came out again on the underside of the churning mist. The stallions leveled off. With every upbeat, their wing tips seemed to skim the dense, dark blanket of cloud. Hokk dropped the arm from across his face. Rayhan leaned over in his saddle. Far below, the Plastlantic Mass still dominated the view, though the two horses had flown far enough to lose sight of the flock of birds circling the spot where they had found Hokk.

Rayhan still felt shaken by their narrow escape. Those fish! How could they be so huge? How could they reach such a height above the water, threatening to swallow everything in their path?

Embarking on a rescue mission was the last thing Rayhan had expected to do today, but soon after he and Blaitz had left the Merreen settlement during the early morning hours, he had been struck by a realization that changed his perspective. Though Rayhan didn't trust Hokk in the least—betting anything the young man would betray him in a heartbeat if it meant saving his own skin—he knew that escaping to Above and leaving Hokk stranded with the Merreens would be reprehensible. He was better than that. Besides, how would he ever be able to face his sister knowing he had not made an honest attempt? While he might not care to admit it, Rayhan had witnessed enough to suggest Hokk truly cared about Elia, and that she probably harbored similar feelings for him too. Did he really want to bear the blame for ruining whatever connection they might have?

Trying to convince his commander to return to Below, however, had been a challenge, but Rayhan was pleased with himself for not giving up. Blaitz worried the plan was too risky and explained that saving Rayhan was the only reason he ventured to Below in the first place. Having succeeded in his mission, the commander was therefore determined they both return to the Noble Sanctuary as soon as possible. Yet Rayhan would not accept this. Though he fully expected to be reprimanded for insubordination, Rayhan finally demanded outright that Hokk be rescued. Surprisingly, Commander Blaitz relented, as if obeying a direct order from a superior.

That conversation, and the eventual decision to return for Hokk, had taken place on a small, barren floating island—the first one they'd encountered after leaving the Merreen settlement. It was here that Blaitz had set up the single tent he had brought along for himself in case the effort to find Rayhan took more than a day.

Rayhan could tell they were heading to that same island now. Of course, with the strong air currents pushing it through the upper atmosphere, it had drifted a greater distance away. After what seemed like several hours of flying, they finally saw the tiny tip of the island poking beneath the clouds. Taking one last look down from this altitude, Rayhan could now see far in the distance where the irregular edge of the Plastlantic Mass ended and the open ocean began, the water extending uninterrupted toward the horizon. Still, he did not see any sign of the solid land that Hokk had described to the Merreens.

The riders pulled back on the reins and the horses changed course. They soared up, almost parallel to the vertical rock, and emerged above the thick mist, where they found themselves once more under a blue sky. It was now later in the afternoon, and the sun's rays were much less intense, though Hokk still had to cover his eyes.

They touched down no more than a minute later beside the simple campsite. Rayhan was the first to jump to the ground. He watched Hokk swing a leg over the horse's back, using his one free hand on the animal's hindquarters for support as he slid off.

"Is there any shelter?" Hokk asked.

"There's a tent we've already assembled," Rayhan replied.

"Take me. I can't let my skin burn and blister like before."

Imagining how easily the sun could fry Hokk's white skin, Rayhan quickly led him inside the tent. It was just high enough for them both to stand.

Hokk rubbed his red, watery eyes. "I can't take it out there."

"I didn't realize how little tolerance you have."

"I actually have none. In these conditions, I'm at a great disadvantage with only one set of eyelids." Hokk blinked a few times, then scanned the tent's interior. "Not much space for the three of us. I guess we have quite a way to go yet before we get back."

"To the Noble Sanctuary, you mean?" Rayhan asked, prompting Hokk to nod. "Yes, I suspect we still have a great distance to cover," he continued. "However, Blaitz must know which direction to go from here."

"But can he really be trusted?" Hokk asked, looking skeptical.

"Of course. Why wouldn't you think so?"

"Because he's an Imperial Guard, to start with," replied Hokk, glancing at the tent's front flap as if the man might suddenly enter. "But I'm also certain he and I have encountered each other several times in the past, though under much more hostile circumstances."

Rayhan was startled to hear this. "Are you sure?"

"I was digging in my memories as we were flying, and I remember some run-ins with a guard whose helmet had that same metal spike protruding from its forehead. How many guards can boast one of those?"

"He's the only one."

"Are you sure?" Hokk asked, throwing the same question back at Rayhan.

"Yes. The spike distinguishes Blaitz from all other guards with a lower rank."

"Just like that man with the mangled face whose helmet had metallic wings on the side?"

Recognizing the description, Rayhan's forehead wrinkled. "Do you mean Commander Wrasse?"

Hokk nodded, his expression grim. "Yes, that's the name. I had forgotten until you just said it."

"From what I've been told, he's dead."

"Dead? Good! He was the one who hunted your sister."

"Wrasse was chasing after Elia?"

"He *hunted* her!" Hokk stressed. "Across the plains of Below. She was terrified of being captured by him. She knew he'd kill her."

"You must be mistaken. If anything, Wrasse was probably trying to rescue her, like Blaitz has rescued you and me. We're lucky he came down to save us."

"Which brings me back to my first question. What makes you think we can trust him?"

Before Rayhan could answer, Blaitz flung back the tent's flap and entered.

"I've given the horses their water," said the commander. "A little rest and they'll be ready to continue on."

Rayhan only nodded. Though he would hate to confess the truth, he felt blindsided by doubt. Was Hokk's concern justified? If so, how much did he know? What was really going on? Did any of this relate to why Elia had jumped from the bridge?

"We've met before, haven't we?" Hokk said abruptly, interrupting Rayhan's thoughts.

Blaitz paused. As if deciding Hokk's blunt, cold manner warranted a more tactful face-to-face response, he took off his helmet. The serious expression on his handsome features softened with the slightest smile. "Yes, we have met," he acknowledged, though his words seemed somewhat cautious. "It was the first evening you arrived at the Sanctuary with Baron Shoad. You were being denied access to the palace until I stepped in."

Hokk's eyes narrowed. "Yes, of course, that was our most recent encounter," he said impatiently. "But what I'm talking about are the two other times before that night."

"I'm not sure what you are referring to."

"Come on, now, don't pretend you don't know," Hokk scoffed. "You were with the first group of guards who descended to Below and tracked us across the prairies. I clearly saw you on your horse when you flew beside that solitary tree, trying to spot Elia in its branches."

"Yes, I knew she was hiding up there. But where were you?" Blaitz asked evenly.

Hokk ignored the question. "Then there was that time you were flying through the streets of my home city, Ago. You were looking for us again, though little did you know Elia was already safely hidden beneath the city. What did you want from us? What do you really want with me now?"

Blaitz pinched his lips together and drew a long, slow breath through his nostrils before replying. "Yes, it was definitely me that day in the city, too. And now that you mention it, I suppose I do recognize you from when I was patrolling the streets. But what you apparently don't realize is that I ran across Elia one other time as well."

The guard's comment seemed to surprise Hokk.

"Before any of those other instances you've just mentioned, I found Elia alone on the grasslands," Blaitz continued. "Yes, there was an entire search party looking for her—or rather for the items she was carrying—but I did not reveal her location when I discovered her."

"I don't believe you," Hokk replied, though without much conviction.

"Elia was trying to hide, lying in the grasses, right there at my feet. I could have picked her up in my arms. Instead, I protected her by not divulging anything to the others, not even when our group returned to the Sanctuary. I tried to go back for her as soon as I could, but I guess, by that point, you had both moved on."

Rayhan had been listening with great interest, yet also with concern. "All that matters to me now is whether or not my sister is safe. Do you know where she is?"

"And how do you even know her name is Elia?" Hokk challenged.

The commander turned first to Rayhan. "I suspect you're already aware that your sister probably never ended up falling to Below."

"Then where is she?" Rayhan asked again, his tone now accusatory.

Blaitz shook his head. "I can't say."

"You won't say, or you're not sure?"

Blaitz simply shrugged, though he appeared to be holding something back. "I'm afraid your sister might have been arrested by now. Supposedly, she was a fugitive in Na-Lavent."

"In the city? How did she manage that?"

Blaitz frowned, then turned to face Hokk. "As for your question, Elia's name became known to a great number of people as soon as she disappeared with that telescope. I'm sure you've already seen it. Have you?"

Rayhan had no idea what the man was talking about, but he noticed Hokk clench his jaw. Obviously, he was holding back information too.

"How does a telescope play into any of this?" Rayhan asked with frustration, trying to connect the pieces. "Elia never mentioned a telescope. How did she get it? Did she steal it? It certainly wasn't from someone in our family. We're too poor."

"The telescope was recently rediscovered and smuggled out of the palace," said the commander. "I doubt if Elia truly understands how important the thing is. She'd be stunned to know how many dangerous people are after it."

Rayhan went rigid. "So then why should we believe you're any better than the rest of them?" he growled. "How can we truly trust you?"

Blaitz grimaced. "For your own self-preservation, you'd be wise not to."

Chapter 33

STANDING AT THE MOUTH of the tunnel, with an immediate drop-off at the tip of her toes, Elia didn't know what to do next. From this cliffside cave, she could see thick mist but nothing else—no blue sky of Above, certainly no view of the threatening gloom of Below, which might have been visible if she had descended low enough to find herself on the underside of the cloud cover.

This couldn't be the place where Naadie meant for them to meet, so far beneath the surface of the Noble Sanctuary. The girl had implied she'd be taking a different route to join Elia, but what could that possibly be? Would she have to rappel from ground level on a rope? Wouldn't that be too treacherous if Naadie could only depend on her one good eye?

Without question, the tunnel behind Elia had been excavated from the rock as a means of escape. During her years in the laundry room, she had heard snippets of gossip about hidden corridors throughout the palace, supposedly built in case members of the Royal Family were forced to flee their enemies. Assuming those rumors were true, it seemed perfectly reasonable the dungeon would also have its own secret passage if an emperor or empress ever found themselves imprisoned and in need of rescue.

But surely the original plan for the tunnel's construction didn't require a royal fugitive to leap to his or her death if pursued to the end of it. Maybe, in the past, a bridge had connected this spot to some place on the mainland—another undisclosed crossing, like the natural shelf Elia had discovered beneath the Grand Bridge. Or, perhaps there had been some form of platform and pulley system by which someone could be hoisted up to the top when the dangers had passed.

Still, Elia couldn't imagine why Naadie would have suggested this escape route for today if the possibility of getting to safety didn't exist.

No, there has to be a way! You're probably missing the obvious.

Elia leaned forward carefully to look along the outer wall of rock, then checked the other side of the entrance before noticing a narrow, horizontal ledge chiseled into the stone—either eroded over time or unevenly carved. Elia might have overlooked it completely if not for a similar step a couple of feet over and higher up. She saw a third one and then, farther still, what she guessed to be a fourth along the cliff face. If the mist hadn't been so thick, she might have been able to see how far the widely spaced stairs climbed. Would they lead all the way up to the top of the Noble Sanctuary?

She glanced down over the edge, knowing this time there would be nothing to stop her from plummeting to Below. And whatever combination of courage and foolishness Elia had possessed yesterday morning when she'd thrown herself off the Grand Bridge was now completely gone. Maybe the effect of the incense on rational thought was more harmful than she would have guessed.

Ah, to light a stick of incense right now would be bliss!

Facing the cliffside, her body pressed tightly against the rock, Elia swung one leg out, hoping her bare foot would make contact with the closest step. Unfortunately, the chain between her ankles prevented her stretching far enough, so she pulled back. Perspiration formed on her scalp like morning dew as she tried to collect herself, picturing in her mind what she had to achieve. Stretching was not going to do it—she needed momentum to make it across.

So Elia jumped.

For that split millisecond hanging in mid-air, with nothing beneath her, Elia didn't think she would make it. Then she landed, though with only minimal space for both feet.

Clinging to the side with toes and fingertips, Elia struggled to settle her breathing and not think about the step crumbling away. She looked ahead at what was coming next. For a person without restraints, the distance would be manageable, but again, the next ledge was too far for her to reach without leaping. She gritted her teeth and launched herself. The swinging chain clanged on the rock, but she found the foothold she needed.

Two steps conquered, but how many more to go? Still, Elia's determination was bolstered. She could do this! However, one miscalculation or a bit of overconfidence could be her end, so Elia continued on slowly, each time carefully judging how far she'd have to jump, then drawing on all her strength to make it happen.

Before long, she had traveled far enough that the tunnel entrance had disappeared into the mist. But as Elia bent her knees, preparing to make another attempt, she suddenly heard what sounded like a person slipping on loose gravel somewhere overhead.

She froze.

An instant later, several dislodged stones tumbled into view only a few arm-lengths away. As the pebbles bounced off the side of the cliff, their momentum slowed until they were hovering like miniature floating islands of Above.

Elia had no doubt somebody was on the stairs just ahead

of her. But which direction was the person going? Toward her or away?

What if people were closing in from both sides?

Now I'm really getting paranoid.

Elia quickly peered down in the direction from which she had come. Nothing.

She glanced up again to where she was headed.

A ghostly foot appeared. Then another one, accompanied by the fluttering hemline of a uniform.

"Naadie?" Elia called out cautiously.

"Elia?" came the girl's response. The rest of Naadie materialized through the fog a few steps higher. She gripped the rock as fiercely as Elia. "Th-thank goodness you've already—already started climbing," she stammered, her voice trembling with anxiety.

"I couldn't just stay there waiting, doing nothing," Elia replied. "But why weren't you more specific about what I'd find on the other side of that door?"

"B-because I didn't . . . I didn't know myself," Naadie replied. "I could only tell you what I had been told."

Naadie shot a terrified glance straight down, then flattened herself even more against the cliff. Though one side of the girl's face was plastered to the rock, Elia could see tears running down her cheek from her one uncovered eye.

Wait, of course—it was suddenly so clear. Naadie would be doubly afraid, not only of the challenging descent, but of Scavengers too. This was the last place she wanted to be. Obviously, Naadie was a minion for whoever was coordinating Elia's rescue, and the poor girl was being forced to do their bidding no matter what it entailed.

Elia knew this was not the time to try convincing Naadie that her fears about Scavengers were unfounded, but she could offer some comforting words. "You don't have to worry. I've been out here for quite a while, with no sign of monsters."

The girl still seemed too frightened to move either up or down. How long had it taken her to get this far?

"So, can you lead us back the rest of the way?" Elia asked gently.

Naadie nodded, releasing the grip of one hand to wipe away her tears.

Elia made her voice sound calm and soothing. "And do we have far to go?"

"We're about a third of the way," Naadie replied with slightly more fortitude in her voice. "The steps curl around the island, then stop just below the Grand Bridge. You won't believe what's beneath it . . . actually, you'll have to see for yourself."

"Good. Then let's keep going."

Elia followed Naadie's lead as they slowly started climbing. After a number of minutes in silence, Naadie paused and looked back, staring hard over Elia's shoulder.

"What?" Elia asked with heightened unease as she too looked behind. "Are you concerned we're being followed?"

"I guess there's no reason to be. We should be fine," said Naadie, though she didn't sound convinced. "You sealed up that door behind you good and tight, didn't you?"

"Yes, I made sure it was closed."

"And turned the key in the lock to reset the deadbolt, right? Just like I said?"

"Of course," Elia replied as a pit of dread formed instantly in her gut.

No, damn it, she hadn't done anything for an actual *deadbolt*! She hadn't even thought to relock the door, let alone stop long enough to look for a keyhole on the other side. Naadie should have told her specifically that the door didn't automatically lock itself!

In all truth, though, Elia had been stupid not to double-check, especially since she'd heard somebody entering the cellblock she shared with Tasheira. Would Tash have kept quiet about Elia's escape, or would she have traded the information for her own benefit?

Filled with guilt, Elia debated whether or not she should tell Naadie the truth. But after coming so far, going back now to check seemed absurd. What if guards had already discovered the tunnel and were waiting for them at the end of it?

"Come on, let's hurry up and finish this!" Elia blurted, startling Naadie with her sudden forcefulness. Gone were the serene, comforting words. "I want to get the hell away from here just as badly as you!"

Chapter 34

HOKK WAS STUNNED. HE had been right all along. This Imperial Guard really could not be trusted—he had just admitted it!—and now Hokk was no better off than a prisoner in the man's custody, stuck on this remote, desolate island where he'd never be found.

But there were two stallions outside the tent, one gray and one black, ready to take flight. He and Rayhan could use them to escape. All they had to do was overpower this guard and get out of here!

Digging his fingernails into the soft flesh of his palms, Hokk glanced around the shelter for anything that either of them could use as a weapon, besides their fists. Unfortunately, the place was empty except for two rolled-up sleeping mats and a few provisions. Maybe there were utensils, preferably some sort of knife, tucked away with the rest of the supplies.

Following Hokk's gaze, Commander Blaitz must have guessed his thoughts. "Hold on," he said quickly. "I think you've completely misunderstood what I was trying to say. When I warn you about ensuring your own safety, I'm not suggesting you can't rely on me. I only mean that you can never be too sure about *anyone* involved in this game that we are all now playing. But I assure you—in fact, I swear upon the sun and shattered moon—that I can be trusted completely. I am here for your protection so we can work together to achieve what we must ultimately accomplish."

Rayhan appeared just as unconvinced as Hokk felt. "How can we know for sure you have our best interests in mind, as well as Elia's?"

"What have I done to suggest otherwise?" Blaitz asked firmly. "Tell me, has there been anything? When have I acted to suggest I mean you any harm?"

Hokk wished he could come up with something specific. Rayhan seemed to be at a loss too.

The commander focused on Hokk. "Yes, you've seen me flying over Below several times, not to mention the one occasion when you weren't even there. But I did nothing to risk either Elia's life or yours. All I was doing was monitoring the situation and reporting back to those who are trying to make everything work out as it's all rightfully meant to be."

"So what role do you play?" asked Rayhan.

"I'm part of a very small group of people who have infiltrated the many levels of the palace's hierarchy, from the highest of the privileged class to the lowest of servants. All of us are acting to protect what's most important, not just for the monarchy, but for our society as a whole. For close to two decades, the telescope has kept its secrets. Unfortunately, for most of that time, we had no idea of its whereabouts. Not until recently, when Elia, your sister," Blaitz added, spinning to face Rayhan, "entered the picture. Then the race was on."

Hokk and Rayhan eyed each other. Were they both in agreement that everything the man had been saying so far seemed to be sincere? That some of his explanations even made sense?

Blaitz sighed. "Let me ask you this before you decide," he said. "Have you considered why it's only me out here? Why there was a group of guards who descended to Below yesterday, yet I'm the only one who returned? Yes, true, I have led many of these missions beneath the clouds, but only so I could lead those people who are most dangerous as far off-track as possible. Can't you see that?"

Hokk unclenched his fists. There no longer seemed to be any need to fight or resist. However, just because he was willing to risk cooperating didn't mean he would let down his defenses entirely. At the moment, the most important matter was returning to the Noble Sanctuary. Hopefully they could then easily locate Elia, whether she'd escaped into the city or ended up imprisoned.

After looking at Rayhan, who appeared to be in agreement, Hokk glanced back at the guard. "What do we do now?" he asked. "Is our first goal to break Elia free?"

"I don't know yet if that's even necessary," Blaitz replied. "But what we have to do for sure is leave as soon as the horses are ready to continue flying."

"And you know how to get us home?" Rayhan wondered.

The Imperial Commander nodded, stepping toward the tent's front flap and flipping it open. The light streaming in forced Hokk to shield his eyes against the brightness.

"I confirmed the coordinates with the Drift Master before I left," said Blaitz. "But don't worry, he's the only one who knows I'm out here. And he doesn't even know the reason why. If we pack up and leave this island as swiftly as possible, all we have to do is follow the direction of the setting sun. Once it's dark enough, we can align ourselves with the right stars and correct our course as necessary. Then, at some point in the middle of the night, depending on how fast we travel, we will see the lights of the Noble Sanctuary twinkling on the horizon."

Chapter 35

THE SPARKLING YELLOW HUE of the clouds had deepened to a much darker shade of orange by the time Elia and Naadie finished climbing the sheer cliffside of the Noble Sanctuary. Finally reaching the platform of stone and moss below the Grand Bridge, they could hear the sounds of workers, animals, and carts crossing overhead.

Elia feigned surprised when Naadie explained where they were actually standing, too exhausted to share how she had already discovered this place yesterday. She collapsed on the ground for a rest, while Naadie immediately set to work to remove her shackles, again with a hairpin. Before long, the metal bands fell from Elia's ankles and she was free.

"Now you won't be so noisy when we slip into the city," said Naadie.

"Where will you be taking me?"

"Some place safe, where nobody could possibly know to look for you."

Beneath the bridge, they crept along the rock shelf until they reached the slope angling up toward the edge of the city. Here, they came across two folded cloaks that Naadie must have brought down with her earlier. The fabric was black, and when Elia put the garment on, it hung all the way to the ground. With a hood that completely concealed her head, it was the perfect disguise for their getaway through the cover of night.

They waited until the sun had set and the sounds above them had ceased before scrambling up the embankment. They rose above the mist and carefully checked that no one was around. Holding back the fringe of her hood, Elia looked at the buildings of Na-Lavent now basking in the blue-silver moonlight.

Naadie crawled out onto the road first, at a safe distance from the Grand Bridge. Elia followed, keeping close to Naadie as they both dashed into the nearest passage. It was not the one where Elia had last seen her father, though she would have loved for the man to know she had escaped—that she had evaded the miserable fate to which he had doomed her for a few measly coins.

Had her father been watching again now as Elia and Naadie stealthily emerged from the clouds? Hopefully the bastard was plagued with remorse.

With footsteps whispering along the cobblestones, they moved deeper into alleyways that were no different from those Elia had experienced on her own the night prior—forgotten homeless people rummaging through the streets while families who could boast shelter shared meals in their dilapidated, multi-story houses lining the way. The same stink of poverty hung in the air too: animal and human waste, smoke, the straw of thatched roofs, the blend of fetid garbage, alcohol, and vomit.

As they rounded a familiar corner, the marketplace opened up before them. The shops were closed and the area empty. Rather than cutting across diagonally, they crept along the plaza's perimeter where Elia noticed several posters of herself still tacked to the walls.

They headed down another narrow passage, but they

didn't travel far before Naadie stopped in front of a particularly rundown, lopsided building. Piles of trash blocked a red door. Its paint was peeling off in strips, and Elia could see deep scratches in the wood, likely the result of a dog's claws.

Naadie shot a glance left, right, and above before knocking with a rhythmic sequence of thumps. They waited. Then Elia heard the unmistakable sound of several locks sliding back. The knob turned, and the door opened only the slightest crack.

"It's me," Naadie whispered, lifting her hood off her face just enough. "And I have her with me too," she added, leaning to the side to show Elia standing there.

Though no one uttered a response, a few more security chains were detached and the door opened. A slice of light poured outside.

As they entered, Elia could not make out the face of the person who stepped back into the shadows. She felt suddenly nervous and naive. What had made her trust Naadie so implicitly? For all she knew, the girl could be obeying the orders of a villainous scoundrel with plans to confiscate the smuggled telescope.

Just as Elia was on the verge of bolting, Naadie pulled her farther inside. The red door closed firmly behind them, followed by the sound of deadbolts sliding back into place.

Elia squinted, trying to adjust her eyes to the light. As she scanned the room's interior, she saw a fire burning in a hearth, a chair beside it, and someone rising off the seat cushion.

Elia gasped, clutching the base of her throat.

The woman limping toward them was the last person she would have ever expected to see.

Chapter 36

THE NIGHT AIR WAS still and crisp. Under the shattered moon's radiance, two large shadows flitted across the silver-dappled clouds below as the horses soared high above the mist.

Hokk and his two companions had been flying together for several hours, ever since the middle of the afternoon when they had left the small island to finish their journey. Blaitz flew by himself on his gray stallion, while Hokk shared the black stallion with Rayhan, who was now the one sitting behind, holding on. The commander had been adamant about the seating arrangement.

"Hokk should ride in front," he had said earlier when they were still inside the tent, finalizing their plans. "It will make him less noticeable."

"How do you figure?" Hokk had asked.

"Right after Rayhan's sister jumped from the bridge, it created a big commotion, but when you followed her down into the clouds, that stirred up almost as much excitement. It's best, therefore, that we sneak you back onto the palace grounds in secret to avoid anyone asking questions. We don't need to complicate the situation more than it already is." Blaitz then cocked his head as if unsure about something.

"You *do* want to come back with us, correct? I'm assuming you'd rather not return to Below."

"Yes, I'd prefer to stay in Above for as long as it takes to find Elia. After that . . . well, I guess we'll see." Hokk had not thought that far into his future. "So, how do you plan to make me inconspicuous?"

The commander began unscrewing the spike mounted near the top of his helmet. Then he held the helmet over Hokk's head. "Let's check the fit," he said, lowering the thing into place. "Comfortable?"

"Fits fine," Hokk replied.

"And you can see all right?"

"No problem."

Polished to a mirror shine, the helmet looked like solid metal from the outside, but the two spots for the eyes were actually pieces of reflective, tinted glass, similar to the dark spectacles Hokk had received from the Baron. The helmet also reminded Hokk of the spherical headpiece that came with the cumbersome white suit that Tash and her father had put on him to protect his blisters.

Blaitz seemed pleased with the disguise. "This way, your eyes will be protected while we fly, and you'll simply look like every other guard when we arrive at the Sanctuary."

Now, hours into the flight, they flew toward the location where the sun had disappeared at the bottom of the sky. The journey had been a long one, and he was ready for it to end. He tried to spot anything shimmering along the dark horizon that would indicate their destination approaching. Finally, he was able to say, "I think I can see lights."

"No, you're mistaken," Commander Blaitz called over, after searching for himself. "Those are just more stars coming out." He waved his hand in a wide circle. "As you can see, they're everywhere."

Craning his neck around, Hokk saw pinpricks of light in much greater numbers scattered across the sky, similar to what he had seen during his first nighttime journey to the Baron's estate. At the time, Hokk had thought the tiny spots looked like the spray of sparks from a fire, though he could not ask what they were while encased in that soundproof, bulky outfit. He wouldn't lose the chance now. "So, what are these little lights—these *stars* as you call them?"

"Each one is a sun," said Rayhan.

"A sun!" Hokk exclaimed, his voice booming inside his helmet.

"That's right. According to stories passed down through the ages, they are as big, if not bigger, than the one that travels our sky each day."

"But there must be hundreds . . . thousands of stars out there."

"It's estimated there are millions of them."

"Millions?" Hokk repeated, but then fell silent, unable to fully comprehend such a number.

Suddenly appreciating the immensity of the world around him, he continued to gaze into the night sky. He felt exceptionally small and inconsequential. There was so much more to the world than he could ever have imagined. Not just the two realms of Below and Above, but the greatness of . . . Beyond! Yes, that was the best word to describe all the mysteries out there he would never understand.

Somehow this new awareness also made him feel incredibly lonely. It reminded him of the cruel isolation he had suffered while exiled on the vast prairies. Threatened with total mental collapse, he had only survived those challenging years because of one special soul in his life. Nym.

Hokk wished the fox could be with him right now. Hopefully, Nym was still waiting for him back at the palace, sleeping curled up in that nest Hokk had made: a blanket tucked in a drawer.

"I was assigned a room for the few nights I spent at the Noble Sanctuary," Hokk abruptly announced, glancing over at the commander. The edge of desperation in his voice was probably obvious, but he didn't care. Nym would be needing food and water by this point. "When we arrive, I must immediately check on something that I was forced to abandon."

Frowning, Blaitz shook his head. "It will be too risky. Whatever you left behind is probably already gone. We'll have more important matters to attend to once we've landed."

Hokk gripped the reins tightly. *Then I'll track down Nym on my own. Nothing these two can do or say will keep me from finding him.*

Chapter 37

"MRS. SUDS!" ELIA EXCLAIMED, her legs threatening to give out. She grabbed Naadie's arm in order to steady herself.

"My dear Elia!" The woman hobbled forward and embraced Elia as tightly as her feeble arms could manage.

"Is it true . . . can it really be you?" Elia sputtered.

"I could ask you the same thing," said Mrs. Suds with a broad smile as she flipped back the hood of Elia's cloak to study her face. "We thought we'd never see you again. I'm glad we were wrong."

"I just can't believe it. They released you!"

Mrs. Suds laughed. "Released me? Ha! Those swine would never do such a thing. Certainly not for the likes of me."

"So then you . . . you must've escaped!" Elia decided, trying to picture the poor woman's frail body struggling up the side of the island, gripping the rock face with her clawlike hands, deformed by arthritis.

"Yes, I escaped, but only with a great deal of help, I'm afraid," said Mrs. Suds. "While I managed to get through that secret door and down the tunnel on my own, climbing those horrible stairs proved to be impossible for an old woman like me."

Elia glanced at Naadie, wondering if the girl had been there to help that day too.

Mrs. Suds must have guessed her thoughts. "No, fortunately for our darling Naadie, she wasn't assigned the difficult task of rescuing me," she said with a warm chuckle. "Instead, I had to wait, balanced on the cliffside. My associates knew something was wrong when I didn't show up as expected at our prearranged meeting spot. Eventually, I was plucked off by a nobleman loyal to our cause who flew down with his stallion. But in your case, everything has worked out perfectly. We owe an immense debt of gratitude to Naadie for successfully bringing you back to us unharmed."

Naadie blushed and adjusted her eye patch. "Thank you, My Lady."

One of Elia's eyebrows shot up. *My Lady*? What an odd thing to say. Perhaps the girl thought somebody as old as Mrs. Suds deserved a certain degree of respect.

Whatever the reason, Elia squeezed Naadie's arm. "Yes, I can't thank you enough, Naadie. Without your efforts, I would have been doomed to spend the rest of my life in that awful dungeon. You took a huge risk to save me, and I am beyond lucky to have my freedom again." Elia then turned back to Mrs. Suds. "Which raises a troubling question—are my mother and brother imprisoned beneath the palace? I suspect it's the only thing that could have happened to them, though now I wonder whether they were able to escape as I did."

The jovial expression on Mrs. Suds's face withered and she swallowed hard, as if her throat had suddenly become parched. "Their story remains a mystery," she croaked, failing to maintain eye contact.

"Oh, I see," Elia replied sadly as she cast her eyes to the ground.

Then from behind, a hand touched her shoulder, and Elia jumped. Spinning, she saw it was the person who had let them in—a thin, timid young woman, most likely a maid, who seemed to prefer clinging to the edges of the shadows near the entrance.

"Can I hang up your cloaks for you?" the servant asked quietly.

"Yes, thank you, Dani," said Mrs. Suds. "And perhaps make something for us to eat while I get these two girls warmed up by the fire."

"Right away," said Dani with a curtsy, another surprising formality.

Mrs. Suds gestured for them to follow, prompting Elia to start taking in her surroundings. From the alley, the outside of the building had looked especially derelict beside its rundown neighbors, but the interior, bathed in flickering light from the fire and a few scattered candles, was the complete opposite. Gold-framed pictures of various sizes had been hung throughout the room, and the walls were papered with beautifully intricate patterns that ran all the way up to the high ceiling. The front windows were tightly covered with velvety, brocade drapes that pooled on the floor. Elia's bare feet sank deep into a plush carpet, and as she was led to the hearth, she noticed that the chairs assembled there appeared to be equally luxurious. Settling into a soft, well-stuffed seat cushion, Elia wondered if perhaps she was actually still in her jail cell, only asleep and dreaming.

Naadie sat in a chair beside her while Mrs. Suds stiffly lowered herself into the one directly opposite. "I bet you have all sorts of questions for me," said the old woman.

"My head is absolutely bursting with them!" Elia declared as she squinted at the dimly lit painting over the fireplace, as well as the collection of ornaments lining the dark mantel. Then she focused on Mrs. Suds. "This is all so unbelievable. Is it just my imagination?"

"It's all very real, I can assure you," the woman replied in a gentle tone. "Obviously, I have much to share, but first, and more importantly, I must hear what has happened to you since we last saw each other. I'm sure it's quite a story."

"It is," Elia sighed. She leaned back and turned her thoughts inward. As she began to recall the many painful memories of the despair and hopelessness she had endured, she felt distressed. "I almost don't know where to start," she barely murmured, fidgeting with her pocket, which still contained Naadie's key to the secret door. Her body began to tremble. Was it fear? Exhaustion? Incense withdrawal?

Mrs. Suds stretched forward and patted Elia's knee. "You're safe with us here, so you needn't worry," she said softly. "No harm will come to you now."

These words helped to calm her, as did glimpsing Naadie's relaxed manner. Yes, Elia could feel safe with these two. She could let down her guard without fearing repercussions—so it was time to open up about everything and finally be free.

She took a deep breath before speaking. "I guess . . . I guess it all began with the earthquakes."

Mrs. Suds nodded. "Ah, yes, the earthquakes. Who could forget those?"

Elia nibbled her lower lip as she reconsidered. "No, I'm wrong," she said, shaking her head. "It actually started when Cook reassigned Naadie and me to hang laundry at the clotheslines. That happened the very next day after you were arrested."

Elia proceeded to explain how their daily duties had unexpectedly changed to escorting the donkey procession into the rolling green hills where the clean laundry was hung and collected. She also explained how Cook began grilling the two of them every afternoon to find out who they had encountered along the way.

Elia then paused as something dawned on her. "But wait—maybe you've already heard about all this from Naadie."

"Yes, she did share many of these details. However, her summary of events ended with your disappearance. It was as if you vanished off the face of the island."

Elia sat up straighter. "You're right, I did. That's exactly what happened." Seeing the old woman's shock, she quickly continued. "The tremors were so strong that last morning, the edge of the island began to crumble away, right beneath my feet! With nothing left to support me, I fell. All the way to Below."

"To Below!" Mrs. Suds gasped. "Surely you haven't been stuck down there this whole time!"

The color drained from Naadie's cheeks. "But Elia . . . the Scavengers! How did you manage not to end up as part of their gruesome collection of corpses?"

"There are no such monsters," Elia replied, carefully watching their expressions. "Our islands of Above float on a thick layer of clouds, but when you break through to the other side, a vast, new world opens up before you. I don't know why we've never been told about its existence, but I have witnessed it with my own eyes!"

Naadie frowned, seemingly unable to accept any shred of truth in what Elia had just said. Mrs. Suds, on the other hand, nodded her head slowly, as if Elia's revelation was not a surprise. Yet despite such different reactions, they both remained silent and attentive as Elia continued.

And there were so many more details to share—she could barely contain the barrage of thoughts spilling forth from her mind, forcing her to jump quickly between topics: from the massive body of water she landed in to meeting Hokk and Nym, and together crossing the empty grasslands covered with rubbish; from visiting the towering skyscrapers in the disintegrating City of Ago to living with the Torkins in their villages surrounded by terraced fields; from the extreme cold and endless cloud cover to the drops of water that fell from the sky as both a solid and a liquid—

A sudden *thump* overhead stopped Elia's storytelling. Her eyes shot up toward the ceiling.

Mrs. Suds waved it off, unconcerned. "It's nothing to be worried about. Just Dani working on the second floor."

Reassured, Elia picked up where she had left off, recounting her life with Roahm and the Torkins, as well as the weeks of hard labor she'd spent to help rebuild their fields and plant crops.

"But somehow, you managed to return to Above," Mrs. Suds observed, just as Dani arrived with a tray of warm pastries and three cups of steaming tea.

"Yes," Elia replied, her eyes devouring the food. "That same young man, Hokk, was able to steal a stallion so we could fly away on it together." She took a mug and eagerly selected the most tempting treat on the platter, stuffing it whole into her mouth. Then she carried on talking, paying no attention to the spray of crumbs landing in her lap. "I was astounded when he showed up, though at first, I didn't recognize him. He had disguised himself and had succeeded in tracking me down over an incredible distance, often over very dangerous terrain. It was remarkable."

Elia's voice faded off as she focused on the flames dancing in the hearth. As she had done many times before, she marveled at how Hokk had put his life in danger for her own well-being. Time and again, he had demonstrated just how wise, resourceful, and determined he could be. She admired him greatly—and admittedly, missed him even more.

Still staring at the fire, Elia began to chuckle. "You know, it's funny, but the horse Hokk rescued me with was the very one Commander Wrasse used when he chased me across the grasslands. Can you imagine a coincidence any more surprising than that?"

"I've heard that Wrasse is dead," said Mrs. Suds.

"Yes, he's very dead," Elia replied smugly, ignoring that small part of her conscience still feeling guilty that someone had lost his life because of her actions.

"So if it was Wrasse's horse, then he must have followed you to Below."

"At first, it was just a small team of Imperial Guards who came down to look for me, but then later, Wrasse arrived in Hokk's city and took over the place as if he had full dominion."

"What could he have possibly wanted with you, I wonder?" Mrs. Suds asked before sipping from her mug.

Elia stiffened. Something about Mrs. Suds's tone made her think the woman was being disingenuous. Perhaps she already knew the reason why. Until now, Elia had purposefully avoided discussing the lady-in-waiting and the telescope that had been entrusted to her care—she was too embarrassed about losing the instrument after so much effort to keep it safe.

"Did you have something he was after?" Mrs. Suds prompted.

Though reluctant, Elia was about to respond when she heard another thump. Again, the sound seemed to come through the ceiling from the second floor—except this time, Dani was still in the room with them.

Elia shot a questioning glance at the old woman.

Mrs. Suds shrugged. "I was wrong. I guess it's coming from one of our neighbors. We're surrounded by a noisy bunch. There are only the four of us in this house."

"I can't help it," Elia said defensively. "I've learned to be suspicious. Everybody's out to pursue their own self interest. I have lost faith in almost everyone I've ever met."

"The same is true for me," Mrs. Suds agreed glumly. After another sip of tea, she opened her mouth as if wanting to say more, but closed it again. She studied Elia in silence for a minute, then reached down on the far side of her chair to grab something off the floor. Before raising it into view, she said, "My whole life, I've had to protect myself from people with questionable intent, often with plans that were downright evil. As a consequence, I've become a reasonably good judge of character, if I do say so myself. However, I always have to remain cautious . . . maybe too cautious for my own good." She hesitated again, appearing to reconsider, then sighed as though she had settled on a decision. "So you'll have to forgive me, Elia, for not showing this to you when you first arrived."

With that, Mrs. Suds lifted something onto her lap.

When Elia saw it, she pushed herself against the back of her seat and clutched the armrests so tight, her knuckles went white.

How the old woman could be holding the telescope in her hand, Elia had no idea. But there it was.

Chapter 38

AFTER BLAITZ HAD CONFIRMED that the newest lights on the horizon were coming from the twin towers, the trip to get there seemed shorter than Hokk would have expected. Maybe the direction of the air currents had switched in their favor.

As they flew over the Sanctuary grounds, approaching the palace, Hokk stared down at the gardens. The last time he had soared over them, a birthday party for one of the emperor's sons was being celebrated outside; the entire area had been lit up and filled with people enjoying food, music, and dancing. Tonight, however, the empty gardens appeared dark and quiet.

Commander Blaitz stopped his horse to hover in the air, and Hokk and Rayhan did the same with their stallion.

"Listen. I've decided I should go on ahead and land first," said Blaitz. "Take your horse to a higher altitude and continue circling until I give you the signal to come down."

"Why?" asked Rayhan.

"I've been giving it more thought, and I'm concerned about who might see us together, especially since Hokk is the only one with a helmet on. It would be best if we were all wearing helmets before we enter the palace. That way, when the two of you are with me, you'll blend in for sure."

"How will we know it's you signaling us to land?" Hokk asked.

Blaitz considered the question for a moment. "Stay above the gardens. Don't fly over the stables or the main courtyard. When you see the flame of a torch suddenly appear, that will be me and you'll know it's safe to descend. Got it?"

"No problem," said Hokk.

The two horses separated. Blaitz's stallion flew straight down, but Hokk banked his horse around, and with his heels, urged the animal to climb higher.

"I guess this is far enough up," he said soon afterward.

"Should be," Rayhan confirmed from behind.

Leveling off, Hokk peered over one side of the horse and Rayhan from the other. After circling the gardens a few times, Hokk pulled back on the reins to encourage the horse to hover again, stopping at a point where he suspected they'd have a clear view of the area beneath them.

They spent the time that followed in silence, listening to nothing except the sound of beating wings. Without knowing how long Commander Blaitz might take, the wait became very tedious and worrisome. Had something happened to him? Was the situation more dangerous than they had originally assumed?

Finally, in the middle of the blackness below, a flame flickered to life. It appeared too small to be the burning end of a torch, but it moved side to side, as if someone was waving it.

"That must be him," Rayhan decided.

"I hope so," said Hokk.

They glided down in a tight spiral. As soon as they touched solid ground, however, Hokk wondered if they had made a grave mistake. An Imperial Guard was charging forward.

"Commander?" Rayhan called out, evidently sharing Hokk's concern.

The guard pulled off his helmet. Indeed, it was Blaitz.

"I didn't intend to take so long," the man explained when he reached them. "But all's well."

"So Elia is okay?" asked Hokk as he and Rayhan quickly dismounted.

"Sorry, I still have no idea," said the commander. "I simply meant that nobody seems to be expecting us." He then offered the helmet he had just removed to Hokk. "Here. Let's switch."

Hokk put the new one on as the commander handed another helmet just like it to Rayhan. The man also gave Hokk a jacket bearing the same design as the one Rayhan was already wearing.

"Now, somebody hold the torch for me," Blaitz ordered.

Hokk took it, and the commander screwed the spike back onto his personal helmet. Once the helmet was on his head, Blaitz took the torch and shoved it upside down into the ground to extinguish the flame. "No need for that now. I don't want anybody to spot us from the palace. We'll have to tread carefully."

"And the horse?" asked Rayhan.

"Leave it. Someone will find it in the morning. They'll assume the thing escaped its stall during the night."

Quietly, the three of them began to creep through the gardens. Their progress was slow. Hokk's eyes were accustomed to seeing with the meager light of Below, so he led the way. When he reached a grove of trees, he stopped to let the other two catch up. This was the same orchard where Elia had climbed into the branches to spy on people with her telescope, which meant the stables were not far away. "If I'm not mistaken, we can cut through here to reach the stable yard and then the palace beyond. Is that right?"

"Yes, that's the way," Blaitz confirmed.

They continued on, weaving around the trees and ducking branches. Light from the few torches burning on the columns of the stable's portico up ahead began to filter through the leaves as they got closer. It was enough to illuminate the area. Despite the time of night, a few horses were still being led into the stable by workers.

Tempted to hold back in the shadows, Hokk reminded himself that he was disguised as an Imperial Guard, so he had no reason to hesitate. Marching confidently with his companions, he crossed to the other side of the courtyard and continued along the path that led to the palace. When they finally reached it, they entered through revolving doors similar to the bank of doors lining the front reception hall.

Hokk quickly scanned the wide corridor that stretched out in front of them. It couldn't be as late in the evening as he had guessed. A number of servants were scurrying about, and a few straggling courtiers still stood around in groups—their dinners had finished, but their conversations had not.

"We've got to head toward the back," the commander murmured before setting off in that direction.

Hokk recognized this quieter section of the palace. Elia had charged through here to escape onto the bridge.

Was the bridge the place where they were headed?

Not so.

"Down the stairs a couple floors," Blaitz instructed, leading the way.

As soon as they started to descend, Hokk got an uneasy feeling. Hadn't Elia described something like this in the past? Yes, seeing the kitchens—where staff were still busy cleaning up from the evening meal—only confirmed it. At the bottom of these steps, they would find only one thing. The dungeon!

Hokk suddenly halted.

Rayhan collided with him. "Hey, why are you stopping?"

If not for his helmet, Hokk knew his face would have given away the sickening dread that had just overwhelmed him.

This was all a trap! If Blaitz didn't know of Elia's whereabouts, there was no need to be here. And they had fallen for the commander's lies so easily, blindly following and taking themselves down to their own imprisonment. Blaitz had hidden them behind helmets so he alone would get full credit for their capture and arrest.

Rayhan pushed him from behind. "Come on. Get going!"

Was Rayhan in on it too? Or was he simply ignorant?

Blaitz, who had continued on a short distance ahead, now realized he wasn't being followed, and he turned to look back. "Keep up, you two!" he ordered. "We're almost there."

Though Hokk took a tentative step, then another, his mind was quickly calculating a plan. He pictured the route through the palace to get back out into the gardens. No, the bridge! Crossing it was a shorter escape route. Nobody would know to stop him at the gate, and then he could hide out in the city.

"Why are you suddenly so slow?" Rayhan hissed, now stepping past him to catch up to the commander.

Hokk caught his arm. "I think we're in danger. Isn't there a dungeon at the bottom of these steps?"

"You're crazy!" Rayhan chuckled with a tinny laugh that seemed to rattle around inside his helmet. He pointed down the staircase. "Look. Blaitz is turning the corner at the next landing. He's not going all the way to the bottom."

This was true. The man had just disappeared.

Still cautious, Hokk followed Rayhan, keeping a good distance behind, ready to charge back up to the main floor at the first sign of anything suspicious.

Arriving at the spot where Blaitz had left the stairwell, they entered a dark cavern that appeared to be chiseled out of the bedrock. The floor was wet and the air dank, with the lingering smell of soot, yet also a hint of fragrance. The commander was waiting for them. Hokk glanced past him to study the rest of the space, though it was difficult to see much deeper inside. He noticed many large objects on the floor—what could they be? Blocks of wood? Crates? Barrels of some sort?

He stepped closer, and then he knew.

Washtubs!

"This is the laundry room!" he exclaimed, recognizing the place that Elia had described in such detail, a place she had always detested so much. Now, looking overhead, he noticed clothes on hangers suspended from the ceiling. "Why have we come here?"

"I could ask the very same question," growled an angry female voice.

Spinning, Hokk saw a large, haggard woman with wild hair and wide eyes. A lantern hung from one hand. In the other, she gripped a large knife. She was blocking the entrance they had just come through, her feet firmly planted as if nothing, not even the three of them rushing forward, could ever hope to push her aside to escape.

Chapter 39

“THAT CAN’T BE THE same telescope!” Elia cried out. “This has to be some sort of mistake.”

“Why?” asked Mrs. Suds.

“Because the telescope I’ve been struggling to protect for so long was stolen! It’s gone! It should be in the hands of Imperial Guards by now.”

“Was yours in any better condition than this one?” Mrs. Suds showed her the damaged end where the glass had been smashed.

Elia began to massage her temples as if she had a sudden headache. “I-I don’t understand,” she groaned, feeling on the edge between sanity and losing herself completely. “My father stole the telescope just last night.”

“Yes, and he was the one who brought it to me first thing this morning,” Mrs. Suds replied in a measured tone.

Elia dropped her hands, and her mouth hung open. Her mind couldn’t stop racing as she tried to piece everything together—yet nothing made sense! “My father was right there when I was being arrested. He turned me in for the reward money!”

“That’s not his story.”

"What?" Elia exclaimed in disbelief. "No, you're wrong. You can't believe anything he says! You don't know all the details. The guards wouldn't have found me if he hadn't decided to betray his own daughter!"

"You can't be sure of that. There were pictures of you on bulletins throughout the city. The posters were what alerted us to start looking for you again. You could have been spotted in the streets by any number of people."

"Then this has to be some sort of trap," Elia declared adamantly, reluctant to give in. "He gave it to you so that when the guards eventually track down the telescope, they'll find it with us, and we'll all be in serious trouble."

The old woman shook her head. "Do you have no faith in your father?"

"Absolutely none!"

"That's a shame."

"I know! It's a damn rotten shame!" Elia bellowed as she rose to her feet. She felt tears welling up, but fought to hold them back. "My father has done no good for me, or anyone else in my family. That's just the painful reality and it's never going to change!"

"But if his plan was to actually hand you over to the guards, then explain this," said Mrs. Suds as she reached down beside her chair once more. She lifted the satchel Elia had taken from Greyit's home. From inside, the old woman pulled out the bag of coins that the Imperial Guards had given her father as a reward. "He specifically made me promise to deliver this money to you as soon as you were rescued."

Stunned, Elia blindly reached back for the chair behind her. She sank onto the silk cushion, her mind numb.

Mrs. Suds leaned forward and placed the sack of coins on Elia's lap.

Elia could only stare at it.

"Does that now change your point of view?" Mrs. Suds asked.

"It does," Elia whispered. She wiped the corner of her eye before looking at the woman sitting across from her. "But what's really going on? How could I have gotten it so wrong?"

"Don't be too hard on yourself. What else were you supposed to think?"

"I feel stupid. Really stupid. And I hate it! So many things have been hidden from me for far too long."

"Yes, that seems to be very true," said Mrs. Suds with a heavy sigh. "There's no reason to blame yourself, however. And I certainly can't see the need for you to be left in the dark any longer. As promised, I have a lot to explain, and I'm sure once you hear everything, it will all become much clearer."

Elia caught herself anxiously picking at the drawstring of the bag in her lap. Was she prepared for this? To finally face the truth was suddenly a daunting prospect. She glanced at Naadie, who was sitting silent but wide-eyed, then at Dani, who hadn't moved from where she had been lingering against the wall.

"All right, I'm ready," she decided. "Tell me what I need to know. Begin with the bone tied with blue ribbon."

"Yes, that's the best place to start," Mrs. Suds agreed.

"And explain why you were so horrified when it first showed up in my washtub," Elia demanded, as if afraid Mrs. Suds might leave out some crucial detail.

"I will, I will," the woman assured her with a lighthearted chuckle. Then she set her face into a firm expression. "The bone with its blue ribbon was a very important sign that I had given up ever seeing in my lifetime." She paused for a moment as if reflecting on how difficult the wait had been. "And I wasn't horrified," she continued. "I was startled, yes, but only because it was so unexpected. The arrival of the bone meant things were starting to happen. That I could finally have hope again. Yet I was also very concerned to learn that Naadie and a number of other workers had found similar bones in their own tubs a few days earlier. I was worried we had missed our opportunity."

"To do what?"

"The bones were a signal that the telescope had been discovered. It had been missing for many, many years, and it contained documents that were vitally important. I suspect you've already seen them, since the end has been broken into. Were you the one who did this?" she asked, holding up the damaged instrument.

"Yes, that was me," Elia admitted. "I hope all the papers are still in there."

"Thankfully, nothing seems to be missing."

"Good. I had been told that the telescope could reveal a secret that would topple the monarchy, little knowing I was actually supposed to look *inside* the thing, not through it. What makes the documents so crucial?"

"You didn't notice what's on them?"

"Yes, except I don't know how to read."

"No, of course, I didn't mean to suggest you could," said Mrs. Suds. "I just wondered if maybe—"

"But I did see that page with a baby's footprints and handprints in ink."

The old woman's face lit up. "Precisely. That page is the most important one of the bunch."

"It had the royal seal on it, too. Why's that?"

"To mark its authenticity. There's also a date stamp confirming the child's birthday."

Elia's brow furrowed. "Is that significant?"

"Very significant, indeed. It proves the child was the first of the royal offspring . . . and therefore the successor to the throne ahead of anybody else."

"Then the prints must belong to Prince Veralion," Elia concluded.

Mrs. Suds solemnly shook her head. "No. They're from a child born several years earlier."

"What?" Elia gasped. "Then that would mean Veralion is not actually the heir to the throne!"

"Exactly," said Mrs. Suds. "That's why everyone is so keen to get their hands on these papers. Some people will stop at nothing to destroy the evidence. Others, like myself, want to keep the papers safe no matter what the cost. The whole affair has been horrendously difficult and drawn out over far too many years. It's affected too many lives as well."

Elia's thoughts were reeling as she began to grasp the gravity of the situation she'd been thrown into that fateful day she met the lady-in-waiting among the clotheslines. And the ramifications of what she had possessed for all those weeks were staggering. "So, where is the rightful heir now?"

"That's what we are trying to determine. The baby was put into hiding shortly after its birth because its life was in grave danger. That was when the documents were concealed as well, with only a few key people knowing that both the baby and the papers even existed."

"But surely Empress Faytelle knows where her baby has been kept."

"Not at all! She's the last person we would want to ever find out."

"Why?"

"Because it's not her child!"

"Are you kidding?" Elia exclaimed, leaning forward in her chair. "But if it's not her child, that would mean—"

Mrs. Suds nodded grimly. "That's right. It was Empress *Mahkoiyin's* baby."

Elia ran one hand through her short hair as she stared into the fire, trying to process this startling revelation. In her mind, all she could picture was the woman she knew as Koiyin, recently tracked down in Below, wrapped in rags, her hair matted, living in paranoid isolation.

As Dani added another piece of wood to the flames, Elia turned her attention back to Mrs. Suds. "So, I assume Mahkoiyin's disappearance is somehow related to this secret about her only child."

"That's what we believe too, but nobody knows for certain how events actually unfolded that day in the gardens. Where did the poor woman end up? What caused Emperor Tael to lose his eyesight?"

Elia clenched her jaw. She knew more about these two questions than Mrs. Suds would ever guess. Yet Elia would bide her time until the old woman had finished sharing her side of the story. "How did you end up getting involved with all this?" she asked, trying to dig deeper. "Was the bone sent specifically to alert you?"

Mrs. Suds tensed up. "Yes, it was meant for me," she said hesitantly.

"But why you?" Elia wondered aloud. "Please, I don't mean anything rude or hurtful by saying this, but you were nothing more than a laundry worker, nearing the end of your work life."

The woman grimaced. Elia noticed Naadie react too, as if Elia's comment was inappropriate.

"I can see how you'd think that," said Mrs. Suds, "but it's not even close to the truth." Again she paused.

Elia's stern gaze demanded an answer. "You said you'd tell me everything."

"You're right," the woman replied. She seemed to be struggling, but finally gave in. "The truth is, I was the person originally charged with the task of placing Mahkoiyin's child in a secure location. I was the one who assembled the documents that proved her baby's existence and claim to the throne. When I concealed the papers in this telescope at the empress's request, I had no idea Mahkoiyin would mysteriously vanish. When that happened, I was forced to share the secret of the telescope with a few trusted people who, I hoped, could ensure its safekeeping." Mrs. Suds wiped away a tear. "That's the last thing the empress would have wanted me to do, but I was desperate. It was my only choice given the circumstances—because I had to go into hiding too."

Chapter 40

“COOK, DON’T WORRY. IT’S just me,” said Blaitz as he removed his helmet.

“And these two?” the sturdy woman demanded, still braced for a fight.

“Let her see your faces,” the commander urged. After Hokk and Rayhan took off their helmets, he introduced them. “This is Hokk, who recently helped Elia return to Above from Below. And this is her brother, Rayhan.”

The fierce lines in the woman’s expression softened. “Her brother?” she repeated with surprise, trying to examine him more closely by the light of her lantern.

“We’ve actually met before, a number of years ago,” said Rayhan.

Cook now appeared to recognize him. “Yes.” She nodded. “That unfortunate affair with your father.”

“Correct,” Rayhan replied despondently.

“The poor man.” She then swung the lantern around to inspect Hokk. “And this one,” she added. “He looks so pale and sickly.”

“They don’t get any direct sunlight below the clouds,” the commander explained. “It’s no different than spending a lifetime living in a cave.”

"I sure know what that's like," Cook grumbled. She started to walk past them, moving deeper into the gloomy chamber. "Follow me before anyone spots us," she called over her shoulder.

Cook approached several cauldrons that hung over the few remaining embers of a large fire pit. She placed her lantern on the floor, stirred the cinders to life with her knife's blade, and added some wood to encourage the reluctant flames.

"Did we wake you?" Blaitz asked as he flipped over a nearby washtub to sit on it. Hokk and Rayhan did the same.

"I was only half asleep," Cook said dismissively, finding a seat of her own. "Normally, I sleep like the dead down here, but *that's* changed now that everything has been rekindled again."

Though tempted to keep his eyes fixed on the growing fire, Hokk surveyed their surroundings, trying to locate where the woman might have a bed. She probably lived day and night in this miserable place.

"You've been missing in action for a bit," Cook said to Blaitz.

"Yes, I have. I had to return to Below again, trying to track down these two," he replied with a nod toward Hokk and Rayhan.

Hokk expected the woman to be surprised to hear this, but she showed no reaction.

"Has my absence been noticed by other guards or anyone else in the palace?" Blaitz asked.

"Not that I've heard myself."

"Good. I was able to keep my trip shorter than I had initially anticipated."

"But I hope it's safe enough for you to visit me right now," Cook said in a worried voice, peering back in the direction of the stairwell.

"I was careful."

Cook grimaced. "Still, though, of all people for you to bring into the thick of things, it's quite a risk."

"I realize," Blaitz replied. He sounded almost apologetic, as if reporting back to a disapproving supervisor.

"Do they know?" Cook asked with a side glance at Hokk and Rayhan as she slid a finger along the dull edge of the knife still in her hand.

"They know what they need to for the moment, but nothing more."

"What haven't you told us?" Rayhan piped up suspiciously. "Come on, you're not being fair. Do you know something about my sister?"

Cook appeared reluctant to say one way or the other.

Blaitz answered on her behalf. "Elia's whereabouts is certainly one of the main reasons why we came here this evening." He turned to Cook. "What have your sources been able to gather?"

Hokk considered this an odd question for Blaitz to ask a mere laborer who apparently lived no better than an exile in this gloomy laundry room. As a commander, shouldn't Blaitz have been the one to know what was going on?

"They found her," Cook said flatly. "They tracked her down before the break of dawn."

"Just last night?"

"Yes, after the posters went up throughout the city."

"And she was arrested?"

"Hauled directly to the dungeon."

Rayhan jumped to his feet. "Elia's in the dungeon?" he asked in horror, which matched Hokk's sinking hopelessness. "Are you sure?"

Cook nodded. "I couldn't sleep—too much on my mind, wondering what to expect—and when I heard guards descending the stairs, I got up just in time. They passed by my floor with Elia in shackles."

"Then we have to get her out of there!" cried Rayhan.

"Can we gain access and free her?" Hokk quickly added. "We have these helmets to conceal us, and no one will question you, Commander."

"You're not letting me finish," Cook growled. "We've already been able to break her out."

"You have?" Rayhan asked in disbelief as he took his seat again.

"That's what I was hoping to hear," said Blaitz. "Has she been brought to Lady Argina's?"

"Yes, she should be there now. Or at least, that's where I assume she's been taken," Cook replied. "I'm hoping I would've heard by now if things hadn't worked out as planned. I have a reliable girl on the inside, Naadie, who was carefully briefed about how to proceed, and as far as I can tell, she made it happen. There's been nothing to suggest otherwise."

"And what about the telescope?" asked Blaitz. "Was it found on her? Have we lost it?"

Cook slouched, looking burdened. "That's our problem. I can't say for sure where it ended up, but since the guards got to Elia first and she wasn't expecting them, I suspect the telescope is long gone. Which means . . ." She sighed as if she had given up hope. "Which means we can't take this any further. It's over, I'm afraid."

"It can't be!" declared Blaitz.

Rayhan looked confused. "What are you two talking about?"

Blaitz ignored him. "I won't accept that it's over until we can confirm, once and for all, what has happened to that telescope. Maybe Elia was able to hide it somewhere in the city, and she can lead us to it."

"Perhaps," said Cook, though she sounded unconvinced. "If she could somehow produce the thing, that would be our only salvation. But I doubt—"

The commander interrupted her. "There's no point wasting time here. We should leave immediately for Argina's."

"Wait," said Cook as Blaitz stood up. "There's more."

"Tell me," he ordered.

"Somebody else has unexpectedly gotten mixed up in the fray. I don't know if she will help matters or complicate the situation further."

"Who's this?"

"The daughter of Baron Shoad. A young woman by the name of Lady Tasheira."

"I've met her," said Commander Blaitz.

"I know her too," Hokk offered. "Elia and I came with her and her father to this island."

"Is there a chance this Tasheira girl has the telescope?" asked Cook.

Hokk's face scrunched up. "I'm not sure. But it's possible. I'm trying to remember whether or not Elia was holding on to it when she jumped. Perhaps she wasn't."

"I'm positive she was," Rayhan replied. "I didn't realize at the time, but if I think back, that's what she must have used to hit me on the head when I tried to stop her from escaping onto the bridge."

"That doesn't mean the documents inside hadn't already been removed and hidden," Blaitz countered. "We must find Lady Tasheira and find out what she knows."

"Unfortunately, she has been imprisoned as well," said Cook.

"She has?" exclaimed Commander Blaitz. "Upon whose authority?"

"From what I can piece together, her arrest was made under the directive of an emperor, but I'm still trying to learn which one. I've had palace staff report to me that Lady Tasheira was questioned yesterday morning by both emperors before she was released and allowed to return to her room. Then others observed her being brought down to the dungeon shortly after, where she's been ever since."

"Has her room been searched?" asked Blaitz.

"I don't know."

Blaitz stood quickly, kicking back the tub he had been sitting on. "Then that's where we start."

Chapter 41

BECAUSE I HAD TO *go into hiding too.*

Mrs. Suds's comment replayed itself in Elia's mind like a persistent echo. Dumbfounded, she could only stare at the poor, crippled woman in front of her.

Was it all just lies?

Probably not—everything she had said seemed plausible. At the very least, it helped explain why Commander Wrasse had shown up in the laundry room that morning to arrest Mrs. Suds. They had recognized each other right away, so they must have shared some sort of history together—of that much, Elia was certain.

"Who are you?" Elia asked after finally finding her voice. "I mean, who are you *really*?"

Mrs. Suds pointed a knobby, twisted finger at a nearby table where a candle was burning. "Dani, please bring the light closer so we can have a better look at what's hanging above the mantel."

Dani obeyed, stepping toward the fireplace with the candleholder. As more and more of the painting over the hearth was illuminated, Elia expected to see a portrait of Empress Mahkoiyin as a young woman looking down on them, similar to the image she had seen outside Baron Shoad's library. Yet the person in the picture was not the empress at all, but rather a finely dressed woman of about forty years. The delicate strokes of the paintbrush captured her sitting on a stately sofa, gazing straight ahead, with a stone arch and layered curtains in the background. One hand was stretched out to pet a perfectly groomed dog, sitting just as regally on its own tasseled cushion.

"Am I supposed to recognize who this is?" Elia asked.

"The years have taken their toll," Mrs. Suds said regretfully. "And perhaps if my health wasn't failing, you'd see the resemblance."

No, it can't be!

"Are you saying . . . that's you up there?"

Mrs. Suds nodded, then laughed a sad, nostalgic laugh. "Yes, if you can believe it. I sat for that portrait on the fifth anniversary of my husband's death."

"Your husband?" Elia said with surprise. She had always understood that "Mrs." was a term of respect; she had never imagined that the woman had been married. "Who was he?" she asked.

"Lord Levyn."

"A lord?"

"That's right. Married to a decrepit old goat like me—can you imagine?" Mrs. Suds joked, though she looked heartbroken as she gazed wistfully at her portrait. "He was a high-ranking advisor to the Empress Mother, highly decorated for his trusted counsel and loyalty. What some people don't realize, however, is that he also played a key role in sorting out the mess with Tohryn and Tael when they were still babies."

Elia knew the story well—it was common knowledge that the Empress Mother and her court had to deal with a huge dilemma when she unexpectedly gave birth to twin sons. During the life-threatening delivery, so much attention had to be directed toward her well-being that nobody kept track of which baby had been born first. This oversight created a monumental problem never before faced in the history of the Royal Family: which of the two boys would eventually succeed his mother?

After much heated debate, the court ministers narrowly approved a decision to allow the twins to share the throne. When Tael and Tohryn took over the monarchy, each chose their own tower on opposite sides of the palace, and ever since, they had maintained a mostly stable truce. Given their very different personalities, however, a breakdown in their precarious harmony seemed a real possibility, and soon after they each got married, gossip quickly spread about a race between the couples to see which empress could get pregnant first. The official decree that originally had been passed years earlier stipulated that the Twin Emperor who produced the first offspring would be the one whose bloodline would carry the monarchy into the next generation.

So when, amidst great fanfare, an announcement was made that Crown Prince Veralion had been born to Emperor Tohryn and Empress Faytelle, it was assumed the race was won.

But just imagine the scandal, upheaval, and violence that could erupt if, years later, it was revealed that Emperor Tael and his wife, Empress Mahkoiyin, had a long-lost, first-born child who could legitimately prove his or her position as rightful heir! It would be devastating for Tohryn's immediate family. Lives would be lost on both sides to either protect this secret or erase it completely.

Elia drained her cup of tea and placed the mug on a side table. "So tell me if I understand this correctly," she said. "Because you were the one who knew the secret of the monarchy's true first-born, as well as where the child was hidden and the location of the documents supporting a claim to the throne, your life was in just as much danger, forcing you to conceal your identity and disguise yourself as a laundry worker."

"That's right," said Mrs. Suds. "Being down in the laundry was certainly not pleasant, and a far cry from the life I was used to, but I considered it my unquestionable duty to Empress

Mahkoiyin. And the arrangement worked, all things considered, since I was still close enough to the inner workings of palace life to catch tidbits of information about court activities, yet, at the same time, impossible for anyone to find."

"Until Wrasse came along."

"Yes, I was safe until he figured out where I was. He must have been tipped off by someone when the telescope resurfaced."

"But for all those years, did none of the other laundry workers know who you were?"

"Only Cook. She knew the truth right from the start."

While this was a startling fact, it also made sense. Cook had tried to prevent Wrasse from dragging Mrs. Suds to the dungeon—a selfless act that had initially seemed very out of character.

"I guess the washerwomen initially assumed you had been demoted to the laundry room because you were no longer capable of being a seamstress."

"That's correct. At my age, it was reasonable to think I was losing my eyesight."

"And you were definitely well established by the time I started working," Elia added.

"Yes, I had already been down there for a long time. And I grew very old, very quickly in that wretched place. But luckily I wasn't stuck there my entire lifetime like a lot of those poor women."

"Which explains why my mother didn't recognize your name. She would have been promoted to the seamstress department years before you showed up. What I can't comprehend, though, is why you originally asked me to bring her that bone with its blue ribbon. You said she'd understand what it meant—that it was a warning to our family. But she had no clue." As soon as Elia said this, Mrs. Suds flinched ever so slightly, and Elia began to feel rising doubt. "What? Am I wrong? Was she not telling the truth?"

Mrs. Suds frowned before answering. "I can't say for sure if your mother was truly clueless, outright lying, or just being cautious. But I definitely know Sulum, and she knows me too, both by my nickname, Mrs. Suds, as well as by my true title, Lady Argina."

Hearing her mother called by her first name—then to be told in the very next instant that Mrs. Suds should be addressed as Lady Argina—made Elia catch her breath. Yet more astounding than anything was learning that the two women indeed knew each other. If that was true, why hadn't Elia's mother been honest from the start?

Elia gritted her teeth and closed her eyes, concentrating hard to remember the exact sequence of events that afternoon when the Imperial Guards had so roughly searched her and her mother while they were trying to cross the Grand Bridge. When the guards discovered the bone in a pocket of Elia's apron, her mother had lunged forward to grab it, then tossed the bone into the clouds. Later, she explained that her impulsive action had been triggered by her concern that the guards would think Elia was trying to steal food. But maybe Sulum only said this to cover up what was really going through her mind. Maybe she *did* understand the bone's significance all along.

Perceptions deceive. Things are often not as they seem.

This was Omi's favorite piece of advice. Elia's mother had reminded her about it right after she denied knowing anyone by the name of Mrs. Suds. But at the time, Elia had no reason to suspect her mother of being someone other than who she seemed to be.

Elia's spinning thoughts were suddenly interrupted as Mrs. Suds—or rather Lady Argina—began to speak again in a soothing voice.

"I can tell how much all this is a surprise to you. But I swore to share the truth, and I don't intend to go back on that promise. Which is why I also have to admit . . . I knew your grandmother too."

Elia's eyes flew open. "How is that possible?"

"She worked in the stables. We knew each other for years, from the time we were both young women. Besides grooming the stallions that belonged to the Empress Mother, your grandmother also attended to the horses owned by Mahkoiyin."

"But if you were from the higher class, and my grandmother was nothing more than a servant, then—"

"Does that mean we couldn't be friends?"

"Friends?" Elia repeated. "I can't imagine how that could ever be an option."

Having stayed quiet all this time, Naadie spoke up from where she was sitting in the chair beside Elia's. "But, Elia, regardless of Lady Argina's social standing, she has always been very respectful and generous to everyone. Surely you must have seen that from her every day in the laundry room when we knew her as Mrs. Suds?"

"Yes, of course," Elia agreed. She turned back to the old woman. "If not for you, working in the laundry would have been unbearable. For many of us. That's why we all found it so devastating when Wrasse came to arrest you. And I don't mean to doubt what you just said about your relationship with my grandmother. You'll just have to be patient with me since there's so much information I'm trying to process."

"I understand completely."

Elia took a moment to reflect, then shook her head as if to clear it. "So, if you knew my mother and my grandmother, did you know my father?"

"Not to the same extent, but yes," said Lady Argina. "That's why he came here looking for my help when you were arrested."

"What about my grandfather and my brother?"

Lady Argina paused for a second, trying to recall, before she replied. "No, I don't believe so."

"Is there anyone else? I ask because recently, I've started developing a strong sense that there have been people looking out for my family for a very long time. Do you know a man by the name of Greyit?"

"Yes."

"He's dead, by the way," Elia said, more bluntly than she had intended.

This rattled Lady Argina's composure. "Is that true?"

"I found his body in his home the other day."

The woman's face sagged with grief. "That's very sad news. I'll miss the poor man."

"I saw no signs of what caused his death, whether it was just old age or something more sinister." Then Elia almost leapt out of her chair. "I'm so stupid. I don't know why I didn't realize sooner—Imperial Guards came to visit my grandmother the same morning they raided the laundry looking for you. It seemed a strange coincidence at the time, but it makes sense now, knowing the connection between the two of you."

A cloud of dread darkened Argina's expression. "What did she tell them? Do you know?"

"I suspect she said very little, if anything. For over a year, her mind had been deteriorating to a point where her words were often incoherent. She had also started wandering off, at all times of the day and night."

"I'm very sorry to hear that," Lady Argina offered, though her face betrayed instant concern not evident in her tone.

"When we returned that same evening, we found my grandmother dead at the edge of the island."

This news seemed to be an immediate relief to Argina, though she said, "My goodness, we've lost her too? The poor dear."

"Everybody assumed she died because of a Scavenger attack, but it didn't take me long to figure out where the blame should really lie—with the Imperial Guards!" Elia now abruptly leaned forward, assuming the role of interrogator. "Obviously, she had a secret to share—or so they thought—and I'm positive you know what that secret was."

Argina sipped tea from her big mug as if to hide behind it. "I have no idea what you're talking about."

"Don't you?" Elia challenged, shifting closer until she was sitting on the edge of her seat cushion, the bag of coins still balanced in her lap. Out of the corner of her eye, she noticed

Naadie squirming in her own chair. "I've been well aware for a while there's some sort of mystery that, for whatever reason, involves my family, and now I'm convinced it's all related to Mahkoiyin's child and that damn telescope."

Argina's expression hardened. "I assure you, that's not the case," the woman hissed through tight lips.

Although caught off guard by her sudden hostility, Elia was not going to back down. She felt certain she was on the right track. Glancing at Naadie, who looked unsure herself after hearing Argina's sharp retort, only made Elia feel more confident.

"I want you to tell me why it was necessary to hide the baby!" Elia demanded.

"That, my dear, is the one thing I'm not going to share with you."

In a flash, Elia reached forward and grabbed the telescope sitting on Argina's lap.

The woman moved too slowly to stop her. "Give that back!" she ordered, holding out a wrinkled, veiny arm.

Elia reached her fingers inside, and as soon as she felt the rolled-up documents, she pulled them out. Riffling through the pages, she found the one with the hand and footprints on it. She glanced at the baby's impressions, then held the paper up. "What are we going to do to track down who these belong to?"

"Nothing," Lady Argina said coldly.

"Nothing?" Elia exclaimed. "After all this—after everything I've been through—we're just going to give up on it? That's insane!"

"We are not going to do anything," Argina stressed. "That's where you're mistaken."

"What do you mean?" she asked angrily, feeling more confused than ever.

"Your role in this whole affair is finished!"

"Because I want answers to my questions?"

Lady Argina softened her stance. "No, my dear girl. What I mean is you are no longer needed. You've played the game well—far better than most, I should add—but the competition has now ended. At least for you."

Elia's mouth dropped open. "But-but—" she sputtered, struggling to come up with a response.

"Surely you didn't think you'd be the hero in all this." The old woman's laugh was now tinged with mockery—with pity too, as if offering nothing more than sympathy to a fool.

Elia sat frozen in place, her mind incapable of thought. She wasn't even aware of Dani coming around behind her chair until the girl reached over her shoulder and snatched away the telescope and documents.

This snapped Elia back into the moment. "That lady-in-waiting I encountered at the clotheslines said it was up to me to deliver the telescope into safe hands."

"Which you have done," Argina replied flatly.

A memory surfaced in her mind. "Then explain this," she challenged. "I remember you saying to me specifically how you thought it was funny that after everything, I was the one to discover the bone in my washtub. What were you trying to say?"

Lady Argina shrugged noncommittally.

Her frustration mounting, Elia wanted to scream. How was she going to win this battle of wits?

"I've come too far to be excluded," she pleaded. "I feel destined to see this through to the end, especially now I know that we're trying to support someone's birthright."

"What you don't seem to understand, my child, is that this is not your fight. You are a nobody. Inconsequential. A hindrance. Are you sweet? Yes. Naive? Yes. But nothing more than a very plain, simple servant girl, who really had no business getting mixed up in these affairs. It's a damn shame that lady-in-waiting had to choose you in the first place. Once my telescope was smuggled out of the palace, it was supposed to have been brought straight back to me here. You just got in the way, dragging everything out much longer than was necessary."

Springing out of her chair, Elia didn't care about dropping the small sack of coins onto the carpet. She also couldn't stop a few tears, though they were tears of outrage. "You are a hateful person!"

"Don't get riled up. Consider yourself lucky that, for you, it's over." Lady Argina nodded toward the floor. "And I gave you the money as your father requested, so now our business together is finished. You can do what you want, but you'll have to take care of yourself. Hide out for a few weeks, grow your hair to a respectable length, take that hideous piercing out of your eyebrow, then report back to Cook to resume your work in the laundry room. I understand they've become rather short-staffed lately."

"You can rot for all I care!" Elia screamed at the old woman as she picked up her empty mug and threw it into the fireplace. She didn't wait to see it smash on the tiles; she only heard the noise of it shattering as she grabbed her satchel and bag of coins, then raced to the front door.

She slammed back the locks, flung the door open, and stormed out into the cold dead of the night.

Chapter 42

"I WILL MEET BOTH of you up in Tasheira's room when I'm done," said Hokk. "First I need to quickly check my old room."

He had just climbed back to the main floor with Rayhan and Blaitz, after leaving Cook in her underground laundry. The commander was carrying the woman's lantern. All three of them were once again wearing their helmets.

Blaitz didn't reply as he looked down the corridor that stretched toward the front reception hall. Hokk wished he could see the man's face to gauge his reaction. Either way, the matter was important enough to keep pushing.

"Most of the palace is sleeping, so the timing is perfect," Hokk added. "And it won't take long. I'll be fast."

He feared that if he didn't take this opportunity, another chance might never present itself. The commander's plan right now was to search Tasheira's room to see if they could uncover anything, then head into the city to locate Elia. This could very well be Hokk's last visit to the palace, so he couldn't leave without retrieving what he'd set his mind on getting. "Whether or not I find what I'm looking for, I'll be joining you again before you've even had a chance to miss me."

"No, we'll go with you," Blaitz finally decided. "I'm not letting the two of you out of my sight. Otherwise, if we separate and come across other guards, we could lose track of who's behind these helmets, and we might never meet up again. But I'm holding you to your promise—you'll have to make it fast."

"I will," Hokk promised, not bothering to worry how he'd convince the commander to let Nym join their group once the fox had been found.

Moving quickly through the corridors, they encountered only a few servants performing their nightly duties, each stepping out of the way as the imposing threesome strode past. They crossed the wide open area beneath the grand atrium of glass and began climbing the stairs on Tael's side of the palace. At the first landing, two guards were positioned outside the blind emperor's private residence. The pair did nothing but stand at attention, apparently recognizing the spike fastened to the front of Blaitz's helmet.

Several flights up, they came to the floor where Hokk and Baron Shoad had been assigned rooms. Hokk found his door unlocked, exactly as he had left it.

As he burst through, his eyes darted toward the bureau where he had made the nest for Nym. Blaitz entered right behind, holding the lantern, and as the room brightened, Hokk could see the lowest drawer was closed.

So where was his fox?

Hokk charged to the cabinet in case Nym had become trapped inside, no matter how unlikely that seemed. Yanking open each drawer, he tossed the contents—mostly towels and bed linens—onto the floor.

Still nothing.

He pulled off his helmet as if it would help him see better.

"What are you missing?" asked Rayhan.

Hokk didn't reply. As he scanned his surroundings, he realized that except for the mess he had just made, the room was in pristine condition. The sheets of the bed were perfectly tucked in, the pillows fluffed and evenly arranged, the curtains drawn—certainly nothing like how he had left it. Obviously, the room had been thoroughly cleaned for the next guest, with all traces that he had ever stayed here removed.

"This is not good," he murmured, trying to imagine where Nym could have been taken.

"You're giving me a bad feeling," said Commander Blaitz, his tone suspicious. "You'd better not be saying . . . damn it, please don't tell me you had them all along!"

Hokk spun on him. "What do you mean?"

"Did you hide the documents somewhere in your room? The ones from inside the telescope?"

"No, that's ridiculous," Hokk shot back, offended by the suggestion. "How would I have ended up with them? And if I did, I would've certainly told you before this."

"Then what are you looking for?" the man demanded.

"Something . . . of great personal value," Hokk offered simply. "It's been part of my life for a very long time. But I guess someone has taken it," he added, throwing his hands up as if all were lost.

"Why won't you say what it is?" asked Rayhan.

Hokk knew neither of them would understand. "We should just get going," he muttered as he put his helmet back on. "I was wrong. It was pointless to come here."

Blaitz hesitated as though trying to assess the situation. "Fine," he said, sighing as he headed back toward the door. "Let's not waste any more time."

They descended to the ground level. Hokk trudged behind as they crossed to the other side and began climbing the stairwell within Tohryn's tower. They passed a similar set of guards stationed outside the emperor's royal suite, and continued higher, floor after floor, until they finally reached the very top.

"Do you know which room was theirs?" asked Blaitz.

Hokk proceeded ahead of him and then stopped. "This one."

It too was unlocked.

Following his companions inside, Hokk was the only one prepared to see the mess.

"Somebody's destroyed the place!" Rayhan exclaimed.

Blaitz raised the lantern to see over the stacked crates. "Damn it, they must have been a step ahead of us."

"No," said Hokk. "The room was like this from the start."

"But surely not in this condition!" Rayhan argued. "I thought that girl, whatever name you called her, was the daughter of a baron. A room in such a state doesn't seem appropriate for a person of her stature." Clearly, Rayhan's expectation of the palace was the same as Hokk's had been—that every room would be lavishly decorated.

"This is typical in the towers the higher you go. The rooms are much plainer than you'd expect, especially for ladies-in-waiting just starting out, or lower members of the court," the commander explained. "But it's the holes in the walls I find most concerning. I wonder if the damage was caused by whoever broke in here first, or whether it was your sister or Lady Tasheira trying to find a place to hide the documents."

"Like I said, the room was like this from the moment the girls first arrived," Hokk stressed.

"Still, we'll have to double-check to make sure nothing important has been overlooked," said Blaitz. Then he pointed to a tray on the floor, surrounded by splattered jam, broken biscuits, and pieces of a smashed saucer, cup, and teapot. "Look," he said. "It appears someone was attacked."

"No, I threw that tray down on purpose the last time I was in here," Hokk replied. "I used it as a diversion so Elia and I could escape from an Imperial Guard who insisted on pursuing me everywhere I went—in fact, of anyone, you'd know exactly what I'm talking about."

"I had received a direct order from Emperor Tael, who was only concerned for your welfare," Blaitz explained.

Hokk snorted. "I doubt it."

As if to show his sincerity, Blaitz placed the lantern on the floor and removed his helmet. "I can't change the past. I was only following orders."

Admittedly, this was true. The commander would have had no other choice but to obey the blind emperor's wishes.

Blaitz stepped around the boxes to approach the door. He closed and locked it, then turned back and began cracking his knuckles as if trying to decide where to start. "I'm curious what else might have been left behind in here, so I want us to search the entire space, including each of these shipping containers."

"And just to be clear, we're only interested in finding those documents?" Rayhan tried to confirm.

"They're most important, but I'm sure we won't be so lucky. However, show me anything noteworthy, just to be safe."

With that, the three of them set to pulling the room apart. Soon, the space was in chaos and piled high with stuff—lids removed, containers tipped over, clothing heaped up on the mattress, chunks of the wall pulled out to widen the holes so that the interior could be inspected.

Yet for all their effort, they could find nothing of importance.

In one of the crates, Hokk discovered a stash of incense sticks, which he guessed belonged to Elia. Though he assumed the incense wasn't worth pointing out to Blaitz, in Hokk's mind, it was still a disturbing discovery. He despised the sight of them, knowing all too well that if the sticks somehow ended up again in Elia's hands, they would cause her much harm. So he carefully broke each one between his fingers and ground the pieces into the floor with his heel until there was little left.

At least another hour elapsed before they were finished searching. They were sweating and the room's large window was steamy.

Rayhan was the first to admit defeat. "I think we have to give up."

"I agree," said Blaitz. "There's nothing. We had to make sure, but in the end, I'm really not surprised."

"So our best bet now is to find my sister and hear what she might be able to share with us."

"I agree, we definitely have to find her as soon as possible," said Hokk. "But I wonder if we shouldn't do something else first."

"What's that?" wondered the commander. "Must we follow you on another personal errand?"

Ignoring the sarcasm, Hokk replied, "This might be our last chance to be in the palace without anyone knowing what we're trying to do or that we're even here. So before the situation worsens, we should break Tasheira free."

His comment was met with silence.

"The girl did a lot for both Elia and me, and now she's become wrapped up in this whole crazy affair," Hokk continued. "She doesn't deserve it."

"It would be too big a gamble to pull off," said Blaitz.

"And all I'm worried about is my sister," Rayhan added.

Hokk shook his head. "We have to do it. It's the right thing. We can all wear our helmets. And I'm sure, Commander Blaitz, that no one would question why you have shown up in the dungeon, demanding her release."

Blaitz frowned. "Eventually, though, and probably in very short order, word about Tasheira's sudden discharge would reach the ears of the emperors, which could jeopardize everything."

"Then maybe we shouldn't involve you. Or you can remove the spike from your helmet. All I know is that at least one of us should show up down there to make the attempt. And there's no better time than right now. Even if it's just me who tries, then Tash and I can meet up with you later."

The commander considered Hokk's suggestion. He opened his mouth as if to say something, thought about it a bit more, and then finally made his decision. "I understand your thinking. And there is certainly a way to pull it off," he said. "But we have to plan our next steps very carefully."

Chapter 43

ELIA HEARD NAADIE CHARGING out into the alleyway, calling her name.

"Elia, stop! Please come back! It's not safe!"

Stupid girl. Did Naadie want to alert the whole neighborhood and get her arrested again?

Elia didn't stop running or allow herself to slow down because of her sore ankle. She pushed on through the pain.

She clutched the satchel close to her chest as she ran, feeling some measure of reassurance when she heard the jingle of coins inside. Having the money gave her an advantage, but it would be too risky to spend it right now on food or lodging. She had to focus on getting out of the city as quickly as possible.

Her destination?

Greyit's.

She had no other option. Though she abhorred the notion of following Lady Argina's advice, the woman was correct. Elia definitely needed to find a remote location to hide out until things quieted down, until it was safe enough to consider coming back to the city, as well as the palace.

But to return to the laundry room? Never! That prospect

was soul-crushing. She had tasted freedom, and now Elia's mind was changed forever.

My story's not over yet!

Elia was glad to reach the outer limits of the city. Fortunately, nobody was trailing her, and as far as she could tell, she hadn't caught the attention of the homeless people she'd seen sleeping on the streets. Yet she didn't feel relaxed until Na-Lavent was behind her completely, and she was traveling once more along the farm roads that were bathed by the glow of the shattered moon.

After entering the woodlands, she eventually found the path leading to Greyit's home, and she hurried down it through the dozing forest, knowing that when she finally arrived, she'd be ready to collapse from exhaustion.

But Greyit's body would still be there.

Damn. The realization made her shiver.

When she reached the faded white-and-blue checkered door, she pushed it open, yet paused on the threshold, holding her breath. She leaned in to take a look, left and right. Though it was dark, everything seemed to be the same as she had left it. Greyit was still sitting slumped in his chair. The smell in the air was stronger and more unpleasant—and it wasn't coming from the leftover food this time.

She couldn't spend the night here until she took care of the man's remains, and she'd have to do it all on her own.

Surely you don't think you're the hero in all this.

Elia cringed remembering Lady Argina's hurtful words.

No, she didn't think she was a hero, or even particularly courageous or smart. But she certainly wasn't a *nobody*. She was a decent person. And just because she feared the dark side of her personality and what she was capable of, that didn't mean she had to succumb to it. While she might have decided the last time she was here that she wouldn't trouble herself with Greyit's corpse, she was back now, and she'd do the right thing.

From a hammock suspended in a corner of the room, Elia took the one thin blanket she found and laid it on the floor in front of Greyit. She tried to ignore the smell and the feeling of his cold flesh in her warm hands as she unceremoniously pulled him forward by his bare feet. He slipped out of the chair and landed with a *thunk*, cracking his head. She stretched the material around him, tightly tucking the sides underneath, then tore narrow strips of fabric from a pillowcase, which she tied at both ends of the body to secure the wrapping. She removed the hammock from its hooks and proceeded to wrap the bundle on the floor like a cocoon.

But now what? Elia had no idea. Even if someone else were around to help her carry Greyit to the Slope of Mourning—or at least to any easily accessible point on the edge of the island—the ritual of sending bodies to Below no longer had any meaning for her. How could she possibly hold the tradition with the same high regard knowing that loved ones ended up sinking into an ocean or landing on the ground in a broken heap, where they would slowly decompose? In the past, before she'd known better, Elia had found the concept of Scavengers troublesome, but like everyone else, had accepted them as an unavoidable reality. Their collection of dead bodies was considered a sacred, albeit macabre, way for the deceased to be revered. It was as if the human remains were being treasured and protected. Now, of course, the very concept of such creatures was preposterous.

Elia had since learned a much better way to deal with the dead, and she wondered if it could work for Greyit. Several weeks ago, Hokk had suggested they actually *bury* her grandfather when they'd found him fallen in Ago—as in bury him underground. While it seemed a strange idea at the time, the concept of burial was really now the most logical and suitable solution. Yet at this moment, Elia had neither the energy nor the means to dig a hole sufficiently large or deep enough to accommodate the bundled man at her feet.

She dragged Greyit to the door, then outside. She left him stretched out beside the wall. Burying Greyit was a problem she'd deal with tomorrow. Where he was now would have to do for tonight.

Re-entering the shack, she closed the door behind her. Her body demanded rest, so she lowered herself into the only chair in the room—the one Greyit had just vacated—hoping for sleep to come to her.

It didn't.

Too much had happened. Too much had been said and revealed, and now she couldn't stop everything racing through her head. A missing empress, whose whereabouts only Elia knew. Mrs. Suds, turning out to be a former lady of the court. A long-lost child, the rightful heir to a throne. A mother, father, and grandmother, each connected to palace life in some mysterious way. And Elia herself, who was perhaps capable of piecing it all together.

Yet she felt as though she was overlooking something important—a link that could be used to pick up the trail where it had ended in the hands of Lady Argina.

She racked her brain.

What was it?

She squeezed the small key that was in her pocket, placed there after she'd opened the door at the end of the dungeon passage.

Tash was still down there. Locked up. Forgotten.

But Tasheira could be a very valuable ally. And she could be freed.

Yes, that was it! This was the next step she had to take. Doing a favor for the Baron's daughter would put Elia in a position to expect the same in return. And it was more than just a simple favor—Elia would be saving the girl's life.

Elia jumped to her feet with a surge of exhilaration, running her hand through her short hair as a plan formed in her mind.

She knew how to sneak beneath the Grand Bridge, then climb down the steps on the side of the island to reach the tunnel. She could wait for the right moment, then break Tasheira out of her cell. She'd simply need a hairpin or something similar to pick the lock. Naadie had done it—how hard could it be?

Maybe Naadie could be convinced to help. Elia had seen the shock on her face when she'd witnessed Lady Argina's hostility. Instead of being stuck doing the old woman's bidding, exposed to the threat of similar retaliation, wouldn't Naadie rather be free too?

Yes, freedom! It suddenly became so obvious in Elia's mind. *Freedom.* That was what rescuing someone as wealthy as Tasheira would allow Elia to negotiate for herself.

She hurried over to the same chest that she had searched through the other day. What she wanted was at the very bottom. The mirrored helmet of an Imperial Guard.

She unwrapped it from the towel and held it up.

Enough moonlight was shining through the window for her to see her reflection on the polished metal. This time, the image didn't bother her. She admired the person staring back.

She tried the helmet on, but it was too big. No matter. What she hadn't expected, however, was how easily she could see through the eye area of the helmet. Nothing blocked her view.

To be hidden behind the mask of a guard was exactly what she needed in order to get back into the city without anybody recognizing her. She would wear the helmet and rescue Tasheira—they could even walk out through the dungeon's main entrance if Elia kept the thing on!

She chuckled, knowing all too well her plan involved great risk. But without a doubt, it was something she had to attempt.

Greyit's trunk still contained several pairs of pants and shirts to choose from. These would be perfect to wear instead of her dress. And the boots too, even if walking in them properly might take some getting used to.

She took the boots out of the chest and pulled one on. The fit was snug—she could feel her toes touching the leather at the end.

It was then that a sudden realization rocketed in her mind, a thought so startling and unexpected, she stepped back and tripped over her other foot.

She lay sprawled on the floor, paying no attention to the pain of landing. For an instant, Elia couldn't accept the possibility her brain had come up with, but the more she considered it, the more certain she was.

And the thought almost made her sick to her stomach.

She scrambled to stand, yanked her dress over her head, kicked off the single boot, and began to get dressed in the darkest shirt and pair of pants she could find, glad that she could disguise herself as a man. The heavy footwear came next, which she tightly laced up, and finally the helmet on top of her head.

Without another moment's hesitation, she strode toward the door and stepped outside. This was not the time to rest. And burying Greyit . . . well, that would have to wait. She had to get back to the city as soon as possible, preferably by the break of dawn.

Though she had missed the clues for far too long, the actual rescue attempt she'd have to orchestrate was bigger and much more important than she could have ever possibly imagined before.

Chapter 44

THERE HAD BEEN NO showers this morning, no need to strip naked in front of the other prisoners. But they had congregated as before, fully clothed, this time holding buckets to collect the soapy water that fell from the pipes in the chamber's ceiling. Again, Tasheira was jostled about, getting wet as she tried to fill her container, not knowing what to do with it when the overhead spouts stopped dripping.

She had just been returned to her cellblock, escorted by a warden who was carrying a torch. She now turned to the hooded man with a questioning glare and held up the pail. "What am I to do with this?"

"Your toilet," he replied, waving his hand toward the corner of Tasheira's enclosure. "Flush it out. Keep it clean."

Stepping inside, Tash removed the board, bent over the cavity in her floor, and dumped her bucket. With a gurgling sound, the foul contents that had been sitting in the hole swirled around, most of it disappearing down a narrow drain that appeared at the bottom. Unfortunately, not everything was washed away. She wished for more water.

"Give me your pail," said the man, holding out a gloved hand.

Tash passed him the container. As he began to close her

cell door, she caught the bars to stop it, then peered down the corridor and pointed. "You know, I'm not the only prisoner down here," she said.

The man turned his head to follow her gaze.

A sly smile crept across Tasheira's face. She was still feeling angry and jealous that whoever had been locked up in there had managed to escape. "Why hasn't that other inmate been taken to have a shower? And shouldn't the person get food like everybody else?"

"We've received specific orders to leave that particular prisoner alone. Far too dangerous and undeserving of attention."

"But are you sure the prisoner is still in there?" Tasheira asked to rouse a spark of doubt.

"Why? What are you trying to say?" the warden said gruffly, though through his hood, his voice sounded uncertain.

"The person's gone. The cell's empty," said Tash. "Go check for yourself."

The man pushed her door shut and locked it before moving down the corridor. At the cell, he held up his torch.

Tash braced herself, anticipating his outrage to see the space unoccupied.

He leaned closer to peer in, then shook the door to confirm it was locked.

He turned and started walking back to her.

"Nice try," he growled.

Tasheira was flabbergasted. "But it's empty, isn't it?"

"He's still in there," the man replied with a snort.

"He?" said Tasheira. "No, it's a she."

"Who cares? He . . . she . . . their head was covered with a blanket. I couldn't tell."

"Listen to me!" Tasheira bellowed. "She escaped! I heard it all happening late yesterday."

The man ignored her as he strode past, on his way to leave.

"Wait!" she called out after him, wondering who the man could have possibly seen. "There's been some kind of mistake!"

He disappeared around the corner.

Boom.

The door to the outside stairwell slammed shut and the darkness swallowed her.

Tasheira's thoughts were swimming. Had the isolation gotten to her? Was her brain imagining things to trick her?

Leaning her head against the bars, feeling a deep sense of despair, she noticed a faint light suddenly appear from the cell the warden had just inspected. The glow grew brighter as if the flame of a match had lit the wick of a candle.

I'm losing my mind!

Yet there was no doubting the gloved hand that she saw extend past the cell's door. She watched the fingers fiddle with the lock, which was quickly released. The door swung open with the same squeal she had heard before.

A foot appeared, followed by the rest of the person's body emerging into the corridor, gripping a thick candle in one hand.

But Tash couldn't see a face.

Only the mirrored helmet of an Imperial Guard.

The Imperial Guard approached Tasheira's cell and stopped. He didn't say a word.

Though his polished helmet was the same as all the others she had ever seen, there was something about this particular guard that made him different. She couldn't pinpoint exactly what. Was it his stature? Something unusual about his clothing?

Before she could figure it out, he started picking the lock of her cell door.

"Are you here to help me?" Tash asked, half hopeful, half expecting to be disappointed.

The guard nodded. He held a finger up to the metal lips of his faceplate, encouraging her to remain silent. Opening the door, he moved aside, allowing her to step out. He took her by the elbow, but his touch was gentle, and it was all she needed to confirm what she was hoping to be true—he wasn't a threat, and she was getting out of here!

Together they climbed the first set of steps, then began winding their way through the other cell blocks as prisoners watched them pass by. Taking more stairs, as if heading back up to the showers, they marched down the final corridor and arrived at the dungeon's main entrance.

A warden was blocking the way, and Tash held her breath. Thankfully, he didn't appear to be the same man who had escorted her with her bucket full of water. This man seemed almost uninterested—definitely not suspicious—to see an Imperial Guard accompanying a prisoner, and without asking any questions, he snapped back the deadbolts to let them both exit.

Only once they were beyond the door and Tash heard it slam behind them did she finally allow herself to breathe again.

It had been so simple. And she was out!

"Can you take me to my father?" she asked quietly as they climbed past the floor of the laundry room, filled with workers.

When the guard shook his head, Tash almost started to protest, but quickly decided for once to hold her tongue. Maybe the Baron had already left, making a reunion impossible. And the guard seemed to be working alone, so perhaps all he could do for the moment was take her somewhere safe.

Ascending higher, they climbed above the kitchen floors before arriving on the main level of the palace. The Imperial Guard led her past the dining room and through to the atrium of the reception hall that connected the two towers. While Tash must have looked atrocious in her prison garb, she was thankful the few courtiers they encountered simply looked right through her as if she didn't exist. But that was perfect. The more invisible she could be to them, the better.

Tash was so focused, however, on who might recognize her that she didn't pay close enough attention as she and the guard began mounting stairs in one of the towers—which tower was it? Thinking back now, she could have sworn they had approached the side belonging to the blind Emperor Tael, but that didn't make sense. Her shabby room was on the top floor of Emperor Tohryn's side, and that had to be where he was taking her.

On and on they climbed. Tash began feeling the burn in her leg muscles but didn't complain. Although she would be with all her belongings, Tash felt anxious to be returning to her room—it would be the first place the guards would search once it was discovered she was missing. She would have to demand a bodyguard and a weapon so she could defend herself.

They finally reached the uppermost level. Moving down the adjoining hallway, the guard stopped in front of her door.

Glancing behind to confirm they were alone, Tash decided there was no longer any need for the guard to continue hiding behind his metal mask. She had pledged to seek revenge on those who had imprisoned her, but on the flip side, she wanted to reward the man who had come to save her.

The guard was about to insert a key into the door to unlock it, but before he knew what was happening, Tasheira reached up and swiftly pulled off his helmet.

The guard recoiled.

Just as startled, Tash backed away. "Oh my goodness, it's you!" she cried out.

The face looking at her frowned.

"I wish you had not done that," grumbled the most unlikely man to be wearing an Imperial Guard's uniform . . .

His Greatness, Emperor Tohryn.

Chapter 45

ELIA STOOD ONCE AGAIN in the shadows of the narrow lane, her gaze fixed on the inconspicuous door of Lady Argina's home.

Wearing Greyit's helmet, boots, and oversized clothing, she imagined she must be a strange sight—shorter, sloppier, and much less menacing than the typical Imperial Guard—but she had still achieved her desired result. Whether she was on the road heading toward Na-Lavent or within the city's streets, nobody had dared to challenge her. Instead, they seemed intimidated by her presence. Even here, the homeless along the alley had cleared away as soon as she appeared. She hadn't anticipated how much more powerful she'd feel behind this mirrored mask. And she loved it!

Now, the next step in Elia's plan involved confronting the old washerwoman—still Mrs. Suds in her mind—so that she could demand the answers she needed.

Yet Elia knew she would have only one chance to get inside. She couldn't remember the pattern of Naadie's secret knock, so she'd have to push her way through. Hopefully, somebody would leave soon to go to the market before it became too busy, though Elia was ready to wait however long it might take.

Thankfully, less than an hour after staking her spot, with morning sunlight beginning to stream down the lane as if to wash away its darkness and filth, Elia saw the door open a crack.

Prepared for this, Elia quickly darted across and flattened herself against the wall, no more than a few feet down from the entrance. She didn't want to be spotted, knowing that whoever was coming out would first check to make sure the passage was safe.

Elia heard chains being unlatched, then the gentle *swish* of the door swinging across the threshold.

She bolted, still clinging to the wall's edge.

Dani was about to peek out into the lane, and at that very moment, Elia was upon her, pushing her back inside.

"Where is she?" Elia barked in a deep, brutish voice, relishing the sight of Dani wide-eyed and trembling. Yet Elia didn't wait for an answer. She spotted Lady Argina rising from her chair by the fireplace. She had the same frightened expression as her servant.

"I'm here for you!" Elia shouted as she stormed into the room, pointing with an outstretched arm at Argina.

Quite unexpectedly, the old woman quickly collected herself and snatched a poker leaning by the fireplace. She started jabbing it in the air to ward off Elia. "Stay back! Who sent you?"

Elia yanked her helmet off and swung it in a wide arc—*clang*, metal on metal—to knock the poker from the woman's hands.

Lady Argina's mouth fell open. "It's you!"

"That's right, I'm back!"

Now, the old woman's face hardened, which only infuriated Elia more.

"I'm so surprised and disappointed to see you," the old woman snarled.

"Shall I go for help?" Dani called out from behind, her voice wrought with anxiety.

Lady Argina waved her hand dismissively. "No, just close the damn door!"

As Dani obeyed, Elia came around and flung herself down into the chair she had used the day before. "Take a seat!" she ordered.

Pinching her lips tight enough to drain their color, Lady Argina stood defiant.

Elia glared at her.

The woman finally shrugged. "Poor girl, you're quite the sight this morning," she observed with a contemptuous chuckle.

"Sit down!" Elia insisted again.

Argina hesitated, but then sighed and grudgingly gave in. Once settled into her chair, she returned Elia's stare with one cocked eyebrow. "Whose clothing did you steal? I must admit, I'm impressed you were able to find an Imperial Guard's helmet. A very clever disguise."

Ignoring her comments, Elia narrowed her eyes. "You promised to tell me *everything*."

"I did."

"You didn't!"

Trying to look unruffled, Argina didn't respond, though she squirmed ever so slightly in her seat.

"You are a liar, plain and simple," Elia said. "Not only do I suspect that you know details about the mysteries that surround my family, but I'm also certain every secret has ultimately stemmed from your involvement."

"Nonsense."

"I pieced it together last night before returning to the city."

Again, Lady Argina remained silent.

"I'm here this morning to confirm my suspicions," Elia added.

"And what are those?" asked the old woman belligerently.

"Let me see those documents that were being stored in the telescope."

Argina gave her a sidelong glance, but did not move.

"I need to see them to know if I'm right. I won't damage them. Just hand them over!"

The woman frowned. "Dani, bring the papers here."

Elia and Lady Argina did not break eye contact, not even when Dani returned and slipped the curled documents into Elia's extended hand. Only after unrolling the papers and flattening them out on her lap did Elia finally look down.

It was the page with the footprints she was most interested in. And to observe again what she remembered seeing made her pulse race. Unless she was wrong.

Perceptions deceive. Things are often not as they seem.

But no, not today. Today she knew to trust her instincts unconditionally.

"It's . . . it's these footprints," Elia murmured.

"What?"

"I recognize them."

"How? They're merely a blob of ink on a page from a baby born many years before you."

"Not born *many* years before me, only a couple. They're a very special set of prints, made unique by their shape."

"What shape? They are just feet," the old woman scoffed.

"No. Look again. The second toe of each foot is so much longer than all the other ones beside it. It's odd . . . and unmistakable." Elia blinked rapidly to catch the wetness brimming along her lower lashes, then pulled her gaze up from the page and stared hard at the old woman. "And I know I'm not wrong. These footprints belong to . . . my brother."

Lady Argina shifted uncomfortably in her seat and looked away.

"Tell me I'm right," Elia barely whispered. "It's my brother, isn't it?"

Argina turned back, this time holding her gaze. "It is," she muttered.

Though fully expecting this response, Elia felt her breath being stolen away as if she had just suffered a heavy blow to the chest.

"Is Rayhan . . . the heir to the throne?" she asked quietly.

"That's not his real name. But yes."

Elia gripped the armrests of her chair. "So what does that make me?"

"I already told you yesterday. *Nothing*."

Another blow. Elia recoiled in her chair.

Then, from overhead, she heard a *thump, thump*—the same sound she had heard the last time she sat here.

Dani was still in the room with them. It could be Naadie moving about up there, but Elia highly doubted it.

Elia's eyes blazed, and in an instant, she was on her feet and charging toward a spiral staircase in the corner of the room.

"Stop! Get back here!" Lady Argina shouted.

Elia ignored her as she bounded up the steps two at a time, circling around to the top.

Upon reaching the landing, she discovered a door, but she didn't pause to find out if it was locked. Instead, she threw her whole weight against it and crashed through, landing on the floor in a heap.

She heard a startled yelp, then "Elia!"

Elia's head spun in the direction of the voice. Scrambling up, she ran forward and launched herself into the waiting arms.

Together, mother and daughter sobbed, hugging each other close as if they would never let go.

Chapter 46

TASHEIRA WAS STILL STANDING speechless in the hallway as the emperor snatched back the helmet from her hands. "Just get inside before anyone sees us," he warned, glancing over her shoulder.

Yet as he turned the knob and pushed against the door, Tash was equally unprepared for the second surprise he now revealed—her room completely transformed. Every shipping crate, all her belongings, even the dirty mattress on the floor had been removed and replaced with beautiful furniture and a staggering overgrowth of foliage. In this huge reception room, decorative pots with flowering plants, vines, ferns, and ornamental trees were arranged everywhere—sitting on tabletops, tucked beside sofas and chairs, spilling onto the floor, cascading from the ceiling, crawling up the walls—making it look as if the Sanctuary's luscious gardens had been recreated indoors. Fresh air blew through the room from one of the large, sliding windows, further enhancing the illusion of exterior space, and the cool breeze fluttered the curls of Tasheira's hair as it swept into the corridor, carrying with it a deliciously floral fragrance.

"This isn't my room," Tash declared, finally finding her voice. Obviously, none of these changes could have been made over the short period of time she had been imprisoned. “What is this place?”

“A spot where you can feel safe.”

“I could have sworn we climbed the stairs to the highest floor.”

“We did.”

“So is this Emperor Tael’s side of the palace?”

“Yes, it is.”

Though Tasheira had never heard of any protocol that restricted the Twin Emperors from being on the property that belonged to the other, it still seemed very odd that Tohryn was attempting to hide her at the top of the tower assigned to his blind brother.

“Does he know I’m up here?” she asked.

“No. And I hope to keep it that way.”

It was just as she expected—to pull off this rescue attempt, Tohryn was working alone. Or at least, without his brother’s involvement.

“What about my father? Is he still on the Sanctuary grounds? Can I see him?”

“I’m trying to make that happen, though it’s very challenging to arrange at the moment,” the emperor replied as he shut the door behind them.

“But does he know what’s happened to me?”

“That’s where the complication lies. He’s been in my brother’s company ever since we questioned you in that meeting room on the main level. You should feel assured, though, that I’m making every effort possible to get word to him without raising suspicions. In the meantime, you’ll be protected here from those who are most dangerous.”

“How can you be sure I won’t be found?”

A third voice—gruff, raspy, and speaking very slowly—answered from somewhere deep within the jungle of plants. “Because nobody ever ventures up this high.”

Tash spun around and scanned the area. Who did that voice belong to?

She walked farther into the room, picking her way through the rampant foliage until she saw the ancient face.

The man sat motionless, surrounded by the room's vegetation, like a cat concealed in a thicket waiting to catch its prey. Looking much older than anyone Tash had ever seen, the man was bald and his scalp was mottled and peeling. His forehead, cheeks, and the skin around his eyes were creased with such deep wrinkles that he appeared to be made of cracked, dry dirt. His mouth was hidden behind a white beard with whiskers that had grown into long wisps, like tangled vines, coiling down to cover his massive belly.

Emperor Tohryn crouched on one knee in front of him. The elderly gentleman raised a sinewy hand. Almost every square inch of the hand's wrinkled skin was covered with tattoos. The emperor touched the man's knobby knuckles to his forehead—a surprising show of reverence normally reserved only for Tohryn himself and other members of the Royal Family—then he stood up again to make his introductions.

"Lord Mack, I'm very pleased to present to you a friend and ally of the court, Lady Tasheira."

Emperor Tohryn gave Tash a look to suggest she should mimic his gesture of respect, so she bowed before the old man in a similar manner. "It is a great honor, My Lord," she said, touching his fingers to her brow.

As she lowered his hand, she could see his tattoos ran farther up his arm, disappearing under his sleeve. The images were so dense they seemed to overlap. The only tattoos Tash had ever seen were those on the foreheads of palace staff, each mark an unmistakable symbol of their servitude. So why did a man with a noble title have them?

"Please forgive my impertinence for arriving unannounced," said the emperor, and once again, Tasheira was surprised by his deference. "But as you know, political matters at court have recently become very serious, and I was hoping Lady Tasheira could stay here with you until those issues are resolved."

Lord Mack nodded slowly and thoughtfully before speaking in a measured cadence. "Of course, you are always welcome. I also extend that invitation to your guests. With such solitude day after day, I appreciate the company of anyone you might deem fit to visit an old man like me." His eyes shifted to examine Tasheira before his gaze returned to the emperor. "But just to be clear—when you say she's a friend and ally of the court—"

"I mean she can be trusted."

"In all matters?" the old man questioned with one eyebrow raised.

"Yes. She and her father, Baron Shoad, have not only helped protect the secret, but they have also returned to the palace with the information that will soon solve my problems."

"I'm not sure I understand," Tasheira interjected with a growing sense of unease.

Tohryn turned to her. "You don't have to pretend anymore. I'm aware just how much you must already know, so there's no need to worry about incriminating yourself with your words. You can relax. You are well protected."

"But yesterday, I was considered a criminal, stripped of my rights. Why the sudden change?"

"Because of the difference your actions have made. Based on the details you've already told us, plus what I've been able to piece together since then, I now understand much more clearly how important your involvement has been. That girl you saved and then brought to the palace is the person who possessed—and perhaps still possesses—everything that I need to correct a great injustice."

Tash couldn't believe what she was hearing, but to be sure she understood, she asked, "Which girl?"

"You used her name several times during our interview," said Tohryn. "Unless I'm remembering it wrong, you called her Elia, didn't you?"

"Elia?" Tasheira repeated with alarm. "There must be some mistake. She's a threat to both you and your brother. Just the other morning, she attempted to assassinate Tael!"

The emperor frowned and shook his head. "No. That's not what happened."

"It isn't? How can you say that? Right afterward, she tried escaping from the palace!" Tasheira exclaimed. "There was all that blood, and the guards chasing after her onto the bridge. Then I was arrested, tied to a chair, and hauled to the dungeon because I was supposedly an accomplice to what Elia was scheming!"

Tohryn's expression clouded over. "That was all very regrettable. You definitely didn't deserve to be detained and treated the way you were, and I'm very upset about what took place. Unfortunately, for both you and Elia, there was too much confusion, upset, and misinformation circulating at the time. People acted recklessly, and the orders we gave were grossly misconstrued."

Tasheira was baffled by this sudden change in the perception of events. Yet she could think of no reason why Emperor Tohryn might want to deceive her. "If I'm to believe all this, then I am very grateful and fortunate that people realized the truth. But to compensate for all my distress, there's something you must do for me," Tash boldly requested. "My cousin Fimal is still locked up. He should be released immediately as well."

"Your cousin? I didn't know," Emperor Tohryn replied, sounding genuinely surprised. "I'll see to it right away. What you may or may not know is that Elia was locked up too. Before I could rescue her, mind you, she somehow managed to escape."

"She escaped? She was down there too?" Tasheira asked in astonishment as she flipped through her memories.

Could that prisoner she saw with the hood and shackles really have been Elia?

Yes, the more Tash thought about it, the more plausible the idea seemed. So why hadn't Elia shown her how to escape too, especially when Tash had been calling out for her help? Tasheira resolved to confront Elia about it, and her explanation had better be a good one.

"With Lord Mack's permission, I'll bring your cousin up here too as soon as I find him," said Emperor Tohryn. "Then you'll both have to remain in this suite until everything has been exposed and resolved."

Up until now, Lord Mack had been watching and listening with great interest. "By all means, whatever you think is necessary. I'll always take more visitors. I'm assuming you'll be locking us in."

"I'll have to," the emperor said. "I have no other choice. I will advise your butler of the situation, so he'll know to bring up extra food. But except for him, I should be the only person granted access to this room. If anyone else does arrive who I haven't specifically brought up here, they should not be allowed to enter."

"Understood," said Lord Mack.

"At all costs, Lady Tasheira cannot be taken away. She should be hidden immediately if any trouble arises," Tohryn added.

The old man nodded solemnly. "After all the protection you've offered me over the years, I will make sure your wishes are met absolutely."

Chapter 47

SULUM WIPED AWAY A tear from Elia's cheek. "Praise the sun," she whispered, letting her touch remain on her daughter's face.

Elia reached up and gently placed her hand on her mother's. "All I've been hoping for is to see you again."

"You look so . . . so different," said Sulum. She ran her fingers through Elia's short hair, then held her daughter at arm's length for inspection. "You seem to be healthy enough. But you'd tell me if you had been harmed in any way, wouldn't you?" Her attention seemed to linger on Elia's eyebrow piercing.

"I'm fine. Don't worry."

Lady Argina's loud protests rose from the floor below, demanding Dani climb up to retrieve Elia. Striding toward the door, Elia looked down and saw the timid servant girl creeping up the stairs. When they made eye contact, Dani froze mid-step and cowered against the railing.

"Leave us alone, or you'll regret it dearly!" Elia growled, brandishing her fist before she slammed the door and turned back to her mother.

"Are you really all right?" Sulum asked.

"Well, I can't say it hasn't been challenging," Elia replied, deciding to spare her mother unnecessary grief with too many details. "But none of that matters now. I'm just relieved we're finally together. And what about you? Surely you haven't been here this entire time?"

"I have."

"Really? So then why wasn't I told?" Elia asked, surprising herself with the sharp edge in her voice.

Remorse darkened Sulum's expression. "I'm sorry. We didn't know where you were. A number of weeks ago, you seemed to vanish completely."

"For goodness' sake, I'm talking about yesterday evening! When I was downstairs, just a few feet below you."

Sulum frowned. "That was very difficult."

"Yet you found it acceptable to do nothing."

"Lady Argina insisted I not come down. I thumped the floor a few times, in case that would change her mind, but I had no other choice. And she was very angry with me after you left because I hadn't kept my promise to remain silent."

"Why promise such a thing? Why would she even force you to? It makes no sense!" Elia exclaimed, pulling away.

Her mother looked hurt by her harshness. "I'm just a player in this whole drama like you, don't forget. The same day you disappeared, Lady Argina arranged to have me brought here for my own protection. She was very concerned I'd be the next target. Though I didn't know what was going on—and really, I still don't—I've had to stay on this second floor the entire time for fear of who might come bursting through the front door to search the place. Even when we knew yesterday that you were probably going to be rescued, Argina was adamant that I remain up here alone, just in case you and Naadie were followed by Imperial Guards. But last night, I wanted to join you more than anything. I tried listening through the door."

"Did you hear what we discussed?"

"Some of it. However, I made Argina fill me in on all the details afterward. But you had me so worried, Elia, when you stormed out of here. Where did you go? What upset you so much?"

"If you have to ask, then I know you didn't hear everything we talked about. Mrs. Suds—or *Lady Argina*," Elia replied sarcastically, "probably didn't mention a word about all the cruel things she said to me." Elia felt her emotions stirring again, but she quickly shut them down. "Never mind, I don't really care about that now," she lied. "Even worse is what she just confirmed for me this morning. About Rayhan."

"What do you mean?"

Elia was astounded that her mother was still trying to hide the truth. "Don't pretend. You know! I'm certain you know everything. Damn it, he was your baby—or he was *supposed* to be, at any rate!"

Sulum's face sagged, and her arms dropped limp at her side. "I'm so sorry," she murmured.

"I just . . . I don't know . . . how can—" Elia sputtered, frustrated by how jumbled her thoughts sounded. Her legs began to weaken beneath her, so she lowered herself onto the floor.

Sulum sank down beside her, pushing out the air that ballooned her skirt. "I've always dreaded this day. The day when you'd find out."

Elia looked expectantly at her mother.

Sulum fidgeted with a button on the front of her dress as she sighed, glanced up at the ceiling, then down to the floor, but said nothing.

Was she just going to sit there, mute?

Elia decided not to wait. "Lady Argina says his name isn't even Rayhan."

"It's not," Sulum replied with a sniffle before dabbing her nose with her sleeve. "It's Jeradon."

Elia repeated the name in her mind several times. "I guess we're supposed to refer to him as *Prince* Jeradon, are we not?"

"Yes." Her mother's voice was a ghostly whisper.

Silence again.

After a long minute or two, Elia finally prompted her. "Please. I need to hear this."

Sulum reached across for Elia's hand. "You have to realize, it's very hard for me. I've had to deal with great sorrow and shame for such a long time, and the words don't come easily."

"Is Rayhan my *actual* brother?" Elia asked bluntly, unable to call him by his true name.

"No."

"Is he your child?'

"No."

"Am I your daughter?" Elia croaked as this new, startling possibility suddenly entered her mind.

"Yes! You are. You're definitely mine."

No sooner were the words out of her mouth than Sulum started weeping. She crumpled and Elia caught her in her arms, though Elia could not ease the tension she felt in her own body.

Wiping her eyes, Sulum tried to compose herself. She sat up straighter. "Oh Elia, I'm so sorry. I've always loved you so much, but a few years before you were born, I suffered a terrible tragedy. It's a loss I've never been able to get over." Choking up, she held the base of her throat until she was ready to continue. "I'm talking about the loss of your older sister."

Sister?

Elia's mouth opened and closed—opened and closed once more—before any words could come out. "I have . . . a sister?"

"You *had* a sister," her mother sadly clarified.

"What was her name?"

Sulum sniffed again. She looked defeated. "I never got the chance to name her," she said with a tremulous voice. "The little girl was stillborn. Dead in my womb. I was able to hold my precious baby for only a few brief moments before she was taken away."

Elia's heart ached for both her sister and her mother. "How come you never told me any of this?"

"I was forbidden to say a word."

"Why?"

"To protect your brother."

"But he's not my brother!" Elia retorted as she pulled her legs up to her chest and hugged her knees.

"Don't say that."

"Who did he really belong to?" Elia asked, already knowing the answer, but wanting to hear it from her mother's mouth.

Sulum glanced anxiously toward the door. The effect of many years of being afraid, trying to keep her secret safe, apparently continued to rule her life.

"Was he Mahkoiyin's baby?"

Her mother was startled by Elia's accuracy. "Yes. How did you know?"

"I've been able to find out a lot over the past little while—enough to start piecing it all together. What isn't clear, however, is how our family got involved with this whole complicated affair in the first place."

"It's all due to a series of unfortunate events, as well as some very unexpected connections that developed with people inside the palace. People of influence who saw fit to interfere with our lives."

"Was it someone important from the palace who disposed of my sister?"

Sulum looked pained. "No, it was only a servant following orders."

"Who gave the orders?"

"Perhaps they came directly from Mahkoiyin, but I'm not sure. I suspect it was more likely from Lady Argina. She seemed to be the one coordinating everything. Her involvement became more evident after the empress was attacked and pulled over the edge of the island. And as you've probably figured out, Argina has held onto her position of control all these years, even when she hid herself down in the laundry room as Mrs. Suds, waiting patiently for the right moment to come. It's just that none of us ever expected it would take this long. I was supposed to take care of Rayhan for only a short period of time."

"But let's go back to the start so I can understand more clearly," said Elia. "How did we, our own poor little family, end up concealing a prince when plenty of other families were better suited for the task?"

"Because of those connections I just mentioned. Believe it or not, your grandmother and Lady Argina knew each other quite well as young women. It was remarkable the relationship that developed—unprecedented, actually, that kind of rapport between a noblewoman and somebody like Omi who worked as a stable hand. But I guess it was their shared love of horses that they bonded over first, and, with time, their connection grew. Maybe it wouldn't have lasted as long as it did, though, if your grandmother hadn't proved to be such a very valuable informant."

"You make it sound as if Omi was some sort of spy."

"Yes," Sulum replied matter-of-factly. "That's exactly what she was."

Chapter 48

EMPEROR TOHRYN HAD LEFT a few minutes ago, first donning his helmet to conceal himself before exiting. Now, with only the two of them in the room, neither Tasheira nor Lord Mack had uttered a word.

Just like her elderly companion, Tash sat surrounded by lush green foliage. The breeze rustled the leaves of the plants. The curling tip of a curious vine, reaching out in search of a new contact point, tickled the back of her neck.

Brushing the flirtatious tendril away, Tasheira turned her head toward the long bank of windows. She could see the other tower in the distance, its mirrored surface reflecting sunlight. She found it remarkable that, just a few days earlier, she had stood over there at her own window, looking across, never guessing a place like this could exist.

Clearly, living this high up would make it tough on someone as old and obese as the man sitting in front of her. Tash could imagine the challenge for him to climb so many steps whenever he needed to come and go. But perhaps the situation was even worse—maybe he was completely incapable of using the stairs and he was stranded at the top of this tower. That would explain why Tash had never before heard of the man or seen him mingling with the other courtiers.

"How long have you been living up here?" she asked, suddenly breaking the silence.

"Well over a century. It's been almost as long since I last left this room."

Tasheira snorted. The man was obviously delusional.

Yet his deeply creviced face grew serious. "You think I'm joking, but I'm being completely honest."

"Ha!" Tash blurted out, now laughing. "That can't be possible!"

"It's the truth."

"So, if you've been here that long, just how old are you?" She knew that asking such a personal question was rude, but if the man wanted to say absurd things, she was willing to play along.

"I gave up counting at three hundred and fifty," he said. "That was many, many years ago, of course. At this age—whatever it is—it really doesn't matter whether or not I keep track. Old is old."

Tash covered her mouth to stifle another laugh. Lord Mack was looking at her with such an earnest expression that she felt somewhat embarrassed by her reaction. Though he sounded senile, his sincerity made Tasheira reconsider her opinion of him. He might have some very interesting stories to share, even if they were pure fantasy. And if he didn't, she was stuck with him for the time being and she'd have to be civil. She was Lady Tasheira, after all, and her manners should reflect her noble status.

"The emperor addressed you as Lord Mack," she said with greater self-control. "Is it appropriate if I do the same?"

"Yes, by all means. My full name is actually Mackenzie Noble, not just Mack."

"Oh," Tash replied, still unable to recognize his name. "Please excuse my ignorance, but I have to admit, I've never heard you mentioned before."

"I'm sure I haven't been the topic of conversation for decades. That's how it's supposed to be, though. It's also why I've been banished up here for so long."

"Banished?" Tash repeated with surprise. "Like a prisoner?"

"Practically. But don't get me wrong—it was always my choice too, right from the start, to have it this way."

"Why?"

"Because a decision was made long ago that the best plan was to keep me separated from everybody else. I fully agreed it was the right thing to do. Too much about our society had changed, and the situation had become very tricky to manage. To have me around risked disturbing the balance that had finally been achieved, so it didn't make sense to aggravate matters. People's beliefs were firmly set to match their perceptions, and we had reached a point where it was futile, even dangerous, to keep reminding everyone of the actual reality of things."

"You've lost me," said Tasheira, furrowing her brow as she crossed her arms. Was the man speaking more nonsense?

Lord Mack suddenly looked uncomfortable and nervous. "Listen to me blathering on. How can you tell I almost never have visitors? The floodgates open and everything spills out like I'm a silly fool."

"It's fine," Tash assured him. "I enjoy this sort of discussion with people who know so much more than me."

"I really should be careful, though, what I say," he muttered to himself. His gaze drifted toward the open window while he rubbed the trailing whiskers from his chin, as if to tame them. "Still, if you're a friend and ally of the court, then you wouldn't have been brought here if I wasn't supposed to share what I know."

Tash only stared at him as he continued to think out loud and debate how much of his story to tell. She had always loved getting swept up by intrigue, and the more he spoke, the more her interest grew. Before long, she was squirming in her seat.

He became quiet. Then, after a few minutes more, he squinted in Tasheira's direction, as if hoping he might see her clearly enough to judge her trustworthiness.

"I believe you were going to tell me more about your history," she prompted, deciding to rely on a well-practiced ruse of innocence to pull him out of his silence. "The emperor actually made that promise to me as we climbed the stairs together. He said you'd leave nothing out."

This lie proved to be the catalyst.

"Good. Yes, that's good," Lord Mack murmured, nodding slowly. "And it will benefit me greatly to explain what I know. Not just bits and pieces, but *everything*! It's been too long. Much too long to keep it all inside."

Perfect. This was exactly what Tasheira wanted. An eager smile tipped the corners of her mouth.

"So, what would you like me to tell you first?" he asked, rubbing his hands on his pants where his thighs weren't already covered by the spread of his belly.

"I'm not sure," replied Tash. "Perhaps you should start at the beginning and I'll stop you if I've heard it before."

"Oh, I doubt very much you've heard any of this before," he said. "Over these many years, I have been forbidden to reveal the details to people—except to a very select few, mind you, just in case I passed on and all my knowledge went with me. Yet I never seem much closer to death. Eventually, everyone else always beats me to it. I suspect I will continue to go on and on, for who knows how many centuries more, in the company of my plants. Really, it's a curse in ways I would never have anticipated."

Regardless of how impossible his comments seemed to be, a very small part of Tasheira was beginning to believe he might be telling the truth. "Who were your parents?" she asked to get him started.

"My father was a computer programmer. My mother was a nurse, but she stopped working at the hospital when my older brother was born. Next came two sisters, then me, the youngest of four. In those early years, we were comfortably middle class and quite happy. Then everything changed. One of my sisters was diagnosed with a very rare form of leukemia, and within a year she had lost her battle and died. How unfortunate for her—tragic, in fact—that only three years later, gene therapy cured cancer for everyone. But in my sister's case, after so many months in the hospital, and faced with mounting medical bills and grief, my parents couldn't handle the stress. They divorced. My mother was left to raise us kids with my father's minimal child support."

Tasheira had no idea what he was talking about. Many of the man's words were ones she was hearing now for the first time.

Lord Mack must have sensed her confusion. "I'm sorry. I've done this before—I forget that when I speak, people struggle to comprehend what I'm saying. You have to realize I grew up in a very different time. You can't begin to imagine how much has changed since then."

"But you must tell me," Tash encouraged. "I want to know everything. Remember, this is what I'm here for."

"Yes, I can see how eager you are to learn. You'll just have to ask me to explain if I say anything you don't understand."

"I will," said Tasheira, leaning forward. "I'm most fascinated to hear what life was like back when you were young."

"It was easier in most ways, yet more challenging in others. If you were wealthy, your life was set and you had little to worry about. If you were poor, you were often absolutely destitute, with not much hope of escaping the clutches of poverty. The shocking divide between people only grew more and more pronounced over the years as technology took over society."

"What's technology?"

"Good question." He considered it for a moment. "It's hard to explain to somebody like you whose exposure to such things is so limited. But technology encompasses all of humanity's shared knowledge, whether it's how to solve problems, create useful tools, or complete tasks more easily and quickly. In my day, as a young man, advances in technology had reached a point where every possible piece of information that existed was instantly accessible to people, with minimal effort. There were even devices invented to entertain us and think for us!"

"Hmm," Tash replied as she tried to process this. "It's difficult to really grasp what you're saying. I mean, I get the general idea, but . . . can you provide an example?"

"Sure. Let's consider . . . a candle," he suggested, pointing to one on a nearby table. "Just imagine the first person who decided that dipping a piece of string into wax might be a smart idea. Think of the benefit we've all enjoyed since then by that simple introduction of a flame to a wick. Now we can brighten our rooms with a candle's light. Such a simple concept, but at some point in time, it was a new invention, a new *technology*, that improved our lives."

"The way you describe the past, though, makes it sound like many of the things you knew back then no longer exist."

"Unfortunately, that's true. A few traces still exist, but not many."

"How can that be?"

"People used to think technology would save us, but in reality, it came close to finishing us off. Besides having depleted almost all of our energy supplies, we were too dependent on stuff, and we had forgotten how to really take care of ourselves without those resources. But before our reckless behavior could cause our complete annihilation, the world changed in catastrophic ways that we were unprepared to face."

"What happened?"

His expression grew troubled, as if the memories were difficult. "The Earth's north and south magnetic poles suddenly switched, wreaking havoc of such proportions—"

"What's the Earth?" Tash asked, interrupting him before he could go further.

"My apologies, I forgot again you wouldn't be familiar with that term. Earth is the place where we all come from."

"Oh, you mean the moon. Before it broke apart, right?"

"No, the Earth is *beneath* us."

"So, the ground?"

The old man chuckled. "I'm talking about what's on the other side of the clouds. What everyone refers to as Below."

Tash's entire body shivered. She immediately recalled the conversation she'd had with her cousin Fimal after he flew to the palace on horseback from her family's estate, desperate to warn her about Elia's attempted murder of Tasheira's loyal servant, Marest. Fimal had spoken of the strange new realm he had visited with Hokk—miles and miles of an endless landscape, dark and cold, with mountains, and meadows, and other features she still struggled to imagine.

Could this place be what Lord Mack was referring to?

"When the poles switched, it nearly spelled the end for all humanity," he continued. "Though no one was sure whether or not the reversal was the cause or simply the result, it happened when the orbits of the Earth and moon faltered, and they moved too close together. Their gravities had devastating consequences on each other—parts of the Earth splintered into the chunks of rock we see floating in these clouds, but the moon suffered the most, shattering into the many pieces that are still strewn across our sky."

"I'm sorry to stop you again, but none of this is making any sense."

"That's understandable."

"I've always been told—"

"Yes, I know what you're going to tell me," said Lord Mack, cutting her off. "The story everyone believes—that our islands are the remnants of the moon that somehow drifted away and became trapped in these clouds to form the Lunera System. Ever since, our people have supposedly been isolated, unable to return to the moon, where the descendants of our common ancestors still live today."

"Yes, exactly. That's the account we've all heard since childhood."

"But none of it is true," he said firmly.

Tasheira shot him a suspicious sidelong glance. "Why should I believe you?"

The old man grunted. "Because I lived through it all. I was a witness to what really happened."

Chapter 49

"YOU CAN'T BE SERIOUS!" Elia gasped. "Omi was a spy?" She couldn't picture her grandmother as anyone except a frail, old woman with a damaged mind.

"When she was working, your grandmother was privy to many things," Sulum began to explain. "Information and gossip were frequently shared between courtiers outside the palace, whether they were arriving at the Sanctuary on official business or leaving the Royal Court to fly off to some secluded location where they could scheme, far away from the ears of those ready to condemn them. However, since Omi was no more than a lowly horse groomer, she was practically non-existent in the eyes of these noble ladies and gentlemen. They would often talk openly in front of her, with little regard to what she might hear as she saddled up their horses or brought the animals water-balls after a long flight. Of course, Omi picked up only snippets of their conversations, but the details were always worthwhile enough for Lady Argina to check in with her for updates. And your grandmother was always very willing to divulge whatever she heard. Sometimes a bit too cooperative, I'd say, especially when it came to matters about our family."

"Like what?"

"Personal things. Such as when I was pregnant with your sister. My belly was so huge I could barely walk, but I was still required to work. Once I reached the point where I couldn't manage the long trek between the palace and home, I spent almost a month sleeping in the laundry room to save me the strenuous trip. That way, I could report for duty every morning, right on time."

"Why sleep in the laundry room? Weren't you already a seamstress on the level above?"

"No, I was only promoted after all this happened. I guess the new position was offered as their half-hearted attempt to compensate me for my involvement."

"And this related to Omi how?"

"Leading up to this, your grandmother had started to overhear grumbling from a number of courtiers—hostile grumbling—that seemed to indicate a budding conspiracy against Mahkoiyin. Fearing it could possibly put the empress's life in danger, Omi naturally told Lady Argina everything, not knowing that the empress herself was pregnant too and almost as far along as me. Mahkoiyin had been purposefully staying out of public view, so only Argina and Emperor Tael were aware that she was expecting to deliver a child very soon—a child who would become the first heir of the Twin Emperors. Mahkoiyin knew her situation could be precarious if Tohryn or Empress Faytelle found out about her pregnancy, so she instructed Argina to circulate rumors that Mahkoiyin was suffering from an illness that forced her to remain in quarantine."

"Good grief," said Elia, shaking her head. "It all sounds so complicated."

Sulum nodded seriously. "Indeed, it was. And very dangerous. Supposedly, a few sympathizers on Tohryn's side started to guess the real reason for the empress's absence, and they banded together to devise a fiendish plot to protect Tohryn's interests—as well as their own—ahead of Tael's. Of course, I had no idea about any of this myself. All I knew was that I was pregnant and very eager to deliver my baby as soon as possible. As for Omi, she would check on me down in the laundry room at the end of each day before returning home to take care of your father and grandfather. I guess one afternoon, she mentioned my condition to Lady Argina, and, as I found out later, this was the reason why Cook began to closely monitor my progress too."

"Cook?" said Elia with a start.

"That's right. You see, we were both using the laundry room as a place to sleep. I'm not sure if you know, but Cook doesn't have a home of her own. Whereas staying in the laundry was a temporary solution for me, she has always spent every night in that wretched place, which she continues to do to this day."

"Really? No wonder the poor woman was always so unhappy."

"Anyway, late one night, my contractions started, and I knew it was time. No doubt about it. Cook woke up as my groaning grew louder, but instead of helping, she suddenly disappeared. I didn't know where she had gone, until the next thing I knew, she was back, accompanied by Lady Argina and some young man I didn't recognize. He must have been an Imperial Guard who Tael trusted. That was the first time I had ever met Argina, and I couldn't figure out why someone of her status was interested in my delivery. But I wasn't allowed to stay where I was. Between the three of them, I was slowly brought up the stairs to the main level. I assumed they were going to kick me out and send me home, rather than let me give birth inside the palace. However, we didn't stop there. We kept climbing."

"How far?"

"I was brought up to Empress Mahkoiyin's private suite just above Tael's. Let me tell you, I was certain it all had to be a dream. I couldn't imagine why I deserved such attention. And then to be inside the empress's room! Well, I had never seen a space so beautifully decorated!"

"So is that where you gave birth?"

"Yes. I was taken to a private bedchamber where the empress

was waiting. Within a few hours, it was over and my baby was out of my body. Dead."

"I'm so sorry."

Sulum took a moment to reflect. When she spoke again, her voice was full of emotion and she stared blankly ahead. "What seemed like a dream had turned into a nightmare. All I could think about was running away, to get as far away from that room where I had held my limp little girl in my arms. But they wouldn't let me leave."

"Why not?"

"Because Lady Argina had a different plan for me. She knew the empress was going to give birth very soon too, so I was held in the suite for several days until it happened. Normally, Mahkoiyin would have been surrounded by many ladies-in-waiting, but they were kept away, probably with the same excuse that the empress was too contagious. I can't think of any other reason why so few people were in attendance to oversee a royal birth."

"Was Cook there again too?"

"No. She hadn't even stuck around for my own delivery a few days earlier."

"And what about Dad? Didn't he wonder where you had ended up?"

"I assume so. But well in advance of all this, Omi had already been ordered by Lady Argina to deal with your father and stress upon him that there was no need to come and visit me. Instead, he was supposed to continue working in the dewfields, helping your grandfather. The poor man—he was told everything was fine and progressing normally, and that he could expect the baby in a few days. Omi promised to keep him informed, but otherwise, he would not have to play any role in the whole process. Your grandmother always felt guilty about lying to her son, but really, she didn't have any choice either. She was just following instructions like everyone else."

"It must have been so hard for you."

"Incredibly hard. I felt so alone. And to make matters worse, I was given Mahkoiyin's baby to take care of. At first, I couldn't believe what they were asking me to do—it was crazy! The original scheme was for me to pretend that I had given birth to twins, but when my daughter was born dead . . . well, the plan changed. They wanted me to act as if Rayhan—or Jeradon—was my own son. Can you imagine me having to do that right after losing my own child? To nurse a stranger's baby? It was heartbreaking. All I could do was cry and cry."

"But if people were scheming to get rid of Tael's first-born son because he had an exclusive claim to the throne, what made Tael and Mahkoiyin think they could trust you?" Elia asked. "You could've so easily exposed the truth."

"They made it very clear, through Lady Argina of course, how important the child was to the whole monarchy. And I didn't doubt it. But it was the threats Argina made against our family that really forced me to agree to her bidding. And as I said, it wasn't supposed to be for very long. I was to protect the baby until Tael sorted out who his enemies were so he could have them exiled or executed. But then that incident in the gardens happened shortly after, and Mahkoiyin was killed, and Tael was blinded."

"Emperor Tael is not blind," Elia declared. She could have added that Mahkoiyin was not dead either, but for now, she'd keep that information to herself.

"He is. From that first moment when he was attacked."

"No, he's not blind," Elia firmly insisted. "I was in the palace, in his very room, with him standing right in front of me, and I discovered, without a doubt, that he can see."

"That's impossible!" her mother exclaimed.

"It's true. We can go down and ask Lady Argina right now."

"Well, I'm not sure—"

"But what worries me is that I always thought Emperor Tael was the dangerous one in this whole affair."

"You couldn't be more wrong," said her mother. "It's Tohryn

and Faytelle who are the greatest threat. And if Tael can actually see—and I'm not saying that he can—then there must be a good reason why that secret has never been revealed."

"Yes, there must," Elia agreed. She thought for a brief moment. "As for secrets, has my father ever found out the truth about Rayhan?"

Sulum looked crestfallen. "Yes. Many years later. He found out from your grandmother. Omi let it slip one day. I think it was one of the first signs she was losing control of her mind. The consequences were horrendous and it almost destroyed your father. He didn't believe it at first, until he confronted me. Of course, I told him everything. I couldn't possibly hold the secret any longer. And he was devastated."

As if in pain, Elia's mother sighed deeply before continuing. "Not long afterward, when your father couldn't bear to look at Rayhan without thinking about all the lies and about the daughter he had lost so many years earlier, he went crazy. He stormed into the palace one morning, drunk, shouting and cursing. He demanded answers about what had happened, but soon realized how much danger he was putting our family in. He then tried retreating to the dewfields as if nothing had happened. But later that same day, after a city-wide manhunt, Imperial Guards arrived in the farmlands to arrest him. Rayhan and Opi witnessed everything. They said it was awful. I suspect it was under the orders of Emperor Tael, ironically enough, that the guards beat your father to within an inch of his life. They imprisoned him long enough for all of us to know, in no uncertain terms, the dire consequences of breathing the slightest word regarding what had been done to conceal Rayhan."

Sulum wiped a tear as she gazed at Elia. "Your father's brain must have been badly injured, because he was never the same again. For weeks afterward, he struggled. The illness in his mind became worse and worse until he decided to leave us. I know, with my whole heart, that if he were the same man I had married, he would never have abandoned the family he loved. However, he simply couldn't deal with things, and he has lived in the streets ever since."

Without realizing, Elia had been holding her breath at length. Now, as her own tears seeped along the edges of her eyelids, she exhaled long and slow.

Noting her daughter's sadness, Sulum said, "This is why it's so hard to tell you everything. I know it's very upsetting to hear. But I want you to understand that your father has always loved you very much. He still does. And, in a complicated way, he loves Rayhan too, but he can't cope with the sorrow or come to terms with what it all means."

Elia could barely find her voice. "And what about Rayhan? Where is he right now?"

"Greyit is handling that. He promised to take action as soon as you disappeared."

"Greyit's dead."

Shocked, Sulum covered her mouth. "Are you sure?"

"I am. I saw his body. I was going to bury him last night—"

"What do you mean 'bury him'?"

"It doesn't matter. I didn't have time to do it anyway because I had to race back to the city after I figured out who those footprints belonged to on the documents that Lady Argina has been hiding all these years."

"And how did you come to that conclusion?"

"When I tried on these boots," Elia replied, pointing to her feet. "I remembered Rayhan complaining about his own boots not fitting comfortably because of his second toes being so long—the same kind of toes I had seen stamped in ink on that royal document. It suddenly became so clear."

"Impressive. I commend you for being so clever."

Convinced that she should've been able to figure out the truth much sooner, Elia ignored the compliment. "But do you think Greyit delivered on his promise to keep Rayhan safe?"

"As far as I know, yes. The plan was to hide your brother by getting him to start his training as an Imperial Guard much earlier than would normally be the case. It was a smart move, putting Rayhan in a position so close to the monarchy, but where no one would think to look for him."

A thought entered Elia's mind. "Which reminds me, there's another thing you might not have heard. Our house is gone too. The suspension bridge was cut."

Sulum nodded knowingly. "I'm not surprised. Greyit probably saw to that right away, to create the illusion that I had drifted off. To remove any traces that I was still around."

Dani's meek voice suddenly came through from the other side of the locked door. "Lady Argina is inviting both of you to come downstairs and join her."

Elia scowled.

"We're coming," Sulum called back, then shrugged at her daughter's annoyance. "We have to go, I guess."

"Or else what?"

"It's not worth arguing. It won't help matters."

"But I hate that old woman," Elia grumbled. "I swear, I've had enough of her meddling and all the trouble it has caused us."

Sulum sighed. "I know. But our freedom will eventually come, even if we have to hold out a bit longer. At least we're safe. So try to be patient and accommodating."

"I'll try," Elia replied resentfully.

She helped her mother stand before they headed toward the door. Dani was not waiting for them on the other side—she'd gone ahead and had already reached the lower floor. Elia led the way as she and Sulum began descending the spiral staircase. Looking at her feet to avoid tripping, she guided herself with one hand on the metal railing. Yet as she got closer to the bottom, she sensed there were more people in the downstairs room than when she had left.

Ducking her head to look in, she saw Lady Argina by the fireplace, then her eyes darted toward Dani, who was now lingering at the front door.

Beside the timid servant girl stood a group of Imperial Guards.

In a flash, Elia spun on her heel and began shoving her startled mother back up the stairs.

"I knew it! Start climbing! It's all just a trap!"

Chapter 50

"I WAS ONE HUNDRED and forty-six years old when the world, as I knew it, began to fall apart," said Lord Mack, continuing with his story. "By that point in my life, I had already made my fortune. After my parents split up, I promised myself that I would never be poor, so early on, as a teenager, I focused all my efforts on getting the very best education possible."

As he spoke, Lord Mack had been lovingly stroking the leaves of a plant growing beside him, as if the thing were a pet. Now he paused and studied Tasheira.

"The most prestigious, fascinating, and lucrative careers in those days involved anything to do with genetics, so of course, that's what I specialized in. Do you know what I mean by genetics?"

Tash shook her head. "I don't."

"Genetics is the study of hereditary traits. By that I mean the personal characteristics we inherit from our parents, as well as from our relatives who lived generations before us. Essentially, it's what makes you different from me, and what creates such diversity in all the plants in this room. Does that make sense?"

"Yes, I think so," she replied.

"Well, in those days, genetics had become a very powerful

tool, or *technology*, as I explained earlier, and people who studied it learned how to manipulate biological traits for specific, desired results. Things could be modified in exciting ways—new kinds of fruit that grew faster and sweeter, enhanced varieties of grains that could thrive in poor soil or low light conditions, high-protein substitutes for meat that could be produced cheaply. But the changes weren't made just to foods. Modifications were also made to animals, such as chickens that would molt all their feathers at a certain stage in their growth, or sheep that would automatically shed their wool at a set time of year. In some instances, qualities of one animal were combined with a completely different species to create new living things, never before seen. That's what I was involved with. I earned my initial wealth by creating horses that could fly with the feathered wings of a bird."

Tash was amazed by such a suggestion, especially given the herds of stallions bred on her father's estate. "Aren't horses with wings a natural occurrence?"

"Not at all! Not even close!" Lord Mack replied with excitement. "Flying horses were originally designed by me to bring a mythical creature to life. Before I came along, they were just a fantasy. As you can imagine, they were very popular right from the moment they were first introduced, though extremely expensive to engineer. Only the very rich were willing to pay the exorbitant price to have a designer specimen for themselves."

Tasheira's mind struggled to process this information. She was so preoccupied that when the pesky vine poked her neck again, she impulsively reached over her shoulder and snapped off a large piece of its stem.

Lord Mack was not pleased. "I can't have you destroying my plants like this!" he barked. "Each one is the result of many years of meticulous breeding."

Tasheira looked at what she was holding in her hand, then glanced up at him apologetically. "I'm sorry. I wasn't paying attention to what I was doing. I'm still struggling to comprehend everything you've been telling me. The notion of animals being modified to produce something new, well, the concept is . . . it's—"

"Mind-boggling, I know," he said to finish her thought. "Even stranger—and I swear this is true—genetic modifications were performed on humans too."

Tasheira's mouth fell open.

He nodded, appearing pleased to see her reaction. "It was only a matter of time before scientists began investigating ways to improve the deficiencies within the human race, especially when such a need for change became vital for our very survival as the environment became more and more extreme."

"Extreme? In what way?"

"The sun, mostly. Its radiation grew so strong that the original human eye could not cope with such intensity, and those people with pale skin would burn and blister. Genes, therefore, had to be altered to fix the problem. Darker skin, with protective pigments, was one solution. Another was the double set of eyelids that inhabitants of Above now have and take for granted."

"No!" Tash said defiantly, shaking her head. "No, that's impossible! I can't accept it."

"Look at my own eyes," he instructed. "Look carefully." He blinked.

"They're different!" she gasped, covering her mouth.

"I was born before the carefully engineered mutation was introduced into developing babies. And look at the horrible condition of my eyes as a result."

Tash had been wrong to assume his cloudy eyes and poor vision were due to his age. "Your single eyelids actually remind me of Hokk's," she reluctantly admitted.

"Who's Hokk?"

"A young man that I recently brought to the palace to meet Emperors Tael and Tohryn. He said he was from the moon and had traveled all this distance with a special message. As it turned out, he was full of lies. And while my cousin already tried to explain it to me, I'm only now understanding that Hokk must have come from this Earth place you just described."

Lord Mack's expression turned quizzical. "What made you think the man came from the moon? Surely the reason had to be more than just his eyelids."

"He looked different because he was so pale. But what really convinced me was the object I witnessed falling out of the sky."

Tash told Lord Mack about the fiery trails she had seen raining down, as well as the massive piece of charred debris that had formed a crater in the sand on the Isle of Drifting Dunes.

"After finding Hokk burned and suffering in the desert, so close to the crash site, I could only assume he had escaped from the wreckage. His ability to survive the crash made sense because of the strange padded suit we discovered inside the craft."

Tash described the suit, including the glass globe that latched onto the top to create a perfect seal.

"At first, I assumed Hokk's name was Isec because of the badge stitched on the front of his outfit."

"Isec?" the old man repeated with a deep-throated chuckle. "How was it spelled?"

"I-S-E-C."

Lord Mack rumbled with a hearty laugh. "Just as I suspected!" he said, wrapping his arms around his huge belly to stop its jiggling. "I'm sorry. That's not fair. I can understand how easily such a mistake could be made. ISEC is actually an acronym—or the initials—for a much longer name."

"I don't understand."

"ISEC stands for the International Space Explorers Confederation."

She stared at him blankly.

"It was an alliance formed by many of the world's countries to support a new age of exploration in space."

"Space? Countries? I don't have a clue what any of those words mean." Tash had never felt so ignorant.

"Countries were separate groups of people on Earth who lived within specifically drawn borders that distinguished their population and territory from others. Think of them almost like the islands floating in our clouds, each one a distinct nation of people, but all part of the same world."

"And space?"

Lord Mack raised his arms, though his stiff joints seemed to limit how high they could go. "Space is what's above us, including the moon, the stars, and everything *beyond*." He paused to let this concept sink in before continuing. "Based on your description, I suspect what you found in the desert was a section of a damaged space station. Stations like that were typically constructed in the shape of a wheel with a central hub. This spinning structure would have been drifting high above Earth, halfway between here and the shattered moon, for who knows how long, before breaking apart. Then gravity would have caused it to fall out of orbit. That's what you saw streaking across the sky before discovering a remnant of it in the desert."

Tash lowered her head and began rubbing her temples. Did this man have an answer for everything?

At that very moment, she heard a key unlocking the door. She looked over just as it opened and a man entered. He was not Emperor Tohryn, but a male servant carrying a tray of food.

"Ah, Weitin, good timing," said Lord Mack.

As Weitin bowed his head, Tash could see the perspiration that had formed on his forehead from the long climb up. He lowered the tray without letting anything rattle. "I brought more to eat than usual because I understood from Emperor Tael that you have a guest visiting today," he said with a courteous nod at Tasheira.

"That's right," Lord Mack replied, eagerly eyeing the selection.

"And shall I plan to bring an extra serving for dinner as well?"

"Indeed. You should expect to do so until you are instructed otherwise. According to Emperor Tael, Lady Tasheira will be spending some time with me until certain issues are sorted out."

"Very good, My Lord," said Weitin with another bow before he backed out of the room, closing and locking the door behind him.

Through his whiskers, Lord Mack crammed a cheesy puff pastry into his mouth. "My butler," he explained when he noticed Tasheira's bewilderment.

Yet that wasn't the reason she was puzzled. Instead, Tash was startled by the exchange she had just heard between the two men. "I think your butler must have been mistaken."

"Why's that?" the old man asked, taking a large bite out of a meat pie and brushing away the crumbs from his beard.

"Because he mentioned that Emperor *Tael* spoke to him about me being with you. That has to be wrong. I was led to believe that only Tohryn and Weitin have access to this room."

"No, that isn't right. Tohryn *never* comes to visit me. Not since he took the throne as a young man. I'm sure he prefers to think I don't exist."

Tasheira's frustration began to soar. "But Tohryn was the one who brought me up here this morning!" she almost shouted, wondering how the old man could be so mixed up. "You saw him yourself!"

Lord Mack stopped chewing. "That wasn't Tohryn. That was Tael, without a doubt."

Tasheira had to hold herself back from launching out of her seat. "But Tael's completely blind! Don't you get it?"

"What? That's impossible!" Lord Mack exclaimed. Then he quickly shook his head as if he had sorted out what was causing the confusion. "Is he still playing that charade? I thought he gave up trying to fool people a long time ago."

Chapter 51

"STOP! DON'T RUN AWAY!" Rayhan shouted as his sister and his mother charged up the stairs.

He hated to see Elia so fearful, but he understood her impulse to escape—he, Blaitz, and Hokk were still hidden behind their helmets. From her point of view, what else could this be except a trap set by Imperial Guards?

Rayhan and his two companions had left the palace a short while ago to cross the Grand Bridge and enter Na-Lavent. Prior to leaving the Sanctuary, Rayhan had thought the commander would first escort them down into the dungeons to save this Tasheira girl whom Hokk had mentioned; however, Blaitz decided the attempt would have to wait, regardless of her noble status. A more urgent matter required attending to first.

The commander had shared nothing about his plan as they navigated the city's narrow alleyways, but Blaitz seemed to know exactly where he was headed. He even used a secret knock when they stopped in front of a nondescript door. When a demure servant girl opened it, Rayhan was amazed to see the lavish interior, and he knew right away this home belonged to someone of great importance. Still, he didn't recognize the old woman who seemed to be expecting their arrival. Even her title, Lady Argina, meant nothing.

Everything quickly began to make sense, though, as soon as he saw his sister and mother on the spiral staircase. This was obviously a hideout where Elia and Sulum were being kept safe for this eventual reunion—a reunion that was probably very carefully coordinated. Now he just had to convince both of them to come back, to not be afraid.

"Please, Elia! Wait!" Rayhan called out as he bolted toward the staircase, yanking off his helmet along the way.

"Quick!" Elia yelped, continuing to push Sulum. "Climb faster!"

Rayhan reached through the railings and grabbed his sister by the ankle.

Elia tripped and fell hard on the stairs. In a panic, she started kicking furiously at his hand with her free foot. "Don't touch me!"

"Elia, stop!"

"Let go!"

"Look! It's just me! Your brother!"

Elia's yelling and kicking halted.

A few steps higher, his mother looked over the banister. "Rayhan!" she cried out, before stepping past Elia to hurry to the bottom landing.

As Rayhan let go of his sister, she leaned forward and peered cautiously at him through the space between the rails. "Rayhan?"

He nodded. "See? There's no reason to be frightened."

Elia slowly rose, still gazing at him in disbelief. Then she nervously glanced in the direction of the front door, where Blaitz and Hokk were standing. They too had removed their helmets. Elia's eyebrows shot up with surprise, and a joyous smile illuminated her face.

"Hokk!" she exclaimed before racing down the steps.

Sulum reached Rayhan and embraced him tightly. "What

a lucky woman I am, getting the two of you returned to me on the same day!"

Though Rayhan hugged her back with equal enthusiasm, he couldn't help being distracted. Over his mother's shoulder, he watched Elia dart toward Hokk, throwing herself at him with such force that when the young man caught her in his arms, he spun around on his heels.

As Hokk set her down, Elia took his face in both of her hands. "Praise the sun as my witness, I never want to be separated again!"

Then . . . she kissed him! Not a warm peck on the cheek like a friend might offer, but a lingering, much more intimate kiss, fully on his lips.

Hokk was beaming, though he looked startled too—just as startled as Rayhan himself felt.

Rayhan also felt snubbed. Certainly, as her brother, he didn't expect the same passionate welcome, but he deserved to be greeted first! After all, he had taken great personal risk to find her!

Yet it appeared her relationship with Hokk was more meaningful than he would have ever guessed or cared to admit. He didn't like it.

Holding his mother in one arm, he stretched his free hand toward Elia. "What, no greeting for me?"

Almost reluctantly, she broke away from Hokk—their fingertips separating at the last possible moment—and she came toward him. She seemed unable to make eye contact.

As Rayhan hugged her, he sensed an unusual tension in her body. "Am I ever glad to see you," he said *with* earnest.

"Me too," she replied unconvincingly.

"I thought we had lost you forever after I watched you jump from the edge of that bridge."

Elia looked surprised and went even more rigid. But at least this time she actually looked at him. "Were you there?"

"I was the guard you ran into as you fled. I tried to hold

on, but you broke free after smashing your telescope against my helmet."

"I had no idea," Elia said breathlessly, still staring into his eyes. He could read pain and sadness in her expression, making him wonder what she had been through.

"How did you survive the jump from the bridge and end up in the city, of all places?" said Hokk, moving closer. "I flew down to Below, thinking that's where I'd find you."

Elia slipped from Rayhan's grip and reached for Hokk's hand. "Yes, I thought you might," she said.

"Actually, all three of us went down to search for you. I followed on horseback right behind Hokk," Rayhan made a point of stressing. "Later, Commander Blaitz came too."

The commander now stepped forward. "It is a pleasure to finally meet you, Elia. If not for your involvement, everything we've been struggling to protect would have been lost or destroyed."

Elia shot a smug glance directly at Lady Argina before turning back to Blaitz. "And I've been very keen to meet you too." She pointed to the helmet he held at his side. "I recognize that spike sticking out from your helmet. You found me twice before on the plains of Below, did you not?"

"You're right. That was me," he confirmed.

"And if I'm not mistaken either," Sulum added, "I believe we met when I was a much younger woman, in labor, and about to give birth for the first time."

"Yes, that was me then too."

By now, Rayhan's curiosity was stoked, but before he could clarify anything, Lady Argina pushed her way into their midst.

"I'm very pleased we are all finally together," she said, almost sarcastically. "But we aren't out of harm's way just yet. With the dangers that remain, we can't be too careful."

Rayhan had no idea what Argina was referring to. And was he wrong, or did she seem more anxious about stopping them from talking than about any true danger ahead?

"Has the emperor been notified?" the old woman asked.

"Not by me," said Blaitz. "As I'm sure you can guess, I've been sidetracked dealing with other issues, so I haven't had the chance. That's why I wanted to come here first in case you had."

"Unfortunately, no," replied Lady Argina. "I haven't had a safe opportunity to leave my home, nor the inclination to take the risk of requesting an audience."

"But I imagine the emperor at least knows the whole situation is about to culminate very soon. That all the pieces are lining up as planned."

"He must, though until just yesterday, it still looked doubtful whether circumstances would finally shine in his favor."

Rayhan shook his head in confusion. For all the words Blaitz and the old woman had exchanged, they had said little of substance. And though Hokk looked as perplexed as he felt, Rayhan found it frustrating that even his sister and mother seemed to grasp the gist of the conversation.

"Which emperor are you talking about?" he now interjected. "Tohryn or Tael? And what do you mean by these circumstances shining in his favor? What's going on?"

Not surprisingly, Lady Argina was the one to speak up. "All in good time," she said soothingly as she placed her gnarled hand against his chest. "All in good time."

"I want somebody to tell me right now!" Rayhan demanded as he shrank away from the old woman's touch.

"Everything that needs explanation will be shared in due course," she said. "You won't have long to wait. As soon as the emperor can be notified that all is in place, this very unfortunate affair will be over."

Rayhan turned to Elia. "Do you understand any of this?"

She looked up at him with hooded eyes. "I do," she admitted.

A snort from Lady Argina diverted Rayhan's attention for only a second before he focused again on his sister. "If you know, El, you can't leave me out. I have every right to be told the truth, especially if everyone else is already aware."

"I agree," said Elia. "You have more right than anybody here. Because it affects you the most."

Lady Argina spun angrily on her. "That's enough out of you. Not another word."

"I don't have to listen to what you want!" Elia shot back. The level of disdain in her voice was like nothing Rayhan had ever heard coming from her mouth. "For you see, what nobody has figured out, except me, is that everything isn't wrapping up as neatly as you all think."

Argina snorted again, but Commander Blaitz's expression clearly showed he was concerned and prepared to take Elia seriously. "What are we missing?"

"There's still the matter of Empress Mahkoiyin."

"Rest her soul, the poor woman is dead!" Argina hissed, saliva spraying from her lips.

Elia solemnly shook her head. "No. You're wrong. She is very much alive. And I know where to find her."

Chapter 52

WAS NOTHING IN THIS WORLD what it seemed to be? Modified humans . . . horses with no wings . . . space and beyond . . . Emperor Tael's deceitful ways—it all made Tash feel as if every perception of reality she had ever held true could somehow be condemned as false. Was there anything left to believe in?

Lord Mack looked guilty as he nervously cracked his tattooed knuckles. "I've said too much. I thought Tael had shared with you the truth about himself since you both arrived up here together. But I should have known better than to take it for granted."

Tasheira stared down at her clenched hands in her lap. "Was his blindness really just a hoax all these years?"

"Nothing more than an elaborate trick, I'm afraid. One, it seems, that Emperor Tael has been faithfully committed to for a very long time. Too long, in my opinion."

"I can't stop going over it again and again in my head . . ."

"Trust me—the man has never been blind. He did suffer some injuries to his face, but that occurred almost two decades ago when he and Empress Mahkoiyin were attacked on the palace grounds."

Tash looked up again. Lord Mack was referring to an event she had heard discussed many times before. "You're referring to that morning when Scavengers pulled the empress over the island's edge."

"Yes, that's the one. But you're wrong—the ambush had nothing to do with Scavengers." He then inhaled deeply through his nostrils, appearing to brace for another revelation. "Those creatures are . . . make-believe." He paused to gauge the effect. Seeing no visible response from Tasheira, he quickly followed up with, "Monsters like that don't exist. They never did."

"So I've been told," Tash replied grimly, having first heard this fact from Fimal. "But if not Scavengers, what happened? Who was to blame?"

"Hard to say. I'm still not convinced Emperor Tael has told me everything about the events that day in the gardens. At the very least, though, I know the attack was orchestrated by Imperial Guards."

"Really?" Tash gasped. "Were they caught?"

"It proved too difficult. How could anyone know who was really responsible when the guards all look the same, hidden behind their helmets? Complicating matters was their near immunity to the law." Lord Mack stopped and cleared his throat, suddenly concerned once more. "But listen to me. Here I go again, still talking. I don't seem to know when to shut up."

"You needn't worry. Besides, what difference does it make now?" Tash asked. "Even you said it yourself—great benefits can come from sharing the truth. I bet you already feel better for having unburdened yourself."

"I suppose," he admitted with a sigh. "Though I'm also the victim of my own weak tongue, which is much too old and loose to know when enough has been said."

Despite his worries, Tasheira suspected he appreciated their conversation more than he would dare to admit, so she ignored his qualms and pushed further. "Can you please explain why Tael pretended to be blind all these years?"

The man hesitated for a brief moment, perhaps to collect his thoughts, then continued. "At the time, the injuries to the young emperor's face, which included severe bruising and swelling, made it appear his eyes had been damaged. I'm sure his assailants wanted him to lose his vision, in all likelihood to eliminate him as a witness to the attack on his wife. It was a vicious, cowardly assault, and while recovering, Tael had to wear so many bandages over his face that he was forced to function without his sight. He managed well enough, yet he was only able to endure those difficult weeks by plotting the best way to seek justice on his wife's behalf. He was driven—consumed even—to identify the perpetrators, so as soon as the bandages came off, his plan went into effect. Naturally, nobody doubted he was blind after what had happened, and his fake disability only heightened the sympathy he received. But much more importantly—something Emperor Tael has mentioned to me often—he was free to observe things with much greater clarity than when people thought he could see."

"I can't imagine undertaking something that would demand such strict discipline every second of my day-to-day life."

"Nor can I. However, from the very start, Tael noticed how differently everyone acted around him when they thought he couldn't see, which revealed their true nature. He learned quickly who was genuine. Who he could really trust."

Tasheira was suddenly struck with the memory of her lengthy interrogation with the Twin Emperors after Elia's alleged assassination attempt. When it was just Emperor Tael with her, before his brother arrived, Tash had been impressed when she thought he could sense the Imperial Guard still standing in the room rather than leaving as ordered. Yet Tael had observed the guard's trickery with his very own eyes, ultimately creating the impression that he had sublime, otherworldly powers of perception.

But what about her own behavior that morning? Tash suddenly felt embarrassed—while tied to that chair, she had rolled her eyes and grimaced, and probably displayed all sorts of incriminating gestures as she struggled to come up with convincing lies against the emperor's barrage of questions. How strange and unsettling to think he had observed everything and had been able to precisely read her body language. If only she had known the truth. She would have acted so much differently.

Surely that was why the emperor kept up the scam. Tasheira could also well imagine the upset and outrage that would ripple throughout the court if the truth were exposed.

Which made Tash now wonder how Elia fit into the bigger scheme of things. Did she know all along about the emperor's ability to see? Since arriving at the Sanctuary, Elia had been afraid of someone who could do her harm, so any threat of her exposing Tael's lies would explain why Imperial Guards had pursued her onto the bridge.

But who else might know the truth?

"What about his brother?" Tasheira asked. "Is Tohryn aware of Tael's deceit?"

"Oh no! He's the last person Tael would want to find out."

"Why?"

"Enough! Enough!" Lord Mack exclaimed, waving his hands. "I'm not going to say anything more, except that it relates to confidential family matters." Then, as if to contradict this oath of privacy, he added, "Supposedly there are secrets that could quite possibly implicate Tohryn, or even Faytelle, in the attack in the gardens. Yet, after all these years, any connection remains unsubstantiated." The old man went rigid, catching himself again. "But that's it! That's all I'll say on the subject!"

Now more curious than ever, Tasheira leaned forward to select a slice of melon from the tray Weitin had brought up for them. Taking a large bite and chewing thoughtfully, she wondered how she could change her angle of inquiry to squeeze just a little bit more information out of the man. "Is it all right, then, if I back up a bit and ask more generally about your relationship with the Twin Emperors? How do you know them, and how did you come to reside up here in this tower?"

Apparently, these questions were acceptable. "Tael and Tohryn are sixteenth-generation great-grandsons to me."

Tasheira almost choked on the second bite of melon she had just taken. "B-but that could only mean . . ." she sputtered, wiping her lips and forcing herself to swallow. "That would make you a member of the Royal Family!"

"Yes, that's right. I'm actually the *founding* member."

Chapter 53

HOKK COULD TELL THAT Elia was pleased with the stunned reaction she had received after her announcement about the empress.

"Of course, I had no idea it was Mahkoiyin when we first met," Elia explained. "I searched her out, high up on a mountain of Below, for the sole reason that she was the only other person who had ever survived a fall from Above. But it was definitely her. Hokk can back me up."

"Yes, I met her face to face. Mahkoiyin is alive," Hokk confirmed with a vigorous nod, hoping to distract anyone who might detect the slightest hint of guilt revealed by his flushed cheeks. He couldn't deny the wickedness of letting go of the woman's hands while she had been dangling over the river, and the whole incident continued to weigh on his conscience. "Elia and I were only able to verify her true identity when we saw a portrait of Mahkoiyin at Baron Shoad's estate."

"And where is she now?" asked Blaitz.

"Still stuck in Below," Hokk replied. "A very regrettable mishap separated us from the empress when we were under attack. There was nothing we could do to prevent it. Otherwise, she would have escaped with us to Above, which was our plan from the very beginning."

Lying was such an easy solution for everything—a familiar crutch he depended on far too often. It bothered him, though, when he had to dodge the truth with Elia. And he knew his remorse for telling her lies would only worsen now that she had openly shown her genuine feelings for him.

That kiss! Hokk was still rattled by it, but in a good way this time, not with the flustered unease he had felt when Tasheira forced an awkward kiss upon him in the palace. Elia's tender touch thrilled him in new ways he wanted to experience again.

"Unfortunately, we had to leave Mahkoiyin behind," Elia continued, her words pulling Hokk from his whirring thoughts. "But Hokk and I made the commitment to return and save her as soon as we could."

"Once we had the necessary reinforcements to pull it off," Hokk quickly clarified. He turned to the commander. "So can a rescue mission be organized?"

"I'm still grappling with the idea that she's alive," Blaitz declared, shaking his head. "But yes, of course, we must coordinate a search party immediately. Are the two of you able to lead a group of us down to the spot where we'll find her?"

"Absolutely," Elia replied. "And if we all go together—"

"No, no, no! I can't let that happen," stormed the old woman who had been introduced to Hokk as Lady Argina. "I'm certain it will be much too dangerous."

"We can't simply abandon her down there!" Elia shot back.

"If you're so confident of her whereabouts, then by all means, leave on your own to go looking down in Below," said Argina. "In the meantime, the rest of us will be dealing with other urgent matters."

"Down to Below?" gasped a fretful, middle-aged woman, who Hokk assumed to be Elia's mother. "You can't possibly be considering a plan like that!"

"Elia will not be going on her own," Hokk announced firmly. "I will *not* be separated from her again!"

His words made Elia smile.

"And I make the same commitment," Rayhan quickly added.

Hokk noticed Elia's smile wither and die.

Lady Argina wore a similarly dour expression, apparently more concerned than ever now that Elia's brother intended to leave too. "I can't allow you to do such a foolhardy thing." She then addressed Blaitz. "Surely, you agree with me. We can't afford to take the chance."

Elia spoke up before the commander could respond. "Of anybody, Rayhan should be the one to rescue the empress. After all—"

"I forbid it!" Argina shouted, spinning on Elia and pointing a deformed finger at her face. "Shut up."

"Lady Argina, do not speak to my sister that way," Rayhan growled. "And you have no control over what choice I make. My decision is final. I'm going with Elia. I mean, let's be reasonable—the life of an empress is at stake!"

Argina seemed confounded by Rayhan's stern gaze. Mouth open and speechless, she reluctantly backed down. "As you please," she murmured, respectfully bowing her head. She turned and glanced up at the commander, and when she spoke, there was ice in her voice. "Then I insist you accompany them."

"There's no reason why our rescue attempt has to be dangerous," said Elia. "On horseback, we can easily dip beneath the clouds—"

"Oh, Elia, I *really* don't like the sound of that!" her mother said anxiously, wringing her hands.

Ignoring her, Elia continued. "We can fly at a safe altitude over the terrain until we come to the Torkinian Mountain Range. That's where we'll find Mahkoiyin. I bet it won't take us very long."

"I'm afraid it might not be as easy as you suggest," said Hokk, wishing he didn't have to contradict her. "Of course, it would be ideal if we could descend below the cloud cover and find ourselves close to Torkin territory. But as we've just discovered very recently," he said, indicating Blaitz and Rayhan, "we might find a completely different landscape beneath us, with no idea which direction to go in next."

"But you always knew your way across the grasslands," said Elia. "It's a natural gift of yours."

"It's not that simple. When we saw you jump from the bridge, we flew straight down after you, but there were no prairies in sight. No mountains either. Only a huge mass of garbage floating on a vast ocean. I had never seen or heard of such a thing. And that time when Tasheira's cousin followed me down, there was ice everywhere. The climate was so extreme, if we encountered it again, we wouldn't be able to stay long enough to properly redirect our search efforts."

"Oh," Elia replied with dismay. "So you're saying the Torkin villages will be difficult to find."

"Or near impossible. Who knows what kind of hostile environment we'll end up in? We've already encountered earth, water, and ice. What's next? Fire?"

"Then that settles it," Lady Argina declared with a smirk. "Making any sort of attempt is pointless, which is what I've been trying to tell you from the start. It's a fine, noble idea to want to save this person whom you *allege* to be the empress, but *clearly* it's a futile mission."

"No! I can't accept that," Elia decided. "Commander, there must be a way."

"I'm sorry, Elia. I'm at a loss for suggestions, but I would be committed and willing to do whatever is necessary," Blaitz assured her.

"Good. Because to find Mahkoiyin, all we need are the coordinates of the general location to begin looking. And there's only one person capable of making those sorts of calculations. I'm sure you can arrange access. You have to bring us to the Drift Master."

Chapter 54

LORD MACK . . . THE FOUNDING *member of the Royal Family?*

Wide-eyed, Tash slowly lowered her hand, which was still clutching the half-eaten slice of melon. Without shifting her gaze, she studied him and considered yet again whether or not he was suffering from dementia. He had said he was well over three hundred and fifty years old, so greater confusion was bound to be natural for somebody of such advanced years—not that anything about living that long could be considered *natural.*

"I can see you don't believe me," the old man concluded, sounding just as coherent as he had all along. "But it's true. Our family's long reign, which has brought us to this point with Tael and Tohryn in power, all started with me."

Tasheira had never heard of the Royal Family's origins. She knew the history only as far back as the portraits that lined the corridor outside her father's library. If her memory was correct, the paintings spanned thirteen generations of royal rulers and their spouses, which meant they did not go far enough into the past to the very beginning of the monarchy. But obviously, somebody had to be the first. Could Lord Mack really have been the one?

"This very islet, where we are now, was christened with my family name," the man continued to explain. "I am Mackenzie Noble and this island is the Noble Sanctuary. *My sanctuary.* And control over it has been passed down through the line of my descendants. I know with great certainty, however, that neither of the Twin Emperors, nor the Empress Mother, nor many of the other rulers before them ever knew the true source of this islet's name."

"People would have just thought it referred to the nobility who lived here."

"Exactly. And in many ways, that was a good thing."

"And the palace. Was that built by you too?"

"Yes, financed by me alone. As I mentioned already, my wealth was immense—practically unlimited—all thanks to my hugely successful foray into genetic engineering. I started to construct these mirrored towers as a retreat, after the Earth and moon drifted closer together. I had finally accepted the fact that environmental conditions down in Below had deteriorated past a tipping point from which there seemed no hope of turning back. It was a very challenging feat, let me tell you, to assemble all the building supplies and transport them up to this floating island. Yet nothing could stop me. It took years and years to build my vision, inspired by great architecture from the past, but eventually, I was firmly established up here in my refuge. By that time, the sun was completely blocked out by the choking, polluted clouds in the sky, and a fifth black plague was running rampant through Below's population."

"I don't understand. There are so many people who live on the islands of the Lunera System; surely, we are not all related to you."

"No, of course not. The overall number has grown with time, and people have migrated to other islands. However, this island was the first one to be populated. I had no problem convincing like-minded people to join me. Though not as prosperous as me, they were plenty rich themselves to pay the fee to live as my courtiers. I fondly called them my disciples. Such a pity the name never stuck."

"And what about the others, who probably didn't have very much money?"

"They weren't allowed to come. We only included those people already employed as our staff, as well as all the tradespeople we knew we'd need to develop our own society. They simply accompanied us when we left Below for good. Really, they were blessed to have the opportunity. Thousands and thousands, if not many millions, would have killed to be in their place, serving my needs and those of my disciples."

The man's emerging arrogance made Tasheira cringe, but she tried not to let it show. "Why do you say many would have wanted the same opportunity?"

"Disease was so widespread, people were dropping dead everywhere. Especially the poor, who, I must say, really had it coming to them considering their filthy way of life."

Again Tash flinched. It was this kind of thinking that left all those lost souls alone and forgotten in the palace's dungeon.

Lord Mack carried on, unmindful of her disapproval. "Not surprisingly, the fifth outbreak of the plague was traced to those people in their slums, just like all the deadly epidemics in the past. However, once I left Below, along with those who shared my vision, it was a permanent exodus. We were creating a new world for ourselves, and there was nothing to tempt us to return to that misery. We cut all ties and made sure no one would ever attempt to go back to Below."

"Did that really warrant twisting our history beyond anything resembling the truth?" Tash challenged.

"It was all very well-intended, I assure you. We couldn't risk people coming and going and carrying disease up here with them. It would have jeopardized everything I had set out to do."

"But as I see it, you created and perpetuated lies to keep everyone living in fear. Take Scavengers, for example. How could the notion of those creatures ever be justified as necessary?"

"Yes, that's an excellent example. I came up with the concept myself," Lord Mack said proudly, as if he had no clue about the point she was trying to get across. "It took only two generations of reinforcing the idea to make it stick, and it worked beautifully. It kept people safe."

"It kept people *afraid.* Myself included!"

"Better to keep everyone away from the island's edges and eliminate their curiosity than to let them explore and learn what was beneath the clouds. Our isolation up here was paramount. It was the only way I could create a society that functioned perfectly, remained self-sufficient, and stayed relatively free of disease. A simpler, more *noble* way of living. And I regret nothing. Think of all the lives I was actually able to protect. Can I really be faulted for that?"

Tash didn't know how to counter his perverted logic, and it made her angrier. Still, she had to say something. "Where did such a concept of monsters even come from?"

Lord Mack pushed up his sleeve to expose his whole arm. As Tash had suspected, a complex collage of multicolored tattoos covered the entire surface of his skin. From where she was seated, she found it difficult to see any one image that stood out from the rest.

The man pointed to a spot on his arm where his biceps used to be, but where sagging flesh now hung from the bone. "This tattoo was the inspiration for Scavengers. Come closer so you can see."

Stepping forward, Tash leaned over to look at it. As the old man stretched his loose skin to make it as taut as possible, she could see the image was surrounded by a random assortment of other pictures: roses, a skull, a pair of serpents. But her eyes focused on the figure he was pointing to in the middle. A monster from her nightmares.

The creature tattooed on his arm was almost identical to what she had always imagined a Scavenger to look like. It was pale, with claws, a curved spine, no eyes, a massive forehead above two holes for nostrils, and a gaping mouth with white lips pulled tight over toothless gums. "It's awful," she said, pulling away.

"Definitely not one of the prettiest of my collection," Lord Mack admitted with a nod as she sat down again. "But I was very young when I got most of these and, at the time, this particular tattoo meant something to me—only wish I could remember what." He pulled down his sleeve. "As for the name Scavenger, it was a term coined during the black plague, and it seemed very fitting to use again. Scavengers were real-life people of Below who were tasked with removing the dead bodies and disposing of them in mass graves to combat the spread of disease. So it wasn't much of a stretch to adopt the same name for the monsters I invented."

Tash nodded thoughtfully, certain that she was on the verge of understanding the whole picture. "It's all starting to come together, but I've got one more question for you."

"I'm listening," said Lord Mack, combing his beard with his fingers.

"It's still not clear why you live at the top of this tower. Why seclude yourself if you're the founding father? I would have assumed you'd still want to bask in the glory."

As soon as the words left her mouth, it suddenly became clear to Tasheira why the man had divulged so much information—he needed praise for his extraordinary accomplishments. His desire was probably so all-consuming, it outweighed any threat of punishment for opening up with the truth.

"It's a fair question," said Lord Mack. "As I mentioned, my society was perfect—I designed it that way—and for many, many decades, it flourished. But in time, one flaw in the system stood out . . . me! You see, I was completely obsessed with the possibility of cheating death. Losing my sister when I was a child was devastating, and as an adult, I devoted all of my time to finding a way of avoiding the same fate . . . or at least delaying it as long as possible. And my studies in genetics provided me with the perfect starting point. Of course, as my discoveries were still in their infancy, I chose myself to be the prime test subject for each experiment. Soon, I had slowed my own dying process to a near standstill."

"Just yours?"

"Yes, just mine. And since I was the only one with that advantage, in the long run, it became a liability. People in high positions at court, pursuing their own expansion of power, could not accept being denied equal longevity. However, I had no intention of sharing my discoveries to let others have almost endless lives. What a monstrous world that would be! But I couldn't let my dream crumble. I had already abdicated my so-called throne to my first grandchild, the daughter of my eldest son, who had already died of old age. In counsel with her, it was decided I should step away from court life and let any memory of me fade. She became the figurehead, while behind the scenes, I still maintained control. I enjoyed that arrangement for nearly another century, acting through whichever one of my descendants was the current face of the monarchy. But eventually, I lost all interest in political wrangling and scandals and power struggles. So I focused my attention and expertise on my plants and on solitary reflection. And as I said, I have no regrets about—"

He stopped himself to listen to a faint noise coming from the door. With the sound of rattling keys came the same guilty look on the old man's face that Tash had seen earlier.

The door swung open, and an Imperial Guard stepped inside. Since only Lord Mack's butler and Tael were supposed to have keys to the room, Tasheira assumed it had to be the emperor.

Except why was he choosing to conceal his identity when they'd know who it was?

Because Fimal entered the room right behind him.

Tash leapt to her feet and ran toward her cousin, trying to avoid Mack's precious plants along the way. "Praise the sun!" she exclaimed as she embraced him, his shirt damp with sweat from climbing so many stairs.

Fimal squeezed her back just as hard. "What a relief to be out."

Tasheira turned to the guard. "Thank you," she said, deciding not to reveal that it was Tael hidden beneath his disguise.

The man nodded, saying nothing.

"And we look forward to finally being reunited with the Baron," she added.

Once more, just a nod, before the guard turned and left them.

Taking Fimal by the elbow, Tash led him toward the sofa where the old man was still sitting. "Lord Mack, this is my cousin Fimal," she said. "As far as I know, he's the only citizen of Above who's ever been to Below."

She felt Fimal stiffen as if she had spilled a secret he didn't want known.

"It's all right," she assured him, pulling a chair forward from where it was partially hidden under the canopy of a huge plant, and offering him the seat. "You're joining us at the best possible time. If Lord Mack is willing—and I'm sure he is—you're going to love hearing everything that he really must tell you."

Chapter 55

IT WAS MIDDAY, AND the four of them strode in unison, single file, just as any observer in the streets would have expected to see Imperial Guards marching. Yet they moved through the city at a hurried pace. Commander Blaitz took the lead, followed by Rayhan, Elia, and Hokk bringing up the rear.

Elia kept checking over her shoulder as if afraid that Hokk might vanish or be stolen away. True, her fears were unfounded, but nonetheless, she wished the two of them could be walking side by side. Someday soon, she hoped it could be hand in hand. Inside her mirrored helmet, she felt flushed every time her mind drifted back to Hokk pledging not to let anything separate them again. And she was so pleased with herself for being brave enough to kiss him! Any other time, she would have been too shy to even consider it. But the opportunity had been perfect, and she was proud she hadn't let it slip away.

They reached the end of the cobblestone road and the view opened up to the Grand Bridge arching above the clouds. Traveling with Blaitz, they met no resistance at the patrolled gates, and they passed straight through to start crossing.

Knowing she still owed Hokk an explanation, Elia took the chance now to describe to him how she had survived jumping from the bridge by landing on the shelf of rock obscured by the clouds.

"And you knew the ledge would be there to stop your fall?" he asked.

"I was lucky."

This made Hokk wince, as if he was imagining what could have happened otherwise.

They stopped talking as they entered the Mirrored Palace. Passing courtiers and servants, they followed Blaitz deeper into the building. Then, while walking along one of the corridors, Elia had a sudden thought—she had often heard mention of the Drift Master, yet she had no idea where to find him, or any clue what he might look like. Did he have a workspace in one of the Twin Emperors' towers?

Apparently not. Blaitz turned past the banquet hall and proceeded in the direction of another exit.

The stables?

Yes, strangely, that was exactly where they were headed.

However, instead of visiting the lower level of the sprawling compound, the commander chose to take them to the second floor, which could only be accessed by a set of stairs around the back.

At the top of the steps, they came to a recessed door. An Imperial Guard stood out front. Again, they received no opposition as Blaitz barreled past and pushed the door open.

On stepping inside, Elia couldn't believe the size of the space. While the level below was compartmentalized to accommodate supplies, feed, and the hundreds of thoroughbreds belonging to the Royal Family and members of the court, up here, it was completely open, like a massive atrium to rival the palace's main reception hall. The ceiling of the Drift Master's workplace was a span of glass, supported by four delicate-looking metal arches that curved up from each corner of the room. Sunshine streamed through, creating countless points of twinkling lights on the floor, like stars in the night sky. Focusing more closely,

Elia realized the sunlight was reflecting off fine grains of sand that had been spread in a thick layer to cover almost the entire area, leaving only a narrow bare perimeter to walk around.

Near the middle of the room, two men were kneeling, studying something in the sand. Each held what appeared to be a long, slender pole, which reminded Elia of the ones Shifters used to push islands away whenever they drifted too close and were at risk of colliding.

The men were concentrating so hard that the arrival of Blaitz and his band of Imperial Guard imposters went unnoticed until the commander spoke up. "A word with our most gifted Drift Master!" Blaitz called out, his voice echoing as he summoned them over with a wave.

One of them raised his arm in greeting, still clenching his pole. Together, the men began to carefully move forward as if afraid to disturb anything or leave too many footprints. They looked almost like two giants, trekking across a miniature recreation of the desert on the Isle of Drifting Dunes. At one point, they stepped over a flat, polished stone, and Elia noticed quite a few rocks just like it scattered about the sand's surface. Then she suddenly understood—the men were walking over a map of the Lunera System!

"I'm sorry to disturb you again," said Blaitz, removing his helmet as they finally drew near.

The older of the two responded with a broad smile. "Not at all. I'm pleased to see you have returned safely from whatever mission pulled you away the other day."

"And now I'm hoping you can help once more, with something of far greater urgency."

The man's expression grew concerned. "Are you aware of an impending collision? Has something been missed with my calculations?" he asked, clearly alarmed.

He must be the Drift Master, Elia decided. His head was practically bald, expect for a blond, frizzy halo that circled above his ears and a patch of hair that sprouted precariously at the front of his head, like a small island of wispy strands drifting across the dark skin of his scalp. His face and body were lean, and he wore two pairs of glasses—one with large circular lenses pushed up close to his eyes, and a smaller set, with narrow, rectangular frames that balanced on the tip of his sharp nose.

"No, it's nothing like that," Blaitz assured him. "We've come to see if you can provide some special coordinates."

The Drift Master proudly bowed his head. "That's why I'm here. What do you need?"

"I'm not the best person to explain. Rather, I'll leave it to one of my companions to tell you." The commander turned toward Elia. "It's safe now to show your face. In fact, you're all welcome to do so," he added.

Elia removed her helmet first, glad to be rid of it. Hokk and Rayhan then followed her lead.

The Drift Master seemed surprised by their youthful appearance and the discovery that one of them was female. He studied each person in turn, but his curious gaze rested on Elia.

She would not let his intense scrutiny bother her. "We're hoping you can tell us the coordinates of this island we're standing on."

Perplexed, the Drift Master's eyebrows moved together until they were almost touching. "You mean the Noble Sanctuary?"

"That's correct," she continued. "But not where it is situated now. We need to know where it was located a few weeks ago."

"A few weeks ago?" he repeated with a start, jerking his head back, which fluttered the island of hair above his brow.

"Is it possible?"

Leaning against his pole as if it were a walking stick, the man pondered her question. "I've never been asked before to calculate a position in the past, but I suppose there's no reason why not. Between my apprentice and me, I'm quite certain we can determine coordinates that will be reasonably accurate. Though I can't imagine how it will prove to be of any use."

"I assure you, it will help immensely."

"Fine," said the Drift Master, appearing ready to take on the challenge. "What point in time were you hoping to go back to?"

"I need to know where we were positioned when those recent earthquakes hit the islands. When everything shook so violently that the ground beneath our feet threatened to crumble away."

Chapter 56

WHEN IT CAME TO the mind-boggling vastness of Below, Hokk had been wondering how Elia would pinpoint the site of the Torkin villages, but now he understood her reasoning. And he was impressed. She obviously needed to know where Kamanman and the Noble Sanctuary were at the time of the earthquakes because that was when the lower tips of the islands had gouged through the grasslands of Below. And while the two huge scars on the prairies were still quite far from Torkin territory, traveling to that mountainous region would not be an insurmountable task. Hokk could easily lead the way if necessary. Soaring above the terrain on horseback would make the distance much more manageable than covering it by foot or gazelk; however, finding the right place to start would never have been possible without Elia's solution to zero in on the right spot to descend through the endless blanket of clouds.

Fortunately, the Drift Master seemed keen to help. "Your coordinates are actually going to be easier to provide than I would have first guessed," he said, pushing the larger of the two pairs of spectacles farther up the bridge of his nose. "Under normal circumstances, if someone asked me about a location at a specific time point *in the past,* my calculations would be extremely difficult to determine working backward. My analysis never happens in reverse. However, the event you're referring to relates to something that has always been an anomaly in the System." With his free hand, he beckoned with a flourish of his fingers. "If you will all please follow me, I can show you what I mean on this map."

The man turned and took a step back onto the layer of sand covering the floor.

At the same moment, compelled to share a thought burning inside him, Hokk leaned closer to Elia. "I have to say, I really admire you," he whispered. "It was such a smart decision to come here. You should be very proud of yourself."

Elia bowed her head modestly, but he was pleased to see a shy smile creep across her face, as well as a sudden flush in her cheeks, which deepened the shade of her already-dark skin.

Ahead of them, the Drift Master started to call back instructions. "Everyone, watch where you walk. Try to step in the footprints of the person in front of you to avoid disturbing the sand too much."

The man's apprentice walked directly behind him to set the example, then the rest of them stepped in line as well, one by one, with Hokk in the last position, trailing Elia.

Now with his helmet off, he had to shield his eyes from the afternoon sun shining through the large panels of glass above. Thankfully, the rays seemed weaker than in the past, almost as if the transparent ceiling was capable of filtering out some of the light's harshness. What he hadn't noticed earlier, however, were the small glass globes suspended from the ceiling, hanging at the ends of nearly imperceptible wires. There seemed to be no pattern to their arrangement—they dangled at various heights high above the floor, grouped in all sorts of inexplicable combinations. He would have guessed them to be bulbs like the ones he had seen in Ago, used to light the Board's courtroom, but these objects overhead appeared to be completely empty.

Dropping his gaze, Hokk watched his stumpy shadow follow the five others ahead of him, each silhouette clinging to its owner's feet as the group crossed the enormous room. Along the way, he became intrigued by the many rounded stones he saw scattered about. Some were large, like a serving tray—others not much bigger than a small teacup. He could only assume each rock corresponded to a particular island of Above. He could also see lines drawn in the sand, which likely represented the direction of air currents.

As if to confirm this, the Drift Master paused to consult with his apprentice, then he repositioned a stone and sketched new swirling lines around it with his pole before moving on. "To reflect changes in my predictions about future drift patterns," the man explained.

When they reached a point near the middle of the gigantic sand bed, the Drift Master halted. The train of people behind him stopped too. Using his pole, he pointed to a distant spot. "Perhaps from here, you can distinguish them. Look far over there, toward that corner of the room. Do you see those two boulders placed next to each other—a large one and a smaller one beside it? Those reflect the current position of Kamanman and the Noble Sanctuary at this very moment. And over here . . ." he added, taking several more steps forward, then swinging around and pointing to the ground beside his feet. "This is where the islands were located when the earthquakes occurred."

Hokk frowned as he looked back at where the islands were now, trying to judge what this would mean for the distance they'd need to travel. Considering the expanse of clouds signified by the sand, they likely had a long trip ahead of them.

"What's most interesting to note is the shape of the lines I've already drawn here," said the Drift Master. "Notice how they circle around and around a central point?"

It was true—like a whirlpool, the tracks in the sand formed a wide spiral.

"For some reason, this vortex in the clouds is always present somewhere on this map. Sometimes it grows, sometimes it shrinks, but it never completely disappears. That's why I consider it an anomaly. Islands that get caught up in it often rotate for several days before they emerge, though others pass straight through, depending on their momentum and the angle at which they hit it. And while the air currents are always changing elsewhere in the System, this spiral formation shifts quite slowly over time. When it moves, it does so independently of anything else around it. At the time of the earthquakes, I recall our two islands were caught in this spiral pattern."

Hokk remembered being on the plains of Below and watching Elia's islands circling overhead for at least two days instead of floating out toward the horizon as they normally would have done. What he had seen exactly matched what the Drift Master was describing.

"But if the vortex shifts, even by only a modest degree, are you sure this is exactly where the earthquakes occurred?" Elia wondered.

"*Exactly*? No, I'm afraid not. But it's my best estimate and as close as you're going to get. And really, given the scope of this map," he said, turning with his arms held wide, "you have to agree that asking for any better is not a fair request. What I don't understand, though, is what caused the earthquakes in the first place. There were no other islands in the vicinity that could have led to a collision."

Hokk noticed Elia glance back with concern in the direction where the Sanctuary and Kamanman were currently drifting. "Do you think we can fly the distance?" she asked Commander Blaitz.

"Fly there?" the Drift Master exclaimed. "Why would you want to? Not a single island is close to that spot at the moment."

"But if we did want to get to that particular location, is it possible?" asked Blaitz.

The Drift Master combed his fingers through the small tuft of blond hair at the front of his shiny scalp. "Well, yes, of course.

With the right coordinates, anything is possible. And seeing that you, Commander, already know how to use the necessary instruments for navigation, it's definitely doable. But even so—" He cut himself off as he surveyed the route they'd have to take. Then he pointed to a single stone about a hundred feet away. "It will take you a full day of flying just to reach that island right there to rest and rehydrate your horses. After that, the last leg of your trip will require another eight to ten hours of flying. Then there's the return trip to add on. How many of you will be traveling?"

"I'm assuming the four of us," the commander replied, looking back at the rest of them. "Though we'll need at least one extra horse saddled up for when we come back. My worry now is whether or not we can supply enough animals for the expedition without drawing attention to our absence or raising questions about why we are leaving." He then spun toward the Drift Master. "But I must stress to both you and your apprentice that nothing about our plans can be shared with anyone. That is a very strict order. You can't disclose any details concerning where we plan to go, when we might be back, or that we were even here to visit you in the first place."

The Drift Master seemed unfazed by the commander's demands. "I understand completely. Nothing will be said, I assure you."

"Good, because we can't let our tactical advantage in this situation be jeopardized."

"And when are you aiming to leave?"

"As soon as possible."

"Of course," said the Drift Master, bobbing his head in agreement. "I suggest, however, that you wait until at least this evening's twilight when enough stars will be visible to guide your travels." He lifted his gaze toward the ceiling. "But right now, I'll start writing down the coordinates for where you'll be heading, as well as the constellations you must follow. It should be easy enough. In the meantime, if each of you could please return to the side of the room, my apprentice and I can start working."

Everyone did an about-face, now with Hokk as their leader. They retraced their steps to where they had first entered, and from there watched the two men, instructor and student, begin their calculations.

The apprentice walked several paces away from the Drift Master. He held his own pole straight up into the air. Raising some sort of instrument to his eyes, the Drift Master peered through it in the direction of his assistant. After adjusting several dials and a few metal arms that angled off from the device, the Drift Master lowered it, took out a notebook from his breast pocket, and wrote something on the page. Then he moved to the same spot where his apprentice had been standing, while the young man shifted closer to where the rocks of Kamanman and the Sanctuary were positioned in the sand. Again, they repeated the process, then another time after that.

"It's very puzzling," said Hokk. "I can't figure out what they're doing."

"They must be mapping out the route," Elia suggested.

"Yes, but how? Why do they keep pointing their poles up toward the ceiling? What are they measuring against?"

"The constellations," replied Blaitz, standing on the other side of Elia.

This meant nothing to Hokk. "I don't understand."

"The word *constellation* refers to how the stars are grouped in the night sky," the commander explained. "You can form distinct shapes if you connect the lines between specific points of light . . . provided you know what to look for."

"So how does the Drift Master use the stars to navigate?" Rayhan wondered.

"It's all based on their set position," Blaitz responded.

Rayhan tilted his head skeptically. "How? I thought the stars were always moving."

"Yes, they're in constant motion across the sky," said the

commander. "But stars are in the same place relative to each other at all times. So when you know where to find them, you can always find your way in relation to them—except I understand the Drift Master has to account for other factors that affect the results, such as the System's rotation." The commander sighed as he then scanned the sand bed. "But what still has me concerned is the distance our horses will have to fly. I hope you're all up for it."

"I am," Rayhan replied. "How about you, El? I know how terrified you've been in the past about the idea of flying."

Hokk could see Elia's instant irritation. "Why would you say that?" she asked.

"Because of that time our home was being towed back to the mainland, that day after the property broke away from the edge of the forest and drifted off during the night. You know what I'm talking about. I was riding on horseback the whole time, and I invited you up to ride too. But you refused to join us. I can't say I was surprised, really, that you wouldn't get into a saddle. You're always so scared of everything."

"I can't believe you just said that," Elia said through gritted teeth, avoiding eye contact with her brother.

"So what about today?" Rayhan added, not picking up on Elia's growing animosity, which seemed so obvious to Hokk. "Are you going to be so scared tonight to ride a horse that we'll be forced to leave you behind?"

"Shut up!" Elia spat back. "I hate you. You don't have the slightest idea about anything. Certainly not what I am capable of!"

Chapter 57

ONLY NOW DID RAYHAN realize he had gone too far with his sister. He should've known better. Like a fool, he had made the situation uncomfortable for everyone, including Blaitz and Hokk.

"I'm sorry, El," Rayhan offered. "I really am. I can only imagine what you've been through. Clearly, you're a different, much stronger person than the sister I remember from even a few weeks ago."

Elia sighed as if considering forgiveness, yet she still seemed unwilling to look at him. After the things he had just said, he could understand why, but for some reason, she had been acting this way since leaving Lady Argina's place. What was her problem?

The awkward silence that settled over them was broken a moment later by Blaitz. "Twilight will be coming soon enough. I should leave now so I can figure out how to assemble the horses we'll be needing."

"Actually, Commander, if I could mention something quickly before you go," said Hokk. "I have an idea that might make things easier."

Blaitz looked intrigued. "I welcome any suggestion."

"It's about Baron Shoad. I'm wondering whether he's still at the Sanctuary."

"I'm not sure. It would be easy enough to find out, though. Why?"

"We flew from his estate with a large team of stallions, most of which he sold upon our arrival. However, he had quite a few other horses that I believe were supposed to be flying back with him and his staff once his visit was over. Perhaps if he's still here, we can use his horses to fly to Below. If Tasheira wasn't stuck in the dungeon, we could have gotten her to ask him for us . . . but maybe it's not even an option if you don't consider the Baron trustworthy enough. He just seemed to be a very generous, accommodating, and respectable man, so I thought it could work."

"Interesting," Blaitz murmured as he considered Hokk's suggestion. "Yes, it's worth a shot. I'll see if he's around, then assess what the chances are for coordinating something with him. Otherwise, I'll just have to take horses from the Imperial Guards' reserve." He glanced out across the bed of sand at the other two men standing out there. "Now listen everyone, if the Drift Master asks any of you where I have gone, simply tell him I'll be back soon."

"Of course," said Rayhan. "And in the meantime, what shall we do?"

"You should all just stay up here until I return." Blaitz took a step to leave, then paused and turned back. "Remember, share nothing, not even if the Drift Master has questions that sound innocent. And remain watchful. If you see anything that doesn't seem quite right, let me know."

"Absolutely," Rayhan replied on behalf of the others.

With that, the commander made his exit, leaving the three of them standing in another awkward silence.

There was little else to do except observe the Drift Master and his apprentice as they worked. Both men had stopped taking measurements and were instead lifting rocks at the perimeter of the sand bed and moving them to the other side of the room. From what Rayhan could surmise, they were repositioning the stones to reflect the continuous flow of the islands as they floated through the ever-changing airstreams. The Drift Master had only the large, flat floor to represent the entire Lunera System—a system that was supposedly spherical—and because the clouds in real life did not terminate at a sudden edge of nothingness, the currents traced on one side of the sand were obviously picked up at a matching spot on the opposite side of his map.

Before long, Rayhan lost interest, and he started chewing the inside of his cheek, trying to think of what he should say to Elia. He'd been hoping to have a private conversation with her, and now he wished Hokk would just leave them alone. Finally, he decided to take matters into his own hands.

"Hokk, I'd like to talk to my sister for a moment in private. So if you could excuse us . . ."

Elia and Hokk glanced at each other. Her eyes seemed to plead with him to refuse the request.

"I'm not asking," Rayhan added. "I'm insisting."

Hokk nodded reluctantly. He scanned the large area, then pointed to a far corner in shadows. "I'll wait over there. It will get me out of the sun and give my eyes a rest."

Watching Hokk walk away, Rayhan struggled to decide what to say first. Clearly, Elia wasn't going to make this easy. She stared straight ahead—motionless, lips pressed together, not even blinking.

"You have every right to be mad at me," Rayhan eventually said. "I wasn't there for you the way I wanted to be."

No response. She was pretending he didn't exist.

He took a deep breath. "I keep thinking back to you and me sitting against the wall at the back of our house, our legs pulled up, waiting for the family to carry Omi to the Slope of Mourning. Do you remember that day too?"

Still nothing from Elia.

"I felt so bad that you were the one to find her body. You

didn't deserve that burden. I would have gladly taken it on to spare you."

Elia bristled, but continued to face forward. "I don't need your pity," she murmured. "I can handle whatever is thrown at me."

"I didn't mean to suggest you couldn't," Rayhan quickly added. "I was merely trying to express how the moment we shared that afternoon was . . . well, it was special in its own way, despite the sad circumstances. It was short-lived, but we formed a bond again like we had when we were younger—you and I looking out for each other, ready to take on the world together. Have you forgotten how it used to be?"

Elia's severity started to melt away. She dropped her head. "No, I remember," she barely whispered. "Those were good days. I wish we could get them back and forget everything else."

Rayhan felt a wave of relief and a renewed connection. "Oh, El, I was so afraid we had lost you forever when you went missing. Then to see you this morning with Mom brought me so much joy, I knew I had been wanting nothing more than for our family to be together again. What's left of us, anyway."

"Yes, our family." Elia abruptly turned to him, except without the same hostility as earlier. "You should know, I saw my father a few days ago."

Rayhan pulled back. He preferred to not waste a single thought on that pathetic man.

Elia must have read his reaction. "We have to forgive him."

"I can never—"

"He's a damaged man, I agree. But listen, he continues to look out for us, in his own simple, little ways. Those efforts still count."

"How could I possibly forgive him?"

"My mother has. And now I do too."

Rayhan's face twisted with frustration. "You keep talking that way, and you just did it again. I don't understand why."

Elia flinched. "What are you complaining about now?"

"You keep saying *my* father, *my* mother. I'm just as much

a part of this family. They're *our* parents, for goodness' sake, so include me when you talk."

His sister looked away. Whether angry or just sad, he could not tell, yet her mind seemed to be struggling.

"This is why I wanted time alone with you," he added. "Why are you acting so strangely? I noticed it first thing this morning when we were finally together again. After all the time we spent apart, our reunion should have been a happy one, but you're treating me like we're strangers . . . or adversaries. I'm your brother, damn it!"

Elia flashed her eyes at him, but tears were starting to well along her lashes. "Oh, how I wish that were actually the case."

Chapter 58

LEANING AGAINST THE WALL, shielded from the sun by slowly advancing shadows, Hokk kept his eyes fixed on Elia and her brother, ready to act at a moment's notice.

What were they discussing that they couldn't talk about in front of him? Was Rayhan trying to warn Elia that he couldn't be trusted? If only Hokk had thought to be first to share with Elia his own misgivings about her brother.

Initially, Rayhan seemed to be the one leading the conversation while Elia simply stared straight ahead. Then Elia lowered her guard and began addressing her brother directly. From their body language, Hokk could tell their conversation was intense. Then she said something that obviously hit Rayhan hard. He dropped his helmet onto the floor and his mouth hung open. The next instant, he threw his head back in anguish, running his hands through his hair.

Whatever it was, Hokk couldn't help feeling pleased—even more so when Rayhan's legs buckled and he lowered himself to the floor. Elia sat beside her brother and put a consoling arm around him. This prompted a different emotion in Hokk. Was it jealousy?

They're siblings, he reminded himself. There was no reason to feel threatened by their closeness.

Still, Hokk had to look away.

Only then did he notice that the young apprentice was no longer out on the bed of sand.

Where had he gone?

Curious, Hokk started walking along one side of the room. He moved into the sunshine again and approached the Drift Master, who was drawing fresh lines with his pole.

"I see you lost your assistant," Hokk called over to him.

The Drift Master stopped what he was doing and looked up with a smile. "I sent him on an errand."

Hearing this rather evasive response made Hokk leery. He wanted to dig deeper, but knew he couldn't without coming across as blatantly meddlesome. Instead, he asked, "Do you need any help?"

The Drift Master shook his head. "No, thank you for offering, but we finished calculating the coordinates we were asked to provide. Though I see Commander Blaitz is now absent at the moment as well."

"He had a brief errand of his own," said Hokk with a weak smile, remembering Blaitz's warning to share nothing. "He will be back soon." Hokk then pointed down to the sand bed to change the subject. "I've been growing more and more intrigued by how you know where to sketch these lines in the sand. Can you make all your calculations from this room, or do you travel outside to confirm your estimates?"

"Traveling is necessary when there's been a drastic, unexpected change in the System's air currents. It helps me to recalibrate and correct the map as necessary. Otherwise, it's only many years of carefully studying this science, starting out as an apprentice myself, that has allowed me to master the skill of making accurate predictions from inside this room. The key is to continually reassess the situation and determine how present conditions might affect the future positioning of each island. I must take into account factors such as changes in the wind, the seasons, gravitational pulls, and even collisions or near-misses, which can all have a ripple effect on things both near and far."

Hokk nodded as if he truly grasped everything the man had just explained. He suspected that a lot of what the Drift Master did involved best guesses. So long as he could give them the information they needed today, nothing else really mattered. "Well, I don't want to interrupt what you're doing," said Hokk. "Please, carry on."

Keen to seek the shade again, Hokk turned around to go back to the spot where he had been waiting alone. Except now he saw Elia approaching from the opposite direction. Farther behind her, she had left Rayhan still sitting on the floor with his legs crossed, holding his head in both hands.

As she came closer, Hokk saw that Elia's features were set into a rigid grimace.

"What's wrong?" Hokk whispered when she was within earshot.

She looked back at her brother before turning her solemn face toward Hokk. "I had to tell him some very difficult news. Something he would never have expected to hear."

"Are you all right?"

"Much better now. It was really bothering me, but what a difference to share the truth and end these secrets."

"And him?"

"He'll be fine. We both will. Of course, nothing between us will ever be the same again, but that doesn't mean we can't be friends. We will be friends—close friends even—once he's had time to process everything. However, the change to his life is going to take a lot of getting used to. I hope he's up for the challenge, the poor guy." Elia then laughed. "No, let me rephrase that. *Poor* is far from the right word."

With curiosity ready to devour him, Hokk laughed too, though somewhat nervously. "Good grief, Elia. You're leaving me hanging. I'm about to burst. What did you just tell your brother?"

"First of all, he's not my brother. He's somebody else altogether. Someone who none of us would have ever guessed."

"I knew it! I knew there was something about him that wasn't quite right."

Elia caught Hokk by the arm, forcing him to focus on what she wanted to say next. "And second of all, I had to explain to him that, someday, he'll be able to claim the throne of this kingdom floating in the clouds."

Chapter 59

IN AN INSTANT, RAYHAN had become an orphan.

No, that's not what I am, he thought. My true parents have just been revealed to me!

Still, *orphan* seemed to fit him best. His connection with the mother and father he had known since his earliest childhood memory was now severed. He felt alone. Lost and confused. Even fearful. On this particular day, this afternoon, only minutes ago, a mere second in time had made all the difference between comfortable ignorance and the wretched truth—now his life could never be the same again.

If he had heard it from anyone else, Rayhan would've rejected the story as a cruel lie. But he had no reason to doubt Elia. Everything she had said seemed irrefutable, especially when pieced together with all the strange events of recent days.

But to be a first-born prince? To inherit a guaranteed position of power from a long line of royalty? It was too much to take in all at once. Too distressing. What did this mean for his future? What would happen next?

He didn't want this. Damn it, he hadn't asked for any of it to happen! Why did things always become so complicated?

Maybe he could decline. Yes! He would turn down the role.

Many other members of the nobility would surely be eager to fulfill his responsibilities. Wasn't Prince Veralion already being groomed to take over the throne? Of course he was. So why interfere with what had already been set in motion?

Yet even as he played with the possibility of denying his destiny, Rayhan realized it would never come to pass. It would be impossible to avoid the expectations that would soon be placed on him—too many lives had been ruined, or lost altogether, to protect and restore Rayhan's birthright.

So who was this exalted person he was now supposed to be? He had no idea. And his name . . . he wasn't even Rayhan anymore. He couldn't remember what Elia had said—Jerehm, or Jerrad, or Jandon or something crazy like that. Losing his name and identity, he felt as though he had been struck a fatal blow.

But perhaps most hurtful of all was the knowledge that his destiny had been kept from him for so long. His phony mother and father, his grandparents, Greyit, and Blaitz—they were all aware of the cover-up, yet none of them had done anything to warn him or prepare him for what was to come. True, they must have felt they had to protect him from enemies who would have much to lose if his existence were known, but did that warrant concealing a secret that would affect him so profoundly?

He almost couldn't stand himself—to be this person with whom he could no longer identify. No wonder Elia had found it so difficult to be around him—she was experiencing the disconnect as well.

Elia.

Just saying her name caused a surge of emotion.

Elia.

He could no longer call Elia his sister. This realization left a heaviness in his chest.

Gazing over at her now, he saw that she had joined Hokk across the room. They were huddled together as if that's how it were always meant to be between them.

No, he couldn't look.

Shifting his gaze, Rayhan was now surprised to see that shadows covered more than half the stretch of sand in front of him. The sun had slipped much lower in the sky.

How much time had passed? How deep in thought had he delved, oblivious to whatever was going on around him?

He debated joining Hokk and Elia but felt compelled to seclude himself. Though it intensified the loneliness he was wallowing in, giving them their space was the right thing to do. He could also appreciate that someday soon—when he found himself standing alongside his new father, Emperor Tael, and his mother, Empress Mahkoiyin, once she was rescued—he'd have to learn very quickly how to handle the isolation that inherently came with their absolute power. Revered, but ultimately segregated from his subjects, he would find his solitude magnified when he eventually took over as sole sovereign.

Hoping to distract his troubled mind, Rayhan shifted his attention toward the Drift Master, who was still obsessing over his map. No doubt the work kept him continuously occupied and removed him from the trappings of court life. What an enviable position.

Then the Drift Master suddenly raised his head. Following his line of vision, Rayhan saw the back door fly open.

Commander Blaitz strode into the room with great determination. However, he wasn't alone. Behind him marched two courtiers.

Startled, Elia and Hokk leapt to their feet as if ready to bolt.

And then it became painfully clear to Rayhan. His entire body filled with paralyzing dread.

Blaitz had gone against his word. He'd never intended to arrange horses for a mission to Below. Nothing would be done to save Rayhan's mother. Instead, the commander was a traitor. He had betrayed their hiding spot up here with the Drift Master to members of the Royal Court—to the very people who would make sure that such a rescue attempt of the empress never took place.

Chapter 60

STANDING BESIDE HOKK, ELIA'S heart pounded against her rib cage. Though it was happening right before her eyes, she still couldn't believe who had just stormed into the Drift Master's workspace behind Commander Blaitz.

"Tasheira!" Elia gasped.

The girl marched straight toward her, wearing a severe expression. She was followed by somebody just as startling—Tasheira's cousin Fimal.

"You!" Tash exclaimed with a piercing glare when she was only a few feet away. "I can't believe I'm finally getting the chance to confront you, face to face."

Feeling angry that Blaitz had allowed the girl to come, Elia braced herself. "What are you doing up here?" she demanded.

"I know everything," Tasheira announced loudly, as if daring Elia to challenge her. "I know what you did! The way you treated Marest and left her for dead! All the lies you told! Then how you left me behind to rot in the dungeon when you successfully escaped!"

Elia swallowed a lump in her throat. Her confidence was wavering, and she knew Tash could see it. Though all of the girl's charges were true, taken out of context, they unfairly painted

Elia as the villain. She had never intended to kill Marest—the servant had simply known too much about Elia's true identity, so the girl had to be silenced with the Torkins' poisonous darts.

Yet before Elia could respond in her own defense, a sly smile curled Tasheira's mouth. "But I understand why you made the choices you did. I was mad before—furious, in fact—except I'm not any more. I have the utmost respect for your cunning. I would have done the very same."

"W-what?" This sudden change in attitude caught Elia completely off guard.

Tash nodded toward Blaitz. "It took some time to hear all the details, but our esteemed commander here explained everything. Of course, now it all makes sense. You did what was necessary to make all this happen. Really, in my eyes, you're a hero."

Elia glanced at Blaitz, who smiled and winked back.

"And I hear my father is more than delighted to assist with your mission. Commander Blaitz has already asked him, and the Baron will supply all the horses you need." Tasheira's expression became serious again. "On one condition, however."

Elia scowled. "What's that?"

"I insisted that Fimal and I be included in your plans. We've been through so much over the past little while, you and I, that it seems all part of a greater plan laid before us. Doesn't it feel as if we were meant to find each other on the desert and follow this adventure together through to its inevitable, successful conclusion?"

That was the impression Elia had been harboring about Hokk's involvement when she thought they would never reconnect. But to include Tasheira? Did Elia want her to have any part in this?

Did she really have any other choice?

Not waiting for her reply, Tasheira approached Hokk and played with one of the buttons on the front of his shirt. "And as for you, Hokk," she said in a more sultry tone, which immediately infuriated Elia, "I've heard so much about Below from the commander, as well as from Fimal, that I absolutely must not be left out on this excursion you're planning."

Elia quickly stepped between them and pushed Tash away. "I suppose we'll have to let you join us, but I only agree because if we're going to save the life of . . ." Elia flashed a glance at the Drift Master, who was hovering nearby, then decided to choose her words carefully. "Because if we're going to deal with this urgent matter, we need your family's horses. But I'm warning you, you can't interfere with our plans, or demand anything, or try to make any of the decisions."

Though taken aback, Tash seemed to respect Elia's direct and forceful manner. "Fine," she said with a decisive nod. "I agree to your terms."

"And if you don't comply, or if you do anything to jeopardize our plans, then you'll have to contend with me!" declared the stern voice of Rayhan, who had come up behind Elia.

"Who are you to speak to me like that?" Tash asked haughtily. "You're nothing more than an Imperial Guard!"

"I'm much more than that," Rayhan growled. "I am Elia's brother. And I won't let a single bad thing happen to her."

Chapter 61

A FEW MINUTES LATER, Hokk was keeping close watch as Blaitz consulted with the Drift Master, presumably to get the flight coordinates they'd need for their trip. There was a lot of pointing toward the constellation models hanging from the ceiling, as well as double-checking the notes that had been written down.

Once the two men finished their business, Hokk caught up to the commander so he could speak with him privately.

"I just wanted to let you know," Hokk murmured, "that while you were gone, the Drift Master's apprentice left."

Blaitz clenched his jaw as he scanned the room. "I hadn't noticed. How long ago?"

"Over an hour, I'd guess. I was told he had an errand to attend to, but there's been no sign of him since."

"It's probably nothing serious, but I'm glad you told me." The commander then tilted his head skyward where the sunlight was quickly fading. "I understand everything will be in place very soon for our departure, so hopefully, we won't be around long enough to have any problems. As Tasheira mentioned, we found the Baron, with Emperor Tael's help, and he was most obliging."

"So the horses we need have been assembled?"

"Almost. They're being pulled from their stables and saddled as we speak. There will be enough animals for all of us, plus one extra."

Hokk glanced toward Elia and the others. "And when you say *all of us,* do you really intend to include Tasheira and her cousin?"

Blaitz sighed. "It would not have been my first choice, but she made the request to Emperor Tael, and he approved it."

"How much does she know?"

"Enough."

"I'm asking specifically for Elia because I know she doesn't believe the girl can be trusted. I have my own misgivings. Tash can be a difficult person to deal with."

"I'll take that into consideration," said the commander. "I definitely plan to keep a sharp eye on her. But the emperor felt that Lady Tasheira and her cousin were already wrapped up in this affair enough to justify their further involvement. Truth be told, I suspect he'd rather not have them hanging around the palace, stirring up controversy, especially since they were wrongly imprisoned these past few days. It will buy him time, as well. Once we get back with the empress—and may fortune shine on us that we actually have success—the emperor plans to have everything in place for his dramatic revelation to the—"

As if summoned by the commander's comments, Emperor Tael suddenly arrived, unannounced and unattended, through the rear entrance.

"—to the Royal Court," Blaitz said quickly to finish his thought.

Holding his white cane, the blind emperor began tapping it on the ground to his left and right.

The Drift Master, who happened to be the closest, hurried over to greet Emperor Tael before taking his arm and escorting him to where Blaitz and Hokk were waiting. At the same time, Elia, Tasheira, Rayhan, and Fimal came over to join them.

"Commander Blaitz?" Tael asked tentatively.

"Yes, I'm here," he replied, taking the emperor's outstretched hand and touching the man's knuckles to his brow.

"Good," said the emperor with a smile. His eyes twinkled, yet still stared straight ahead. "Is everyone assembled and prepared to go?"

A chorus of voices confirmed their readiness.

"Perfect," said Tael. "Because the time to leave is almost upon us."

Chapter 62

ELIA INITIALLY FOUND IT curious that Emperor Tael was still pretending to be blind, though she quickly realized why he considered the charade necessary. Besides Rayhan, she was probably the only other person in this group who knew the truth. Tasheira and Fimal certainly wouldn't have a clue, and neither would Hokk—how could he? She had been planning to tell him, but there was so much else to explain about her family's secrets. She would let him know, however, as soon as she had the chance.

Right now, her full attention was on the moment at hand—this first opportunity for Tael to behold his son.

And admittedly, she was impressed. The emperor played his role as a blind person perfectly. Though Elia could tell the man was looking at Rayhan with his well-practiced, off-kilter, vacant gaze, she doubted anyone else would be able to pick up on it. Not even Rayhan, who couldn't take his own eyes off Tael. Standing silently, looking almost haggard, the young man she used to call her brother was closely observing every movement the emperor made, hanging on each word as if trying to capture the essence of this stranger to whom he was related.

“Commander, a brief moment before you lead the troop out,” the emperor now requested. “Could you quickly remind me again who is assembled?”

Blaitz obliged, starting off with Tash and Fimal. Then Rayhan.

“Rayhan, is it?” said Tael. “If I’m correct, I’ve never had the pleasure of an introduction.”

“The honor . . . the honor is all mine,” Rayhan croaked.

“I understand you have very recently begun your training as an Imperial Guard.”

“Yes, that is correct.”

“And you come highly recommended. As it turns out, I’m looking right now for someone to be my close personal aide and bodyguard. Someone extremely loyal who can take on this coveted position. I would like very much for that person to be you.”

“Uh . . . thank you,” said Rayhan, appearing both startled and confused. “That’s very gracious, Your Excellency.”

“Do you accept?” Tael enquired more directly.

Rayhan hesitated. “Yes, I suppose I do.”

“Excellent! Then I’m pleased to say your services start immediately. Which means, of course, that you won’t be needed for this mission today.”

“What?” Rayhan exclaimed, his eyes quickly darting between Elia and Commander Blaitz as if hoping one of them would intervene on his behalf. “But I’m already committed to going.”

“You just committed yourself to me!”

“Then I decline!”

Tael’s nostrils flared. “That is not an option!” he growled. “I am not making a request. Consider it an order.” The emperor then swung around on Blaitz and demanded just as harshly, “Now, who else do we have in our company, Commander?”

To appease the emperor, Blaitz continued on down the line. “Next is Hokk.”

“Our man from the moon!” observed the emperor, speaking more diplomatically.

"And lastly, Elia."

Emperor Tael smiled broadly. "Ah yes, Elia, the girl who made a surprise visit to my suite the other day. My dear, I'm so sorry you had to leave in such a hurry." He reached forward and gestured for Elia's hand. When she offered it, he kissed just below her wrist and gently squeezed her fingers. "I'll be forever grateful to you and everything you've done in service to the Royal Family and our well-being."

"You're very kind, Your Excellency. I look forward to celebrating a successful outcome."

"As do I," he replied, nodding solemnly. "As do I." Tael then turned in Blaitz's general direction. "Speaking of which, Commander, I don't mean to hold you up any longer. It must be twilight by now."

"It is, indeed."

"Then the hour has come for all of you to take to the air and fly away," said the emperor. "And I pray to the sun and moon for your speedy and safe return, as well as for the fates to shine in our favor."

Chapter **63**

GUIDED BY COMMANDER BLAITZ, they left the Drift Master's quarters as a group of five, and quietly descended the stairs to ground level.

Tasheira felt her excitement increasing with each step, knowing she was finally going to see her father. A reunion with him had been promised by Blaitz and Emperor Tael when they'd shown up together in Lord Mack's suite to collect both her and her cousin. At the time, Tasheira had been concerned about leaving the security of the room too soon, but the two men had assured her they'd be perfectly safe. Tael and Blaitz also said a very important matter had surfaced that required Tasheira and Fimal's immediate assistance. They told her they had already met with the Baron to explain the mission and to request the use of his horses. Naturally, Tash was intrigued and determined that she would not be left out.

Except right now, she suddenly had doubts. Blaitz was not leading the group toward the front of the stables where Tasheira would have expected to find the Baron. Instead, the commander darted through a thicket of trees located at the back of the building, before racing into the Sanctuary's gardens beyond. The manicured grounds, almost dark with the onset of dusk, appeared empty.

Tasheira hurried to catch up with the commander. "What about my father?" she asked, grabbing his arm in an attempt to swing him around. "You said you'd take me to him."

Without halting, Blaitz pulled free of her grasp. "Where else do you think we're going?"

I don't know, but I don't like it! she wanted to shout, wishing that in the dim light she could see the man's face more clearly to gauge his sincerity.

She debated turning around and heading back, but as Hokk, Elia, and Fimal caught up to her too, she decided to keep running—because despite all the things she could feel anxious about, Tasheira loved nothing better than an adventure. She certainly wasn't prepared to be left behind like that young man, Rayhan, who claimed to be Elia's brother.

There was still something about Rayhan's personality and how he fit into the whole scenario that didn't sit right with Tasheira. It wasn't just the lack of a family resemblance between two people who were supposed to be siblings. More troubling was that strange request from the emperor, who wanted Rayhan to be his bodyguard. It didn't make any sense. Why offer such a prestigious position to someone he had never met before? And why did the emperor continue his pretense of being blind? Tael had an ulterior motive—that much Tasheira was sure of—but what it could be, she had no idea. Obviously, Lord Mack had told her only one part of the story; now she was determined to find out what was really going on.

It must all somehow relate to Mahkoiyin's rescue.

If Tash had been told yesterday that today she'd be asked to help save such an important woman, missing for nearly two decades, she would have laughed it off as preposterous. But after her conversation with Mackenzie Noble, nothing surprised her or seemed impossible now. She was also glad Fimal had been able to spend enough time with Lord Mack to hear for himself the many remarkable things that the centuries-old man had to say. Though Fimal hadn't had the chance to hear everything, Tash looked forward to filling him in on the remaining details once they had returned from Below.

Below! Finally, a chance to see it for myself!

Her pulse began to race faster than could be blamed on the running. She was definitely the Baron's daughter—the urge to explore, to comprehend greater truths about reality, past and present, was a trait she had undeniably inherited from her father. It was a yearning that drove most of her decisions, and she was convinced a similar fever coursed through the veins of her favorite cousin. How appropriate that she and Fimal would experience this adventure together.

And I will have redemption!

Whatever tarnish to her reputation Tasheira might have suffered recently as a result of her association with Elia and the girl's rumored assassination attempt, it would soon be cleared by the glory of having been selected as a member of this search party. She could imagine it all so clearly: proudly flying back to the Sanctuary with the empress in their protective care, the jubilation of the court, each one of the rescuers hailed a hero. After such a success, how could Mahkoiyin not insist that Tasheira become her highest-ranking lady-in-waiting, saving Tash from her duties with the contemptible Empress Faytelle?

"Almost there," Blaitz called back to them, pulling Tash from her musings.

Adjusting her double eyelids so her pupils could function better in the moonlight, Tash now saw horses farther ahead. As they approached, she could also distinguish two men with the herd. One was the livestock foreman from her family's estate. The other was her father.

Tasheira rushed forward, sprinting past Blaitz to reach the Baron first.

He opened his arms just in time to catch her. "You're trembling," he observed as they embraced.

"Oh, Father, it's been just awful," she whispered into his ear before pulling back as the rest of the group arrived.

Though she couldn't explain more to him now, her comment was enough to raise his concerns. "Everything all right?" the Baron demanded of Blaitz.

"Of course," said the commander. "Why? Have you seen anything out here to be worried about? Were you followed?"

Tash squeezed her father's hand, and he seemed to understand that he should let the issue go. "All quiet, as far as we've been able to tell," said the Baron. "And no questions were raised as we escorted our horses out of the stables. It was really very easy."

"Perfect," said Blaitz. "And I see we have the six horses, as requested."

"You do, indeed."

"Then everyone select the steed you'll be riding and get mounted." The commander turned back to Tasheira's father. "And Baron Shoad, you can have faith that you'll be rewarded handsomely for your efforts, just as the emperor promised."

Delighted to hear this, Tasheira felt a tingling sensation surge to the tips of her fingers and toes. With Emperor Tael's sponsorship, the Baron was finally going to rise above his somewhat undignified status as a horse merchant, furthering Tasheira's own campaign for greater prominence within the Royal Court. And to think, before this afternoon, she'd had every intention of returning to her family's estate and giving up life at the palace completely. How quickly things could change.

"The emperor is very generous, but it is all unnecessary," said the Baron. "Though it's my duty, I also consider it my great honor."

Tash clenched her fists. Surely her father wouldn't foolishly give away what was rightfully coming to him!

She was about to recklessly jump in and say something when her father leaned close and spoke in a low voice. "But most importantly, you be safe, my dear Tasheira. I almost don't want you to leave."

"I'll be fine. Besides, it was Emperor Tael's wish that I go too. He was adamant, so I had no choice but to agree," she whispered, knowing full well that stretching the truth was often necessary and forgivable.

The Baron inhaled as if preparing to say more, but the commander suddenly became tense and interrupted him.

"Shh! Everyone silent!" Blaitz hissed, holding up his hands for quiet.

Each of them froze to listen.

Above the swish of tails, and one horse shaking its head, they heard pounding footsteps drawing near.

Tasheira turned in the direction of the sound, immediately making out a dark figure running toward them in the moonlight. It was an Imperial Guard.

No! This can't be happening!

Chapter 64

"IT'S JUST ME!" RAYHAN gasped, struggling for breath after running so hard to catch up.

He had put on his mirrored helmet so he wouldn't get caught or identified as he fled, and only now did he sense the panic his sudden arrival had caused. No one could recognize him.

He whipped off his helmet.

"Rayhan, what are you doing here?" exclaimed Elia, who was already sitting up in the saddle of one of the horses.

"I'm coming with you."

"Really? You've been allowed to join us?" asked Blaitz, sounding very skeptical. "I'm surprised Emperor Tael changed his mind."

"He agreed—after some persuasion—and told me to chase after you."

Of course, it was an outright lie. Rayhan had bolted before Tael could stop him, charging down the stairs behind the stables to flee the emperor, whose angry voice shouted for him to come back. Though Rayhan had no regrets, he also couldn't believe he had defied the orders of a man who was both his sovereign and newly introduced father. But whatever consequences he might have to pay for this disobedience, he would gladly face them upon his return. All Rayhan counted on now was that nobody, particularly Commander Blaitz, would bother wasting precious time returning to the palace to confirm whether or not he was telling the truth.

"Will you need another horse?" asked a nobleman whom Rayhan didn't recognize. "I followed your earlier instructions with the understanding that you would need one extra steed saddled for a passenger you'll be picking up later. But there are six of you now and only six horses."

The commander sighed as if frustrated by this new complication.

"It's not necessary," Rayhan answered for the commander. "I can ride back with Elia."

"I still have my reservations," cautioned Blaitz. "I'll be held responsible if anything—"

"Enough talk! Let's just get out of here!" Rayhan demanded, glancing over his shoulder to make sure Imperial Guards weren't already charging through the gardens. "You have the coordinates, everything is packed, so my order to you is that we leave right now before we're discovered!" There was a new hardness in his voice.

Everyone in the group was startled by Rayhan's deliberate insubordination. Remaining still and silent, they all seemed poised, waiting for the commander's response.

"Then it's the six of us," Blaitz reluctantly agreed, caving in just as Rayhan had expected.

Because if Rayhan was truly a royal heir, then there was no better time than the present to start exercising his authority among those people who had no choice but to obey.

Chapter 65

THEY FLEW ALL NIGHT above the cloud cover without stopping. Commander Blaitz wanted to make as much progress as possible while it was still dark enough for the stars overhead to guide them.

Elia was exhausted by the time the sun started to rise over the horizon, shining like a radiant crown of light that flecked the clouds with hues of orange and pink.

Two more hours of flying were necessary, however, before the first island came into view, appearing as a hazy mirage floating on the mist. By this point, the sun had climbed higher into the sky and everyone seemed ready for a much-needed break, especially Hokk, who had begun wearing his helmet again to protect himself as soon as the morning blazed awake.

The island was small, but thankfully inhabited. A tiny village, situated at its center, had a cluster of buildings ringed by fields of varying shades of green that stretched to the rocky edges. As they approached, Commander Blaitz encouraged everybody to put on their helmets if they had one—only Tasheira and Fimal did not. Through her own, Elia could see men and women already out tending to their crops. Many of the workers looked up to watch the horses arrive and land within their hamlet.

As soon as they touched down in the derelict village square, residents from the surrounding homes and farmers from the fields all quickly congregated to see who these unexpected visitors might be. From their expressions, Elia could tell they didn't know whether to be curious or afraid.

To help allay their concerns, Blaitz removed his helmet before he explained to the island residents that they were a band of Imperial Guards escorting two dignitaries, played by Tash and her cousin. The local people were easily convinced, and the commander's request for food and waterballs, particularly for the horses, was met with very generous hospitality.

After a simple meal, the six of them napped for a few hours, resting in beds offered up by several villagers. By early afternoon, though, it was time to leave. Elia could have slept longer, but her eagerness to continue traveling quickly erased any lingering drowsiness. Saddled up, refreshed, and loaded with additional supplies, the group was soon airborne again.

• • •

PIECES OF THE MOON glowed in the evening sky, but it was against the twinkling stars that Commander Blaitz now aligned his navigational device. He explained they had drifted off course because they had needed to fly during daylight hours, but he assured them that with a slight correction in their path relative to some point overhead, they would soon be traveling in the right direction again.

Yet how much longer would it be until they reached the spot marked by the Drift Master's coordinates? Elia felt as if they'd never get there. Only when she was on the verge of falling out of her saddle from fatigue—as another glorious dawn was about to break along the skyline—did Commander Blaitz make the announcement that she had been waiting to hear.

"I think this is it!" he shouted. He consulted the notes he had received from the Drift Master, then checked his instrument once more, lining it up with the few stars still bright enough to sparkle in the early morning sky. "Yes, I'm right!" he said triumphantly. "Forty degrees north, one hundred and seventeen degrees east. This is where we start our descent!"

Everybody roused themselves and sat straighter. The next moment, upon the commander's lead, their horses dove down into the thick mist. Darkness enveloped them yet again, but soon, they cut through the underside of the cloud cover into a slightly brighter atmosphere.

Elia glanced quickly at Tasheira. Shock spread across the girl's face to see Below for the first time.

Elia looked down too, and was surprised to feel just as stunned by what she saw.

No endless prairies with grasses blowing in the wind.

No craggy peaks forming a treacherous mountain range.

All she could see was a huge body of water, from horizon to horizon, with large barren islands of rock sticking above the surf.

"There's been a huge mistake!" Elia shouted.

Hokk yanked off his helmet, looking equally startled as all six horses hovered while their riders took in the view below.

Despairing over their failure, Elia started to panic. "What are we going to do?" she yelled as she flicked the metal blade in her eyebrow.

"What do you mean?" Rayhan called over. "Isn't this where we're supposed to be?"

"No, not even close," she replied. "The Drift Master must have gotten it all wrong! Now we're completely lost!"

Chapter 66

THE HORSES HAD DESCENDED a bit farther, and now they flapped their wings with little effect, having become caught in the atmosphere's band of weak gravity between Above and Below.

Hokk felt unexpected relief and a sense of inner peace to return to this realm beneath the clouds. His home. A place that didn't try to burn his skin or blind his eyes. But he ignored these pangs of wistful longing for all things familiar to focus instead on the problem at hand. With their descent momentarily stalled, he carefully studied the sprawling seascape.

"I think we'll be all right!" he exclaimed.

"How can that be?" Elia shouted back. "It's hopeless!"

"No, you're wrong."

Commander Blaitz didn't know whom to believe. "Which is it? Have we found the correct spot or not?"

"This isn't where I landed when Hokk first found me," said Elia, shaking her head as she surveyed the scene. "I can't even begin to guess which direction we should go from here if we want to find the grasslands."

"Are we at least close?" asked Tasheira.

"We're closer than you might think," said Hokk, feeling increasingly confident.

"I don't see how that's possible," Elia replied.

"The Drift Master only promised us his best *estimate* of where we needed to go," Hokk explained. "He didn't guarantee a perfectly accurate result."

Elia, however, had come to her own conclusion. "I bet he gave us the wrong coordinates on purpose to sabotage our efforts. Imperial Guards could have already arrived at the spot where we should actually be right now! If they beat us to the empress, who knows what they'll do to her!"

"Believe me, that's probably not the situation we're facing," said Hokk. He pointed down to the ocean, then out toward the horizon. "Do you see that string of islands stretching all the way into the distance?"

Elia's eyes followed his finger. "Yes, but how does that help?"

"I'm guessing these aren't random islands, but actually the peaks of submerged mountains that form the most easterly tip of the Torkinian Range. Doesn't it look like that's what they are, jutting out of the ocean?"

"Well . . . maybe," Elia replied, though she certainly looked doubtful.

"Is that a good thing?" Commander Blaitz sounded more optimistic.

Hokk nodded. "The Ancients passed down many legends to my people. One tells how, centuries ago, the climate changed, water levels rose, coastlines moved inland, and valleys became so flooded that the mountains appeared separated from one another. I remember my uncle telling me how the Torkinian Range ran right into the sea until the tops of the mountains looked like mere stepping stones. I think that's exactly what we're seeing here. If I'm right, it means this is the same body of water that Elia first fell into before getting washed to shore. So we should follow these peaks to see where they bring us."

Hokk looked around the group. Tasheira, Fimal, and Rayhan obviously hadn't grasped much of what he had said; Elia and Blaitz still appeared unconvinced. Hokk pointed to an island directly below and explained further. "Look closely. Can you see that impressive stone wall running along the island's ridge line?"

All confirmed they could.

"And do you notice too how the wall runs right down into the water at either end . . . then how it seems to pick up at the shoreline of the next nearest island and run along the crest there as well?"

"It's amazing," said Tasheira. "It seems to go on forever."

"Almost looks like a serpent rising in and out of the water," Elia added.

Fimal pressed his feet into his stirrups to lift himself out of his saddle. "But how far does it really go?" he wondered aloud.

"According to the Ancients, it used to run an incredible distance," said Hokk. "And if we follow the remnants of this Great Wall far enough, I'm quite sure we'll discover the point where the ocean meets the mainland and where the peaks of the Torkinian Range reach their highest altitude." He noticed Elia had become very quiet, as if lost in thought. "What is it, Elia? What are you thinking?"

"Do you remember that Torkin warrior, Roahm, who brought me back to live with his people? Well, when he and I were in North Village, just before setting out to find Mahkoiyin, he pointed out a large formation on the mountain across from the settlement." Her face began to light up, as if the memory was becoming clearer. "It was mostly covered in snow and it looked like a long rock ledge to me, but if I remember correctly, Roahm called it a *great wall* too."

"That's perfect!" Hokk exclaimed. "Then it's simply a matter of flying along this wall's path until we reach one of the two Torkin villages, either North or South, where we'll—"

"Where we'll be able to rescue Mahkoiyin!" Elia interrupted with a surge of excitement.

"Exactly. The spot where we should find Mahkoiyin waiting for us."

Provided the woman survived her fall into the river.

But Hokk couldn't let himself dwell on the guilt he still felt for deliberately letting her go—not until he knew for certain the outcome of one of his most recent regrettable decisions.

Chapter 67

THEY FLEW ABOVE THE water for countless miles, following the incredible man-made structure beneath them. Rayhan watched in amazement as it snaked up and down the slopes of the islands. At regular intervals, they also flew over square fortifications—either intact or in ruins—that dotted the entire stretch. He marveled at just how many people would have been needed to construct such a monumental barrier. How long had it taken them to finish? For what purpose had it been built? And what must the wall have looked like before the flooding, when it was one continuous strip of rockwork from beginning to end?

Distracted by this ancient landmark, Rayhan forgot to keep watch of what might be flying behind them. Since leaving the Sanctuary, he had been vigilant, all the while fighting a nagging fear that troops had been dispatched by his father to follow and bring him back. Up until their descent through the clouds he had thankfully seen no cause for alarm.

But what a sickening feeling when he suddenly reminded himself to be more attentive, only to swing around and observe what he had been frightened of seeing all along.

Still at a great distance away and much higher up, a dark formation was visible beneath the clouds. He couldn't deny, though, what it signified—a large team of stallions, with Imperial Guards in their saddles. Counting the exact number was impossible, but there were definitely far too many.

Tugging his reins, Rayhan forced his horse to break formation and hover in the air. Everyone else in the group immediately noticed and pulled back on their own steeds to turn the beasts around.

"What are you doing?" Elia called out, instantly concerned.

"Go on ahead without me," Rayhan instructed, trying to sound as calm as possible. "I'll catch up soon."

"What's wrong?" asked Commander Blaitz.

Rayhan was reluctant to answer, but he also knew he couldn't endanger this mission. The others would have to carry on to find his mother, while he flew back to intercept these Imperial Guards who were hunting him.

Discouraged, Rayhan pointed up. "I hate to say it, but we're being followed."

Mouths dropped open.

"How is that possible?" Fimal wondered. "We've covered such a huge distance. Have they been tracking us the whole time?"

"Hard to say. I've just noticed them now," Rayhan replied. "But it doesn't have to change anything. They are here only for me."

If he was forced to return to the Sanctuary, then all was not lost. The empress could still be saved from Below, just without the help of the son she had never known.

Chapter 68

HOKK HAD A DIFFERENT theory to explain the sudden arrival of the Imperial Guards, but he was still sorting everything out in his mind as Blaitz took charge of the situation.

"Are you sure the guards are chasing you, Rayhan?" the commander challenged, having stopped his horse in mid-air like everybody else.

"I'm afraid it's the only explanation," Rayhan replied.

"Not unless—" Hokk started to say.

Blaitz angrily cut him off. "But I thought you had full permission from Emperor Tael to come with us. Were you lying?"

"I had no choice," Rayhan said defensively. "I was determined from the start to join you and nothing was going to stop me. Certainly not any fears about my safety."

"That is not an acceptable excuse!" the commander barked. "Especially since I'll be the one to pay the price if you suffer any sort of harm or don't return."

"But Empress Mahkoiyin is my mother, damn it all!" Rayhan shot back. "What else would you have expected me to do?"

With a sudden intake of air, Tasheira clutched her chest. "Your mother!" she wheezed in disbelief.

Rayhan ignored her. "If my father wants to lay blame, then I'll assume full responsibility. You were only following my orders."

Blaitz grimaced, but appeared reluctant to dispute this further. For a moment, he said nothing as he glanced back up at the guards, still a distance away but swiftly approaching. "So give us your orders. What do you propose we do?" he asked. "Our time is quickly running out."

"It's simple," Rayhan suggested. "I accept defeat. All I have to do is leave you and return to the guards so they can escort me back home. They want nothing more, so it doesn't have to mean the end of the journey for this group."

"I worry it might not be as straightforward as that," Hokk interjected. "We could all be facing a very serious threat."

The commander's eyes narrowed. "How so?"

Hokk turned to Rayhan. "How long has it been since you discovered these guards following us?"

"Like I said, only just now. But I have been keeping careful watch from the start just to be sure."

The commander snorted, shaking his head in dismay. "And yet you said nothing this entire time to prepare us for what we might expect."

"Wait, I'm not finished," said Hokk, holding up his hand as he squeezed his saddle with his thighs. "I doubt very much the guards were sent by Emperor Tael to find Rayhan. I'm willing to bet that these men were dispatched by someone far more dangerous—an enemy who hopes to ruin what we've set out to do."

"Explain," the commander demanded.

"How could guards have followed us undetected for such a long journey? It's not possible. We would have seen—or at least Rayhan would've seen—these men on horseback long before now. And why wouldn't they have caught up to us when we stopped at that small island yesterday morning for a rest?"

"So what other explanation could there be?" asked Elia.

"This all has something to do with the Drift Master," Hokk said decisively. He turned to Blaitz. "Remember how the Drift Master's apprentice left soon after the two of them figured out our coordinates? Yet the young man never came back. That's because his errand was to share our plans with whoever wants to stop us. And from what I've heard from Elia, that person could only be Tael's twin brother, Emperor Tohryn."

"Which means the reason we haven't seen the guards until now—" Commander Blaitz started to say.

"—Was because," Hokk interrupted, "they didn't have to actually track us the whole time to find their way. They simply had to follow the same coordinates. Or perhaps the Drift Master plotted a more direct route so they'd quickly end up at this exact spot. But we're lucky. We could have discovered them flying ahead of us, not behind, putting us in a far worse situation."

Rayhan nodded. "Which could still happen."

"Yes. We can't waste the head-start advantage we now have."

"I agree with Hokk," Elia announced firmly. "We have to act quickly! I'm flying onwards!"

"And as promised, I'll head back to intercept the guards and try to slow them down," said Rayhan.

"I'm joining you!" said the commander, pulling on his helmet as if preparing for battle.

"Count me in too," Fimal offered.

"Then take my helmet, Fimal," said Hokk, tossing it through the air to him. "As for you, Tasheira, come with us. I'm staying with Elia no matter what to show her the rest of the way to the Torkin villages." He then turned to Blaitz. "But remember, success is your only option. At some point, Commander, you'll have to return and follow the Great Wall to locate us. Otherwise, without you and your ability to navigate by the stars, we will have no way of knowing how to find our way back to the Sanctuary once we have the empress!"

Chapter 69

ELIA LEANED FORWARD IN her saddle as she kicked up her heels with sharp thrusts to urge her horse to fly faster.

Glancing behind repeatedly, she shuddered to think what perils Rayhan, Fimal, and Commander Blaitz would soon be forced to confront when they met the Imperial Guards head-on. If the guards were not stopped, nothing would prevent them from ultimately capturing or killing all of them, including Mahkoiyin.

Swinging around to look back once more, Elia could not tell what was going on, but the guards seemed to be narrowing the distance. She wondered how quickly they might catch up. Were they five minutes behind? Ten? Twenty?

By now, the islands in the ocean had finally merged into an undeniable mountain range. They were still following Hokk's Great Wall as it coiled over the increasingly steep terrain, and many parts of it were covered with snow.

Somewhere in these mountains were the two Torkin villages. Mahkoiyin had been living in North Village all these years, after falling from the clouds into a huge snowbank. However, more recently, the woman had plunged into the river below Hokk's cliffside cave when they were trying to save her, so the current would've swept her down closer to South Village. Would Mahkoiyin have stayed there, or headed back north, to more familiar territory?

Elia knew she had to decide quickly where they should start their search. Of course, they would have to deal with more than just Mahkoiyin—there'd be all those villagers too. Seeing the horses arrive from the sky, every single inhabitant would panic, thinking that a second airstrike was upon them. Little more than a month had passed since Imperial Guards had flown down the first time, looking for Elia and setting fire to the villagers' crops in a futile attempt to flush her out of hiding. Surely the Torkins would now be better prepared to fight back and prevent a similar catastrophe.

And their warriors will have those same poisoned darts, thought Elia. They'll attack and kill us before we can even touch down on the ground.

Chapter 70

"REACH BELOW YOUR RIGGINGS," the commander ordered. "Our saddles are supposed to have an inner sheath on the left-hand side where Baron Shoad promised to hide knives, just in case."

After seeing Blaitz pull a blade out from under his saddle, near the left stirrup, Rayhan reached down and found a weapon of his own.

"Listen carefully, though," the commander added. "We must avoid, at all costs, any sort of combat, especially since it's just the three of us. The only outcome we can hope for is to slow these guards down, not stop them altogether. Keep in mind, Elia and the others will be better off if we can buy them the extra time they'll need to find the empress. And that won't happen if we end up dead! So no heroics out here today."

This was an easy thing for Rayhan to agree to now, but he could only guess what desperate acts he might need to perform to save himself.

And he was about to find out very quickly. Staring through the lenses of his metal faceplate, he couldn't tear his gaze away from what was approaching.

As if propelled by the escalating, headlong wind, there had

to be at least two dozen Imperial Guards coming straight for them. And they were all carrying spears!

With measly knives as their only defense, fighting these men off would be a futile undertaking. Even if they weren't already so grossly outnumbered, Rayhan knew their efforts would likely prove to be inadequate and fatal.

"Brace yourselves!" Commander Blaitz shouted as final words of advice.

Closer and closer the guards advanced.

Neither side appeared willing to yield.

Impact was imminent.

"I am Commander Blaitz!" the commander yelled as they were almost within their midst.

Whether the guards could not hear him or they simply chose to ignore him, they gave no visible reaction. The wings of their many horses still flapped with great force as they drove forward with unwavering determination.

"I am Commander Blaitz!" the man repeated with a note of desperation in his voice, no doubt surprised these men did not seem to recognize the spike on his helmet or his superior rank. "Stop! You are forbidden to go any farther!"

And then the swarm of horses was upon them. Rayhan instinctively ducked in his saddle, watching on all sides for spears trying to impale him. However, none came. There was nothing but a confusing flurry of feathers everywhere, with just barely enough space between wingtips to keep the animals from colliding.

An instant later, the Imperial Guards had passed them by completely without any clash or quarrel—almost as if Rayhan and his two companions were invisible.

Blaitz immediately banked his horse and pulled on the reins to force the beast to hover. He yanked off his helmet to watch the backs of the guards flying away. His expression was sheer bewilderment.

Fimal and Rayhan brought their stallions alongside the commander's.

Rayhan removed his helmet as well and tucked it under his arm. "That was it? Nothing more?"

"It's like they didn't even see us!" said Fimal.

"So, what now?" Rayhan wondered.

Blaitz shook his head to clear his shock. He stared after the regiment, then turned his attention to Rayhan and Fimal with a sense of urgency. "We have to follow before they get too far ahead of us. Somehow, we must cut them off. I just pray Hokk, Elia, and Tasheira can act quickly enough on their end before this horde arrives to defeat them."

Chapter 71

TASHEIRA ADMIRED THE INCREDIBLE view. To her eyes, the gloom of Below was beautiful. Like a dark aura that had settled on this mysterious realm, the perpetual twilight painted a very dramatic panorama. Menacing? Yes. Cheerless? Absolutely. Yet powerful too, and spectacular in a way that Tash could certainly appreciate.

Then, all of a sudden, the heavy blanket of dark clouds parted enough to create a small opening through which the bright blueness beyond was revealed. Beams of light from Above cut through like daggers, bathing a nearby mountaintop with intense, golden sunshine.

However, as quickly as the shaft of brilliance appeared, it began to fade as the clouds pressed together again, until just a warm glow remained—then nothing at all.

A stunning sight. But what had caused it?

They flew farther. Eventually, Tasheira spotted smoke rising from the chimneys of a village up ahead. The settlement clung to the side of a mountain directly across from where they were following the Great Wall.

Hokk motioned for them to land on top of a small section of the wall, one of the only parts not covered by a strange drifting whiteness.

"But we can't rest for long," he warned. "Just long enough to decide which village we want to start with. North or South?

"South," Elia said firmly. "I have to trust a hunch we'll find her there."

Hokk nodded. "Then I suggest we skirt around North Village completely and fly low along the valley basin for the rest of the way."

Tasheira had been listening, but her attention was also drawn to the banks of white powder that had formed along the edges of the wall. Unable to resist, she slipped off her saddle, reached down, and laughed with delight when she felt how cold it was in her hands. "What is this stuff?"

"Snow," Hokk said simply.

"Snow?" Tash wondered.

"Frozen water that falls from the sky."

"I hope we get none of that today," said Elia with a shiver as she gazed skyward. "And what about those clouds opening up earlier while we were flying?" she added, wide-eyed. "Have you ever seen anything like it before?"

"Only once," Hokk replied. "That morning after the Torkins' banquet, when I found you asleep in your tent."

"Why would something like that occur in the first place?" Tasheira asked.

Hokk shrugged. "I have no idea. But I don't like it one bit. Just another indication that things are changing. Makes me wonder too if the sight was a good omen, or a bad one."

"I take it as a positive sign that we'll have success," Elia offered.

"Let's hope so. But listen, let's not waste any more time."

Tasheira promptly mounted her stallion and they were soon airborne again, flying at an altitude where the tips of the evergreen trees below looked close enough to tickle the bellies of the horses. As they followed a series of valleys, a frigid wind whipped up and tossed Tasheira's curls into her face. She was glad Blaitz had given her a thick cloak to wear—she definitely needed it.

After a while, they began flying over green terraces cut into the mountainside. When they crossed a wide ribbon of tumbling water, Hokk shouted, "There's the river. Not much farther now."

For some reason, his tone was far from reassuring. Back when they had landed so briefly on the Great Wall, Tasheira had picked up on the anxiety in Hokk's and Elia's words, and now, as they neared their destination, she was growing concerned—for the first time since starting this adventure.

And then they were flying above huts and tents that speckled the hillside.

South Village.

The few people Tash saw must have noticed them because she could see a lot of pointing. Many also appeared to be shouting excited greetings as the stallions soared overhead. *Good, they are happy to see us.* No reason to be worried. The three of them would be welcomed with the same warm reception offered by the inhabitants of that small island they had visited yesterday.

Yet they didn't land in the Torkin village. Instead, Hokk redirected his steed, and the other two horses followed. A short distance farther, they came upon more terraced fields; these ones were filled with farmers bent over their crops.

Workers immediately noticed the horses in the sky, and the same kind of reaction accompanied their arrival. However, as the majority of the people began to flee, Tash realized they were responding not with excitement, but with pure panic.

Both Hokk and Elia leaned over in their saddles to examine the chaos.

"Do you see him?" Hokk yelled.

"Not yet!" shouted Elia.

See who? Tasheira wondered.

Their horses swooped past the fields entirely, then Hokk and Elia veered their steeds around for another flyby. Tasheira's stallion was right behind them.

This time, gliding very low over the terraces, Elia pointed ahead. "There he is! I see him."

"Got him!"

Simultaneously wrenching back on their reins, they slowed their horses. Tash was too slow to respond, and hers shot well past before she could swing her stallion the right way again. By that point, the two animals belonging to Hokk and Elia were on the ground.

Tasheira's horse landed beside Hokk's. Elia had already dismounted and was swiftly walking toward a fierce-looking young man who had a large wound slashed down his face, from one eyebrow to the middle of his cheek.

While most of the farmers had scattered—except for a few who stood defiant—the person who Elia was now approaching had his feet planted wide apart and his arms crossed. A sneer twisted his face as if to challenge anyone who might dare to trespass.

Everything about him warned of danger.

"Is this who we've come to see?" Tasheira quietly asked Hokk.

"It is."

"And he can help us?"

Hokk glanced at her doubtfully and sighed. "Elia sure seems to think so."

Chapter 72

ELIA COULD SEE TENDONS bulging at the side of Roahm's face as he clenched his jaws. His eyes were mere slits, spewing pure hatred.

The last time they had seen each other was along the riverbank, blood oozing down his cheek after Elia furiously yanked out one of his eyebrow piercings. She remembered very clearly his betrayed expression that morning, warranted after all the protection he had provided while she lived among his people. Just moments later, Mahkoiyin had knocked him unconscious with a shovel.

Now, the few Torkins nearby who hadn't run away stood frozen in their spots, ever watchful, holding various farm implements as if prepared to transform instantly into warriors to protect the Chieftain's son.

"I can't believe it!" Roahm growled, baring his teeth with a vicious curl of his lip. "Of all people who I'd least expect to show their face, it's you. You're either a damn fool too stupid to know any better or a wicked swine who loves to wreak havoc with everyone's lives. Either way, you're not welcome here. The same goes for your two companions."

"You have every reason to be hostile," Elia said in a measured tone.

"Just leave!"

"But I was hoping you could—"

"Don't even bother to beg for forgiveness. You're wasting your time. I'll never forgive you!" he spat with disgust.

"I'm not begging for any such thing. I certainly wouldn't forgive me either if I were you. But you have to also realize that I simply acted in self-defense. I was scared."

"Scared?" he scoffed, flexing his fists as if ready to tear her apart.

"You shouldn't have grabbed me the way you did by the river!"

"I did nothing of the sort!"

"That's not true, and you know it! You tried to wrestle me to the ground. You didn't want me escaping."

"Because I thought you had lost your mind and you were a danger to yourself! You were with that crazy woman, Koiyin, and acting so peculiar. Is *everyone* from Above as mad as you two? But I swear, under no circumstances would I have ever harmed you."

"How was I supposed to know that?" Elia retorted. "I saw you kick Hokk in the head like you were a cold-blooded savage! Your anger boiled completely out of control, and I was afraid you were capable of far more violent acts, even against me."

"You're not so innocent yourself, my dear," Roahm snarled. "Don't forget—you're the one who nearly killed me when you hit me over the head with that shovel."

"That wasn't me! Koiyin was the one who did it! She snuck up from behind, and before I knew what was happening, you were knocked out. I told her it was a terrible thing to do."

Roahm moved close to Elia. She could feel his breath on her face. "Almost as terrible as this?" he asked, pointing to the long crusty scab on his cheek that still hadn't healed.

Elia felt too repulsed to look directly at the wound.

Between his fingers, Roahm suddenly took the metal blade still pierced in Elia's eyebrow and gave it a tug. "How would you like me to do the same to your face?" he asked.

Elia caught her breath, waiting for the pain of Roahm ripping the piercing through her skin.

Roahm gave another tug, harder this time, and she gasped.

Then he dropped his hand.

Elia exhaled, trembling . . . and ashamed.

She hung her head. "I still can't believe I did something so despicable. And you're right. You're absolutely right. I can be a horrible person. I frighten myself sometimes by what I do. I feel just sick to think your injury is a result of me. Now you'll be marked for life as a constant reminder of my savagery. However, maybe it will be of some consolation to know that my own heart and conscience is equally scarred."

She paused, hoping he might say something. He remained silent.

After a moment, Elia looked up at him apologetically. "I'm so sorry, Roahm. I truly mean it. There's no excuse except that I did what I thought was necessary to survive. I was hoping you might understand what I'm trying to say, but I accept that you can't."

Did she see the slightest hint of him softening?

Without breaking eye contact, she gingerly reached forward to touch the hole in his eyebrow where the piercing used to sit. Then she let her hand slowly caress the side of his torn cheek.

Roahm sighed deeply, taking hold of her hand as he gently lowered it. Yet he didn't let go. He looked to the side and shook his head as if struggling to process his thoughts. "You know, we're more alike than either of us would care to admit," he finally said. "Which, I guess, is why I found you so fascinating from the very start. It's why I admired you so much and fought for you to be accepted as a member of our village. And maybe it's also the reason I felt so betrayed by your actions."

Elia took a breath, wanting to say something more, but Roahm tenderly placed a finger on her lips.

"Maybe I scare myself too because I understand exactly where you're coming from," he continued. "Would I have done the same? For sure. In fact, I would've probably committed far worse acts in order to protect myself and my people. My only regret, however, is that during our weeks together, I knew how important it was for you to return to your home on the other side of the clouds, yet I did nothing to offer any support or sympathy. For that, I apologize."

"Thank you," Elia said sincerely. "You're being kinder than I deserve."

Roahm bit the corner of his lip as he studied her intently. "But explain to me, why are you here? It's more dangerous for you now than ever before."

"Because we need your help. You're the only person I can count on."

Roahm frowned as he glanced over Elia's shoulder. "Is that Hokk with you?"

"It is, plus another girl from Above. However, we've come for only one purpose." Elia reconsidered this for a second before correcting herself. "No, actually two."

"What are they?"

"To ask for your help to find Koiyin. I must bring her home, just as I originally intended."

Roahm nodded. "And the other?"

Elia's expression fell grim and she looked him hard in the eyes. "To save your life. To warn you and your villagers that another attack will soon come from the sky."

Chapter 73

STILL IN HIS SADDLE, Hokk sat with pinched lips and crossed arms, his steely glare focused straight ahead. He despised everything about the scene he was witnessing.

He forced a lungful of air through his mouth, as if he had been holding his breath for far too long, and followed it up with a deep groan that rumbled in his chest.

They keep touching each other on the face!

Elia had stroked the Torkin's cheek. Then, just now, the young man had pressed one finger to her lips. Why? Why was any physical contact even necessary?

Yet Hokk could not ignore an indisputable fact. Elia had lived with this Torkin, Roahm, for over a month, which meant they had been in each other's company much longer than the total combined time that Hokk and Elia had spent together on the prairies, in the City of Ago, and above the clouds. And while Hokk would have preferred to believe none of that mattered, the truth was now painfully evident—Elia was much closer to Roahm than she would ever be with him.

That's fine, Hokk tried to convince himself. She's better off without me anyway.

Tasheira must have picked up on his frustration, because

she spoke with unexpected encouragement. "Don't worry. She likes you the best."

Flustered and red-faced, Hokk turned to her. "Huh?"

"You keep sighing," said Tash, as if this was enough of an explanation.

"So what if I am?" he snapped, embarrassed to think his feelings were so evident.

"I realize you're angry, but there's no reason to be. Not when it comes to Elia."

"I'm just ready to get out of here. We're running out of time."

Tasheira chuckled in a way he found maddening. "Deny the truth all you want, but I can read it on your face. I know you don't like that young man she's talking to. It's driving you crazy."

"*You're* the crazy one!"

"Don't turn your anger on me. I'm simply telling you not to waste energy being upset because it's very clear how much she likes you. I could tell right from the start, when she fussed over you on the Isle of Drifting Dunes and was so worried about your health. Honestly, it's obvious she cares for you as more than an average friend. Perhaps, it's even love."

"Ha!" Hokk snorted. "I've never heard anything more absurd!"

Immediately, though, he regretted the outburst. Was this truly what he thought? Or was it simply a defensive reaction to protect himself? His body slumped as his thoughts spiraled. And the more he stewed over it, the more insightful Tasheira's observation seemed to be. Perhaps he had just needed someone to point out what he had been avoiding all along . . . his feelings for Elia.

It was flattering to know that she was fond of him—after all, there was that kiss at Lady Argina's—but another side of Hokk felt strong resistance to the idea. In truth, he couldn't imagine sharing his life with another person. He had experienced enough disappointment and heartache to know human connections never lasted. In the end, he'd be alone. Wasn't it better to be realistic now, when he was already accustomed to loneliness? Why change the only way he knew how to live?

"It appears she wasn't able to convince him," Tasheira now observed, pulling Hokk's attention back to the present.

He looked up and saw Elia running toward them. Behind her, Roahm finished shouting an order to the nearby farmers before he started chasing after her.

Hokk swung his leg over his horse's back and leapt to the ground. Regardless of everything else, he was still committed to Elia until the end of this mission. She must not suffer any harm!

"Hurry!" he shouted, madly gesturing for Elia to join him so he could help her up into her saddle.

Yet Elia halted a few steps in front of him, looking perplexed at his outstretched hand.

Hokk was astounded. Didn't she understand the urgency? He frantically looked past her toward Roahm, who was only a short distance away. "Come on! Before he reaches us!"

"Stop! You're mistaken," Elia exclaimed, her eyes wide as she grabbed his hand and squeezed. "We can't leave without Koiyin!"

"We can find her later! Let's just get out of here!"

"No, wait! There's no cause for panic."

The next instant, Roahm was standing with them.

Pulling Elia behind him, Hokk stood defiant with fists raised. "Stay away from her!" he bellowed.

The young man was startled, and he shot a confused look at Elia. "What's his problem?"

Elia grabbed one of Hokk's shoulders to get his attention. "Hokk, listen to me. Roahm is going to help us."

Having been so convinced they were in danger, Hokk now struggled to process her words. "I thought he was after you."

"I asked him to fly with us to confront the Imperial Guards and stop their advance. We just have to wait for two of his men to return before we can leave."

Roahm glanced skyward and his expression blazed with the fierceness of a warrior. "And it will have to be soon. I don't like what I'm seeing. This is going to be a close one."

Everyone else raised their eyes too. The Imperial Guards and their horses were clearly visible against the dark clouds, and they were closing in quickly.

"We have three other members of our group who have flown back to intercept the guards and hopefully slow them down," Elia explained. "But how long will we have to wait for your men to join us?"

"They'll be fast. They simply need to supply us with enough darts."

"What kind of darts? The ones with yellow feathers?"

"Of course."

"So you intend to kill people?" Elia asked with dread.

Hokk was not surprised to see a ruthlessness burn behind the Torkin's eyes.

"If that's what it takes," Roahm replied. "I plan to stop this invasion dead in its tracks."

Elia wrung her hands as she noticed two other Torkins now approaching with satchels and long blowpipes. "But my brother is up there," she said. "And he's with two other good, decent men. All three of them absolutely must return with us to Above once this is finished. It's the only way."

"You can try pointing them out to us, but whatever happens will just be the unfortunate cost of war," said Roahm, showing no trace of emotion.

"Please! You can't be so reckless!" Elia pleaded.

"Elia, listen to me. I have to do whatever it takes to save my people. I already guaranteed to you a few moments ago that somebody will locate Koiyin and bring her to South Village. She'll be waiting for you here when we return. However, this is a serious battle we face. I can make no other promises about what my men and I will be forced to do, or not do, in order to protect our territory. I can't promise that innocent lives won't be lost."

Chapter 74

RAYHAN LOOKED OVER AT Blaitz, who gave him a thumbs-up signal. They had been urging their horses on, pushing them to near exhaustion, and they were indeed gaining on the Imperial Guards. Without wasting a precious moment, Blaitz, Rayhan, and Fimal demanded a final burst of speed from their horses as they cut through the guards' formation.

Shouting erupted this time as the team of Imperial horses scattered in all directions, the same way a flock of startled birds would abandon their roost in a tree.

In the chaos, Rayhan momentarily lost sight of Fimal and Blaitz. Craning his neck around, he saw a horse swoop by at a steep angle. From the spike on the rider's helmet, he could tell it was Blaitz making a second pass, his animal's wings nearly clipping those of an adversary's horse.

As Blaitz and Fimal's steeds kept flapping around the guardsmen, Rayhan flew higher above the fray, then dove, aiming his horse at a cluster of guards still trying to fly forward. In seconds, he was upon them. They dispersed with more yelling as he soared right past, narrowly avoiding a collision.

While the majority of the scattered horses attempted to regroup into the same flying pattern they had been maintaining earlier, several other guards at the rear suddenly broke free of the team to launch a counterattack.

Spears were held at the ready.

Knowing his own knife was useless, Rayhan tucked it under his saddle so he could hold his reins tightly with both hands.

One guard singled him out. The man maneuvered his horse close to Rayhan's and stabbed with his spear. With every attempt, Rayhan either ducked or forced his stallion to swerve out of the way. Fortunately, he avoided the sharp tip each time, although just barely.

Then another spear came at him from a different direction, as one more horse and rider flew alongside.

Rayhan flattened himself, though the saddle horn dug painfully into his chest. Still, it was better than a spike through his heart.

But how long could he keep this up? Surely the odds would quickly turn against him. He needed to shake off his two aggressors. However, whether swooping up and down, or banking hard to the left and right, nothing he tried made a difference. The guards were always right there next to him.

Rayhan sensed that similar pursuits were being waged against Fimal and Blaitz, but he was too focused on his own escape to gauge how they were faring.

Then, suddenly, he caught the briefest glimpse of three additional horses heading straight for them. Twisting around, he saw that each of the new stallions was carrying two riders. Could this be Elia, Hokk, and Tasheira with reinforcements from the village?

Thwtt.

Something yellow shot past Rayhan's face.

Thwtt.

A second one. This time, it hit its mark. Across from him, Rayhan saw a dart with yellow feathers embedded in the flank of the Imperial Guard's horse flying just ahead of him. The animal immediately faltered, its rider slipping precariously sideways in his saddle. Rayhan veered off, leaving the man to his fate.

Thwtt. Thwtt.

The air began to fill with yellow projectiles, fired from all sides by whoever was riding with his sister and her companions.

The chaos escalated.

Horses began to fall out of the sky, careening down toward the green, rocky terrain far below, their once graceful wings now awkward and useless. Some of the guards were able to hold on as they plummeted. Others fell out of their saddles to make their own fatal contact with the hard ground.

Then it dawned on Rayhan that these Torkin warriors would have no way of distinguishing him from the rest of the regiment. Until now, he had feared being killed by a spear, when in reality, a dart could just as easily be the end of him.

"Blaitz! Fimal! Helmets off!" he screamed as he removed his own. "And climb! Climb higher into the sky!"

He hoped both men would hear him and understand his warning. They had done all they could do here. Now, it was time to escape.

Chapter 75

HOKK ASSUMED THE TORKIN sharing his saddle had never ridden a winged horse before, let alone flown so high above the ground. This made the man's accuracy with his blowpipe even more impressive.

Yet the warrior's shots were indiscriminate. Clearly, anybody flying in front of them who was wearing a helmet was considered a threat to be taken down. Holding the blowpipe up to his lips, the man would deftly take aim—usually over one of Hokk's shoulders—then *whoosh,* a burst of air from his cheeks would send a yellow flash zipping toward its victim. Again and again, he loaded another projectile and launched it with only the power of his lungs.

But which of these horses carried Rayhan, Fimal, or Blaitz on their backs? It was impossible to tell. At first, when the whizzing darts started hitting their intended targets, Hokk worried the three men could be struck by the small, deadly barbs without anyone knowing. His concerns intensified when paralyzed horses and Imperial Guards started falling toward the ground. What if one of them, especially Elia's brother, was already among the casualties?

At this rate, the entire sky will soon be emptied.

Fortunately, Rayhan must have figured out the dangers because Hokk spotted him removing his helmet. That one decision made all the difference. Hokk noticed the other two men follow suit, and now the three of them were finally distinguishable.

"Aim only for the ones who still have helmets on!" Hokk shouted over his shoulder at the Torkin.

If Elia had observed this too, she was probably sharing the same advice with Roahm, who was sitting right behind her—hopefully a similar exchange was also happening between Tasheira and her passenger.

Hokk knew he was just as likely to be hit by a stray dart, though he forced himself to ignore the possibility. Instead, he carefully maneuvered his horse through the swirling skirmish, trying to keep track of everybody's whereabouts amidst the shouting and flapping wings.

Then he saw Rayhan's horse suddenly climb into the air. The commander and Fimal quickly joined him. A wise move. Now, flying at this higher altitude, they were safely above the curved trajectory of any rogue dart.

As for the Imperial Guards, armed only with their spears, they were woefully ill-equipped for the Torkin barrage. Before long, those with enough sense to acknowledge the futility of the battle called out for their comrades to make a hasty retreat.

The guards fled with no semblance of order, and it was clear that their numbers had been cut in half. Each man was focused only on saving himself. Their horses, battling both exhaustion and gravity, struggled to carry the men up to the clouds. One by one, the animals disappeared into the thick mist until even the stragglers were gone.

We've done it!

Now, not a single yellow dart pierced the air. Instead, large feathers from the horses' wings, knocked loose during the turmoil, floated slowly down toward the mountain slopes below, where the bodies of men and animals were visible, either crumpled on the rocks or caught in the trees.

A cheer erupted from Roahm. It was matched in volume by the shouts of the other two warriors.

A grin spread across Hokk's face. Having stopped this second ambush from Above, the Torkins had every reason to celebrate. And he too felt the same exhilaration at such unexpected and swift success. Elia's goal had almost been achieved. No further obstacle could possibly prevent it from happening now.

But aside from rescuing Mahkoiyin, Hokk could not forget one large, looming decision that still had to be addressed. He had discussed it with no one, and while his thoughts favored one alternative over the other, he kept debating the options.

Either way, the impact would be significant, and the time was coming very soon when he'd be forced to face his difficult choice.

Chapter 76

JUST AHEAD OF HOKK, Elia's horse was the first to touch down in the middle of the tents and huts of South Village.

The area appeared to be deserted.

By the time Hokk's stallion had landed too, along with Tasheira's, Roahm had already catapulted himself from Elia's saddle.

"Victory is ours!" Roahm hollered, triumphantly raising his blowpipe with one hand. "Come out! The threat is over! We're safe! We have battled the metal-faced demons from the sky and driven them off! Their dead now litter our mountainsides!"

Summoned by his shouting, Torkins began to cautiously emerge from the protection of their shelters. All of them looked up toward the sky as if not believing his words. Many held weapons of all sorts—blowpipes, tools, pieces of wood—fully prepared to wage their own battle.

The excitement of the villagers grew steadily as Roahm and the two other men were proclaimed heroes. Everybody clamored to hear their stories.

Hokk saw the Chieftain appear and stand beside Roahm. He recognized the man not just from the Torkin banquet, but from that time when the Chieftain had been brought to see him by the river: Hokk had been overpowered by young Torkin men, thrown into the icy water, and buried up to his neck in dirt and gravel—all, apparently, on Roahm's orders, to punish him for trespassing. The Chieftain had shown no mercy. Now, looking very pleased, the man proudly put an arm around his son's shoulder.

Then a deathly silence swept over the villagers, traveling like an ocean wave.

Three more horses could be seen arriving. With slowly beating wings, the visibly weakened animals landed shakily at the edge of the assembled crowd. Surely every set of eyes was focused only on the mirrored helmets that Rayhan, Blaitz, and Fimal were holding in their hands.

As if sensing the tension, and fearing violence, Elia immediately rose up from her saddle, straight-legged, with her feet braced in her stirrups. "Wait!" she shouted. "These men aren't who you might think they are! They are *not* the enemy! They have been helping us fight off the invaders, but are only just arriving now because their exhausted horses couldn't travel any faster."

"Don't believe her!" someone yelled out.

"That's my brother!" she hollered, pointing toward Rayhan.

"Who cares?" another Torkin challenged.

"They're all the same. Just kill them!"

"No, she's telling the truth!" Roahm vehemently replied, holding up his hands for order. "They helped delay the metal-heads so that my men and I could prepare for a counterattack."

"We don't want any of you to be here!" spat an old woman. Standing close to Hokk's horse, she whipped its hindquarters with a stick.

Startled, the animal bucked and tossed its head, which only provoked a crowd already on the verge of erupting.

In a frenzy, the villagers swarmed. Arms reached up to yank Hokk from his saddle. As he hit them away, he caught glimpses of his companions trying to fight off Torkins too.

A female voice screamed above the fray.

Fearing it came from Elia, Hokk looked up and watched in horror as she was pulled from her spooked horse. The next instant, he lost sight of her completely as she was dropped on the ground.

She'll be trampled!

Hokk quickly jumped up on his stallion's back, scarcely managing to keep his balance as he kicked at the hands trying to grab his feet. Looking for an opening, he spotted one and launched himself over the riotous mob.

Fists, sticks, and farm implements pummeled his body. Fingernails scratched at his face. But he let none of this stop him as he plowed forward, hoping to reach Elia before it was too late.

However, she had been able to stand on her own. She was fighting off Torkins coming at her from every side, yet taking a beating all the same.

Then Hokk saw Commander Blaitz hauled off his horse too. He couldn't see Tasheira or her cousin anywhere. Only Rayhan was still on horseback, though just barely managing as Torkins hung from the frantic animal's wings to prevent it from flying away.

Hokk feared the worst. They were all doomed. In the end, their mission would fail at this last possible stage before finally getting the chance to rescue Mahkoiyin.

But not so.

"Enough!" boomed an imposing voice.

Only a few of the Torkins paused.

"Stop! All of you!" the Chieftain bellowed. "I will have none of this!"

The vengeful villagers seemed unwilling to obey as they threw a few more kicks and punches. Hokk touched his cheek and felt several bloody scratch marks.

"Return to your homes or to your work in the fields!" Roahm demanded with just as much authority.

Everybody hesitated as if unsure whether or not to listen to the orders of the Chieftain's son. But his father commanded complete obedience.

"I will not tolerate unnecessary bloodshed!" the man roared. "There's been too much! Give these people their chance to leave our territory. We are not barbarians!"

"Why are they even here?" asked a voice from within the throng.

"To burn our crops like last time!" somebody else shouted in response.

"No!" barked a woman who was standing on the fringes. "They have come to rescue me!"

There was a moment of silence as the Torkins looked around for the source of the voice.

"Let her come forward!" shouted Roahm.

As the villagers parted to let her through, there was no mistaking the woman whose hands Hokk had deliberately released, dropping her into that frigid river—hair matted with leaves, heavy jowls, a missing tooth, the easily recognizable triangle of three moles above her mouth. Yes, this was Mahkoiyin.

But what a relief! She had survived plunging into the raging water! One less thing for Hokk to feel guilty about.

As she passed by, Mahkoiyin glanced briefly at Hokk with accusatory eyes and a watch-out-I'll-get-you kind of sneer. She continued on, though, and stopped in front of Elia, who was nursing a swollen lip and several bruises on her face.

"Your Excellency," said Elia, bowing before her.

The woman's head jerked from a neck spasm, yet she quickly recovered and reached forward to place her hand on Elia's stallion. "So the time has finally arrived, has it?"

Elia nodded. "We've come for you, and you alone. We're taking you back with us to Above."

"Careful, careful," Mahkoiyin mumbled as she glanced at the other horses and riders. "Too many people around."

Hearing this, the Chieftain repeated his son's earlier instructions. "Return to your homes everybody, or else resume your work in the fields! The danger has passed. Carry on as normal."

The villagers, now calmer after having released their pent up fear and anger, reluctantly dispersed until only the Chieftain and Roahm remained.

By this point, Mahkoiyin had spotted Commander Blaitz on his horse. She moved purposefully toward the man as he simultaneously slipped from his saddle. He bowed in front of her, just as Elia had done.

"Is my vision playing a cruel trick on me?" the bedraggled empress wondered.

"I assure you, it's me," said Blaitz. "Though I'm almost twenty years older than the last time we saw each other."

Mahkoiyin then scrutinized the battered faces of Tasheira, Fimal, and Rayhan, clearly oblivious to the significance of the young man, last in line, whose steadfast gaze was fixed only on her.

Hokk wondered if Elia would introduce her brother. Or would Rayhan say something himself? It seemed unlikely. Perhaps the timing was not right for such a momentous reunion.

Running her fingers through her tangled hair, Koiyin appeared to be doing a headcount to compare the number of horses to people. "Well, I'm ready to leave," she then announced. "But who will I be riding with?"

"Take my stallion," Elia offered. "I can easily ride back with someone else."

"No, let Mahkoiyin have my horse," said Hokk.

"That works too," said Elia with a grin. "And you can travel with me."

Hokk gravely shook his head. The dreaded moment had come. "Thank you, Elia, but no, that won't be necessary."

Her happy expression vanished and her dark skin seemed to pale by several shades. "W-what do you mean?" she stammered. "Why not?"

Lowering his gaze, Hokk stared at the ground, not wanting to see her disappointment. "Because I'm not going back to Above."

Chapter 77

"NOT GOING BACK?" ELIA gasped.

The impact of Hokk's harsh words was more painful than a physical blow.

"How can you possibly say that?" she asked, her anger surging. "Damn it, Hokk, you promised you'd never let anything separate us! I felt the same way. Now you're telling me this!"

Hokk took her arm and pulled her around to the other side of his horse for some privacy. Elia shook him off.

"Please don't be upset," he said.

"It's too late!"

"You have to understand. It's already a tough enough decision. Don't make it any harder."

"So then change your mind!"

"But remaining in Below is my only logical choice. I've considered it all very carefully."

"With absolutely no thought for me, I see!" Elia hissed.

Rubbing his temples as though he had a headache, Hokk didn't reply fast enough for her liking.

She shoved him in the shoulder to provoke a response. "Do I mean *nothing* to you?"

"Of course you do!"

She didn't believe him. He was a damaged person. The signs had always been there, right from the start. He always looked out for himself. She was foolish for expecting him to change his nature. Still, Elia felt on the verge of breaking down. She summoned her rage and frustration to hold herself together.

"Then why did you lie to me all this time, if you always intended to leave?"

"That's not true. I didn't lie. I just didn't know what path to take. It's only now that I've seen the journey through to its end that the right course of action is clear to me."

"So that's it? I'll never see you again?"

"What else were you expecting? We come from different worlds. I can't survive in yours, just as much as you can't live in mine. Besides, what would we hope to achieve if I followed you back up to Above? Would we just be friends? Develop some sort of relationship? We barely know each other. You've spent more time with Roahm than you have getting to know me. He has much more to offer you, and I can understand perfectly why you'd prefer him."

"You're an idiot!" she spat, furiously wiping away a tear before it could run down her cheek. "I bloody well hate you. I'm glad now to realize how I truly feel. I must have been blind before."

She started to walk away.

He caught her by the wrist. "Stop. Wait. This can't be how it ends. We've been through so much together. I wasn't expecting this sort of goodbye."

Elia pulled her arm free. "*I* wasn't counting on this sort of thing either!"

Circling around the horse, Elia saw that Mahkoiyin, Blaitz, and the rest of them had already mounted their stallions. They were waiting for her. Everyone avoided eye contact, as if to suggest they had not overheard her exchange with Hokk.

"Good, I'm glad to see we're ready to leave!" Elia exclaimed with false cheerfulness.

As she was about to place her foot into the stirrup of Hokk's stallion, he came up right behind her.

"Elia please. Let's—"

She swiftly spun on him. "As for you, you can return to your solitude on the prairies. Die out there, for all I care!"

Hokk's wounded expression was heart-wrenching, but Elia stopped herself from apologizing. If they had to part ways, it was easier to be ruthless. Just cut the ties and be done with him.

Preparing once more to mount, Elia suddenly reconsidered such a hasty departure. One person truly did deserve her thanks.

Ignoring Hokk, Elia strode toward Roahm, who was standing beside his father.

"I am very grateful for everything you've done. You sacrificed a lot to bring me into your village and keep me from harm. I will be forever indebted to you."

"I would do it all again without a moment's hesitation," said Roahm, beaming with that same wonderful smile Elia had always admired.

"And I'm sorry for bringing a near catastrophe to your people for a second time," Elia added. "I also apologize again for the injury I caused to your face."

His smile didn't diminish. "The scar will be a fond reminder of our time together."

Moved by such a generous comment, and with tears welling up in her eyes, Elia boldly stepped forward and hugged him.

Roahm tilted his head enough to whisper into her ear for nobody else to hear. "I don't want to say goodbye either. Would you consider staying here in this village? Are you really returning to something better above the clouds?"

Elia leaned back enough to gaze into his eyes. "I like to think I will be, but I can't say for sure," she replied, speaking just as softly. "But I have to go back now to finish what I've started."

"I understand. But someday, I will try to find you to make sure you're all right."

He then kissed her sweetly on the lips, catching Elia completely off guard.

She felt her face flush and her heartbeat race. Her lips tingled. Did she dare lean forward for a second one? She wanted to. Then, for some reason, her thoughts turned to Hokk. She hoped he was finding this difficult to watch.

Feeling too awkward to attempt another kiss, she instead made a request. "Can I ask you for a favor?"

"Of course," said Roahm. "What is it?"

"Could you please guarantee safe passage for Hokk through your territory when he returns to the grasslands? He deserves at least that much."

"Absolutely."

"Thank you."

With that, Elia slipped from his embrace and returned to her horse, passing Hokk with her head down so she wouldn't have to look at him.

But he held out his hand to catch her attention. On his open palm was Opi's orange princess jewel, which Elia had given to Hokk at the Baron's estate. She was surprised he still had it. Rather than acknowledge his offering, though, she slapped his hand away and saw the piece of polished glass go flying. Where it landed, she couldn't care less.

She hoisted herself up into the saddle and was relieved when Blaitz immediately took control by commanding everyone to get airborne.

Her horse's wings began to flap. She stared at the ground falling away from her as they rose higher. She saw Roahm and the Chieftain gazing up, but she avoided catching one last glimpse of Hokk.

Soon, the mountain range was quickly passing by below them, and she saw the Great Wall running its course toward the ocean.

Elia then raised her gaze to the clouds, knowing that she would never again have to return to Below—a realization that brought immense relief and a feeling of happiness.

So it must have been the wind, alone, blowing into her eyes that was causing the tears to run down her face.

Chapter 78

THE MORNING SUN HAD not yet risen high enough to banish the shadows that stretched across the ground. In the shady spots, glistening pearls of dew still clung to each blade as Elia strolled barefoot through the cool grass toward the farthest post of the clothesline.

A donkey obediently walked behind her. It followed without any need of a tether, threat, or encouraging word—the animal knew no other way to behave.

Baskets were tied to its back with straps that restricted the donkey's long-forgotten wings. Elia felt tempted to remove the bindings completely, though it would make no difference for this trusting creature. Carrying cargo and trekking along a well-worn trail were the only things the animal had to be concerned with—certainly not the possible freedom it could enjoy by flying away from its bondage and daily toil.

Since this was their first trip of the day into these beautiful rolling green hills, the two baskets were empty, as were the others hanging from the backs of the herd of donkeys, waiting for Elia, closer to the main path. Soon, however, all the baskets would be filled with the sweet-smelling bed sheets from yesterday's laundry, which now billowed and snapped in the playful wind.

But before removing the first clothespin, Elia paused to stare out over the clouds. Standing right at the very edge of the island, with her toes sticking past the end of the rock, she fiddled with her eyebrow piercing and tried to imagine once again, as she had done many times over the past several weeks since returning, how much farther the island used to extend before that day when the ground crumbled beneath her feet.

Had all that really happened? The memories existed, but they seemed rooted in a dream world. Perhaps because she found herself again among the clotheslines, as if there had been no interruption, it was easy to trick herself into thinking she was the same person she'd always been. Yet nothing could be more false. The girl Elia used to be no longer existed.

As she stood daydreaming, a silhouette overhead briefly blocked the sunlight. Elia didn't bother to look up. From the sound of the beating wings, she knew it was a flying stallion traveling toward the Royal Stables.

Soon, she would be working inside those very stables, tending to the regal animals. She couldn't wait. Though a promise had been pledged when she first returned, the arrangements were apparently still being made. And she was fine with waiting. All that mattered for now was not being forced to slave over a washboard and tub, stuck underground in that dark palace chamber she had always hated, one floor up from the dungeon. She was much happier to be outside, escorting the donkey procession in the mornings and afternoons to collect and hang laundry.

Naadie didn't accompany her out into these hills anymore. In fact, Elia hadn't heard of the girl's fate. Cook didn't seem to know either, or was perhaps reluctant to say. Instead, another young worker from the laundry room had been given the task of helping her at the clotheslines. Elia made little effort to talk to her—except for a casual greeting at the start of each day—because she hoped to avoid questions about her extended absence. Unfortunately, this solitude also meant she had many quiet moments to think about Hokk and Roahm, both of whom she missed greatly, for very different reasons.

The only wound that time's passage had almost healed was the grief she'd felt over Hokk's refusal to return with her to Above. She knew his decision was the right one because everything he had said was true. He didn't belong above the clouds any more than she belonged beneath them. Now she just wished she hadn't been so cruel to Hokk when they'd parted ways. She should have been brave enough to graciously face a tough goodbye. In the very least, she should have taken Opi's princess jewel from the Isle of Drifting Dunes as a memento of both her grandfather and Hokk.

Thankfully, a distraction now arrived to save her from these regrets. Sniffing his way from the next row of laundry, Nym wandered over and stopped at her feet. The little fox looked up, happily licking his muzzle as if to taste the freshness of the air.

Elia bent down and scratched behind his ears just the way he liked it. "My dear Nym," she said softly. "Thank goodness for you."

He still brought joy to her heart every time she saw him. She had even shed a few tears when they were first reunited, all thanks to Tasheira's efforts. Shortly after returning to the Sanctuary with Mahkoiyin, Tash had found the fox in the possession of Faytelle, just one of the empress's latest accessories. In a genuine act of kindness, Tasheira had decided to steal Nym away with the hopes of surprising Elia.

"I knew you would want him," Tash had explained. "I couldn't let that Faytelle woman have him. Soon she'd be wearing the poor thing."

That was the last time Elia had seen the Baron's daughter. She often wondered what the girl was doing—even right now, as Elia gazed into the distance toward the twin skyscrapers of the palace, she tried to imagine what was going on behind the mirrored glass.

What were any of them doing, for that matter? Blaitz, Fimal, Baron Shoad, Mrs. Suds—or rather Lady Argina? None of them were a part of Elia's world anymore.

But she didn't care. Good riddance. She was glad to be away from them, away from all the complications and dangers they had introduced.

Except for Rayhan.

Rayhan's abrupt exit from her life was very difficult to accept. He and Elia had been granted only the briefest moment together after their horses touched down in the Sanctuary courtyard before both he and Mahkoiyin were whisked away by Emperor Tael. She hadn't heard from her brother since.

Everything about their homecoming was disappointing and not at all what Elia had anticipated during their long flight back from South Village. She had expected great fanfare to celebrate the return of a lost empress and a newly discovered prince—at the very least, some form of recognition for the people who had helped make it happen. But to this day, nothing had been said or done. It was as if none of the recent events had ever occurred. The closest Elia got to any acknowledgement was when she and her mother were briefly summoned to Lady Argina's residence to be lectured and threatened on the importance of remaining silent. According to the old woman, the documents from the telescope had been safely delivered to Emperor Tael, but the situation with Rayhan was still very serious and highly confidential. The secret of his return, as well as Mahkoiyin's, could not be revealed until everything was in place, otherwise assassination attempts might be waged by the supporters of Tohryn and Faytelle, who would do whatever necessary to one day see Prince Veralion on the throne.

But the truth about Rayhan's birthright was bound to come out soon. And when that moment came, Elia hated to think of the turmoil that would be unleashed. In the meantime, all she could hope for was that her brother was being well protected as he learned to become accustomed to a very privileged, noble life. A life of limitless possibilities.

Was she jealous? No, Elia didn't think so. She was destined for a much simpler existence and she could accept that. The only thing she wanted was to occasionally see the person she used to call brother.

And it would happen. Rayhan would make sure of it. He would not forget about her, even if the rest of the courtiers were blind to her existence. Rayhan was actually the person who had promised to get her a new position working with the horses at the stables. He knew how much it would mean to her, especially because Elia's grandmother—no *their* grandmother—had spent her adult life performing the same duties. It would be a very fitting tribute to Omi. And hopefully, Rayhan would also be able to make the same arrangements for their mother, Sulum, whose failing eyesight would soon limit her usefulness in the seamstress department. Anything to prevent the woman's banishment to the laundry room.

It's shocking how much can change so quickly.

It was just Elia and her mother now, the two of them living together in Greyit's home in the same forest where Elia had spent her solitary childhood roaming unsupervised among the trees. Living there required a longer bicycle ride to and from work every day, but Elia enjoyed the time she could share with her mother. And while it also meant they arrived home much later than usual on the days they went to the market, they still made the effort to find Elia's father in the streets to provide him with a meal. Elia now stood side by side with her mother whenever they handed him his bundle of food. Sometimes a few words were spoken. Often, nothing at all. Little had changed with her father's situation, but Elia was beginning to find peace with that too.

Amazingly, for all the imminent dangers brewing within the palace, a general sense of calm and contentment had been able to settle over Elia's life in a way she had never before experienced. She had lived through so much that no future challenge could possibly undermine her confidence. She was strong. A survivor. She had overcome her fears and weaknesses. Even her hands were now steady. Denied access to incense, she had beaten her addiction, and she was proud of herself. Admittedly, her mind occasionally drifted to memories of the pleasures incense could provide, yet those temptations were always trumped by her relief that her bouts of anxiety were gone and the trembling in her limbs had mercifully subsided.

Now, it was Nym who offered the comfort she craved.

Still crouched beside him, Elia noticed the fox turn his head toward the row of laundry hanging nearby. His nostrils and large ears twitched. Elia gazed over in the same direction.

The frisky wind teased the nearest sheet and blew the bottom of it up from the tips of the grass. On the other side, exposed only to the knees, stood someone wearing boots firmly planted on the ground.

Elia's heart jumped.

Unable to pull her eyes away, she watched as a gloved hand was placed on the line and the sheet was drawn aside to reveal an Imperial Guard standing there, wearing his helmet.

Elia quickly stood straight.

The nightmare was starting all over again.

In a blur, she saw the guard advance.

Elia staggered backward as Nym ran off.

Bumping into the donkey behind her, Elia knew she could not step out of the way fast enough. The man would be upon her any second.

Yet the guard stopped in his tracks. He lifted off his helmet and tossed it to the ground.

Elia gasped, pressing her hand against her pounding heart. Then a sudden head rush made her vision swim and her head bob.

He must have noticed, because as Elia struggled to maintain her balance, he hurried closer and slipped his arm around her waist, embracing her with a hug as if he would never let go.

Clinging to his body, she inhaled his scent and felt his warmth envelop her.

She could scarcely believe what was happening.

Then they separated and she gazed into a pair of sparkling eyes.

Reaching up, she caressed his cheek and gently touched his eyebrow piercing. "I can't believe it's you," she whispered.

"I could say the same. Now that your hair has started growing out, you look so different."

"Hopefully, less like a boy," Elia chuckled as she brushed away a few of the longer strands tickling her forehead. "It's been over a month, so it really makes a difference. But tell me, how did you find me after all this time?"

"While working in one of the fields, I spotted your two islands floating overhead through the clouds."

"You recognized them?"

"Of course, right away. Their image is forever emblazoned in my memory. I'll never forget how much you longed to return to your home when you thought there was no hope—when I was an uncaring fool who told you it would never happen. I'm sorry for not bothering to help you from the very start."

"My goodness, no apology is necessary. You did so much."

"What I didn't know was how you'd react to see me again. I feared the worst, but I couldn't let that stop me."

"I'm glad you didn't," Elia replied gently.

"So it's all right that I came up here?"

"Most definitely. I'm just so amazed. I still can't believe I'm looking at you now, standing right in front of me. I have so many questions. How were you able to fly up above the clouds? How's it possible you're wearing an Imperial Guard's full uniform? You don't just have the helmet—you're even wearing the boots!"

"After advising the Chieftain, I led a group into the mountains so we could scavenge the dead bodies of the men who fell to the ground after our attack with the blow darts. We took their clothes, but we also found a few horses among them that hadn't died from the poison or the fall. I was able to nurse them back to health with help from the medicine woman. In recognition of my efforts, I was presented with the best specimen to keep for myself."

"Was that you just now, flying overhead above these clotheslines?"

"It was."

"And what about the piercing?"

"The villagers were convinced I deserved it," he replied, gingerly touching the small, curved blade. "Now you and I match."

Elia smiled.

"So I'm forgiven?" he asked, smiling back with a grin much broader than she had ever witnessed on his face.

"Yes, of course I forgive you. We *both* do."

He looked confused.

Elia glanced down at their feet. Nym had returned and was patiently waiting.

The fox rose on his hind legs, licked his muzzle, and pedaled his front paws, begging for attention.

"Praise the sun and moon!" cried Hokk, choking up with emotion. Bending down to lift Nym into his arms, he cradled the fox and buried his face in the animal's fur.

Elia felt a depth of happiness she had never before experienced.

But then, as she saw the sun shining on the top of Hokk's head, a problem came to mind that she couldn't ignore, and her joy vanished in an instant. "But Hokk, I'm worried."

He looked up. "What's wrong?"

She sighed as though it was all so hopeless. "We're fooling ourselves. No matter how much we want it, how will you be able to live up here above the clouds? You said so yourself. It can never work. You'll spend the rest of your life suffering. I can't let you pay that price, regardless of the way I feel about you."

"Don't worry about me. I'll be just fine. I've managed before, and I'll do so again." He then pulled her close, with

Nym nestled between them. "Because all I care about in this life I'm holding in my arms right now. And wherever I find you and Nym is where I'll call home, whether I'm in Below, Above, or someplace Beyond."

END OF BOOK THREE

Acknowledgments

I HAVE SPENT MANY BLISSFUL moments immersed in the worlds of Hokk and Elia, so engrossed with my writing that each hour of my workday slips by as quickly as a heartbeat. Though eventually I must always pull myself away from the page to return to reality, it's the following individuals in the real world who deserve thanks for making it possible for me to soar with my imagination to Below, Above, and Beyond.

I am especially grateful for the dedication of Daniel Lazar, my unrivalled agent from Writers House in New York City. Dan, it is an honor to work with you, and I'm continually impressed with your keen insight and literary expertise. I look forward to our future projects with great anticipation.

It has been a privilege and a sheer pleasure once again to collaborate with the distinguished team at Turner Publishing Company, all made possible by Todd Bottorff, President, and Stephanie Beard, Executive Editor of Acquisitions. On this third instalment, I was delighted to continue working so closely with my esteemed editor, Jon O'Neal, whose knowledge in his field is second to none. My appreciation also goes to Caroline Herd, my publicist with a treasure trove of marketing ideas that are always at-the-ready, as well as her colleague, Maddie Cothren, a masterful artist when it comes to creating stunning cover designs.

In my extended writing community, five exceptionally talented individuals also deserve my high regard. Thank you very much to Hadley Dyer, Maria Golikova, Catherine Dorton, Suzanne Sutherland, and Catherine Marjoribanks. My success as an author stems from your support, guidance, and inspiration.

For those beloved people in my life who I absolutely adore, know that you are always in my thoughts. Much love to Shawn Shirazi, my dear parents, Jo-Ann and André Chabot, my brother, Jeff, his wife, Jennifer, their children, Jack and Kate, and my friend, Jazz Rai. May everything that I write, every dream that I pursue, be a tribute to how much each of you mean to me.

CPSIA information can be obtained
at www.ICGtesting.com
Printed in the USA
BVOW04*0808030517
482918BV00014B/38/P